IMPASSIONED YOUTH

'Maria!' he said softly.

'Don't say it, Hugo, I beg you,' she stammered.
'I am nigh on thirteen and nearly grown. I do not
think like a child, I do not feel like a child. Oh
Hugo, I need to know how you think of me. I
beg you – say something to comfort me. My
mind is torn to shreds with wanting you, and
that's the sum of it.'

Hugo looked at her as she stood in the darkened
room, wraith-like in her pale gown.

'I'm sorry –' he began.

'You do not care for me?' she whispered.

He shook his head.

LOWERING SKIES

Being the Third Volume in the classic Heron Saga

Pamela Oldfield

This title first published in Great Britain 1998 by
SEVERN HOUSE PUBLISHERS LTD of
9–15 High Street, Sutton, Surrey SM1 1DF,
complete with new text by the author.
Originally published in 1982 in Great Britain by
Macdonald Futura Publishers Ltd
under the title of *After The Storm*.
This title first published in the U.S.A. 1998 by
SEVERN HOUSE PUBLISHERS INC of
595 Madison Avenue, New York, N.Y. 10022.

British Library Cataloguing in Publication Data

Oldfield, Pamela, 1934-
    Lowering skies
      1. Kendal family (Fictitious characters) - Fiction
      2. Domestic fiction
      1. Title
    823.9'14 [F]

    ISBN 0-7278-2205-5

Printed and bound in Great Britain by
MPG Books Ltd, Bodmin, Cornwall.

CHAPTER ONE
Devon 1552

A slight breeze lifted the grasses and freed the pollen, which rose in gauzy clouds into the air and drifted across the meadow into the orchard. Here Maria sat beneath a plum tree, her lap filled with the firm, golden plums. Sunshine filtering through the leaves above her set a burnished gleam to her dark head as she bent disconsolately over the fruit. Lifting her blue skirt, she reached for a layer of petticoat and rubbed the dust from one of the plums until it was to her satisfaction, then nibbled the warm fruit without enjoyment.

'I hate Margaret Kendal,' she repeated tonelessly. 'Hate her, hate her, hate her!' The muscles of her face sagged with misery, but her eyes burned with the intensity of her feelings. 'I *hate* her!'

A nuthatch appeared on the trunk of the next tree, making its way erratically downwards, picking earnestly among the tiny insects that lived in the crusty bark. Impulsively, Maria snatched a plum and threw it with all her might. It went hopelessly wide of the tree, but the small grey-blue bird noted its passage and took flight, in a sudden flutter of wing beats.

'Stupid creature!' she muttered.

She cleaned another small plum on the hem of her petticoat and put it into her mouth whole. As she bit into it, the juice trickled from the corner of her mouth and she wiped it away with the back of her hand, which she wiped in turn on her unfortunate petticoat. She wondered where they would be, what they would be doing, what they would be saying – even how they would look at one another. Her bitterness grew with each fresh image.

'And you're a stupid creature, too,' she told the absent Margaret. 'A stupid, shallow –' she racked her brain for further faults, but temporarily unable to marshal any, she spat the plum stone with great force into the grass and marked its position for future reference. The next plum was popped into her mouth without the benefit of petticoat and the sweet flesh hustled off the stone by Maria's small even teeth. She swallowed the fruit hastily and spat again, but the stone fell short. The small failure increased her wretchedness.

'And boring,' she added. 'How Hugo can bear to live with you, I cannot imagine.'

She scrambled awkwardly to her feet. She had been sitting there for nearly an hour and her legs were stiff. She held onto the tree and straightened up, smoothing her skirt. The last of the plums from her lap had fallen onto the grass, and she now stepped on each one, slowly and deliberately, hearing with satisfaction the slight sound as each skin split under the pressure of her small shoe. A voice, rough and low, surprised her.

'Temper, temper!'

One of the farm labourers stood nearby, watching her with obvious amusement. Maria considered him for a moment and then said coldly, 'I am not in a temper.'

'Seems so to me,' he said.

'Then seeming's wrong,' Maria snapped.

This answer appeared to delight him. A huge grin spread over his moon-like face and he laughed loudly. For all his size – and he stood over six feet tall – the laugh was that of a young boy, eager and unselfconscious, like a puppy sensing a game. He leaned on the handle of his scythe and rubbed the dust from his eyes with a grimy forefinger.

'What they ever done to you?' he persisted, nodding his head in the direction of the trampled plums and glancing again at her face. Ignoring his remark, Maria wiped her

8

soiled shoe on the grass, adding a green stain to that of the plum juice. Smoothing her hair back from her forehead, she pulled forward a lock of her hair and began to twist it around her fingers as she studied the young man before her.

Already the sun had burned his body a warm brown, which went some way to hiding the pock marks, the familiar legacy of an early smallpox attack. His brown hair was bleached also, and hung untidily around his head and ears like an insecure thatch. As Maria looked, disappointment crept into his eyes. The anticipated conversation was not going to materialise. There would be no game. The broad grin wavered, and a further humorous remark died on his lips. Reaching up into the tree above her, Maria plucked another plum and held it out for him. He hesitated, stretched out his hand and then, changing his mind, withdrew it.

'For you,' said Maria. 'Take it.'

'For me?'

She nodded impatiently, and stepping forward took hold of his large hand and placed the fruit in it. The grin returned to his face as he ate it noisily, his head on one side, the better to assess its flavour.

'Catch!' cried Maria, and threw him another. His large hand flashed outward and he caught it easily. Now the promised game was developing. He laughed, and leaning the scythe against a tree, prepared to enjoy himself.

'You watch this,' he told her, and tilting back his head, tossed the plum into the air and caught it in his mouth. 'That's a rare trick!' he told her excitedly. 'A rare trick! See, I'll do it again –' He picked himself a plum and repeated the performance, following its successful conclusion with a further outbreak of boisterous laughter.

Maria watched him, and her eyes narrowed slightly as she recognised the boy's laughter in a man's frame.

'Can you catch this?' she asked him wickedly, and ran to pick an apple. Seizing it from her he threw it up. Determined to impress her, he threw it higher than before and its extra weight brought it down with a painful thud against his waiting teeth.

'*Ow!*'

With a cry of surprise and pain, he released the apple and cursed under his breath, comforting his teeth with the back of his large hand. It did not occur to him that Maria was to blame for his pain and he nodded to her amiably over his hand; but the hurt in his brown eyes reproached her, and she watched guiltily, a slight frown on her face. He kicked the offending apple and it sped towards a tree, struck the trunk, and split open.

'That serves 'un right!' he cried triumphantly, his good humour immediately restored.

Maria smiled at him. 'What's your name?' she asked.

'Matt.'

'Matt what?'

'Cartright.'

She laughed. 'That's a rare name,' she mimicked. 'Mine's Maria – and aren't you supposed to be working?'

He looked vaguely around as though the question puzzled him.

'Working,' Maria repeated. 'Like this –' She swung an imaginary scythe, and saw a flicker of understanding in the brown eyes, but still he stood irresolute, his face screwed up with the effort of concentration. She waited patiently.

'I'm sent on a errand,' he said at last.

'Then you'd best be off,' she said.

He considered her remark for a moment, his head on one side. Then he said, 'Well, I'd best be off,' as though it was his own idea. With a cheerful nod, he picked up the scythe and made his way out of the orchard to the field beyond.

Maria, left alone, regretted her words. Any company was better than none, but it was too late now. He had gone. She sighed deeply.

'Oh, dearest Hugo,' she whispered fervently. 'Please come home. I can't live without you, indeed I can't!'

Maria Lessor was eleven years old, a passionate and

headstrong child. She was tasting, for the first time in her short life, the exquisite agony of unrequited love.

The mid-day meal at Heron was taken in the Hall. Thick walls kept out the bright autumn sunshine, and it was pleasantly cool within. Maria and Hannah dined alone, for Simon was at the mine as usual, and Luke, bed-ridden, would dine upstairs.

Maria ate her lunch in a preoccupied silence, summoning Hugo's dimly remembered face into her memory and giving free reign to her fancies.

'You have eaten so little,' Hannah remonstrated. 'Try another mouthful of the almond cream. I have promised to fatten you up, and here you are fading away before my eyes. I don't know what your mother will say to it!' She smiled encouragingly at her guest, but Maria shook her head.

'I'm full and more!' she said. 'Another mouthful and I shall burst like a ripe puff ball.'

'Oh, very well, I shall eat it myself. But the Lord knows what Simon will say. He calls me his "plump pigeon" already!'

Maria frowned slightly, irritated by Hannah's well-meaning attempts at humour. They disturbed her train of thought and obscured the hazy image of Hugo.

'When will he – they – come back?' Maria asked suddenly.

'Who?'

'Why Hugo, of course,' said Maria, 'and Margaret. They have been gone an age. When will the King pardon them?'

Hannah shook her head. 'Who knows what the King will do,' she said, 'or when he will do it! Tis out of fashion to be a Papist.'

'But many people are –'

'*Ssh!*' said Hannah, her tone unintentionally sharp. 'We

don't discuss such matters. They are dangerous. Suffice it that Hugo displeased the King and must suffer for it.'

'But tis scarcely just,' cried Maria. 'Minnie from Ladyford says that Simon also –'

'You must not listen to servants' gossip,' said Hannah. 'It may be well enough in London, but here in Devon we behave differently – and with *dignity*,' she added reprovingly, for their young visitor was proving herself not a little wilful and Hannah was already looking forward to her return to London.

But Maria was not reproved.

'Minnie says that Simon and Hugo *both* displeased the King –' she began, 'and if that be so, why then, Simon should also be exiled – or else,' she added hastily, seeing the look on Hannah's face, 'Hugo should be pardoned and allowed home.'

Hannah's expression had hardened. 'Hugo is very lucky to be alive,' she said. 'Without Luke's intervention they would have hanged him.' Then she looked into the girl's eyes and read her infatuation. Her tone softened a little. 'He will come home some time,' she said. 'Never fear.'

'But when?' she persisted. 'When will he – they – come home?'

Hannah shrugged. 'Who knows?' she said. 'Maybe soon. Maybe not.'

'And where will they live?'

'In London perhaps,' said Hannah, 'or here in Devon. They will buy a house, no doubt, and –'

'What with?' cried Maria, her voice rising. 'Minnie says they have no money. Minnie says they should live here rightfully! She says that –'

Suddenly Hannah brought her small fist down on the table, so that the pewter rattled. 'Stop this!' she said, her tolerance at an end. 'I will not allow you to talk this way. How dare you chatter with the servants on such a matter. Minnie shall go! She has no right –'

Suddenly her voice faltered and, to Maria's astonishment,

she burst into tears, and, jumping to her feet, hurriedly left the room.

Maria raised her eyebrows. So there *was* some truth in what the maid had told her. Hugo *did* have some claim to Heron! She relished the thought for a moment, and then her flash of temper was gone, leaving her repentant.

'But I do so long to see you, Hugo,' she told his ghost. 'I pray you do not stay away too long.'

Sighing, she stood up. Thoughtfully, she dipped a finger into the almond cream which Hannah had abandoned and sucked the cool custard from it. Then she went in search of Hannah, determined to make her peace. It would never do for poor Minnie to lose her place.

The following day found Maria in the kitchen, a large apron covering her gown. She was making a 'love twist' for Hannah, who had still not quite forgiven her for yesterday's outburst. She rolled a triangle of pastry until it was wafer-thin, sprinkled it lavishly with currants and cinnamon, then trailed a spoonful of honey backwards and forwards over the fruit. Then she rolled it up and twisted it into shape.

'That's fine,' said Beth. 'Now into the oven with it, and there's an end to it. And maybe I can have back the use of my table!'

Minnie and Maria exchanged delighted grins.

'I put plenty of honey on it – to sweeten her!' said Maria slyly.

'Then let's hope you didn't over do it,' said Beth, 'for the Mistress has a troublesome tooth and too much sweetness will aggravate it.'

Somewhat chastened, Maria watched the oven door slam shut. Beth departed to discuss the following week's menu, and the two girls were left alone.

'I'll make one for him when he comes home,' said Maria. 'A love twist for Hugo! I'll put even more honey on his – and I'll add a few nuts.'

Minnie sighed admiringly. She enjoyed Maria's romantic fantasies almost as much as Maria did herself.

'What'll you say to him?' she prompted.

Maria hesitated, then smiled. 'I'll say: *A love twist with love*,' she said.

Minnie giggled. 'And what'll Margaret say to that?' It was her favourite question.

'She'll never know,' said Maria. 'I'll give it to him when she's out of the room. She won't hear me say it.'

'I reckon she'll see the crumbs round his mouth when he's ate it!' cried Minnie. 'There'll be summat said then!'

Maria tossed her head. 'Then twill be for him to think of an answer,' she said. 'He's a grown man, not a child. I shan't cosset him.'

The little maid sighed again. 'I wish I was in love,' she said wistfully. 'I'd like that.'

'There's always Jon the stable lad,' said Maria.

Minnie wrinkled her nose thoughtfully. 'Jon? I do like him a little,' she said, 'but I don't think I love him. How do you know if you love someone? How do you know you love Hugo?'

'Because I can't forget him,' said Maria, rising to the bait. 'Because although I haven't seen him for three years, I hold his memory dear. Tis more precious to me than emeralds! More precious to me than –'

'But you was only seven!' protested Minnie. 'Only a babe.'

'I was not a babe,' said Maria earnestly. 'I'm mature for my age. And I recall so clearly . . . He played with me, tossing me up into the air and feigning to drop me, so that I screamed aloud for mercy!'

'I wager I'd scream louder!' cried Minnie, whose bleak childhood had lacked such luxuries. 'I'd swoon away!'

'I came near to it,' said Maria. 'And he chased me and – and searched for me while I hid – and threw rose-hips at me.'

'Jon never throws rose-hips at me,' said Minnie. 'He once threw a horse brush.'

'Tis not the same thing at all,' said Maria impatiently. 'A lover throws rose-hips and petals – and kisses. Oh, if only he was a King! He could come home and divorce Margaret and wed me!'

They eyed each other gleefully at this glittering prospect.

'And what would Margaret say to that?' asked Minnie in mock dismay.

'What indeed!' cried Maria, and they burst into shrieks of laughter until wisps of smoke curling from the edge of the oven brought them down to earth. The love twist, when they rescued it, was blackened and inedible.

Hannah sat at the long oak table, covertly eyeing Maria. The child was growing tall, outgrowing her strength. Her movements were clumsy and awkward, like an untamed colt. Her small oval face was pale and her large grey eyes full of shadows – haunted almost. Half child, half woman, thought Hannah. It was a difficult age. Maria was unpredictable, her mood swinging like a pendulum from deep gloom to wild excitement. She had been at Heron for three weeks, and all that time Hannah had tried to reach her, to understand her; but without success. One minute Maria would melt their hearts with her innocence; the next, she would wound them with her honesty. She was, Hannah mused, like a locked book: one day the lock would be unfastened and the story would be there for all to read. But for the present its contents must remain a mystery.

'So, Maria,' said Hannah cheerfully, 'shall you read to me? You read so well.'

'I have a slight soreness in my eyes,' she lied easily. 'I think it was the dust blowing from the cornfield yesterday.'

'A walk, then?' suggested Hannah. 'We could gather some lavender.'

'The truth is I am out of sorts,' said Maria.

'A sight too many plums, I'll warrant,' laughed Hannah. 'They play havoc with a young lady's constitution.'

'Not so young,' said Maria. 'I am eleven years old.'

'Eleven, is it?' Hannah smiled. 'You'll be choosing a husband soon.'

'I shall never wed,' said Maria, a secret smile on her lips.

'Never wed?' echoed Hannah, pretending wonderment. 'Now, there's a thing to say! And your mother happily wed before she was fifteen. Your mother will find a good husband for you, and –'

'Never!' said Maria firmly.

Maria leaned her elbows on the table, propped her head on her hands and looked at Hannah, who was re-threading her needle with blue silk. Then she slid slowly along the bench until she could see past her, through the open window and into the garden. This was large and symmetrical, as was the fashion, its lawns arranged in squares and circles, dotted with rose bushes and separated one from another by a gravel path or neatly clipped hedge. Statues graced many a corner, and the time of the day could be determined, in sunny weather at least, by a variety of sundials placed at strategic intervals. Further over there was an aviary, and beyond this was the orchard with its formal rows of trees and small cluster of beehives.

Abruptly, Maria left the table and leaned out of the window. Scents of rosemary, tarragon and thyme hung in the air from the herb garden below. She breathed in deeply, but her exhalation of breath became an unintended sigh. She closed her eyes, imagining herself to be once more with the only person whose company would satisfy her. Her lips moved silently.

'*I* would bear you a *live* son, Hugo.' This to remind him of Margaret's failure – a stillborn son. She was aware of Hannah joining her at the window. Still she did not open her eyes.

'Such a perfect day,' Hannah said. 'I shall walk in the garden.'

But as she turned from the window, a small movement beside the nearest hedge caught her eye, and she turned back and stared.

'What is it?' asked Maria.

'There's someone behind the hedge – I'm sure on it,' said Hannah. 'I saw something move.'

'Someone behind the hedge?'

As they watched, a tousled head appeared and disappeared, to reappear again further along.

'And again!' whispered Maria delightedly, her troubles momentarily forgotten. 'Someone is crawling along behind the –'

'Tis Matt!' said Maria. 'It must be. Tis Matt Cartright! Whatever is he about?'

'Cartright?' said Hannah. 'The lad that you were with yesterday?'

'Maria smiled. 'I wasn't with him – he was with me. There's a deal of difference . . . Oh, how funny. He thinks no one can see him!'

'Bless the boy!' said Hannah. 'He's a simple lad, but a good worker and strong as an ox. What's his name again?'

'Matt. I suppose he was baptised Matthew.'

'Ah yes, Matt. I always want to call him Martin, but that's his father's name.'

'He's seen us!' said Maria and waved impulsively as Matt caught sight of the women at the window and rose sheepishly to his feet. He stood undecided as to how to cope with this new turn of events, his round face pink with embarrassment, one hand shielding his eyes from the bright sun as he squinted towards the window.

'What are you doing?' called Maria. 'You look so foolish creeping along there.'

'Maria!' said Hannah reprovingly.

'Well, he does so,' she retorted. 'You think so too.'

But Matt was stammering out his explanation. 'I'm –
no, I'm not – well, I'm not rightly – I'm –'

Maria burst out laughing. 'Are you "sent on a errand"?'
she mocked.

He considered this suggestion for a moment, began to
nod his head and then shook it, scratched his ear and stared
at the ground.

'I'm going out to him,' said Maria, and gathering up her
skirts, darted out of the room before Hannah could stop
her.

Maria ran out of the house and into the garden, but then,
aware that Hannah would be watching, slowed down to a
more lady-like pace. Down the wide stone steps, across the
grass – and there she was, face to face with him again.
Overcome by her sudden appearance and the stern gaze of
the watcher at the window, Matt looked nervously over his
shoulder and around the garden, as though hoping for
assistance of some kind.

Maria smiled and his large grin reappeared. Shyly he took
something from his pocket and offered it to her. It was a
large greeny-blue egg.

'I found it,' he said. 'Twas by the pond. Laid it in the
grass, she did. I didn't steal it.'

'I'm sure you didn't,' said Maria, touched by the gift.
'It's a beautiful egg. Thank you, Matt.' She hesitated and
then added, 'It's a strange colour, though.'

'Duck eggs do be that colour,' said Matt, surprised at her
ignorance. 'That's a duck egg, that is.'

'Oh, how lovely! Is that why you were creeping about
behind the hedge? To bring me this egg?'

He nodded. 'I didn't want – well, I mean, I just wanted
to – like – well –' He stopped and sighed deeply.

'You didn't want anyone else to see you?' prompted
Maria. 'Never mind. They won't take it amiss – and thank
you.' She stepped forward, took hold of his hand and kissed
it lightly. 'There.'

Matt's eyes widened, and a crimson blush slowly spread

18

over his tanned face. He opened his mouth, shut it again and turning abruptly, stumbled away along the path, his large feet scattering gravel onto the close-cropped grass on either side.

'That was very foolish of you, Maria,' cried Hannah from the window. 'Come in at once.'

Maria turned towards her, her eyes closed. With an effort she could still feel Matt's hand on her lips, could still taste the faint tang of salt.

'Do you hear me, Maria? Come in at once!'

Only when taste and feel had faded, did Maria open her eyes. 'I'm coming' she said, and began to imagine how Hugo's hand would feel.

Hannah lay beside Simon and stared wide-eyed into the darkness. She was thinking about Hugo. Maria's words had disturbed her more than she cared to admit. Was Hugo ever likely to return to England and claim Heron? Did he have a legal right to it, as Maria had suggested? The possibility frightened her immeasurably, and her fingers tightened, seeking reassurance from the feel of Simon's hand in hers. Their love-making had been good – slow to start and fierce to the finish – and her beloved husband now lay relaxed, already half asleep; but she knew she must talk to him, or else lie sleepless beside him through the long hours of the night.

'*Simon*,' she whispered. 'Talk with me awhile.'

He grunted an acknowledgement but made no move.

'Simon, I beg you stay awake awhile,' she said softly, and he turned over and took her into his arms.

'What is it?' he asked sleepily.

Hannah knew that if she did not catch his attention quickly he would be asleep again. 'Something is troubling me,' she told him. 'You will call me foolish to fret about it, and mayhap I am, but Simon, I must talk to you.'

'Aye. I'm listening,' he said. 'What is troubling that dainty head of yours?'

Hannah took a deep breath and prayed silently, *'Don't let him be angry, dear God.'*

'Tis about Hugo,' she said.

'Hugo?'

She sensed that he was instantly alert and chose her words carefully. 'Twas Maria's idle chatter,' she told him. 'She asked me today when Hugo would return, and –'

'Who knows?' said Simon. 'Edward will reign for a long time yet – he is only a boy. Poor Hugo may never return.'

'Maria says –' she faltered into silence.

'Maria says,' he repeated. 'What does Maria say?'

'That if he returns he will claim Heron.'

'Claim Heron? Why, what is she thinking of? He would not dream of it! The child romances as usual. Is that all that troubles you?'

'Oh, but Simon,' she said earnestly, 'I am so happy here with you – I can't bear to think of leaving.'

Simon had propped himself on one elbow, and now, in the half-light, she saw that he was shaking his head as if amused.

'And Maria has told you this?' he teased. 'Oh, Hannah, why do you listen so readily to such nonsense? She's only a child and understands nothing. Hugo has no direct claim on Heron except through his father. I am Luke's son and have first claim. While I live there is no –'

'Oh Simon, dearest, don't speak of dying, tis bad luck,' cried Hannah.

Simon laughed gently, and his finger traced the outline of her face. 'I spoke of living,' he said, 'not dying. You are too anxious. How should I die? I am young and fit. No, Hannah, you may sleep sound in your bed of nights. While I live, Heron is ours. Luke would not have it otherwise, you may be sure of that.'

Hannah was silent for a while. Then she said, 'Maria says tis unjust that he is exiled while you remain in England.'

'I agree with her,' he said abruptly, 'but Hugo will not bend the knee – that is a fault in him. He will not be silent, but must speak his mind. Poor Hugo – he's a Papist and proud of it. Many of us pay lip service to the new religion and escape persecution. He would not do so and pays the price.'

'But if Edward dies?' she asked fearfully.

'Ah then, who knows?' He laughed lightly. 'Mary might come to the throne and send *us* away! But no! I only tease you. Do not give it another thought.'

Hannah relaxed. If Simon could laugh, then surely her fears were groundless.

She had been his wife now for nearly three years and had grown to love the man dearly, for all that he was arrogant, self-willed and not one to suffer fools gladly. She had meant to tame him, but instead he had tamed her. Her body, once given so unwillingly, now craved his; her rebellious spirit had surrendered, her hostility had melted away like snow in the warmth of his smile. She had come resentfully to her wedding, but now she wanted only to be with him, to share his life – and to love him. Her one desire was for heirs, and she prayed nightly that God would quicken her body and give her tall, blond sons in her husband's image.

Simon kissed her nose and laughed again. 'And now you must put aside your fears and go to sleep,' he told her. 'The physician calls early tomorrow to see how Luke fares. Twould never do for him to find the lady of the house still asleep.'

But Hannah was still not quite content.

'Simon, when is Maria returning to London?' she asked him. 'She has been here three weeks. I enjoy her company, and yet with all the good will in the world I cannot match her energy. This week we have walked by the river, ridden out over the moors, flown the merlins – oh, *and* travelled into Exeter in search of blue silk for madam's new gown! I swear I'm quite exhausted by it all.'

'My poor, sweet Hannah,' he said softly. 'I cannot have you wearied in this way. Indeed, I've been thinking on the matter and meant to speak to you about it before. Maria shall go home as planned, at the end of the week. How will that do?'

'Very well, Simon, and thank you.'

'You will go to sleep now, you promise?'

'I will.'

'Then goodnight, sweet wife.'

He kissed her gently and turned over, and she smiled faintly into the darkness. Simon, as usual, had put her world to rights again. Within minutes his breathing changed and she knew he slept.

'Goodnight, my love,' she whispered and kissing his smooth shoulder, she too settled herself for sleep.

Luke sat up in bed, propped up with pillows, and waited for Minnie's tap at the door. Each day she came to see him, and always her visits raised his spirits.

Tap, tap.

'Enter, child,' he called, and the door opened to admit her.

She was still small for her age, and all their efforts to put flesh on her bones had failed. Minnie was puny, with stick-like arms and legs; but her heart was large and her spirit generous. All her affections were reserved for Luke, who had first brought her to Heron. She had been a fiercely wayward child then. Now she was growing up; but though less wild, she was still inclined to be unpredictable.

Luke smiled as she came towards him, holding something cupped in her hands.

'A surprise,' she told him gleefully.

'A surprise for me?'

She nodded and reaching the bed, threw her hands wide and scattered the bed with rose-petals.

'What do you think of them?' she asked. 'Melissa says –'

'The Mistress!' he reminded her. 'Not Melissa. You must call her the Mistress.'

She scowled briefly. 'The Mistress,' she amended dutifully. 'The Mistress says you liked to walk in the rose garden. Since your legs no longer carry you, I have brought the roses to you! See: there are two colours – the pink ones are from Heron beside the lawn, the small red ones from Ladyford. Melissa –'

'The Mistress!'

'– The Mistress doesn't know I brought them. I waited until she was busy in the bedchambers. I did but tap the stems and the petals fell into my hand. They were loosed already and waiting to fall.'

'They're beautiful,' he said. 'And such a kindly thought.'

Minnie looked at him anxiously. 'And are you well today?' she asked. 'Do they take good care of you, or shall I come back to Heron, mayhap?'

Luke hid a smile. Minnie had lived at Ladyford since Melissa and Thomas had moved in there, but she remained unimpressed with the arrangement. Heron had been her first home and she considered Ladyford a poor second.

'There is no need, child,' he said gently. 'Hannah cares for me well enough. I am content.'

'But does she feed you well?' Minnie persisted. 'Your face has a pinched look.'

'I am very well apart from these useless legs of mine,' he told her. 'They are swollen and stiff and trouble me at nights, but otherwise I am well and cared for most kindly.'

Minnie sighed and then sniffed loudly. 'The air is stale,' she said. 'Tis well I brought you scented petals.'

'Tis well indeed,' said Luke. 'And how is Oliver today?'

Minnie beamed. 'He leaves his wet-nurse next week,' she said, 'and will be home for good. I shall have my hands full then – but I will still come to see you.'

'I hope you will,' said Luke. 'Is there news of your grandfather?'

23

'He is still in prison,' she said, 'and serve the old pig right. He may rot there all his days for aught I care!'

Luke raised his eyebrows, but said nothing. The old man was an incorrigible horse thief and was lucky to have escaped a flogging, or worse. There was no love lost between Minnie and her grandfather.

'Is the water in your flagon cool enough?' she asked. 'Should I plump up your pillows?'

She looked at him hopefully with her dark button eyes, but he shook his head. 'A little bird tells me,' he said, 'that you have distressed poor Hannah with your idle gossip. No, don't scowl so! I know that look of old.'

A sullen look had settled on her face at his mention of this delicate subject.

'I only spoke the truth,' she said defiantly. 'Maria asked me and I told her. She had no right to tell Hannah. She told me twas a secret between us. I never shall tell her anything more, though she may beg and plead on bended knee! Twas to be a secret – and then she must needs blab it all to Hannah, and Hannah must blab it all to –'

'Hush, child!' said Luke. 'There's no need to take on so. Maria should not have asked you, that is true enough. I'm not angry, but I don't wish it spoken of. Simon is my son and a Kendal, and this is his home.'

'But if he died?' cried Minnie. 'Would Hugo then come to Heron? And if so, would I return? I would serve Hugo and Margaret with all my heart. I would serve Hannah if she would have me, but Hannah hates me.'

Luke sighed. Minnie's one desire was to find a way back into Heron. 'She doesn't hate you,' he explained patiently. 'I have told you before. Hannah brought her own maid with her. She did not need you. Melissa had no one.'

'But if Simon died, and Hugo came to Heron?' she persisted.

'Do not speak of Simon's death,' said Luke sharply. 'Such talk invites disaster. Simon will have heirs, and they will inherit Heron.'

Minnie groaned inwardly. Her chances of reinstatement seemed slight. 'But if he has no heirs, why then, might young Oliver move into Heron?' she asked. 'I would serve Oliver – *Master* Oliver – most devotedly, I swear it.'

Luke shook his head. 'Oliver is a Benet, not a Kendal,' he said. 'No, I will not dwell on such a morbid subject. Simon is fit and in his prime – and you come to Heron each day to visit me. Be content, child – and now leave me, for the medicaments make me drowsy and I must sleep awhile.'

She darted forward, rearranged the pillows solicitously and smoothed his sheets.

'And you are not angry with me?' she asked.

'No, child. I'm not angry. Come and see me tomorrow.'

'I will.'

Already his eyes were closing. Minnie tiptoed to the door, threw him one last adoring glance and let herself quietly out of the room.

CHAPTER TWO
France, May 1553

Margaret clung to the window-ledge, her knuckles white with effort, as she fought off the dizziness and nausea. Behind her in the large oak bed, Hugo slept soundly, his face still tanned from last summer's sun, contrasting with the white linen of the pillow. He lay sprawled across the tousled bed, abandoned and unaware. Margaret envied him his oblivion. She had been awake for nearly an hour, woken as usual by the church bells, which rung at six o'clock to summon the faithful for their first prayers of the day. Soon the small church would fill with dutiful villagers, the young eager to be done with the service and on with the day, the elderly in their sombre clothes, savouring it, enjoying the relaxation before the day's labours began in earnest. Margaret felt guilty that she joined them so rarely, and sensed their disapproval. She could hear them whispering about her when she passed them in the village. Some talked openly, knowing that she understood little of the language – perhaps even aware that she made no effort to learn it.

The people did not like her, but Margaret did not care. She was utterly miserable, incurably homesick for England, and she blamed Hugo for her plight. She shared *his* exile and in her heart she believed that he had brought the punishment upon his own head. Everyone had warned him to curb his tongue and moderate his ways, but he chose to disregard them all with a fine show of defiance. The rebellion in Cornwall had ended disastrously, and many fine men had been hanged for their part in it. Hugo himself had come near to suffering the same fate, and only the intervention of

Luke Kendal had saved him. Instead of death, he had been banished from the country of his birth – and Margaret with him.

She sighed heavily as she watched him turn in the bed with an abrupt movement that tangled the sheets even further. His sleeping face had, she thought, a childlike quality about it, and for a moment she found herself wishing that she could love him now as she had once loved him in England. But her deep misery and black resentment overrode every other emotion and hardened her heart against him.

Outside the window, the village of Béduer straggled down the hillside to the highway which served as a main street, where the 'boulangerie' was to be found. Margaret rarely baked bread now, preferring to buy it from Madame Laffries. Alice, her maid from England, could sometimes be persuaded to turn her hand to it, but this morning she lay sick in bed with an unnamed fever, which had burned her flesh for the past ten days and showed no sign of letting up. Instead of Alice, she now had to make do with Marie, a dull-witted girl who came in daily and spoke not a word of English, forcing them both to rely on gestures, to their mutual irritation. And the girl reeked of garlic! Breath, hair, clothes. It offended Margaret's fastidious nose to such a degree that she contrived whenever possible to be in a different room from her and opened the windows frequently to clear the air. But, if Marie was aware of Margaret's prejudices, she allowed no sign to show in her face, merely gazing impassively at her mistress, her narrow eyes black in her pudgy, grey face. She was a true peasant, thought Margaret bitterly and could not excuse her for that.

Throwing a last glance at her husband, she steadied herself, then threw a shawl over her shoulders and made her way out of the chamber and down the stairs. Gently she drew back the bolts on the heavy wooden door and stood outside on the top step. Later it would be very warm, perhaps even hot. It was already April and the weather was unpredictable. A north-easterly breeze would bring cold air and cloud, but from the south-west the breeze could blow gently in a clear blue sky. The weather was the only thing with which Margaret could find no quarrel.

She looked past the boulangerie to the saddler's workshop, and beyond that to the blacksmith. Monsieur Duprés had at least tried to be kind to her. He had waved his fat hands, unleashing a torrent of words punctuated by nods and smiles, inviting her to sit and watch as he shod a large brown horse. She had wanted to accept, but stubbornly had resisted the impulse, pretending not to understand his pantomime. She refused to let herself be seduced by this alien land with its strange, volatile people and unfamiliar customs.

Beyond the grey shingled rooftops the flat, broad valley lay green and fertile in the early morning haze. The first of the cherry trees were in blossom, more were still bare, and other trees wore a sprinkling of green leaves, lacy against the brown earth. A man drove two black cows along the winding road towards Figeac, accompanied by a small brown dog. Above one of the houses a tiler was already at work, clambering along the ridge of the roof, whistling unconcernedly. In the farmyard to her left, chickens fluttered round a young boy, who was scattering corn from a bowl; a pig, unseen, grunted hungrily. Outside the cottage to her right, the three nanny goats would be grazing along the roadside, tethered on long chains that chinked interminably as the goats' paths crossed and re-crossed. Their milk was coarse, but the greyish cheese was full of flavour and Hugo consumed large quantities of it. He had a fair appetite, thought Margaret, and it was no easy task to satisfy him on the limited money they were allowed to receive from England. Plainly, the young King Edward did not intend them to enjoy their exile.

A flutter of wings from the small loft above her carried the pigeons on their first flight of the day. She must remind Marie to collect the eggs – the wretched girl had a memory like a sieve. Margaret sighed again and wondered if she should go inside and re-read the small bundle of letters from England. There were four from her mother, three from Simon. Ah, Simon. The frown on her face deepened into a scowl. Simon, Luke Kendal's bastard! He sent letters to them as often as he could find a willing carrier – and well he might, she thought bitterly. Simon, pardoned for his part in the rebellion, was still able to live in England, in Heron. Yet Hugo was a true Kendal, a Kendal by birth, the only son of Stephen Kendal, Luke's older brother. On Stephen's death, Hugo had been given his stepfather's name, for he was a wealthy man and had only one son by his previous marriage. Only under the threat of death had Hugo reverted to the name of Kendal.

A woman in black passed, shooing a flock of geese before her, and waved a hand in greeting. *'Bonjour*, madame!' she cried cheerfully.

'Bonjour' said Margaret.

She forced a smile to her lips, but her eyes remained cold. She knew what would follow. The old woman waved her hands and began a lengthy tirade. Foolish old crow, thought Margaret. Didn't she realise that the words meant nothing to her? The old woman paused, awaiting Margaret's reply. Margaret hesitated, then nodded.

It was the wrong answer, apparently. *'Mais non, madame!'* cried the woman, *'non!'* and launched once more into the story. It was always the same. If Margaret appeared not to understand, she would repeat the same tale at twice the volume. Margaret waited for her to finish and said 'Tut, tut,' and shook her head.

'Ah!' the old woman smiled delightedly. *'Vous comprenez, madame!'*

'Oui.'

'Ah!' she said, and was beginning to elaborate on her theme, when one of the geese strayed too far and she was forced to wave farewell and hasten after it.

'Thanks be for small mercies!' muttered Margaret,

wondering idly what the news might have been. Not that it mattered: Hugo would ferret out anything of interest for her. Any scrap of information about England would be carried to him by his many French friends for Hugo was well liked despite his unapproachable wife.

Ironically, it was she, Margaret, who had French blood in her veins: her father was a Dubois, although he had been born in England. The Dubois family still lived in Figeac, less than six miles away, and it was Margaret's grandfather who had found them the cottage in which they now lived and the Dubois family and their friends who had furnished it for them. Naturally they had been immensely grateful. So why, she asked herself for the hundredth time, could she not like them – her own kinfolk? Whatever the reason, it was too late now. She had lived in Béduer for several years but still hated it, finding no beauty in the landscape and no charm in the people. To Margaret Kendal it could never be home. She wanted only to go back to England. Every night she uttered her own special prayer: please let the Protestant Edward die and let the Lady Mary come to the throne at last. Many others thought as she did. The unhappy Margaret was not alone in her deep and treasonable despair.

A letter from Simon later that week brought startling news. Hugo read it aloud.

'". . . Tis said the young King Edward lies sick in Greenwich and confined to his bed. Rumour has it that he suffers a fever, is deathly pale, and his body thin and twisted. Other rumours, more grave, say that his legs are covered in ulcers and that his lungs are infected and him not yet sixteen and at a sensitive age . . ."'

Hugo lifted his eyes from the letter and looked at Margaret.

'The King mortally sick?' she gasped. 'Is that what he means? Is Edward like to die – so young?'

'Twould seem most probable,' said Hugo, 'else why is the succession being discussed?'

Margaret felt a wild rush of hope, but hastily crossed herself and muttered, 'Poor boy. To die so young.' Yet she could not keep the excitement from her voice. 'Read on, Hugo,' she begged.

'"... Men say openly that Lady Jane Grey will wed Northumberland's son and will be Queen before the year is out –"'

Margaret gasped, and her joy faded.

'The Lady Jane Grey!' she exclaimed. 'But what of Mary, the King's own sister? Surely her claim is greater? What trickery is this? What does it mean, Hugo?'

Hugo shook his head slowly. 'Northumberland does not give in so easily,' he told her. 'For five years they have brought about Protestant reforms. They will not want a Catholic Queen. Northumberland would be signing his own death warrant.'

Margaret put a hand to her heart, which was pounding with a new and sudden fear. 'But Hugo,' she whispered. 'Our return to England? I have so long prayed for – for –'

Tears filled her eyes, and Hugo drew her gently towards him.

'What will be, will be,' he said. 'There is nothing we can do but wait and pray. Who knows? The Lady Jane Grey may well pardon such as us. They do say she is an intelligent girl and well-read. A tolerant girl, mayhap. So no tears, I beg you, until we know our fate more surely.'

But Margaret clung to him. 'Hugo, I think I am with child again,' she whispered. 'Twill be a boy, I know it. I want our son to be born in England.'

'With child? You did not speak of it before!'

'I wanted to be sure. I feared to disappoint you again,' she said. 'Oh Hugo, tis my deepest wish to give you a son. Tell me this time that God will spare our child. I am so frightened.'

Hugo patted her back comfortingly. 'You must not be so

31

fearful,' he reproached her. 'They say an anxious mother is bad for her child. Put your trust in God, and this time all will be well, I promise you. You are quite recovered from the last birth and much stronger now.'

'So you are pleased, Hugo, at my news? Say you are pleased.'

He kissed her gently. 'I'm delighted with my clever wife! When will it be?'

'December most probably,' she told him eagerly. 'A Christmas gift from me to you.'

He laughed, and his pleasure lifted her own spirits.

'Christmas,' he said wonderingly. 'Who knows? Much can happen in seven months. We may be home by then. Imagine that! Our first son born in London. What do you say to that, eh?'

'I say Amen to it,' said Margaret fervently, and they clung together once more, a new and desperate hope in both their hearts.

Across the Channel, events moved steadily. Edward's condition grew worse, and Northumberland was forced to accept the fact that the King's death was approaching. Another month passed, and still the succession was not secured. The King's doctor was sent away, and a wise woman was brought in to rally the unfortunate boy by any means at her disposal. Her 'miracle cure' lasted long enough for Northumberland to ensure that the crown would go to Lady Jane Grey, bypassing the two Tudor sisters. By the time the young King's physician was allowed back to tend him, it was already too late: gangrene had developed. Three weeks later the pathetic Edward's wasted body gave up the ghost.

Whatever the weather, the market place in Figeac was always crowded, for the stalls were set up under a roofed area in the middle of the square. In wet weather it afforded shelter from the rain, and now, in late August, it provided a shade from the glare of the mid-day sun. Margaret, accompanied by Alice, moved slowly, conserving her energy. The worst of her morning sickness was past now, and her body, accepting its growing burden, had rounded out so that even the outline of her face had softened. There was a new brilliance about her eyes that revealed her inner happiness.

She paused at the fish stall and bought some mackerel. She would marinade them in oil and vinegar – it was one of Hugo's favourite dishes. An old woman sat beside a huge pile of yellow melons and smiled toothily at Margaret as she felt the fruit, pressing top and bottom to test for ripeness. She bought two, and Alice took them wearily and stowed them in the wicker panier that would be strapped across the saddle of her horse for the return journey. Normally she enjoyed the weekly ride into Figeac, but today her head ached dully and her eyes itched uncomfortably.

'Have we forgotten anything, I wonder?' said Margaret. 'In this heat we might forget our own names? Ah – cheeses! I thought there was something else.' She noted for the first time her maid's apathy and smiled at her kindly. ''Twill take me a few moments only,' she said. 'You go back to the horses. By the time you are loaded up I shall be with you.'

The girl scuttled off thankfully, and Margaret sought out the old man who sold goats' milk and cheese. Today he also had ewes' milk cheese, and she bought a small quantity. Wasps buzzed interminably, attracted by the smell of broken peaches or damaged oranges, but the old people in their sombre black either swatted them without interest or ignored them altogether. Ragged children ran in and out, stealing where they could; others, neatly dressed, trailed after their mothers, wide-eyed.

A small black dog sprang yelping under Margaret's feet, making her stumble; instinctively she put out a protecting hand to her belly. Uneasy memories of her miscarriage came into her mind, with the image of her little boy, perfectly formed, but dead within minutes of the birth. 'No!' she whispered. 'I'll not think on it. I have promised Hugo.'

Taking a deep breath, she relaxed and straightened her back. Ahead of her the lacemaker tried to catch her interest, but she shook her head and made her way out of the shade into the full heat of the sun. At least the crush of bodies was less here, and the wasps fewer. She walked quickly back to the rail, where Alice waited with the horses. She was already mounted on the large cob, but slid to the ground to assist Margaret onto her sober dappled mare.

As they rode through the town and out into the country at a leisurely pace, both were busy with their own thoughts. Alice had seen a young farmer who had winked his eye at her for the third week running, and her mind wove delightful fantasies around him. Margaret's thoughts divided themselves between her coming child and dreams of England. In silence they covered the first two miles along the road to Béduer, barely registering the greetings or stares of the people they passed – a young girl collecting snails along the roadside; a jovial carter whistling the journey away, a flagon of wine on the seat beside him; an old woman who sat knitting in the hedgerow, while a small flock of black-faced sheep grazed around her.

'Who's this coming hell for leather?' said Alice suddenly. Margaret relinquished her dreams to shade her eyes and stare ahead at the two horsemen who approached. For a moment fear leapt within her, but she gave no sign to Alice, merely advising her to 'stay close and say nothing'.

Alice however, her eyesight keener than that of her mistress, cried out in her excitement, 'Ma'am! Tis the Master and another gentleman.'

Margaret gasped. They were waving their hats and hallooing. Oh, dear God, what could it mean?

Conscious of her condition, she resisted the urge to spur

her horse forward, and Alice, too, held back, waiting for the two men to reach them.

'Hugo!' cried Margaret 'and – Simon?' she stared at him, astonished.

'Simon Kendal in person and at your command, sweet cousin!' he cried, and drawing alongside, made her a small bow. Then he took her hand and kissed it almost passionately.

It gave her a strange feeling to look once more upon the blond head and arrogant blue eyes of this young man whom she could not love. His head was thrown back, his lips parted in a smile of triumph, and Margaret noted the contrast between the two men – Simon so fair and Hugo so dark.

Hugo's brown eyes flashed with a barely suppressed excitement. 'I will let you tell it, Simon,' he cried, 'for you have come so far with your news.'

'Tell what?' cried Margaret. 'What news, Simon?'

Hugo turned his horse abruptly so that he sat alongside her, taking her hand in his as though to share physically in her reaction. 'Tell her, Simon, for God's sake, or I swear I shall tell her myself.'

Simon smiled at her. 'Why, that the King is dead –'

'Dead? So soon?'

'Aye, and out of his misery, poor wretch. Lady Jane Grey –'

'Ah no!' cried Margaret.

Simon grinned at Hugo conspiratorially. 'Lady Jane was England's Queen – but for ten days only. The Lady Mary is to take her rightful place on the throne of England! What say you to that news, sweet Margaret? Was it worth a Channel crossing to tell?'

'Oh, I can scarce believe it,' she cried. 'Oh Simon! Hugo! Our beloved Lady Mary, Queen at last. God bless her. Can we go home, then? Tell me, Simon. Can we go home?'

'You can, sweet lady. The Lady Mary has pronounced that she will tolerate all her subjects to follow their own

35

conscience without restraint. Those are her very words. So we, too, may serve God in our way.'

'You, too? Then you are – have embraced –' She broke off, slightly embarrassed.

'Aye, we are more Protestant than Catholic,' Simon admitted. 'Half England is also. Times change, and we have had a Protestant King in England for nearly six years now.'

She looked at Hugo and he smiled reassuringly. 'England will still be England,' he told her. 'Protestant or Catholic, it is still home. We shall leave France within the month and take lodgings in London. Simon has arranged it well. Did I not tell you he was a true friend? No man ever had truer.'

'My deepest thanks, Simon,' said Margaret. She turned to the maid. 'There, Alice, we are to go home at last. Are you pleased?'

'Aye, ma'am. Never more so,' said Alice.

'Are you certain sure?' asked Simon, teasing. 'We cannot offer you such sunshine as this. Indeed, when I left Dover it was raining, and the wind blew hard in the Channel.'

'I care not,' cried Alice recklessly. 'England may have snow in July, but I will want to be there.'

As they turned their horses homeward, Margaret asked for more details of the past month's events. 'Lady Jane – her reign was so short. Is she dead, also?'

'No, no. Not dead,' Simon told her, 'but a prisoner in the Tower, her husband with her.'

'And the little princess – Elizabeth?'

'In London with her sister. Twas quite a sight, they say. She rode into London at the end of July with a thousand horsemen in green and white, and the crowds went wild with joy. Queen Mary met her at Wanstead and they rode together, bells pealing, bands playing and flowers falling like rain over them.'

'I wish I had seen them,' said Margaret wistfully.

'And so you shall, one day,' Hugo comforted her. 'When we are home . . .'

'*Home!*' echoed Margaret wonderingly. 'Such a little

36

word!' She stretched out a hand and touched Hugo's arm. 'We're going home,' she said,and as she did so, the tears welled up in her eyes. Hugo leaned over in the saddle to put an arm round her shoulders and so they rode homeward, Hugo comforting, Margaret weeping unashamedly.

Margaret stood in the ship's waist and looked out across the grey sea towards the faint, smudged line of grey that separated water and sky. That line, thought Margaret, is home.

'It looks good, ma'am, does it not?' said Alice.

'It looks very good,' agreed Margaret. 'Our ordeal by sea will soon be at an end and we shall stand on firm ground at last. I wonder if anyone will be at the quayside to greet us. Tis hard for them to guess when we shall make landfall, but twill be good to see a familiar face.'

The thin grey line thickened imperceptibly as the ship closed the distance between them. The French coast had long since vanished like a bad dream; England loomed ahead, and with it the glittering future.

'The Captain says we shall probably make Portsmouth,' said Hugo, joining them at the rail. But if the wind drops, it may be Plymouth.'

Simon followed him and the four of them stared out, eyes narrowed in an effort to pick out details in the land mass slowly being revealed to them. Hugo sighed luxuriously and took a deep breath.

'Tis English air,' he told them, laughing, 'and it smells so good.'

Simon drew a deep breath and considered it. 'No trace of garlic!' he said. 'I do believe him. Tis English air.'

'Even the Thames at low tide would smell good to me,' said Hugo. 'So many years on foreign soil, and now tis over at last! We shall be there before nightfall.'

'And shall we sleep over, in Portsmouth?' asked Margaret.

Simon nodded. 'We shall take lodgings for the night and rest well. Tomorrow I shall find a carter and we shall go by wagon to London. I think twill be simpler with so much luggage. A train of pack horses can be a source of great aggravation if tis hot – the idle nags will not move themselves and we should grow hoarse shouting at them.'

Behind and around them, other exiles now crowded the deck, all eager for a sight of England as the grey line took shape and colour and the distant red cliffs of Devon slid by, topped by green fields and wooded slopes. A silence fell on the watchers as the sails above them flapped and billowed in the capricious wind and the halliards snapped and hummed under the strain. Alice, who was a poor sailor, retired once more to groan unheard in the dark, cramped quarters belowdecks, while England drew nearer minute by minute.

The *Rose of Sharon* docked in Portsmouth harbour at exactly ten minutes past eight on September the twentieth 1553. Half an hour later they stood together on the quayside, shivering slightly in the cool evening air.

'Thanks be to God,' said Hugo. 'We are home at last.'

It was almost dark. Hurriedly, they sought out the hospitality of an inn, where they found a small log fire smouldering in the hearth – a concession to the cool autumn evenings. A well-scrubbed tableboard held cold meats, bread and cheeses, and a selection of fruit tarts. Their friendly host cleared an end of the table for them, pushing the previous diners aside with a few cheerful but pointed remarks to the effect that they had supped well enough already.

'There we are, my friends,' he told them genially. 'Food fit for a King – or should I say Queen! And what'll you have to wash it down? Our own good ale? Or a flagon or two of Bordeaux wine?'

'We'll take some of each,' Simon told him, 'and bid your wife see to the beds. We are desperately weary.'

'I will see to it,' he promised. 'But as to the beds, there's just the two in the one room: one for the lady and her maid and the other for you two gentlemen. Tis either that, or two of you must sleep over the stable.'

Simon looked enquiringly at Hugo, but Margaret intervened.

'Tis of no matter,' she said. 'We will all sleep like innocents tonight. The two beds will serve us well enough.'

They ate well and in wonderful spirits. Even Alice seemed to have recovered from her seasickness and found an appetite. After the meal, Margaret and Alice retired to bed – a straw mattress laid on a wide truckle bed.

'But at least it will not rock from side to side,' said Alice, 'and we shan't hear the ship's rats squeaking behind the woodwork.'

'And there's a warm brick apiece,' said Margaret, investigating. 'Wrapped in flannel to comfort our toes.'

Alice helped her to undress, and Mistress and maid were soon in bed. Their conversation flagged and grew disjointed and they were asleep within minutes of each other. Meanwhile the two men walked along the quayside, making plans for the future.

'I'll travel with you to London,' said Simon, 'and see you safely installed in your lodgings, which I hope will please you. Then the Lessors will look after you until you find your way. Your mother will be back at Sampford Courtenay by the middle of October, so no doubt you will visit her.'

'Was she much affected by my stepfather's death?' asked Hugo.

'I fear you will see a change in her,' Simon told him, 'but she goes into retreat twice a year and insists that she benefits from it.'

'And your father, Simon?'

'Most anxious to see you again,' said Simon diplomatically. 'But I fear he is greatly aged since his fall. His legs are quite useless now, and he never leaves his bed. But his mind is as active as ever it was, and I think he is as happy as can be expected.'

'It has been a long time,' said Hugo. 'No doubt you find us changed.'

'I do,' laughed Simon. 'Indeed I do. You are wiser and calmer! And your charming Margaret has changed from a girl to a woman – and is with child. I envy you most heartily.'

Hugo put a finger to his lips. 'We must not tempt fate,' he said, 'but we are full of hope.' He hesitated, then said, 'And what of Hannah?'

Simon sighed. 'So far her womb remains stubbornly empty, and yet she desires a child most passionately. But there is plenty of time and she is very young.'

'And will Hannah welcome us to Heron?' asked Hugo.

'Most willingly,' said Simon, surprised at the question. 'You must visit us before the winter sets in and makes the roads impassable.'

They turned and walked back to the inn where the shutters at street level were now closed against intruders.

'Goodnight to you both,' said their host, and they went up to bed.

Simon fell asleep as soon as his head touched the pillow, but Hugo lay awake for a while longer, savouring to the full his first night in England.

'And what now?' he thought. 'What to do and where to go?' But sleep robbed him of an answer.

CHAPTER THREE
London 1553

Maria's discomfort grew with each passing moment. The floorboards were cold to her knees. The door made a hard resting place for her forehead. Her hands, clasped tightly together, were cramped and the knuckles white. She disregarded these discomforts, however. Her eyes were closed, and her lips moved almost soundlessly in fervent supplication.

'. . . So will you please let Margaret die, dear Father in Heaven. Or run away, perchance . . . But take her away from him, I beseech you, if you care for me at all. She does not make him happy, I know it. Look down, dear Father, and see for yourself! Because she does not love him as I do. Nor ever could do. Nor does he love her, I am convinced of it. Oh, dear Lord and Father, take note of this prayer, I beg you, and act upon it in your infinite mercy and wisdom . . .'

Maria was slimmer now, with large, dark eyes, long thick hair and a full mouth. She was generous, wilful – and still passionately in love. She relaxed briefly to rub at her knees, but almost immediately resumed her kneeling position against the door of Hugo and Margaret's bedroom. 'I have done Thy will,' she confided earnestly, 'and have not lied, nor committed an adultery – nor yet a murder. But Thou hast not –'

'Whatever are you about?'

The girl spun round, alarmed, to find her mother beside her, a candle in her hand.

'I am saying my prayers,' she said hastily.

'At midnight? And at this door?'

'Yes.'

Well used to Maria's spirited ways, her mother folded her arms purposefully. 'Back to bed!' she said. 'And speedily.'

'I haven't finished the prayer!' Maria protested.

'Then finish it at your own bedside, you saucy baggage.'

Slowly, reluctantly, Maria rose to her feet. There was a small damp mark on the door where her forehead had pressed against it, which she now rubbed at with her finger.

'Leave the door alone!' said her mother sharply. 'I can't imagine what you're thinking of – traipsing about at dead of night in nothing but your nightgown. You'll catch your death of cold, and you'll have no one to blame but yourself.'

'Not in October!' said Maria.

'Don't answer back! Now, are you going, or do I box your ears?'

'I will go back to bed,' Maria said hurriedly, 'but I shan't sleep.'

'Then you shall have a sleeping-draught. I'll fetch it at once.'

Reluctantly, Maria padded back along the narrow passage to her own room. Once there, she flung herself onto the bed and pounded the pillow with her fists. Stopping abruptly, she cast a look heavenward, and whispered, 'So *do* something, I beseech you. I will make him happy, I swear it. Amen.' Then she dived under the sheets and, stretching out full length, lay quite still until her mother returned.

'What were you asking Him for so fervently?' she asked curiously, as Maria sat up and sipped the warm draught.

'It's a secret,' she said triumphantly.

'And why outside Hugo and Margaret's door? Were you looking through the keyhole?'

'No, I was not.'

'Well, that's a mercy. The very idea! Visitors in our house – and Margaret so good to you, too.'

'I tell you I was not.' Maria finished the draught and handed the cup back to her mother. 'I shall have a nightmare now,' she grumbled, sliding back under the bedclothes and allowing her mother to tuck her in. 'I always do.

I have a nightmare every night. Shall I tell you of it?'

'No, you shan't,' said her mother. 'I have nightmares enough of my own without hearing yours. You just settle yourself to sleep, and no more wandering.'

Maria put out her tongue at the retreating figure as the light from the candle dwindled and finally died with the closing of the bedroom door, then she turned onto her side and closed her eyes. Her mother's words returned to prick at her conscience, and she turned over, wrenching the bedclothes with her. She tried to delay the effect of the sleeping-draught by concentrating her thoughts on Hugo, staring into the darkness and willing her eyes to remain open. But to no avail – five minutes later they fluttered and closed and she slid despairingly into her familiar nightmare.

She found herself on a broad, quiet beach at night, the dry sand crusted and cold beneath her bare feet. The moon shone fitfully at the whim of passing clouds, and the tide, a long way out, rolled sighing onto the beach. A long way behind her, rounded cliffs rose to a great height, and large misshappen rocks lay tumbled on the sand. As she walked, Maria gazed intently around her, searching the long shadows for something unspecified. The braying of a donkey broke the silence and she glanced over her shoulder, but the beach remained empty. Turning now towards the sea, she quickened her steps, hearing the sound of waves grow louder. Beneath her feet the sand grew firm and damp, and around her the hated whispers started. They grew louder with each step – fierce, angry words, hissing sharply through the cold, dark air like unseen arrows. She quickened her steps again, but the sand grew wetter and her feet sank deeper with each step. The donkey brayed again, and the sighing of the waves became a low, rhythmic roar. Maria gasped as the sand became a thick, cloying mud. The whispers became shouts, the waves became breakers racing towards her, their crests curling white in the moonlight. The rocks, ugly and distorted now, doubled and then trebled their size and number until they covered most of the beach and hid the approaching sun. The mud sucked at her ankles, and she could no longer free herself. The sea broke against the wall of rocks with a crash of glittering spray which fell around her, cold as ice, driving against her face like hail. The shouts gave way to frenzied roars as, soundlessly, Maria began to scream . . .

As the carriage rolled uncomfortably along the cobbled streets, Maria lifted a corner of the leather curtain and looked out. Rays of sunlight filtered down into the narrow street between the wood and plaster houses which overhung the cobbles. Dust swirled into the air from the carriage wheels, and flies buzzed over the rubbish, which lay in the central gutter awaiting the arrival of the rakers, whose job it was to cart it away.

'I swear that London is even more crowded than I remember,' said Margaret.

Maria sat with a perfumed handkerchief to her nose to block out the street smells. Looking out of the other side, Margaret withdrew her hand hastily. A ragged beggar had appeared alongside and was thrusting his hand in at the opening that served as a window, crying 'Alms! Alms!'

Maria, turning, shuddered at the sight of him, his teeth blackened with decay, his face disfigured by ugly sores. Margaret shouted to the driver who gave the wretch a flick with his whip. With a cry of pain, he fell back, cursing, to await the next carriage.

'Poor man,' said Maria.

Margaret shrugged helplessly. 'How can we help them all?' she asked. 'If we gave so much as a groat we would be beseiged before you could wink!'

The carriage stopped suddenly, and there was a deal of shouting and swearing. Where the narrow street crossed another, the driver of a large brewers' cart sat with his arms resolutely folded, impervious to the threats and insults being hurled upon him by two other men, one pushing a

44

handcart full of fish and one driving a wagon. To add to the noise, a man in the corner house was yelling angrily to them from an upstairs window to 'get their ramshackle heaps moving and let honest folk have a bit of peace'. The various drivers then united in abusing *him* and a crowd of delighted urchins joined in, weaving in and out between the wheels, tormenting the horses, who were beginning to champ and snort restlessly.

Maria took great delight in this exchange, but Margaret grumbled impatiently. A passing orange seller saw his chance. 'Oranges! Sweet oranges!' he called cheerfully. Maria's eyes lit up.

'May we buy some,' she asked, 'to eat while we wait?'

Margaret laughed. 'Just one each, then,' she told her, 'but we shall be beseiged, you see!'

It was just as she predicted. As soon as money changed hands and the oranges were passed in through the window, an old pedlar sidled up offering laces and ribbons, to be immediately shouldered out of the way by a large woman carrying a tray of meat pies. They were just beginning to argue good-naturedly, Margaret having refused their wares, when the carriage jerked forward and the passengers were rattled on their way once more.

Madelaine le Breton opened the door, a smile illuminating her pale face. She was small and thin and wore a simple grey dress with a single red rose tucked into the bodice. Her dark hair curled naturally all over her head, defying all her efforts to coax it into a fashionable style. There were flecks of grey in her green eyes. Maria thought her the most beautiful woman she had ever met, and stared at her, forgetting even a greeting until Margaret nudged her.

'And you must be Maria,' said Madelaine.

'Yes – er – *oui, ma'mselle*,' said Maria, hoping that Margaret would be impressed by her command of French.

45

Madelaine smiled. 'And Maria is to have a new gown?'

'Yes. It is a present from Hugo and Margaret,' Maria told her.

'For her birthday,' said Margaret. 'She is twelve on the seventeenth of this month.'

Madelaine smiled. 'Twelve!' she echoed. 'Oh, what a fine age! I remember how I fell in love when I was twelve. Such delight! Such feeling! It is never the same again, because you are never twelve again. How I envy you, Maria.'

Maria was enchanted. The dressmaker had interpreted her own mood perfectly. Madelaine waved a hand in a sweeping gesture to indicate the bed at the far side of the room. A sheepskin rug was draped over it for daytime use, for there was little furniture and the bed doubled as a seat. Maria and Margaret sat down.

'Thank you, Madelaine,' said Margaret. 'I'm sorry we are a little late, but the roads are hopeless. You cannot move, now, for carts and waggons. And so many people! It really is quite scandalous the way nothing is done.'

The dressmaker raised expressive hands. *'C'est terrible,'* she agreed. 'The little daughter of the landlady – she has a new hoop and cannot bowl it, poor little one. But I'm forgetting my manners. You will have a glass of wine, yes?' They both nodded, and Madelaine went off to busy herself at the kitchen end of the room.

Maria looked around her, fascinated. It was a large room, but very cluttered. A basket stood nearby, overflowing with ribbons, laces, cottons and wools. Several lengths of material lay across the table board. There were several unfinished garments hanging along the wall: a small green dress minus sleeves, a damask coat and an embroidered waistcoat awaiting buttons and buttonholes. Beside the bed was a small plain cupboard, and on it Maria was thrilled to see a hand-painted miniature of a young man, dark, handsome and unsmiling. He must be Madelaine's current lover – she was sure of it. She studied the face, and acknowledged grudgingly that it compared very favourably with

Hugo. A single yellow tulip grew in a small earthenware pot beside it, its petals almost translucent in the sunlight. Maria stared at it. The dressmaker, seeing her interest, smiled.

'*My* birthday present,' she said. 'I have always wanted a tulip.'

'And when was your birthday?' Maria asked.

'October the ninth.'

'So you were born under Libra,' said Maria, 'with Venus as your planet in your element. Was your first love Gemini?'

Madelaine shook her head. '*Mais non!* He was a Capricorn.'

'That's why it didn't last then,' said Maria, accepting her wine.

Madelaine laughed. 'I will take more care in the future,' she assured her.

Greatly daring, Maria asked, 'Is *he* your new love – the man in the picture by your bed?'

'Maria, please!' cried Margaret, embarrassed. 'You know better than to –'

But Madelaine was not offended. She shook her head. 'That is my brother, Philippe,' she told Maria. 'He cares for me now that our father is dead. Tis Philippe who gives me the tulip.'

'Does he live with you?' Maria persisted.

'He travels between France and England, but he is in England now. He was with me yesterday and brought me this rose.' She indicated the rose in her dress.

Maria was instantly seized with a longing for Hugo to give *her* a rose and decided that when they were married, he would have to bring her a flower every day for her to wear in her bodice, next to her heart. Forgetting Madelaine and Margaret, she drifted happily into a romantic reverie, but was soon recalled to the present by demands that she consider the design for her new gown.

The dressmaker had made several sketches, and she studied each of them eagerly. One showed alternative styles for the sleeves and a note at the side suggested ribbon or

47

braid where the fullness ended. The waistline could be worn two ways – either straight, or curved down to a point in the front. A rose-coloured damask had already been chosen, for it was to be a warm dress for chill winter days. The dressmaker produced a selection of lace, and they tried them one after another against the damask, until finally Maria had made a choice.

'I shall need a new gown soon,' Margaret confided to Madelaine. 'I am with child, and already my –'

Maria gave a slight gasp. Her breathing quickened and she felt hot and then cold, hearing the two voices as if from somewhere a long way off. She closed her eyes. Margaret with child . . . Margaret and Hugo, together . . . Hugo, her adored Hugo, giving Margaret a child!

She opened her eyes. She heard Madelaine's congratulations, but interrupted her, her voice shrill.

'Why didn't you tell me?'

Margaret stared at her, surprised at her tone and expression. 'Why Maria, I would have spoken of it shortly, but –'

'I do not want you to be with child! Do you hear me! I do not want it.' Her eyes blazed in a face suddenly pale.

The room was suddenly quiet. Margaret and Madelaine looked at her, dismayed. Margaret put out a tentative hand to comfort her, but it was thrust fiercely away as tears filled Maria's eyes and spilled down her cheeks.

'Don't touch me,' she wept. 'I hate you.'

'Maria, I beg you, don't speak so wildly,' began Margaret, but Maria sprang to her feet and seizing the damask, snatched it up and threw it on to the floor. The braid followed.

'Oh, Maria, I beg you,' cried Margaret again. 'Will you not be pleased for us and say that you love us? For indeed, we love you.'

'I don't want your love,' shouted Maria, her face streaked with tears, her voice harsh. 'And I don't love you or Hugo.'

'My dearest child –'

'I am *not* a child.'

48

Her voice had risen almost to a scream. Madelaine watched helplessly as Margaret tried to put her arms round the weeping girl.

'Don't touch me,' sobbed Maria. 'I do not want the dress. I want nothing from you. Nothing.' And she ran to the door and stumbled blindly down the narrow stairs.

'Let her be,' said Madelaine. 'Poor little one – she is jealous.'

They found her five minutes later, sitting on the bottom stairs, her face rigid with despair and misery. She mumbled an apology and followed Margaret out into the street. Silently, they made the return journey in a deep and uncompromising gloom.

Her mother was slicing oranges in the kitchen next morning when she heard movements overhead and the click of a door told her that Maria was about. 'And not before time,' she muttered irritably, having suffered the previous day, along with the rest of the family, from the girl's depression. Maria's mood had set a chill on all their spirits, for she had shut herself away in her bedroom, refusing to eat anything or to speak to anyone.

There were footsteps on the stairs and Maria appeared in the kitchen doorway, her face pale, her eyes red-rimmed from anguished weeping. Her mother gave her a quick glance, then returned to her task.

'Where is everybody?' asked Maria.

'Out,' said her mother unhelpfully, scooping up the sliced oranges and dropping them into a large earthenware crock which stood on the floor beside her. Then she fetched a large kettle of water from the fire and poured it over the oranges until they were covered.

'Orange wine?' said Maria.

Her mother nodded. 'And how's the temper today?' Maria shrugged. 'A little sweeter than yesterday, I hope.'

'I dare say.'

Taking a jar of sultanas from the cupboard, her mother added three handfuls to the hot orange mixture and stirred it all briskly with a large wooden spoon.

'What's for supper?' asked Maria.

'Oh, it's supper now, is it? Condescending to eat today, are we? Well, it's roast kid and quince tart – yes, you may well look like that! Your favourite meal – and specially chosen by Margaret, bless her, "to comfort you", she says. Comfort you, indeed! A beating might serve you better.'

She glanced at her daughter to see if these chastening remarks were having the desired effect. Maria looked suitably crushed, but her thoughts were busy elsewhere. Aware of the bad impression she had created by her behaviour the previous day, she was concerned to reinstate herself in Hugo's eyes as swiftly as possible. Her mother took up two lemons from the table, made a cut in each and squeezed the juice into the crock. A small pot of yeast and water was warming on the hob; this was well mashed and spread on a thick slice of bread.

'I'm going to apologise,' Maria announced.

'I should think so too.' She floated the bread and yeast on top of the liquid in the crock and topped it up from the kettle. Her reaction was not all that Maria had hoped for, but at least so far she had made no sarcastic comment.

'Where are they gone?' she asked at last, unable to hold the question back any longer.

Her mother covered the crock with two layers of butter muslin and straightened up, her hands on her hips. 'Hugo has taken Margaret to the physician,' she told her. 'She's been suffering of late with twinges and cramps – it's early days yet, and not natural.'

'It's to do with the baby, then?'

'Seemingly.'

A wild hope leapt in Maria's breast, and wicked though it was, she nourished it. Margaret might die in childbirth – it was a frequent enough occurrence, after all. Hugo would be left desolate – and *she* would be the one to comfort him!

Hastily she lowered her eyes lest her mother should see the gleam in them. Then her conscience pricked her and she made an effort to think kindly of Margaret.

'Where is this physician? I think I will walk to meet them on their return.'

'Other side of the town,' her mother told her, 'below the bridge. First landing stage, I reckon. Aye, walk down and meet them and sweeten your expression as you go. Mayhap the fresh air will sweeten your temper too.'

The 'fresh air' proved, in the event, to be a misnomer. The tide was half out and the grey-green slime which clung to the wooden posts and planking gave off an unpleasant smell in the still, warm air. Maria wrinkled her nose in disgust and kicked at a rotten orange, which sped into the water with a satisfying plop.

A line of barges was making its way slowly upriver, where the water was deepest, and conversation and snatches of song drifted across the water in many different tongues. Skilfully a waterman steered his wherry to avoid them and pulled alongside the landing steps to allow his passengers to disembark. The craft bumped and swung against the wooden steps but the man made no effort to help his passengers as they clambered awkwardly ashore, instead watching with rather grim amusement and whistling the while. As the disembarking passengers climbed up the steps, those about to replace them scrambled down. There was never any shortage of passengers for London Bridge; it was the only bridge across the river and it more closely resembled a street, with market stalls set up daily along its length so that horses and wheeled traffic of any kind met with frequent delays. Idly Maria watched the people board the boats, fascinated as always. She had lived in London all her life but the river had never lost its appeal for her.

As she watched, she heard a flower seller behind her.

'Sweet violets! Buy my sweet violets!'

51

Maria's face lit up. The ideal peace offering! Quickly she checked the occupants of the next incoming boat and, satisfied that Hugo and Margaret were not on it, set off towards the flower seller, from whom she bought a small bunch of violets tied with white ribbon. 'For your sweetheart?' the woman teased, and for a moment Maria wished she could give them to Hugo instead. Reluctantly she decided against the idea. Holding the fragrant flowers to her nose and sniffing appreciatively, she then held them out at arm's length and nodded with satisfaction. She returned to the steps and waited impatiently, until she finally saw two familiar figures in one of the boats which slipped towards her through the placid brown water. Maria shouted until Hugo caught sight of her and pointed her out to Margaret, who waved cheerfully.

As the boat drew nearer, Maria moved to the top of the steps, holding the violets behind her back. At the bottom of the steps a young lad in a rowboat untied his boat and slid the first oar into its rowlock. The waterman cursed.

'God's death! Get out of it, you young scum! How am I to pull alongside – get yourself out of my way, and make haste about it!'

Not at all disconcerted, the young boy put his tongue out. 'Since when have you owned the river?' he taunted. 'I'll go when I'm right set up and not before.'

'The Devil you will! You'll go now or feel my fist when I catch up with you!'

'Which will be never, codsbelly!'

Maria giggled. The waterman, his face reddening, shook his fist.

'I'll give you a rare hiding,' he roared. 'Teach you a few manners, you young vagabond! I'll give you "codsbelly", if I lay hands on you. Now move, I say.'

The lad laughed gleefully, aware now of his audience on the steps, and with his free oar reached out and gave the waterman a fierce poke in the back, which set the boat rocking. Margaret cried out fearfully and Hugo, no longer amused by the incident, joined the waterman in his curses.

At that moment the day became suddenly unreal for Maria. The sunlit scene was inexplicably charged with an atmosphere that defied her comprehension, and she became strangely aware of the approaching catastrophe. She stood motionless, her eyes on Margaret, surprised that it all seemed to be happening so slowly. The waterman, turning, dropped one of his own oars and reached out at the one wielded by the boy, trying to jerk it from his grasp. Both boats rocked violently and the boy was forced suddenly to let go his oar in order to save himself from over-balancing. The waterman fell backwards, the oar caught Margaret on the side of the head, the boat rocked again – and she was overboard! Her thin, despairing cry hung echoing in the warm air, and before Maria's terrified eyes, she sank slowly under the muddy brown water.

In contrast, everything that followed happened quickly. The young boy suddenly leapt from his boat, stumbled through the mud, dashed up the steps past the people waiting there, who were too shocked to stop him, and lost himself among the crowd. Hugo dived into the water after Margaret, and the waterman began to holler to the occupants of various other boats and ships.

Maria, scanning the smooth surface of the river, suddenly saw Margaret's head and one arm upflung in its sodden sleeve.

'She's there!' she screamed at the top of her voice. 'Hugo! I saw her! Further down! No – much further! Oh dear God! You will never reach her!'

She began to run alongside the river, keeping pace with the place where she imagined Margaret to be. She could see Hugo's head and his arms as he swam desperately, spurred on by Maria's shout. Not looking where she was going, Maria collided heavily with a man and woman, walking arm in arm along the river bank.

'Whoa there, young lady!' the man reproved her, and the woman smiled.

Maria cast them an anguished look and ran on. Now her view of the river was blocked by more and more ships and boats, some moving, some at anchor. She realised suddenly that she had almost reached the bridge. It was obvious that the drama had been seen, for windows were being flung open along the buildings on the bridge and people were leaning out and calling excitedly to each other, pointing to the water – to something they could see that Maria could not. Out of breath, and with a painful ache in her side, she stared down at the water, one hand held to her side. After a few moments she realised that a crowd was forming by the steps at the bridge. She forced herself to run on, but by the time she arrived, the crowd had grown so large that she could see nothing of what was happening and had to fight her way to the front.

'Tis a drowning!'

'Young woman's drowned herself!'

'Threw herself in, most like.'

'Drowned?' cried Maria. 'Oh – not dead!'

The man beside her shrugged. 'She'll be under the bridge by now, they reckon, and no hope of saving her. Like a mill race it is, through those arches. Smash a body to –'

'Don't,' she begged. 'And the husband – the man who dived in after her. Is he safe?'

'Couldn't rightly give you an answer to that,' he said.

Suddenly there was a gasp from the crowd, and they all pushed forward for a better view.

'What is it?' cried Maria. 'Let me through for pity's sake!'

The crowd suddenly parted as two men came up the steps, supporting a third.

'*Hugo!*'

Ashen-faced, he coughed weakly. His clothes were filthy with mud and slime and he dripped water. He opened his eyes, saw her and tried to speak, but was racked by a fit of coughing. Maria put out a hand, but his head fell forward and he slid to the ground, unconscious.

Somehow, amid the chaotic moments that followed, a carriage was summoned. While they waited, they loosened his collar, and a woman in the crowd rubbed his hands. Maria watched him anxiously and was eventually rewarded by seeing him open his eyes briefly. But soon they were closed again. Unable to look at him, she turned away. Her right hand was clenched uncomfortably, and she realised that she still clutched the posy of violets.

'Oh, Margaret!' she whispered. 'I did not mean to do it – I swear it.'

Running to the river's edge, she pressed the flowers to her lips and threw them as far as she could. They curved lightly down and fell into the brown water, flowers upwards. As she watched them carried away, she whispered, 'For your grave,' and began to weep.

CHAPTER FOUR

Margaret's body was not recovered immediately. Hugo, chilled by the water, developed a fever, and the physician called daily to keep a close watch on his progress. Meanwhile, letters were despatched by the postboy to the respective parents. Wisely Maria's mother kept her busy, to allow her less time to grieve. So it fell to her to bathe Hugo's face and hands and stir the broth which was his sole source of nourishment – the doctor having prescribed 'a little light gruel three times daily', plus a variety of draughts to 'cool the fever'. For these Maria was sent on countless errands and soon struck up a friendship with Master Backworth the apothecary. It was there that she found herself once more on the fourth day after the accident, waiting impatiently while a large woman in front of her stared around at the shelves to make certain she had not forgotten anything.

'. . . Oh, and some more dragon-water,' she said. 'I do recall we were almost out of it – and that is all – except maybe a little wormwood. Yes, a very little.'

The apothecary reached up to the second shelf, took down a bulbous green bottle, tipped out the required amount of wormwood and handed it to her. The dragon-water he poured into a small bottle.

'I hope your poor mother is no worse,' he said.

Maria groaned inwardly as, thus encouraged, the woman began a spirited account of all her mother's ailments. 'It's not so much in her guts now,' she explained, 'but in the chest, poor soul. Cough, cough, cough – all day and half the night, but cannot loosen the phlegm.' She turned to

Maria, to include her in this interesting account. 'Have you never had a tightness or constriction here?' She held a hand to her left side, below the heart. Maria shook her head. 'Well, that is where the tightness lies – and won't be shifted except by fumigation. A pinch or two of wormwood in the fire of nights. Works like a charm, that does!' She turned back to Master Backworth. 'Now, what do I owe you?'

He told her, and she counted out the coins from a drawstring bag at her waist.

Maria stared impatiently round the tiny shop. The walls were lined with bottles of various colours and shapes. There were earthenware pots, a rack of spoons of varying sizes, bunches of drying herbs and round pill-boxes. A set of scales and a pestle and mortar stood on the counter.

'And how is Master Kendal?' asked the apothecary, when at last the large woman departed.

'Mending,' Maria told him earnestly. 'The fever is past – but he is still very weak.'

'He has a devoted nurse, I hear,' he said slyly, and Maria laughed self-consciously. She handed him the prescription and watched as he assembled the ingredients in the pestle and began to pound them.

He looked up at her cheerfully. 'You're growing fast,' he said. 'Before long you'll be a woman and have a husband of your own to fuss over. Have they found you a good man yet?'

She shook her head. 'They may find one,' she told him, 'but I'll not have him.'

'Is that so?'

'Aye.'

'And why not, may I ask?'

'My heart is set elsewhere,' she said with a toss of her head. 'But none shall know of it.'

He laughed. 'A secret love, eh?'

Maria nodded eagerly.

'Now, I wonder who that might be,' he mused, but she made no answer. The prescription completed, he watched her run off through the crowd, the medicament for her beloved Hugo firmly clutched to her chest.

On the fifth morning after the accident, Hugo was declared 'beyond all hazard', and Maria was content at last. Just before noon a hammering on the front door sent her running to answer it lest it wake Hugo from the peaceful sleep into which he had fallen. A young constable stood outside.

'Does a Hugo Kendal live here?' he asked.

'He does but –'

'I have news for him regarding a woman declared missing believed drowned –'

Maria clapped her hands over her ears. 'Don't tell me,' she begged. 'I don't want to hear it! Hugo is sick. I will fetch Mama – Oh no, she is gone to her sister's.'

The man waited, uncomfortably aware of the unpleasant nature of his errand.

'You'd best tell me,' Maria said at last, lowering her hands. 'Is it Margaret?'

He nodded, thankful that his news was obviously anticipated, and began his prepared speech: 'We have news, ma'am, of a young woman's body washed up by the tide at Greenwich, which may be that of the missing female late of this address, one Margaret Kendal, believed drowned.'

Maria said, 'I'll tell my mother on her return.'

He shook his head. ''Tis the body, ma'am. It must be identified as soon as possible and buried with all haste. You understand, it –'

Maria lowered her eyes and he paused, uncertain how to phrase what he had to say.

'Your father, mayhap?' he suggested. 'Where might I find your father?'

'My father is dead.'

'Ah – my condolences, ma'am. But *someone* must identify her. Is there no one else? Yourself, mayhap?' She hesitated, and he went on. 'Tis but a moment's work. A quick glance is enough to recognise a face, and oft times there's a ring or locket . . .' As she still stood irresolute, he added persuasively, 'You'd be doing the poor woman one last favour, God rest her soul.'

'At Greenwich, you say?'

'Aye. You can ride behind me if you've a mind and take another mount for your return.'

Maria took a deep breath. Her own prayers had brought about the disaster. Was this God's punishment? Was it her chance to atone? Maybe her only chance?

'I'll do it,' she said at last.

The mortuary was a small, drab building tucked away in a side street. A peeling, painted sign nailed beside the door announced that this was the public mortuary serving Greenwich. The door stood open and after a moment's hesitation, Maria stepped inside and waited for her eyes to become adjusted to the dim interior. The room in which she found herself was small and gloomy, and a dark wall-hanging made it appear even smaller. There was a wooden bench along one wall, and a table and chairs completed the furnishing. On the table stood a pot of ink, one of sand, a quill pen, a book, a candle and a small brass handbell. There was no one in the room.

After a moment Maria rapped on the table but receiving no attention, rang the bell. A door opened to admit a small, thin-faced man, who eyed her suspiciously and then opened the book.

'Name?' he asked.

'Maria Lessor.'

He ran his finger down the page and shook his head. 'There's no Maria Lessor here,' he said.

'*I'm* Maria Lessor,' she said hastily. 'The person – that is, the body – is Margaret Kendal.'

The stubby finger retraced its path and stopped abruptly halfway down the page. 'And you are Maria who?'

'Lessor.'

59

He took up the pen, wrote her name and sanded it. 'You the sister of the deceased?'

'No. No relation, but a friend. She was lodged with us.'

'Where's her husband? He should do it, by rights.'

'He is ill.'

'Hmm.' He considered her for a moment and then re-read what he had written. 'How old are you?'

'Fifteen,' she lied, 'but small for my age.'

'Hmm.' He wiped the ink from the pen with finger and thumb and used it as a toothpick. 'What of your parents?'

'My father's dead. My mother's away for the day, visiting.'

He sighed deeply. 'Happen you'll do, then,' he told her. 'Follow me.'

He lit the candle and led the way through a door and down some rickety steps to a cellar. Here the walls and ceiling were roughly whitewashed and the only pieces of furniture were two low wooden tables. A cloth-wrapped body lay on each of them. Maria shuddered involuntarily and crossed herself.

The man passed the first table with a jerk of his head. 'Killed himself, that one. Poison, it was. This one's yours.'

Deftly he began to uncover the body, but Maria turned abruptly away, delaying the moment when she must look at the decaying corpse and thus lose forever the memories of Margaret alive and happy.

'What d'you say? Is it her or isn't it? I haven't got all day.'

Slowly she turned to look at the body – and cried out! She had tried to prepare herself, but what she saw was much worse than anything she had imagined. The bloated body upon which she now gazed in horror was naked! She closed her eyes momentarily.

'Where is her gown?' she stammered, trying desperately to regain her composure.

The man shrugged. 'Stolen, most likely. That's the way she was brought in.'

He sounded impatient. With an effort Maria forced

herself to look at the face, but was immediately reduced to a state approaching nausea. The man watched indifferently as she clapped a hand to her mouth. Margaret's jaw hung crookedly, splintered bone protruding through the left cheek. The nose was flattened to an unsightly pulp. One eye showed, bloodshot and staring. The hair was matted with scraps of bone.

Maria put out a hand, signalling feebly that the man should cover the body. He did so with a few expert flicks of the cloth.

'There's an ear missing, too,' he volunteered. 'Torn off –'

'Oh, no! I beg you!' cried Maria. 'Spare me your details.'

'It's my job,' the man told her triumphantly. 'You must be advised of all known facts relating to the corpse, lest –'

'I must go upstairs,' she interrupted, and stumbling from the room, began to climb the dark stairs. As soon as she reached the room above, she slumped onto the bench, burying her face in her hands. The man followed her into the room, blew out the candle and picked up the pen.

'Yes or no?' he asked.

At last she said, 'Was there a ring or other jewellery?'

'No. Stolen, too, I wouldn't wonder.'

'Her face – her poor face!' Maria whispered.

'Likely crushed between two boats.'

'Dear God!'

'Well? Is it her?'

'I – I *think* so. I could not swear –'

'Was she that age?'

'I – I suppose so.'

'And pregnant?'

Maria started. 'Aye,' she said. 'I had almost forgot.'

The man shrugged. 'And in the water about five days?'

She nodded.

'Then is it her?'

Maria hesitated. Then she nodded her head.

'Sign, please,' he said briefly, turning the book towards her. When she had done so, he closed the book and left the room without a backward look. Maria took a deep breath, passed a trembling hand across her eyes and stood up on trembling legs.

'I *must* go now,' she told herself, and stepped out into the sunlight. She deeply regretted her earlier decision and wished most fervently that she had never come.

Late that evening in her bedroom, she sat at the mirror brushing her hair with long careful strokes, considering her reflection in the light from the two candles beside the mirror. She thought about Hugo and tried to imagine his state of mind. Since Margaret's death he had said nothing – not a word. No reference to the accident or his grief, and no hint of his plans for the future. Since he would not talk, how was she to interpret his thoughts? That Hugo knew of her affection for him she had no doubt. But what of his feelings for her? Was his reluctance to talk a shield for him to hide behind? Or did he really not care for her at all?

Maria put down the brush and stared at herself in the mirror, wondering how she would appear in his eyes. As a child, or as a young woman? Her skin was good, for she had so far escaped the smallpox, but her eyes, she decided, were set too close together. Her mouth was altogether too big – the lips were too full and wide – and her hair grew too low on her forehead. No, alas – she was no beauty, nor ever would be. But – nor was she ugly. Perhaps 'comely' would be a fair assessment, or even 'pleasing', when she was looking her best. She sighed deeply, stood up, irresolute, then flung herself face downward on the bed, grinding her teeth in an agony of frustration and indecision.

More than an hour passed. She turned over at last and sat up, reaching for her nightgown. She heard her mother come up the stairs and enter her room. As she pulled the night-gown over her head a terrible thought occurred. Hugo might fall in love with another woman! Dear God, it was unbearable! She groaned aloud, climbed into bed and lay staring up into the darkness.

Five minutes later, having decided what must be done, she climbed out again. She listened carefully. There was no sound from overhead, which meant that Martha was safely asleep. Without waiting to put on her slippers or a wrap, she opened the door, closed it behind her and tiptoed along the passage. Outside Hugo's room she hesitated. If she knocked, someone might hear her. With a thumping heart she opened the door and stepped inside. There was no sound from the bed. She closed the door, the tell-tale 'click' sounding desperately loud. Still no sound came from the bed, although she could just make out Hugo's form, motionless below the covers. Suddenly he moved.

'Who's there?'

Maria tried to answer, but her throat was dry – no words came.

He sat up on one elbow and looked towards her. 'Is that you, Maria?' he asked.

She nodded and with an effort managed a husky 'Yes.'

'What's wrong, little one?'

Little one! In the darkness she closed her eyes and clenched her fists until the nails hurt her flesh, but all she managed to say was, 'Naught.'

He reached out and fumbled for the candle.

'Don't light it. I beg you!' she cried.

'Come here, then,' he said. 'I can't see your face.'

She crossed the room and stood beside him and gently he took hold of her hands.

'Unclench these little fists,' he told her. 'What ails you, child? Is it bad dreams? You ought never to have gone today.'

''Tis not that.'

'What, then? You must tell me, for I am done with guessing.'

Her eyes, growing used to the darkness, could make out

63

the familiar face, and Maria longed to kiss him. He patted the bed.

'Sit beside me – why, look at these poor bare feet. Tuck them up.' And he lifted a corner of the bedcover and wound it round her feet. 'No slippers and no wrap. You want to catch a chill, is that it? You are jealous of all the attention I'm getting!'

'No.'

'Then tell me.'

'I cannot.'

'Then I shall sit up all night in wait for it – and lose my beauty sleep,' he teased. 'I shall be old and ugly by the morning!'

She struggled for words, but a deep and unexpected sigh swallowed them up. Hugo took a lock of hair and wound it round his finger.

'Is it that I shall be leaving soon? When I am recovered. Be brave and tell me,' he said kindly, 'we need have no secrets between us.'

'And you will not be angry?'

'I doubt it.'

'You promise?'

'I do.'

She slid off the bed and took a step back from him. Frantically she sought for the right thing to say, the right place to begin, before her courage finally failed.

'It was my fault,' she stammered. 'Margaret, I mean . . . drowning like that. I asked God to let it happen . . . although I didn't mean like that. I didn't mean it at all – no, that's a lie. I did mean it, but then –'

Her voice faltered and stopped. Hugo said nothing, and made no move to help her.

'. . . And now I'm sorry that she's dead, and I have truly tried to make amends as God is my witness. But twas because I love you, and I want you, and I will be so far away you will forget me –'

'Maria!' he said softly, and in the half-light she saw the

gleam of tears in his eyes. He held out his hands to her, but she took another step back.

'Don't say it, Hugo, I beg you,' she stammered. 'I am nigh on thirteen and nearly grown. I do not think like a child, I do not feel like a child. Oh Hugo, I need to know how you think of me. I beg you – say something to comfort me. My mind is torn to shreds with wanting you, and that's the sum of it.'

Hugo looked at her as she stood in the darkened room, wraith-like in her pale gown. So passionate and so vulnerable, he thought – a thin, dark-haired child. So unlike his poor Margaret.

'I'm sorry –' he began. 'Indeed I am.'

'You do not care for me?' she whispered.

He shook his head.

'And will you ever? Next year, mayhap, or later still?'

'I cannot say. My pet, you are twelve. You are still a child, but one day you will –'

'Then let me sleep with you tonight! Let me comfort you just this once. Oh, Hugo, I beseech you – if I am still a child, take me into your bed. Into your arms. Tonight I will be a child.'

He shook his head despairingly.

'Don't shake your head, Hugo! I declare I will not leave you. I *will* sleep with you! No one will know. In the morning, at first light, I will go back to my own chamber. I promise.' She racked her brains frantically for a way to persuade him. 'You have not wept for her,' she said, 'and your heart is so full. Everyone must weep for a loved one. Everyone must mourn a death. Weep for your Margaret, Hugo, and I will comfort you. I think Margaret would wish it.'

He turned away from her and was suddenly shaken with sobs. Maria went round to the far side of the bed and climbed in. He made no protest when she lifted his head and slid her arm round his neck. She wiped his tears on the sheet, patted his shoulder and made the unintelligible

65

sounds that a mother makes to a crying child. When at last his sobbing ceased, she kissed his eyes and said, 'Good night.' Holding him close with her child's body, she loved him with her woman's mind.

Maria sat in the workroom behind the shop in Gutter Lane. Two other people shared the tiny room – Nicholas Benn, the older of the two, and William Ferris, the apprentice. The former, a talented young man of twenty-two, was working at a gold watchcase, painstakingly inscribing the ornate design which bordered the prospective owner's initials. Head bent, his fingers moved delicately across the metal, and his concentration was such that Maria's idle chatter made scarcely any impact on his consciousness. Will, however, a mere sixteen, was enchanted by the girl's company and could hardly keep his mind on his work at all. He was buffing a large agate, which would shortly be set into the silver collar of a gentleman's ring.

'I could do that,' Maria offered hopefully, but Will shook his head, jerking his head meaningfully in the direction of his senior.

'Best not,' he said reluctantly. 'Anyway, tis skilled work and –'

'Skilled work!' Maria teased him. 'Holding a stone against a polishing band! I could do it with my eyes shut.' She picked up the heavy silver ring and turned it over, letting it lie in the palm of her hand. 'One day I shall commission a ring for Hugo –' Will groaned, but she ignored him. 'But twill be gold, not silver. Aye, and a heavier shank – and not agate, but a ruby. The finest ruby to be found in London. And his initials shall be entwined with mine, here below the stone: 'H' and 'M', where no other eye shall see them or guess of their existence.' She closed her eyes, imagining the scene as she presented Hugo with the ring, seeing his face alight with wonder, gratitude and love.

'You and your Hugo!' scoffed Will, who was halfway to loving Maria himself and jealous of this paragon of virtue who filled her thoughts so completely. 'He'll as like be wed to another by the time you've money enough to buy rings and suchlike. He'll most likely –'

'He will not!' said Maria, her eyes flashing. 'He knows I love him and he will wait for me, I know it. He will mourn for Margaret for many years yet and I'll be a grown woman by then.'

'Your mother will have you betrothed by that time.'

'I shall never wed another. She may say what she will. She may beat me, starve me –'

A bell jangled in the shop, and Nicholas glanced up at the clock on the shelf above him.

'That will be Mistress Tanner,' he told Will in a low voice. 'Tell her I am not here but that the locket will be ready by tomorrow noon.'

Will slid from the stool and went through the curtain into the shop. Maria, robbed of her audience, looked hopefully at Nicholas, but he was huddled once more over his work. With a sigh she looked round the familiar room. The grimy walls were lined with shelves and racks of instruments. Jars, bottles, boxes and pans littered the workbench, and a strong brass-bound chest containing gems and precious metals stood in one corner. Several hammers lay on the table, and Maria picked up a leather mallet and rapped out a tattoo, humming a few bars of a ditty which all the apprentices were singing.

Nicholas looked up sharply. 'That's not a plaything,' he said and reaching out, plucked the mallet from her surprised hands. He dusted it lovingly, blew on it and set it down again on the table.

Maria felt her cheeks burn. Such insolence! And from a hired man! Her mother paid his wages and her father had taught him his trade – how dare he treat her so! She was on the point of snatching the mallet up again when the shop bell jangled once more and Will came back into the room, peeling off his apron.

'Time for a bite to eat,' he announced. 'I wouldn't say no to a mug of ale if I found one in my hand. Are you coming, Nick?'

'Later, mayhap.'

'Maria?'

'I'll come,' she said gratefully. 'I find it suddenly stuffy in here,' she added. 'Mayhap tis the company.'

Will looked puzzled by this barbed remark, but Nicholas pretended not to hear and appeared quite oblivious of their departure.

'I don't know why Mama employs him,' Maria fumed as they made their way along the crowded street. 'He has no manners and no respect. He has always been so. Papa used to say he was insolent, and so he is.'

'Hoity toity!' said Will, grinning, as she lashed out with a neatly shod foot at a stray dog who ventured too close. 'What has Nick done to offend your worthy self?'

'None of your business,' said Maria. 'And don't smirk so. Your mouth goes up at one side higher than the other. It makes you look foolish!'

'Oh, so I am out of favour too,' he said, quite unabashed by her ill humour. 'Forgive me for existing. What a miserable undeserving wretch I am.'

He threw her such a rueful glance that she had to try very hard not to be distracted from her grievance. They continued for a while in silence, but the cobbles were slippery after the night's rain and although she picked her way carefully, she almost lost her balance once or twice.

'Allow me,' said Will with an elaborate bow, and offered her his arm. 'Gladden the heart of your humble servant,' he implored her. Finally she gave in to his good humour and took his arm thankfully.

The alehouse was full of noisy customers snatching a welcome break from their labours. Many had eaten no breakfast, but had purchased a pie or pasty from the numerous street vendors. They now ate hungrily with a careless scattering of crumbs and scraps, which were promptly snapped up by a small dog. Two glasses of ale were passed up from the cellar. Maria sipped hers cheerfully, her earlier irritation forgotten.

'If your mama could see you in here!' said Will.

Maria rolled her eyes heavenwards and said, 'Don't speak on it. She'd be mortified, and I'd get my ears boxed.' She leaned back against the wall and raised her mug. 'Here's to true love,' she said, thinking of Hugo.

'I'll drink to that,' said Will, thinking of her.

They had scarcely put the mugs to their lips, when a familiar head passed by the window. Maria gave a gasp.

'Why, tis him!' she cried. 'Tis Hugo himself!' and she handed the ale to a disappointed Will and rushed outside in pursuit.

'Hugo! Tis Maria! Oh, do wait for me –'

He reined in his horse, turned, and his handsome face broke into a smile. 'I was looking for you,' he told her. 'Nicholas said you were gone shopping in the market.'

Maria made a mental note that Master Benn could not be all bad if he had so kindly covered up for her. 'And here I am,' she said, taking the hand he held out to her and revelling in the sensation it aroused within her. Clambering up behind him, she asked, 'Why are you looking for me? Is there news from France?'

'Aye, and good news at that,' he said. 'My business looks promising and I shall be able to export as I planned.'

'And will you be rich?'

'Hardly rich,' he said, 'but comfortable. In my position I count myself fortunate.' He reached forward and struck at an urchin who had stumbled drunkenly against his stirrup, startling the horse; the boy staggered off, shouting obscenities. 'These wretches!' Hugo exclaimed. 'They steal to buy drink and then, cup-shotten, become a public nuisance. He might have had us both off then.'

'So your future is secure,' said Maria, her arms round his waist. 'And what plans now? Will you stay in London?'

'I'll return to London,' he said, 'but first I must go down to Sampford to visit my mother. She grows impatient at the delay, and I have no further excuse now that I am fully recovered from the fever.'

'Thanks to your nurse,' Maria prompted.

'Thanks to my nurse, indeed,' he said. 'I will be gone several weeks – a month maybe, but then I'll come back to London and find lodgings of my own.'

So he was going. She bit her lip and tried to keep her voice steady. 'And will I be welcome there – at your lodgings?' she asked. She had known he must go. She had prepared herself for such tidings, expecting them daily. Why, then, did the news come as such a shock – indeed, almost as a physical blow?

'Welcome? Why, most certainly you will,' said Hugo, sensing her dismay and glad that he need not see the misery that he knew was in her eyes. 'I shall entertain you and your mother to dinner and we shall eat, drink and be merry.'

'And if I come alone – when I am older?'

'Ah – we shall see,' he said.

'You will not seek a new wife, Hugo? Not yet?'

'No, no.'

'When are you leaving?'

'Tomorrow – but I have a farewell gift for you.'

'A gift? Hugo, what is it? Should I make a guess?'

'Guess away. I shan't tell you, but it waits at home for you.'

'Oh, Hugo!'

My love, she whispered, and turning her face, she laid her cheek against the brown velvet which covered his broad back.

As soon as the way was clear, he urged the horse into a trot, and before long they were dismounting outside the house. Hugo's parting gift was a tabby kitten, nine weeks old and still yearning for its mother. He put it into Maria's arms and watched her young face soften with instinctive caring.

'To keep you company,' he said softly, 'while I am away.'

As she hid her face in the soft grey fur, he saw that her hands trembled. When her feelings were once more under control she looked up at him and smiled.

'Thank you, Hugo,' she said. 'Does he, or she, have a name?'

He shook his head. 'You'll find a name for her,' he said. 'There was a black kitten also, but this one reminded me of the cat we had in Béduer. We called her Minou.'

'Minou,' repeated Maria. 'Why tis a perfect name. I'll call her Minou.' She kissed the soft fur. 'Little Minou shall lead a life of luxury. I shall kill her with kindness. And when you come back you'll see how big she is grown and how sleek her coat. Minou, Minou! How do you like your name? And your new home? Do you think she is thirsty?'

'I dare say she is,' said Hugo, delighted with the success of his gift. As he watched her leave the room intent on the business of the kitten's survival, he began to feel easier in his mind about her.

Poor Maria, he thought to himself. You have so much to learn of the ways of the world, and so much heartache ahead of you.

Two days later her heartache began. Hugo Kendal left for Devon, and through the night Minou's fur grew wet and spiky with Maria's scalding tears.

CHAPTER FIVE
Devon

Ladyford lay white and silent under the first snow of winter. Melissa, shivering, opened her eyes and reached up to pull back the bed drapes. The room was unusually bright, and outside the astonished birds were hushed.

'Snow!' she groaned, and let the drapes fall. She snuggled down under the blankets. Snow! On Dartmoor it would lie for weeks, deepened by successive falls and blown into drifts against every hedgerow. Ladyford, only miles from Heron, would be cut off from it, isolated. Thomas must set the boy to clearing a path to the water pump, and another to the woodshed – but how the lad would grumble! She sighed. Poor Minnie's chilblains would torment her, and Thomas's cough would be aggravated by the cold air on his lungs. She must see to it that he dressed warmly to favour his chest, and if his boots leaked, then his feet must be given a mustard bath before he took chill. He was not an old man, but he was not young either, and he had never been robust. He lay beside her now sleeping on his back, his mouth open slightly, his breathing shallow. If *only* he would wear the sheepskin vest under his shirt – but vanity prevented him.

She listened for sounds of young Oliver stirring in his bed, but all was still in the next room. Minnie, his fierce champion, slept beside him. All the hounds in hell might bark and never waken her, but a sound from Oliver and she would be half out of bed to attend to him before she had even opened her eyes. Melissa sighed contentedly. She had a loving husband and a beautiful son. Let it snow! She closed her eyes and tried to snatch a few moments' more sleep before the day began. Her hopes were suddenly dashed by a commotion outside.

A passing fox, excited by the smell from the chicken coop, had stopped to investigate, and the two dogs were clamouring to be freed from their chains. Melissa groaned as the household awoke. Oliver's piping voice cried for a favourite toy, which had fallen out of his bed during the night – a wooden horse carved for him by his Uncle Simon. Melissa heard Minnie hushing him. Meanwhile, beside her, Thomas rubbed his eyes blearily.

'Such a commotion,' he protested.

'Something has disturbed the dogs,' she said. 'A fox, most likely. Stay awhile, Thomas. Jacob will see to it.'

'Ah, Jacob. I forgot.'

She smiled at him and kissed him lightly. 'Such luxury – to have a Jacob,' she teased.

'Mmm. He's a nice enough lad – surly at times, but I trust him. The last few months have been much easier. You were right, Melissa, twas money well spent.'

'I think it has snowed in the night,' she said. 'You said it would.'

'So early in the winter?'

'Still, we have done all that needed to be done –'

He slid out of bed and crossed to the window. 'Aye, a few inches, no more.'

'We are well stocked with provisions,' said Melissa. 'I'm glad we put down that extra barrel of fish.'

He returned to the bed and sat on the edge, stretching his thin, freckled arms above his head. Seeing his narrow frame, Melissa wished he would eat more. He turned suddenly to her.

'What of Hugo? Wasn't today set for his visit to Heron?'

'Tomorrow,' said Melissa, 'but he will surely not attempt the journey from Sampford in this weather. A pity, for I long for news of London and France – and I want to show him our son.'

'I trust Hugo will not bring his mother with him when he

73

comes,' said Thomas. 'Luke has never liked Hester, and she grows worse as she grows older. Twill be an uncomfortable meal with the both of them present.'

They both laughed easily. Their marriage was a good one, despite the difference in their ages. Melissa enjoyed the simplicity of life at Ladyford and had found there the peace of mind that had always eluded her while she lived at Heron. Thomas, for his part, had never ceased to wonder at the good fortune which had changed his role from lonely observer to a much-loved man with a home and family of his own. He was less diffident in his dealings with people now, and he laughed more readily. He adored his wife and idolised the son she had borne him. Thomas Benet, bailiff, was a happy man.

Now he threw a log on to the embers of the fire and shouted down the stairs for Jacob to bring up a jug of hot water, and while he waited he drew Melissa with him to the window. Together they looked out across the white landscape. In the garden the branches of the young plum tree were weighed down with their unfamiliar burden of snow. Thomas 'tutted' anxiously: the fruit trees were his latest acquisition.

'I shall shake them,' he said, 'else the branches will snap under the strain.'

A line of thinner snow marked the course of the brick path, and the skeletons of shrubs showed dark against the white. Along the far side of the garden wall the beehives stood snow-capped, and beyond the wall the moor itself rolled smoothly for mile after mile, the heathers and lichens hidden and only the stunted, windswept trees breaking the expanse of white snow.

A knock at the door signalled the arrival of the water, and Jacob entered the room, still clad in his outer garments but with his feet bare for fear of treading snow into the house and earning a reprimand from Melissa. He was a stocky boy of thirteen with short legs and a long body, with dark, curly hair, brown eyes and a thin mouth which rarely smiled. He was the youngest of eight, and his mother had died giving birth to him.

'Is the fire going well?' Thomas asked him. 'And the porridge on?'

'Aye, tis.'

'And the pump – not frozen?'

'Twas froze, but I warmed it with a brand from the fire,' he said, proud of his initiative.

'That was well done,' Thomas told him. 'Take a broom now and clean the paths where we shall need them. If the sun comes out, it will likely thaw in no time, but we'd best be sure.'

'Shall I salt the step?' Jacob asked Melissa.

'Only if tis slippery, and then be sparing with it,' she said. 'We'll have a long hard winter with snow in December, and we must eke it out.'

He had no sooner departed than Minnie appeared. She took no notice of Thomas who, naked, stood splashing water over his face and neck. Only Melissa protested at the intrusion.

'How many times must I bid you knock at the door?' she chided. 'Do I have to tell you every morning?'

'Oops!' said Minnie, clapping a hand to her mouth, and withdrew to knock loudly on the door.

Melissa laughed. 'Sweet heaven, tis too late now!' she said. 'You have surprised the master already. But what is it?'

Minnie came in again.

'Young Oliver,' she said hopefully. 'Should I dress him up warm and take him out into the snow? The wee lamb has never seen the stuff and longs to play in it.'

'And so do you, I'll be bound,' said Melissa, reading her thoughts correctly. 'And you'll both get wetter than a sheep in dip and we shall be all day drying your clothes. I think tis too early in the day. Give him his breakfast and I'll think on it later, if the sun comes out.'

The girl withdrew, disappointed, but moments later they

heard giggles and squeals from Oliver, and knew that she had resigned herself to wait.

'Will you wear the sheepskin vest?' Melissa suggested, putting her arms round Thomas's slight frame and hugging him. 'I made it especially for you. It was a labour of love.'

Her husband grinned and tried gently to prise himself free, but she clung on, laughing. 'I shan't let you go until you agree,' she told him. 'I'm so fearful for your chest in the cold weather. Say "Aye" to please me.'

'I will not! There's naught wrong with my chest, and four inches of snow will not harm me.'

'But your cough will –'

He managed to wriggle free of her embrace, snatched up his shirt and pulled it on over his head. 'You cluck over me like a broody hen,' he teased. 'Now I have given you a chick, go cluck over Oliver – he will revel in the attention.'

She gave up good-humouredly and moved to the bowl to wash her own face and hands. 'Shall you ride over to the mine today?' she asked.

'I think so. I'll take the mare; she is more sure-footed.' He pulled on the rest of his clothes and combed his hair. 'There is some unrest,' he said thoughtfully. 'I thought to see and hear for myself.'

'Unrest?' Melissa looked up, surprised. 'What kind of unrest? You did not speak of it before.'

Thomas shrugged. 'It may be nothing, but the rumour is that the men take sides against each other. Two brothers, Samuel and John Riddle, have a grievance between them and it seems to spread among the others, some taking Samuel's side and others John's.'

'And Simon –' said Melissa, 'is he aware of this argument?'

'Aye, but treats it lightly. Yet some say there was a fight in one of the galleries and a man was hurt and might lose the sight of his eye.'

'Dear God! Simon treats this lightly?'

'He may not know of that, give him his due.'

76

'He is too easy,' said Melissa, frowning. 'He jokes with the men and is too friendly. Papa has told him often. They take liberties with him.'

'I will see what I can discover,' said Thomas, 'and have a word with your father, if I think it will help. Simon is not to blame. He was not brought up to rule. Still, no need to fret. We shall resolve it somehow, I don't doubt. Now I must leave you and snatch a few mouthfuls of porridge before I go. I'll be back before long.'

He kissed her and hurried downstairs. Guiltily, Melissa slid back under the bedclothes, hugging the blankets round her, stealing a last few moments' comfort before the empty bed grew cold. She let her thoughts dwell on Simon. Once he had meant so much to her, almost more than life itself. She had loved him with the first passion of adolescence, and he had loved her too. Too late she had learned the truth: that he was her father's illegitimate son and therefore denied to her. When her own brothers had died, Luke had installed him at Heron, declaring him to the world as his rightful heir and arranging his betrothal to Hannah. Helplessly, Melissa had watched them wed, knowing that she could no longer stay on at Heron to witness the growing affection between man and wife. Instead she had moved into Ladyford, a cottage on Heron land, taking her father's bailiff with her.

Now she smiled faintly, remembering Thomas's consternation when she laid her proposition before him. Sweet, gentle Thomas. What had he said about Simon? That he was not bred to rule? That much was true. He had been a baker's apprentice before the ripe plum of Heron fell into his lap. The Heron lands reached across Dartmoor, rich in tin. There were rich yields for the right man. But was Simon strong enough to control the growing numbers of tinners needed to mine the precious ore? Frowning, she saw him in her mind's eye; slim, arrogant, fair. She also saw the tinners; swarthy-skinned, dark-eyed, their bodies short and muscular, their emotions untamed, their moods unpredictable. She sighed. No, Simon was not the stuff that leaders are made of. But at least he had Luke and Thomas to advise him . . . She shivered, hunching her shoulders. The log spluttered on the fire and a new flame leapt into the chimney. Melissa threw back the bedclothes and crossed to the fire, reluctantly deciding that she must let the day begin.

The early fall of snow did not lie long, and no more snow fell to take its place. The following Friday Hugo made his promised visit to Heron, and Saturday found the entire family seated on either side of the long table in the Hall. Simon sat at the head, his face flushed with wine, the angles of his face softened by the firelight and warmed by the rich red of his doublet. Hannah sat beside him, in a dress of green velvet and Luke faced him from the other end of the table, having been carried from his bed, well-wrapped in furs for the occasion. Melissa, in russet brown, sat on Luke's right hand, Thomas on his left. Hugo and his mother faced each other across the middle of the table, so that Luke's hostility towards her need not be too apparent. 'She is only coming to plague me,' he had confided previously to Melissa, 'else she would have stayed home where she belongs.'

The conversation had been awkward, even stilted, at the beginning of the meal, but plenty of wine and a veritable feast had improved their spirits and loosened their tongues. They had despatched large amounts of bread and fish, goose and mutton, vegetables and fruit with great enjoyment, and now cracked nuts and nibbled raisins, each professing to be over-full and like to burst, yet still managing another mouthful.

'So what news of Abby and her brood?' Melissa asked Hugo. Her sister lived at Rochester, and the two families met infrequently.

Hugo smiled. 'Your Abigail is blooming,' he told her, 'and her husband grows quite fat, he is so contented. The babes are as bonny as anyone could wish —'

Hester, still without grandchildren, interrupted this eulogy. 'I hear they live close to the Medway,' she said. 'Very close, Hugo says. Surely not, I said amazed, with all the foul humours and river stench! Do they choose to live so near, or is it force of circumstance? They choose, says Hugo. Then they'll surely regret it, I said. Foul air can do naught but harm to a man's lungs. And as for the babes, tis a wonder they –'

Luke, leaning forward, looked at her sourly, his bushy brows meeting over his faded blue eyes. 'Foul humours? River stench?' he repeated. 'Tis obvious you don't know the Medway, or you'd not talk so foolish! Tis a wholesome, fast-flowing river, and the wind blows in hard from the sea. Good, fresh sea air, to rid the lungs of all its impurities and bring a healthy colour to the cheeks. Foul Humours, poppycock!'

Hester's own cheek had taken on a brighter colour during this outburst, and now the conversation faltered. Hannah, embarrassed, looked appealingly at Simon, while Melissa's hand sought her father's knee under the table and pressed it warningly. But it was too late. Hester's eyes narrowed angrily, as Luke added, 'You talk through the back of your head, woman, the way you always did!'

'And you have the manners of a prentice!' she snapped angrily, '– as *you* always did. Tis a malady with you that your kith and kin can do no wrong – no, not so much as to live in the wrong place. I never did know if twas your brain or your judgement that was at fault, but no children of mine – nor grandchildren neither – would live in such a place. Rochester may be –'

'Trash, woman!' cried Luke. 'Your tongue's taken control of you! Time enough to prate on –'

'Papa, I beg you!' whispered Melissa anxiously, but Luke had drunk too well and his own tongue was running away with him.

'– *when* you get grandchildren,' he continued pointedly. 'I've a fair sprinkling, you see, and you've none. I hear that

79

other boy of yours has been wed three years and bred nothing but sheep –'

Hester half rose to her feet, but was tugged down again by Hannah. 'If my Horace were still alive –' she began.

'Mama, let it ride,' said Hugo evenly. 'We owe a great deal to Luke, remember, and the Medway and its humours is a poor thing to argue over.'

'But he –'

'Mama!'

'More wine, Hester?' asked Thomas hastily, refilling her goblet without waiting for an answer.

'She's had more than enough –' Luke began, but Melissa tugged at his sleeve and whispered urgently in his ear. He lowered his voice to a mumble, and everyone breathed more freely.

Hannah said brightly, 'They say the Queen will soon be wed, God bless her!'

They all raised their goblets and murmured, 'The Queen!'

'And not before time,' said Melissa. 'She must be nearer forty than thirty, and England needs heirs.'

'But Philip of Spain?' said Luke. 'We do not want Spanish heirs to the English throne. Why does she not wed Courtenay? He's handsome enough, and she has made him Earl of Devon.'

'But she is half-Spanish herself,' Hannah reminded them, 'so tis natural enough for her to look on Philip with special favour. Her mother was from Aragon – they say Mary speaks fluent Spanish.'

'Tis all politics,' said Thomas. He glanced at Luke, who frowned into his plate. 'What do you say, Luke?'

But Luke refused to be drawn into the conversation, preferring to nurse his ill humour with Hester. Taking a large mutton bone from the table, he tossed it to the dogs, who sprang on it with delighted yelps and began to push it around the floor.

'The poor woman has my sympathy,' said Melissa. 'They

80

say her health is poor, and she is no beauty. Elizabeth outshines her whenever she is at court, and for all that they pretend friendship, there cannot be any real love between them. Who will Mary have to love if she cannot have the husband of her choice?'

'She *is* the Queen!' laughed Hugo. 'She must love England above all else. She must love us, her loyal subjects.'

'And others not so loyal,' said Simon quietly, and Thomas shot him a startled look. 'While the young Elizabeth lives there will always be uncertainty. She is Henry's daughter by Anne Boleyn. I wonder Mary has allowed her to live this long.'

'The Queen is merciful,' said Hester piously.

'Some say the Queen is weak,' said Luke suddenly. 'Oh, do not look at me that way, Hester. I merely repeat what others say – that Elizabeth and Courtenay would make a prettier match. Both young and handsome, and both English. The people would love them. Aye, it pays to think kindly on Elizabeth, for she may be Queen yet.'

'If she keeps her head!' cried Hugo, and there was laughter at the hidden meaning within his words.

'Yet tis no laughing matter,' Simon persisted, 'if a marriage to Philip means war with France.'

They all groaned. 'No more wars!' cried Melissa. 'Let us keep our sons, I say. I've no wish for Oliver to spend his youth in the mud of foreign parts, in constant danger of his life.'

Hester smiled thinly. 'I think he is a mite too young for that,' she said. 'They will scarcely enrol boys against the French.'

'He will not be a boy forever,' said Melissa. 'The years slip by –'

'Aye, they do,' said Luke, putting a hand gently on her shoulder. 'But rest easy, my little Lissa. With God's intervention, we will be done with fighting by the time young Oliver is grown. The world will be a better place.'

'Amen to that!' cried Hannah, raising her goblet briefly before she drank.

'Amen to that!' chorused the others, and Beth was sent out for more wine and another dish of raisins.

'War with France! War with Spain!' said Thomas. 'And wars with Scotland! If tis not one, tis another. Luke is right. Tis time England settled down. We will never grow prosperous while we fritter our wealth away on fighting.'

'Perhaps with a woman on the throne we will be less quick to take up arms,' said Melissa. 'Unless she is ruled by her husband . . .'

'I doubt any man would overrule Mary,' laughed Hugo. 'She is hardly a shy young bride. Why, she is nearly forty – and from such a mother! They say she has inherited Catherine's stubborn ways. I warrant Philip won't find it easy to influence her once her mind is set.'

'He will not need to,' said Melissa shrewdly. 'If Mary is besotted with him, as they say she is, why then, she'll do all things to please him. He will have his own way without a fight!'

'Philip of Spain can bring the whole weight of the Roman Catholic Church to bear on us,' said Simon, 'and most likely will.'

There was an uneasy silence in which Catholics and Protestants avoided each others' eyes. As Beth brought in the wine and raisins, she noted with surprise the chastened looks and wondered at the cause.

'Take out the dogs, Beth,' said Simon. 'They have stuffed themselves on scraps until they can hardly move. And are the fires lit in the bedchambers?'

'They are, an hour since.'

'Good.' He smiled at Thomas. 'Are you sure we can't persuade you to sleep here overnight? Tis no trouble to warm another room?'

'I thank you, no,' said Thomas. 'We don't care to leave Oliver alone all night with only Minnie and the lad. If our horses might be saddled in a quarter of an hour, we'll be on our way.'

'See to it, Beth,' said Simon. 'And send Jack in. The Master is tired and must be carried up to bed.'

It was a polite understatement. Luke had, in fact, dozed off and sat sprawled forward on the table, his head resting on his arms. His breathing was laboured and the fingers of his right hand twitched in sleep. Jack appeared promptly, and he and Simon woke the old man, who made his goodnights, before allowing himself to be helped upstairs.

'He looks sickly,' said Hester as soon as he had left the room. 'He's no more than skin and bone, and he has an unhealthy pallor. What ails him?'

Melissa looked at her in alarm. 'Sickly?' she repeated. 'Do you think so? I thought twas only his age.'

Hester was triumphant over this small victory. 'Are you all blind? He has an air of sickness. Tis evident in his eyes. Does his physician call regularly?'

'He does,' said Hannah, 'and came only last week. He is well satisfied.'

'Well satisfied, is he? Then I'd find a new physician. That man is sick, mark my words.'

Melissa turned to Thomas, but he smiled reassuringly and shook his head very slightly to dispel her doubts. Outside they heard the dogs bark excitedly as they raced in pursuit of something, and the logs shifted suddenly in the hearth, sending up a shower of sparks.

'And will you wed again, Hugo?' asked Hannah gently.

'Of course he will,' chimed in Hester. 'And the sooner the better. A man alone is prey to morbid fancies. Poor Margaret is gone, God rest her soul –' she crossed herself – 'but she would not want him to mourn forever.'

But Hannah still looked at Hugo, waiting for his answer.

He shrugged expressively. 'I will wed again, but I am in no haste to do so. At present I have a business to establish. I must find myself an office and a clerk.'

'You have found lodgings, I hear.'

'Aye, in Cheapside. I could not stay longer with the Lessors, much as they wished it. They have been good to me, but I wouldn't want to outstay my welcome there.'

'We had thought you might settle in Sampford,' said Hannah. She hoped the remark sounded artless, in fact it hid a keen desire to know Hugo's true position with regard to the Bannerman estate. It was rumoured that when Hugo changed his name back to Kendal, his stepfather, infuriated, had disinherited him in favour of his own son. If that were the case, Hugo had nothing.

'My mother would like that, ' he answered, with a smile in Hester's direction, 'but I made so many useful friends in France, it would be folly not to make use of them. Imports are of growing importance to the economy and there is money to be made.'

'Your step brother,' said Hannah. 'Will he take over your stepfather's interests when he is old enough?'

'It seems probable.'

Hannah laughed. 'I know someone who hopes you will settle in London. A little bird tells me that Maria was a most devoted nurse while you were ill with the fever. Abby wrote that when they visited you the child's eyes never left your face. You must be very flattered.'

Hugo laughed. 'She is a funny little thing. Half-woman, half-child – and so wayward! I warrant her mother will have her hands full with that one. She could be a rare beauty some day and a breaker of many hearts. She has such dark eyes, full of mystery and passion.'

'Aha!' cried Melissa. 'He speaks like a lover, doesn't he, Hannah? You have fallen under her spell yourself, Hugo. Confess it!'

'Maria's lover? Spare me such a fate!' he said. 'She will need a husband and a half to tame her impetuous ways.' Then he paused and said more softly, 'And yet the child has a loving heart.'

'He blushes!' cried Hannah. Melissa joined in the teasing and the two women giggled at his denials. Only Hester failed to see the humour in the suggestion.

'Maria Lessor? The daughter of a goldsmith? You can do better than that, Hugo, so stop this nonsense and answer me: how old is the girl?'

But the two younger women were finding the proposition quite hilarious and paid her no attention.

'If Maria has designs on you, you'd best reconcile yourself to it,' Hannah spluttered through a mouthful of wine that had gone down the wrong way. 'Wouldn't you say so, Lissa? Why, if the Queen herself were in the running, Maria would oust her!'

'Now, there's an idea!' cried Melissa. She blew an imaginary trumpet-call. 'Loyal subjects and whomsoever else it may concern – a marriage is announced between Mary Tudor of London Town and Hugo Kendal of Heron –'

'Heron?'

The laughter suddenly faded from Hannah's face, and Melissa cursed her own stupidity. 'I mean Sampford,' she amended lamely. 'I fear the wine has addled my poor brain.'

'It has indeed,' said Hannah coldly.

Hugo waved a hand casually to dismiss the point. 'Heron, Sampford – it's one and the same,' he said. 'I fear the Queen Mary will never consider me a suitable suitor –'

'A suitable suitor,' repeated Melissa foolishly, trying to reinforce the idea that her blunder was indeed due to the wine and not to the inner workings of her mind. 'A suitable suitor. I like that phrase, Hugo. It has a certain ring to it. Suitable suitor. Aye, I like it.'

Hester looked at her with an expression that Melissa found quite unfathomable, and she was relieved when Simon came back into the room and Thomas took the opportunity to get to his feet.

'We ought to leave,' he said. 'We have enjoyed ourselves well – mayhap too well – but we have a cold ride home ahead of us. Will you excuse us, if we make our way?'

There was a chorus of protests, but Thomas insisted, and Melissa was in agreement. She looked forward to such occasions and found them stimulating, but the following day would find her exhausted and only too happy to slip back into the quiet routine of their everyday life.

The first half of the ride home passed in silence, each of them busy with their own thoughts. Melissa broke the silence.

'Did you enjoy the evening?'

'I did, aye. And you?'

'Aye . . . Did I talk too much, Thomas? I do prattle on.'

He shook his head.

'You are certain I didn't? That stupid slip! I could have bitten my tongue –'

'Twas nothing. Put it out of your mind, little one.'

'I fear Hannah won't forget.'

'Tis no matter, I tell you.'

After a pause she said, 'Thomas Benet –'

'What now?' he laughed.

'You are a great comfort to me, Thomas.'

He reached out and took her hand. 'That's how it should be,' he said.

Christmas came and went, and in the New Year Maria visited Ladyford, where she was surprised to learn from Minnie that 'poor Master Oliver' had been given only a set of skittles for a Christmas present. But on the fourth day of her visit, Thomas called her.

'I am riding into Ashburton and Oliver is to come too. Would you like to come with us? We will loan you the mare and Oliver shall ride with me.'

On the way, Maria did her utmost to discover the purpose of their ride, but Thomas, smiling mysteriously, would say only that he 'had business in the town'.

The Devon countryside looked its wintry best under an almost clear sky, but the warmth of the sun was offset by a cold east wind as they whiled away the journey. Oliver, unaware of the mystery, chatted interminably, keeping Maria and Thomas amused, until at last they reached a saddler in the outskirts of the town and Thomas reined in.

Dismounting, he lifted down his son, then turned to help Maria. She, however, had already been assisted by the saddler's son, who was hovering nearby, enjoying the sight of·Maria's rosy-cheeked face framed by the dark fur lining of her hood.

Embarrassed by his interest, she hastily turned away, letting her gaze roam over the large raftered workshop. A door stood open to the rear and led on to a small kitchen garden, and beyond that she could see the house – a small cottage with a shabby thatch. A bench ran along one side of the workshop with shelves under it, and more shelves lined the other walls. Leather was everywhere, and the agreeable smell hung in the air. Whole hides lay stretched taut on a frame, with part hides hanging over a wooden rack. Several were spread out on the bench, with large circular shapes cut from them, and various cutting and measuring tools lay nearby. Snippets and off-cuts littered the floor and lay in heaps against the walls. Newly-turned wood and several saddle-trees lay on a smaller bench below bundles of wool flock and bales of rye straw. The sweet smell of polish imparted a special fragrance to the air.

'Good morrow, good people' said the saddler, a burly man with a bushy grey beard. 'So this is the young Oliver that I've heard speak of so often. How d'you do, young man? My name's Jim Rudd, and this here's my son Sam. Are you going to shake my hand, young Oliver?'

'If you wish it.'

The boy placed his small hand in the smith's large one and looked up at him with serious grey eyes. He had Melissa's looks, large eyes in an oval face under soft brown hair.

'And did you have a nice Christmas?' the smith asked, winking at Thomas. 'Did you have any presents?'

Oliver nodded solemnly. 'Aye. A fine set of skittles, carved in wood – and I can knock down seven or eight of them. I can knock down more than Mama and more than Papa and more than Minnie and more than –'

'Can you indeed? Then you're a mighty clever boy.'

Oliver looked at Maria to see if she had registered this last remark, and Maria nodded.

'Indeed you are, Oliver,' she confirmed. 'Along goes the wooden ball, and crash! Down go the skittles.'

Thomas, watching proudly, suddenly knelt down and drew the small boy towards him. 'I have a surprise for you,' he told him. 'There's another present for you.'

The saddler handed him a small saddle of pale yellow leather and Thomas held it out for Oliver's inspection. The boy looked at it, puzzled. Then the smith took down a bridle from a hook on the wall behind him and handed that over also.

'There we are,' said Thomas, his voice full of suppressed excitement. 'A saddle and bridle! What do you say to that, eh?'

Oliver hesitated, his expression blank. 'Thank you, Papa,' he said dutifully.

Thomas gave a broad wink to Maria, who was equally mystified. Then the saddler glanced at his son. 'Heigho, Sam! You can bring it in now!' Sam disappeared briefly and returned, leading a small, very shaggy brown pony with a cream mane and tail.

'*Oh Papa!*' The boy's voice was almost a whisper. The adults exchanged looks that were almost as excited as Oliver's.

'This is the rest of your present,' Thomas told him. 'From Mama and me. His name is Bracken.'

'A pony of your own, Oliver!' gasped Maria, and Sam, catching her eye, smiled at her enthusiasm. The pony stood patiently twitching its ears, apparently unconcerned by all the attention as Thomas put the saddle on its back and adjusted the strap. Nervously, Oliver took a step backwards and clutched Maria's hand.

'Such dark brown eyes he has –' said Maria encouragingly.

Sam leaned towards her, looked straight into her eyes and

whispered: 'I warrant yours are darker!'

She felt her cheeks burn at this unexpected compliment. She was flustered for a moment, but so that no one else should notice, went on '– and long, long lashes.'

'But yours are longer,' Sam whispered. 'In truth, you're a pretty filly.'

Slowly she allowed herself to turn and take a proper look at him. His hair was so fair it was almost silver, and hung in tangled curls almost to his shoulders. His face was grimy with smoke from the fire and his teeth gleamed white as the full lips parted in a broad grin. His eyes were steely blue. His bare arms rippled with muscles, and his broad back tapered to narrow hips and long legs. Maria's young senses reeled. And he was only a lad – no more than fifteen, judging by the pale downy hair on his upper lip. What a handsome man he would make! But handsome or not, she must surely put him in his place.

'I'll thank you to keep your remarks to yourself,' she said in a low voice.

But Sam seemed amused by this reply and not at all abashed. 'I speak as I find and meant no offence.'

'None taken then,' she said.

Meanwhile Thomas was putting on the pony's bridle and they were joined by the saddler's wife, a large, jolly woman who brought a pocketful of small apples for Oliver to feed to his new pet.

'There, hold it in your hand, so,' she told him, '– on the flat of your hand. He won't bite your fingers then. No, don't clench your fingers, little man, keep them straight and stiff. Your flat hand is like a platter, see? Oh, bless the little lad! Just see his eyes – nigh on popping out of his head, they are. That's the way of it, my lamb. You've got the idea real fast. Ah, he likes apples, don't he just?'

Maria's thoughts were painfully divided by the two rival attractions – the charms of the pony, and the undeniable appeal of her new-found admirer.

'So he is your father?' she asked him, nodding towards

the smith, regaining a little of her composure.

'That he is,' said Sam, 'and there's five more like me, though none so good-looking! Three sisters, too. He's a lusty old devil, my father.' He leaned nearer and added, 'I take after him in that respect.'

'Oh.' She was definitely flustered. 'Er – *do* you?'

He nodded, watching her reaction, savouring her confusion as she tried desperately to think of an answer that would impress him. Before she could think of anything, he said, 'And I could prove it to you if you've a mind.'

His impudence astounded her. 'I'm certain you would,' she said tartly, 'but you'd have to catch me first.'

'Oh, I'd catch you, never you fear.'

'I'm a fair runner.'

'I'll wager I'm a better,' he grinned.

To her dismay Maria discovered she was beginning to enjoy the exchange. 'If your running's as good as your bragging, you doubtless would,' she told him.

'I'm good at everything I do,' he said. 'And that's no boast – more like a promise.'

Maria dared not meet his eyes for fear of him seeing the spark in her own. Her heart was pounding and she was aware of his nearness with every nerve in her body. But Oliver was tugging at her hand.

'Oh, he wants *you* to help him up,' laughed the smith's wife. 'I won't do, it seems, nor no one else. It must be Maria.'

Hastily Maria turned to him. 'Why, so I shall and gladly,' she said. 'Let me see now, come round this side, Oliver. That's the way, and take up the rein in your left hand –'

'Good, good,' said Thomas. 'He grasps it quickly.'

The saddler's wife positively beamed. 'Oh he'll make a fine horseman, mark my words.'

Oliver did exactly as he was told, his large eyes fixed on Maria's face.

'Now see, this is the stirrup,' said Maria, 'and your foot goes in there. Now, take hold of the saddle edge to steady yourself. Ah, no need to fret, love. Bracken won't hurt you. She is only fidgeting a little and shakes her head – and *up* your go! Swing your leg over and slip the other toe in the other stirrup.'

Nervous but triumphant, Oliver sat astride his first mount, a tremulous smile on his lips, a gleam of satisfaction in his eyes.

'What a perfect pair!' cried the saddler, as his wife clapped her hands delightedly. 'Pony and boy were made for each other, wouldn't you say?'

Thomas nodded. 'So you won't need to ride up front of me any more, Oliver,' he told his son. 'We will make a fine rider of you. What do you say, Maria?'

'He will indeed.'

'A very pretty sight,' said Sam slyly. 'So fair a filly will be a pretty ride, I'll warrant. I confess I envy the rider.'

He spoke so earnestly that Thomas looked at him suspiciously, but Sam assumed an expression of such innocence that Maria almost laughed aloud and was forced to turn the sound into a cough.

But the saddler's wife was not so easily fooled. Seeing Maria's flushed cheeks, and knowing her son's forward nature, she hurriedly sent him into the house on another matter to be rid of him until the visitors had gone.

The ride back to Ladyford was a slow one, for they were all forced to match the leisurely pace of Oliver's new pony. But the journey gave Maria time to think over the events of the past hour without interruption, for Thomas was totally engrossed with his son and quite unaware of the new direction of her thoughts.

Maria was truly amazed at the effect the young man had on her and astonished that his words could move her body so mysteriously, rouse her emotions so completely. Her thoughts were still chaotic, and her head was spinning as though she had drunk too much wine. The hands that held the reins trembled and there was a strange new feeling inside her – a great emptiness like a hunger. But no – not quite like it. Tentatively, she let his image return bright and strong in her mind, and was shocked to find that her feelings intensified. With every moment that she thought on him the sensation grew – a sensation that was both sweet yet agonising. Faintly, she marvelled at it, aware for the first time of the pleasure that her own body could provide. And yet she was also diffident about it, as though the new-found joys were sinful and not to be discussed. Was there anything in the Scriptures to guide her? She could think of nothing. Her mother had never hinted at such delights. Perhaps she had not felt them. Was she, Maria, alone in this matter? No, she could not believe that. But if others experienced it also, why was it kept so secret?

'Maria! You will be left behind!'

Thomas and Oliver were some distance ahead and waiting for her. Guiltily, she waved a hand and urged her horse into a trot to rejoin them.

'A penny for your thoughts.' Thomas laughed, but she shook her head.

'I'd sooner stay poor and keep them to myself,' she told him when they once more rode alongside. And indeed, by the time they reached Ladyford she had given the matter a great deal of thought and had come to a decision. She would speak to no one about her newly awakened body and its dimly understood promise. She would share it with no one. Her heart and soul were Hugo's, and her body would be his also. But the glorious confusion within her lingered on, weaker but still recognisable, and she prayed he would not be too long in claiming her.

CHAPTER SIX

'Written this thirteenth day of January 1554. Greetings from your devoted sister Abigail to Melissa. As usual your letter made me weep for joy. Tis nearly seven months since we last met, and I crave sight of you and Thomas. My sweet Adam suggests you might both travel to London when Maria returns, and stay here awhile before returning home, which would please me greatly. The winter months depress my spirits. Do write me what you say to this idea as promptly as may be. I am impatient for your answer.

'The main cause of my poor spirits is Janna, who last Thursday slipped away secretly to wed a waggoner, who in turn did vanish from his lodgings so that yesterday she did return saying she was betrayed and would I take her back. Adam will not hear of it and has sent her away. I must therefore find a new maid – a worrisome task in which I take no pleasure.

'In Rochester all is excitement and rumour. The marriage treaty was signed yesterday between Queen Mary and the Prince of Spain, yet the people clamour they will not have him. We saw the Spanish envoys landed at Tower Wharf with all ceremony and a salute of guns, but the people were silent, none of them smiling, and none raised a cheer to greet them, but many muttered for the Princess Elizabeth. Tis said that Sir Thomas Lovatt will raise arms in Kent and other men likewise. What news of Sir Peter Carew? I cannot believe he will stand idle. What troubled times we share. What will become of us?

'As to Hannah's news, I pray you give her my warm congratulations. To be with child and in such robust health!

I envy her and pray God she may continue so, for tis early yet and 'many a slip twixt cup and lip' has sadly much truth in it. For our part we are fit and Adam thrives, also the babes, bless them. The Queen's Navy grows apace and we boast a small share in it, with one galley near completed and another due before the year is out. In haste now to dispatch this letter. Write if you will come. And so God be with you all.'

Two months later, Hannah, pale and tight-lipped, ran through the grounds at Heron in search of her husband and found him in the garden by the river, in earnest conversation with a younger man. Catching sight of her, the man coloured slightly and muttered something to Simon, who turned guiltily. Neither men spoke as she went down the steps; then Simon said, a shade too heartily, 'Then I thank you for your news and am sorry you will not stay longer.'

'Simon,' Hannah said. 'I must speak with you.'

The man avoided her eyes. 'You are welcome,' he said in answer to Simon. 'Now I must away. Farewell to you, ma'am.'

'Wait!' cried Hannah, but with another low aside to Simon the man turned and sprang onto his horse, which waited knee-deep in the river. In silence, Hannah watched horse and rider cross the river and scramble up the bank on the far side, where the stranger gave them another wave, cried 'God be with you', and cantered his horse across the grass, away through the trees and up onto the highway where it crossed the bridge.

'What does this mean?' asked Hannah, trying in vain to steady her voice as she faced her husband. 'Maria tells me you are willing – nay, have *offered* to escort her back to London! And yet only a week ago you were advising Melissa that –'

'Hannah, please. A moment –'

'No, let me speak,' she cried, the words continuing to

94

tumble out. 'You told them the capital was unsafe, that times were perilous. You said there was rebellion in the air and twas best to stay out of London. Let her stay a few weeks longer, you said. Now she tells me she will go and you are ready to accompany her!'

'Hannah –'

'And that man, Simon? Who is he? Why does he come secretly, instead of arriving at the house? Why, Simon? You have behaved most strangely of late and I swear I do not know you any more.'

Her fear lent an angry tone to her words, and her pale face was now flushed. Simon made to take her hands, but she withdrew them, shaking her head. 'Answer my questions first,' she insisted, 'for when that is done I may not want to hold your hands. I'm suddenly fearful of what you will say.'

Simon swallowed, trying not to let his feelings show too plainly in his face. 'Come back to the house,' he began. 'Tis chilly –'

'Tell me, Simon. I do not feel the cold.'

He shrugged and took a deep breath, 'As you wish. The man you saw is a friend with news from Adam of affairs in London. As to –'

'Affairs in London? What does that mean?'

'Affairs of State,' he told her.

'What are such affairs to you? No, *tell me!*'

'They are of interest . . . to us all.

'*I* will be the judge of that when I hear it.'

Simon looked taken aback by her defiant expression and the intensity of her questions. 'Matters of government,' he said.

'Of rebellion, more like! You mince words, Simon, thinking to allay my suspicions, but I will not be misled. Speak truly, for God's sake, if times be perilous, as you say they are.'

Simon sighed. 'Twill be in confidence?' She nodded impatiently. 'Then listen carefully, and I will tell you. Not all, but all you need to know.'

She was frightened, despite her brave words, and suddenly took hold of his hands and let him hold her close.

'You know England has a Catholic Queen who now persecutes the Protestants? She would have us all return to Popery, but the people will not tolerate it. Some even die for their beliefs. She would repeal all the reforms, undo all that Henry and Edward have done. She would turn back the clock.'

'But you and Hugo – you fought against the reforms.' She looked up at him, bewildered. 'Hugo was exiled for his part. So few years ago!'

'But that's in the past,' he assured her. 'England is now a Protestant country. We have all changed. Tis the way of the world. Progress, if you will. We do not want a Pope. We want to rule our own land in our own way. England does not want meddling foreigners to tell us how we must live. Nor do we want a Spanish King – and Mary is set on wedding Philip in defiance of the wishes of her subjects.'

'But if she truly loves him –' cried Hannah.

'Loves him? In God's name, woman, she has never *met* the man. How can she love him? She has seen a painting of him which no doubt flatters him, and received a few letters. She cannot love him, and he does not love her. But he needs England's support. He and Mary will drag us into an endless war with France. Is that what you want?'

'Is it so certain?' She was troubled by his words and suddenly fearful for her unborn child.

'Aye, most certain. England will gain a Spanish King and lose her sons and all her wealth – all in a foreign cause.'

'I see. And will she not wed an Englishman? They say young Courtenay is highly born . . .'

'She will not have him. Is quite adamant on the subject. In truth, he is not suitable, poor wretch. He spent his youth and early manhood shut up in the Tower at Henry's instigation and knows little of the ways of the world. But even were he suitable in every way, I doubt she would agree. The Queen is nervous and hedged round by intrigue. Her mother was Spanish and she will not feel safe until she is assured of Spanish protection.'

'Poor woman,' said Hannah. 'In spite of all you say, I feel for her. She has had a sorry life so far and deserves some happiness.'

'But not at England's expense.' His tone was sharp. 'Some people favour the young Elizabeth, who might wed Courtenay. They are more of an age, and Courtenay would be comely enough if only he could polish up his manners and find shrewd men to tutor and advise him. Who knows? His grandfather was a King. The young man might surprise us all.'

'And the man who came here, who spoke with you?' Hannah prompted.

'He brought news of a rising in Kent, and I would add my strength to it. Devon will not rise now, not with Carew fled to Normandy.'

'But you are only one man,' said Hannah. 'They will not miss you. I beg you, do not go, Simon.'

'I have a duty, Hannah. We all do.'

'And what of your duty to me – and our first child?'

'I'll come back to you, Hannah. Never fear. We may not even fight.'

'How will you overthrow a Queen without fighting?'

'We do not need to overthrow her – just reason with her. Wyatt is convinced that with a great show of strength we shall convince the Queen of our determination – persuade her to take new advisers and forgo the Spanish match. We do not intend her harm, yet we cannot sit idly by while England is forfeited to Philip of Spain.'

'Oh, my dearest love, your words do nothing to allay my fears.' She looked at him beseechingly, holding herself away from him in order to read his expression. ''Tis always thus – that men march to the King in peace, wanting no bloodshed, to air a grievance or resist a new tax. Always it ends in fighting. Think on Exeter – and your Uncle William. He died on just such a peaceful demonstration! Send money if you must, Simon, and pray for them. But do not go, I beg you. Stay with me – with us!' She took his right hand and laid it across her belly. 'Your child grows there, Simon. Maybe a son. Soon he will kick me and pummel me with his little fists. I want you to be here to share it with me.'

Simon was silent, then drew her close. 'I swear I will come back,' he told her, 'but I am determined to go. I would rather take your prayers with me for a safe journey.'

'So be it,' she said quietly. 'You shall have my prayers, Simon, but not my approval. When will you go?'

'This very night. Wyatt has over two thousand men gathered at Rochester, but he waits on Isley, who will ride up from Sevenoaks with another five hundred. I shall deliver Maria to her mother and then cross the Thames, and head either direct for Rochester, or if it be too dangerous, then –'

'Dangerous? In what way dangerous?'

He laughed quickly. 'That was a poor word to use. Forgive me. There will be no danger. Let's say if more *expedient* then I shall either drop down to Sevenoaks, join Isley and ride the rest of the way with him, or ride straight to Rochester and seek out Adam. I dare say he is of a like mind.'

'But Hugo? What of Hugo, then?'

'Hugo is newly returned from exile. Mary was his salvation, Hannah. He will admit no fault in her.'

Hannah suddenly clung to him, unable to say what was in her heart. A dark dread chilled her body even more than the raw January air, and she shivered violently.

'What am I thinking of!' exclaimed Simon. 'To keep you out here while I prattle on, boring you with politics. I insist we go in. We'll have a hot drink and you shall help me pack. The sooner I am on my way, the sooner I shall knock some sense into Mary's head.'

'You alone?' Hannah smiled faintly.

'Aye,' he said as they walked back towards the house. 'Your Majesty, I shall say. I, Simon Kendal, your most obedient servant do bid leave to explain your follies and recommend the remedy. How think you she'll react to that?'

'She'll box your ears, most likely,' laughed Hannah. 'I would if I were in her shoes, and a pipsqueak appeared from Devonshire with so much impudence! Oh, Simon! Promise me you will take all care and come home safely.'

Pausing at the door he kissed her forehead, the tip of her nose and finally her lips.

'I love you more than life itself,' he whispered. 'I do most earnestly promise I shall be back.'

While Wyatt fretted in Rochester, the Queen's forces were being organised elsewhere, but the rebels' propaganda had left its mark, and many of the gentry in Kent were reluctant to take arms against them. Wyatt had already made the rounds of the surrounding village with alarming stories of the imminence of Spanish interference and the dire outcome of such interference. He had assured his listeners that they intended no harm to the Queen's person and categorically denied that they intended to bring about her downfall. Elizabeth and Courtenay were never even mentioned.

When the call to arms finally came from London, Sir Robert Southwell and Lord Abergavenny, for the Queen, found it difficult to rally the men of Kent to their cause, and when they finally set up camp at Malling, they had only six hundred men between them. The Queen herself had better success. It was announced that she would address the citizens at the Guildhall in London, and Simon, arriving in the town with Maria, was persuaded by her to make a short detour to hear her speak.

'Twill not take us far out of our way,' urged Maria, 'and Mama need never know we did not come straight home. Are you not anxious to see the Queen for yourself?'

'Indeed I am,' he confessed. 'I have never seen this

daughter. They say she is like her mother in will and temper, but has Henry's hair.'

They joined the crowd at the Guildhall in time to see Mary arrive with her escort, a slim, slight figure with a neat head set on narrow shoulders. Her clear grey eyes shone in a face which glowed in the cold air and was framed by bright red-gold hair. She was warmly dressed in heavy velvet with full sleeves cut in the French style, and her head-dress and mantle were decorated with rich jewels.

Maria was enchanted. 'She is every inch a Queen,' she breathed.

Simon was too kind to argue with her, but his thoughts were far less charitable. He considered how much power lay in this slight, proud figure, who was even now turning to speak to them.

A murmur ran through the crowd and they fell silent. The Queen's bearing was dignified and her expression calm. If she feared inwardly that her reign might be abruptly ended by the rebel forces gathering outside the city, she gave no outward sign. Her courage was both impressive and infectious. The Council had urged her to flee London and ride to Windsor, or else set sail for Calais, but she had refused even to consider such action. Her decision to stay was widely reported and the people were impressed by her courage and set great store by her example.

'I am come in my own person,' she began, 'to tell you what you already see and know, that is, how traitoriously and rebelliously a number of Kentishmen have assembled themselves against us – and against you!' Her voice was low but strong as she continued. She was convinced that her enemies must be heretics, and declared earnestly 'that the matter of the marriage seems but a cloak to hide their pretended purpose against our religion.' When she told them that the rebels meant to seize control of the government, there were angry murmurings among the crowd and here and there a fist raised above a head. But Simon, surveying this cross-section of her subjects, wondered how many others felt as hostile as he did and hid their true feelings behind their smiles.

'. . . Now, loving subjects, what I am you right well know. I am your Queen . . .' There were a few ragged cheers '. . . to whom at my coronation when I was wedded to the realm . . .'

Maria leaned closer to Simon and whispered, 'She has no notes, you see. She speaks right from the heart, and looks so beautiful. Aren't you pleased we came by?'

'Aye, pleased enough,' he lied, but just then a man in front of them turned, scowling, and they fell silent once more, their eyes on the Queen, who was now speaking passionately of her inheritance of the English crown.

'. . . My father, as you all know, possessed the same regal state which now rightly is descended to me . . .' Referring to her forthcoming marriage, she made light of the fact that her husband-to-be was not an Englishman and spoke of her love for the people, stressing her determination to produce an heir. It was a shrewd and moving speech, and she concluded it dramatically.

'. . . And now, good subjects, pluck up your hearts and like true men stand fast against these rebels, both our enemies and yours, and fear them not, for I assure you *I* fear them nothing at all!'

As the cheering began, she stood before them, her arms flung wide as though to embrace them all, her eyes flashing triumphantly. The Council, astonished at her success, could only stare at one another as feet stamped and hats and gloves were thrown into the air by the ecstatic Londoners. No longer frightened and confused, they knew where their duty lay and what they must do. Mary was their own true Queen and the treacherous rebels must be beaten back. As she marched out again, flanked by her white-coated troops, the hall rang with cries of 'God save Queen Mary' and 'God bless our Queen'. A few cried 'God save the Prince of Spain' but a dismayed Simon was not among them. His face grim, he took Maria by the hand, and forcing a way through the crowd, led her off to find their horses. The mood of the crowd incensed him. The sooner he delivered Maria to her mother, the sooner he could be off about his own dangerous affairs.

London was now in a state verging on seige, and the streets were full of scurrying citizens making whatever preparations they could to protect their families and properties from the expected disruptions of battle. Shops were hastily shuttered as word came that Wyatt and his men were camped on the Southwark side of London Bridge, which was itself heavily defended by Mary's troops and four cannons. In Gutter Lane and Cheapside, the gold and silversmiths ceased trading and secured their premises with extra locks, some even took down their signs, so that possible looters should not be aware of the rich pickings to be found within. But the sign of the Golden Plumes was still in place when Simon banged on the door.

'Who's there?' came a cautious voice from within.

'Tis only us, Mama – Simon and Maria. Let us in.'

Her mother opened the door and, admitting them, barred the door again.

'But tis so dark in here!' cried Maria. 'Why are the windows shuttered, Mama? Anyone would think the rebels were in the town already.'

'They're not so far away,' she told them, 'and the two lads are off roaming the streets with their eyes out on stalks. I told them to stay close, but they don't listen. But you must be hungry, and here's me rattling on. Sit yourself down, and I'll get you –'

'I'd rather be away,' Simon interrupted her hastily, knowing how much she rambled on when given the opportunity. 'I've a mind to ride down to Rochester and talk with Adam.' Unsure of the Lessors' allegiance, he thought it wise not to mention the true reason for his journey to London.

The old woman shook her head. 'You'll not make Rochester,' she told him. 'They say the rebels are at Southwark, camped at the bridge foot – thousands of them. You'll not get through to Rochester. You'd best stay here with us until the fighting's done. We can find you a mattress.'

'What of Isley's men?' he asked. 'I heard they were gathering at Sevenoaks and Tonbridge to ride against the Queen.'

'Oh, they did, but met with the Queen's whitecoats at Wrotham. Lost the day, by all accounts, and sixty prisoners taken. There'll be some hangings, I warrant.' She shook her head at the prospect. 'But they're to be reckoned with for all that. Isley has seized some of the Queen's own ships, so my neighbour says, that waited to sail out and greet the Spanish prince. Aye, and some cannons, also. I said to my neighbour, Mistress Cavitt, I said, you have to admire this Wyatt's impudence.' She laughed. 'Stealing the Queen's ships from under her very nose! And hundreds of her soldiers fled to join Wyatt. I don't know what to think on it all, and that's the truth.'

When Simon had finally elicited all the information she could give him, he politely refused her offer of hospitality, remounted and made his way towards London Bridge. He had no doubt that Adam would be among the rebels camped on the far side.

Everywhere windows were shuttered and doors barred. The market stalls, hurriedly dismantled, were missing from the streets, and the shoppers with them. In their place men crowded together at every corner, self-conscious in their battle harness, their hands straying nervously to their swords or daggers or such weapons as they had been able to procure. Above them, the women leaned from upper windows exchanging the latest rumours, some weeping openly, others praying aloud for deliverance. The usual bands of homeless children roamed among the soldiers, their eyes wide, their hands outstretched for any coin that might be begged or scrap of food that might be stolen while the men's attention was engaged elsewhere.

Simon made his way slowly, afraid of attracting unwanted interest. He passed the Mayor and a group of aldermen, all mounted, their mail clinking and glinting in the pale winter sunshine. At last he came to the bridge. To his surprise he crossed unchallenged by the Queen's men, although the shops and houses on the bridge were also heavily secured and many had been evacuated. No doubt, he thought grimly, it would be a different story if he were trying to ride *into* the town. On the south side of the river, Wyatt's army, four thousand or so strong, thronged the High Street, Banner Street and Maid Lane, and sat or sprawled in every available area of waste ground almost as far as Lambeth Marsh. Horses were tethered among the men and tents and pavilions were pitched indiscriminately. Standards fluttered in the cold air, and smoke rose from countless fires where men crouched to warm themselves and cook whatever food they had been able to buy from the bemused citizens of Southwark. A few women moved among the men; some no doubt from Southwark, others from further afield, accompanying their husbands until such time as the fighting began and they were forced to watch from a safe distance or return home to await the outcome. Simon asked for news of Adam Jarman.

'He hails from Rochester,' he told them. 'Boatbuilder. Not tall, with a ruddy complexion. Some would call him stout.'

But no one seemed to have heard of him. Nearly a quarter of an hour passed and Simon was on the point of giving up, when a familiar figure darted in front of his horse, causing it to lunge sideways and toss its head in alarm.

'Maggie!'

The woman turned, and a wide smile lit up her face. 'God a'mighty, Simon Betts!' she cried. 'Or rather Kendal. I forget, you're a gentleman now.' As he slid to the ground she ran to him and flung her arms round his neck. 'Oh, tis good to see you. I might have known you'd be here. Never could resist a fight.'

Laughing, he looked round anxiously, afraid that Adam would choose this inopportune moment to materialise beside them. ''Tis good to see you, Maggie,' he said, 'so far from home. What brings you here – or shouldn't I ask?'

She winked wickedly and jerked her head towards a group of young men who sat playing cards nearby.

''Tis the lad,' she told him. 'Now wouldn't you know it? The lad grew tired of kneading dough – he's the one with brown hair and a feather in his cap, cheeky young devil. I'm off to the wars, Maggie, he tells me, to fight for the Princess Elizabeth. Who'll roll my dumplings then? I asked him.' She nudged Simon and laughed again. 'Who'll fill my pastry? I asked – and he was hard put for an answer, poor young man. 'Tis a shame, but they do so love a battle. So here I am.' She stood, hands on her hips, surveying him with a provocative smile on her homely face. 'And here *you* are,' she added softly. 'Now who says the good Lord don't move in a mysterious way.'

'Oh, Maggie,' he laughed. 'You are just the same sweet woman. Not a day older – but prettier.'

'Prettier? Oh, now I *know* you're flattering me, Simon Kendal – *sir*.' She dropped an elaborate, mocking curtsey.

Simon laughed; but the sight of her stirred his body, bringing a rush of memories – himself and Maggie on a pile of flour sacks, the first time he took her, when he was still Simon Betts, Luke's bastard son. And in the loft above the bakery where her father slept. So sweet, so generous and so uncomplicated. Looking into his face, she read his thoughts and smiled mischievously.

'If you should want your weapon polished before the battle,' she whispered, 'I'd be glad to shine it for you.'

He pulled her to him suddenly. 'And what of the lad?' he asked. 'Would you let him fight with a dull sword?'

She tossed her head and the shiny curls danced. 'His sword's so shiny already he could see his face in it,' she protested. 'The poor lad needs to save his strength, or he'll not make the battle at all!'

He kissed the top of her head and remounted his horse. 'I'll give your offer my best considerations, sweet lady,' he told her. 'And my thanks. Now I must be on my way. I'm looking for a certain Adam Jarman, my brother-in-law from Rochester.'

She pointed towards the church of St. Towles. 'There's a crowd of men from Rochester and Chatham in the church-yard. You might find him there.'

'I'll take a look directly. Goodbye, sweet Maggie.'

'God be with you, Simon,' she said. 'I'll pray for you.' The laughter was suddenly absent from her eyes as she watched the man she loved ride off through the crowd.

Simon found Adam propped up against a grave stone, eyes closed, mouth open, breathing noisily.

'Too much wine,' said one of his companions, and Simon sat down on the grass beside him without waking him, and accepted gratefully a hunk of bread and cheese and a few mouthfuls of ale from Adam's friend, whose name was Marcus Allen.

'Tis the waiting,' he explained, 'and wondering. They say the Queen pardons us all and begs us go peacefully home. Pardons us for what? We have done naught wrong – as yet. Time enough for that, eh?'

Their laughter roused Adam and, the greetings exchanged, the three men opened another flagon of ale and the talk turned to an assessment of their situation.

'The bridge itself is heavily defended,' said Marcus. 'Four cannons to our two. And the city walls are crawling with soldiers. Ludgate and Newgate – indeed *all* the city gates – are so fortified, tis a wonder the stones don't give way under the weight.'

'He's right,' admitted Adam. 'I reckon we'll hope for a friendly reception. If the landowners are truly with us, as the whitecoats say they are, then they'll open the gate to us and let us in. If not, twill be a bloody business and a lot of men lost.'

'On both sides,' said Simon.

'Granted,' said Marcus. 'But let's hope it doesn't come to that. I've a little girl at home – three she is in March. The apple of my eye, she is.'

'I told him to stay at home,' said Adam, 'but no, he would come. I'll wager your Hannah was down in the mouth at your leaving, too.'

'Aye,' Simon agreed.

'And Luke? How did he take the news?'

'Of my coming? I didn't wait to find out,' said Simon. 'Poor Hannah must break it to him, or Thomas Benet. I hope he doesn't take it too hard, he's an old man and tied to his bed. His thoughts grow morbid and he'll be fearful for me. But what of Abigail?'

Adam smiled sheepishly. 'Ranted like a fishwife! I didn't know she *knew* such words! And then when she sees I am determined, bursts into tears and won't be comforted. Poor Abby. Still, she's got the children to keep her busy, and anyway I'll be home again before she can count to a hundred. Wyatt says this will end well and speedily, and London will come over to us. I hope he's right.'

'If we cannot approach by the bridge,' said Marcus, 'we'll probably march downriver to Kingston, cross there and march back on the other side.'

Simon groaned. 'So far? Thank the Lord for horses, I say! Who'd be a foot soldier?'

They finished off the ale, and Marcus wrapped himself in a blanket. 'I had no sleep at all last night,' he told them, 'and tonight will be no better. So cold, and the camp so noisy. I'll follow Adam's example and snatch a few hours now while I still can. Once the daylight goes, the air cools rapidly. Wake me if more food arrives – I've no mind to fight on an empty stomach.'

'You should sleep also,' Adam told Simon. 'I'll watch for all of us. A rich merchant from Bermondsey Street sent two hundred fowls yesterday – the air was so thick with feathers twas like a snow storm.'

Adam took his advice. He fed and watered his horse and then set about his own bed. It was already growing dark as he unrolled his straw palliasse and lay it on the ground close to Marcus. He had brought two blankets and these he threw over himself. The saddle served as a pillow, and the smell of leather was the last thing he remembered as he drifted into a fitful, shivering, sleep.

When he awoke it was dark and he was alone. Above him, the stars shone brightly and there were no clouds. He was shivering so violently that his teeth chattered. A few yards to his left, a large group of men huddled together round a blazing fire, singing the latest bawdy ballad about the Spaniards, and his lips moved in the beginning of a smile as he listened to the familiar words. Beyond them in the darkness, other fires glowed orange, shooting out wavering columns of sparks into the blackness. Horses whinnied restlessly, occasionally pounding the hard earth for attention. In the distance a fox barked and set howling the many stray dogs that had adopted the rebel army. There was a burst of laughter, a snore, angry voices raised in a drunken brawl, the rattle of dice. Suddenly Maggie was kneeling beside him, silhouetted in the firelight.

'Are you hungry?' she demanded. 'I've brought you a lump of mutton still hot.'

'Mutton, do you say? You clever girl – but where did this come from?'

'A well-wisher,' she said. 'Me. I stole it on the way across from a fat old man who was too drunk to eat it. That'll do my man more good than it will you, I told him, but all I got for answer was a belch. Well, make room inside that blanket, Simon Kendal. A true gentleman doesn't leave a lady out in the cold, especially one as brings him a chunk of hot meat for his supper.'

'You are a baggage, Maggie!' he laughed, as she squeezed in beside him. 'Kind and warm-hearted, but a baggage.'

'I've been called worse,' she said. 'Well, I never thought to sleep in so strange a bed – a gravestone at my head and a stray dog at my feet. Shoo, you mangy cur.' The dog crept closer, attracted by the smell of the mutton. 'Look at the poor creature – one ear half gone and the other in tatters! Give it the bone when you're done, Simon – and do make haste. If I'd known you were so slow an eater I'd have saved the meat till after.'

And so, bantering lovingly, she wormed her way into his affections once more until they reached the oneness of mind that leads to passion. Her hands coaxed his cold, tired body into a rich awareness of her own. Her lips caressed his face, neck and ears, her fingers reached under his clothing to the soft skin, stroking it with a sureness of touch born of experience and a desire to please. Her tongue reached for his, and her mouth closed over his, muffling the small sounds that a man makes at the beginning of ecstasy. At last they could wait no longer and clung together in the ultimate joy, unobserved by any but the dog, who glanced at them enquiringly from time to time with his head on one side.

When Simon woke next morning she was gone, but a red-edged daisy from the grass was tucked into the fold of his shirt.

As Marcus had predicted, London Bridge would not yield, and Wyatt was forced to move his army upstream. They crossed the Thames at Kingston and then marched back, finally reaching Ludgate hungry and footsore by way of Temple Bar and Fleet Street, meeting only token resistance. They passed many armed men in battle harness, but encountered little real hostility. The rebels cried repeatedly, 'We are all Englishmen!' and the patriotic words drew forth a sympathetic response. They also cried that the Queen had pardoned them, insisting that she was prepared to give them an audience. Many citizens lowered their weapons and they passed almost unmolested as far as Ludgate.

'Pray God our luck holds out,' muttered Simon, and Adam said, 'Amen to that!'

But Ludgate was held by Lord William Howard, and to the rebels' dismay, he steadfastly refused to unbar the gates.

'Dear God!' cried Marcus. 'The fool will undo us all. There can be no retreating.'

The rebels waited while Wyatt remonstrated, but Howard remained obdurate. Word soon passed through the ranks. Hardly able to believe this last-minute setback, the men turned back, disillusioned and apprehensive.

'The people will not tolerate us now,' cried Marcus. 'You'll see. Howard's rejection has signed our death warrants.'

He was right. The people, previously in two minds, now saw only too clearly that the Queen did *not* accept Wyatt, and their attitude hardened. Fighting broke out almost immediately, and the cry went up that the Queen's soldiers, led by the Earl of Pembroke, had sealed off the rebels' retreat.

'Trapped, by Christ!' said Simon. 'Twill be a bloody route home.'

Soon the air was shrill with angry shouts, clashing steel and the screams of the wounded. Terrified horses reared and men fell under their flailing hooves, to be trampled underfoot by their fellows. Blood flowed from hacked limbs, and bones cracked and splintered under the impact of staves and cudgels. One moment Adam, Marcus and Simon were fighting side by side. The next they were separated by the milling men. The fighting grew fiercer and the pandemonium of battle increased. Simon caught a fleeting glimpse of Wyatt, stunned by the rapid change of fortune, slumped on a bench, helpless to deliver himself or his army from the carnage that threatened them. Simon knew that Wyatt would have to surrender to avoid further fruitless bloodshed. It was Ash Wednesday, it was raining, and the rebels' cause was lost.

When it was over, Maggie came, picking her way along

streets still littered with the débris of war – pools of blood, an occasional broken sword or abandoned bow. The lower windows of a few houses remained shuttered, awaiting the return of their frightened owners. She looked for Simon among the many wounded, but could not find him. Fearfully, she moved on to search among the dead, and there she found him with his neck broken, his sword still grasped in his hand.

'Oh, my sweet man, what have they done to you?' she whispered.

While her tears flowed, she kissed the cold face and smoothed the soft blond hair with trembling fingers. Then gently she closed the proud blue eyes forever. She was still sitting beside him when Adam found them nearly two hours later. Awkwardly she stood up on cramped legs, brushed down her skirt and pulled her shawl over her head. Adam tried to see her face, but she kept it averted and walked away without a word.

CHAPTER SEVEN

Maria dreamed that a wolf had seized her by the arm and was tugging her screaming across the moor. Her screams grew louder until they found a voice, and at once a hand was clamped over her mouth and another voice urged her to 'wake yourself up and stop hollering.' When at last she opened her eyes, it was to find Minnie beside her, shaking her by the arm.

'You sleep like a log,' the girl grumbled. 'For Lord's sake rouse yourself, Maria. I've summat to show you.'

'At this hour?'

Maria looked round the small bedchamber. It was still barely light, and the small window was no more than a pale grey square against the shadowed wall. 'Tisn't morning yet,' she protested. 'You can show me later –'

'But I *can't*. Outside in the garden – there's someone prowling. I've heard him, Maria. Do come and see.'

Since Simon's death, Hannah had withdrawn almost entirely and kept mostly to her room, hugging to her the unborn child which her husband had given her. Maria had been invited to stay over for a few weeks as company for her and to help Beth. Now the baby was due, and Minnie, too, had been loaned. The two girls shared a room from choice – according to Melissa, so that they might lie awake half the night exchanging confidences.

'In the garden?' cried Maria, wide awake at last, and she scrambled out of bed and ran across to the window.

The bedchamber was at the back of the house and looked out over the herb garden and vegetable plot. Further over to the right was the orchard. The shrubs and trees lay shadowy and indistinguishable in the half-light. Maria craned her neck but could see nothing moving.

'Are you certain?' she asked Minnie. 'I see no one.'

'I heard someone, I swear I did,' cried Minnie. 'First it was like a curse, then like a voice saying "Maria". Leastways, I think twas "Maria"!'

Maria's eyes widened. 'Maria? Calling my name? You didn't tell me that before.'

'I wasn't certain of it,' said Minnie, leaning out to have a look.

Maria pulled her back and thrust her own head out again. 'There's no one there, you ninny,' she said, disappointed. 'Where did you think the voice came from? The orchard? Straight below us?'

'I don't rightly know,' said Minnie. 'I didn't wait to look – I was too frightened.'

'Mayhap you were dreaming,' said Maria, but Minnie denied it hotly, declaring that she had been woken by the dogs and had then heard the voice. They looked at each other, uncertain what to do.

'I wish Simon was still here,' said Maria. 'He'd take a light and go down there. Or Thomas – or Hugo.'

Minnie gave a little jump of excitement. 'Mayhap tis Hugo!' she squealed. 'Come to carry you off and make you his own. His child-bride! Oh Maria, d'you think it may be Hugo?'

'Hugo? Oh, I can't believe it! No, Minnie – but let me look again. Oh! There *is* someone there – I see him by the orchard gate. He's looking up here! Sweet heaven, who can it be?'

Minnie tried to look out, but the window was too small for both heads and she was forced to watch Maria's back and experience the excitement at second-hand.

'He's waving up at me,' whispered Maria, hardly daring to trust her own eyes. 'He's calling "Maria" – but softly, so no one else shall hear him!' She jerked her head in so swiftly that she struck it on the window-frame, but pausing only to rub the spot, she snatched up a shawl and made for the door.

'I'm going down to see him,' she told Minnie. 'You had best come with me in case he means me harm. Bring the warming pan.'

'The warming pan, ma'am?'

'Aye, twill serve as a weapon.'

Speechless with excitement, Minnie did as she was told, and draping herself in a blanket from her bed, followed Maria downstairs. Maria was already at the back door, unbarring it. Gently they slid back the bolt and opened it a few inches. A large figure stood silhouetted against the pale sky.

Minnie opened her mouth to scream but Maria hushed her impatiently.

'Tis only Matt after all,' she said. 'Matt Cartright with something hid behind his back.'

She opened the door, and the boy grinned widely, taken aback to see two girls. Minnie giggled, but Marie stepped on her toe to silence her.

'What is it, Matt?' she asked primly. 'Why do you come bothering folk at this hour of the night?'

He glanced up at the sky, surprised. 'I reckoned twas morning. What difference does it make?' He looked at Minnie, frowned, then looked at his feet. 'No difference – leastways, I dunno about a difference.'

'What's that behind your back?' asked Minnie, unable to hold back the question any longer.

'Tis nothing for your eyes,' he said sharply. 'Tis for Maria.' Slowly he held out a small branch of hawthorn. 'Tis a May branch,' he said. 'I made it pretty for you, for to make you my May girl.'

His round moon-face was set in an earnest expression under the pale hair. Maria bit back the words that sprang to her lips: that a poor farm lad had no right to come Maying after a lady. The branch was decorated with tufts of sheep's wool and yellow ribbon was tied round the stem.

'A May branch!' cried Minnie enviously. 'Oh, I wish some lad would come a-Maying after me!'

Maria hesitated. If she accepted the token he would plant it, and then she would have to go with him to the celebrations on the village green later in the day. She would be his partner. Suddenly he laid the branch at her feet.

'I'd like it real well if you'd take it,' said Matt. Seeing that she still hesitated, he added, 'Oh, I nearly forgot,' and snatched off his cap. Hugging it to his chest, he fell on one knee and cleared his throat.

> *'I come to say, this first of May,*
> *Tis thee I want the livelong – er –'*

'Day!' prompted Maria.

'Oh yes – day.'

Minnie giggled again, but at a warning glance from Maria hid herself behind the door, where she continued to splutter helplessly.

> *'This branch I bear –'*

He scratched his head and replaced his cap. Then he stood up and glanced anxiously around the garden, to make sure there were no unwelcome witnesses to his performance.

'I can't rightly recall the rest,' he said, 'but tis a right pretty verse.'

'Who taught it to you?' asked Maria curiously.

'The lads,' he said. 'They're all going Maying, so I says "Teach me the verse", and they laughed at me and said, "Who'd go Maying with the likes of you?". But I never told 'em. Tis my secret, I said. And I learned it right well and I made the little branch. And then –' He shrugged and gazed at Maria appealingly with his large blue eyes.

Maria sighed. She bent down and picked up the bush. 'Tis a fine May branch,' she said. 'Plant it for me, Matt. I'll be your partner for today.'

His mouth fell open and he stammered for words, but Maria turned to Minnie, who was almost as surprised as

Matt. 'Go fetch a mug of ale and a biscuit,' she whispered.

Matt found a patch of soft earth, dug a hole with his large hands and planted the little branch. Smiling shyly, he wiped his hands on his breeches and accepted the ale and biscuit. When he had finished, Maria gave the mug to Minnie and sent her, albeit reluctantly, to return the mug to the kitchen.

'Now, Matt,' she said. 'Haven't you forgotten something?'

He shook his head. 'I aint forgot, but I – I daresn't!' he muttered, scuffling his feet nervously.

'But if I want you to, Matt! Tis part of the Maying.'

Matt took a step towards her, and she stepped into his arms and turned her face up to his. As he bent his head they heard Minnie returning and he hastily snatched a kiss, barely brushing her lips. A slow, delighted grin spread over his face. 'I like Maying!' he whispered, and his mouth met hers again, more firmly.

'Ooh ma'am!' squealed Minnie, and abruptly Matt released her. With a last radiant smile he stumbled away across the rapidly lightening garden, back the way he had come.

Maria watched him go, her heart pounding with a strange exhilaration. For a few moments to hide her confusion, she admired the little branch.

'That Matt Cartright,' said Minnie slyly. 'I reckon he's real clumsy at kissing.'

'Well, he isn't then,' said Maria, taking the bait. 'If you must know, it was –' She searched for a phrase that would impress the little maid. 'It was most delicious! Now, my feet are cold. I'm going back to bed.'

When Hannah looked into the room, Luke was lying back against the pillows, his head to one side, his eyes closed. As the door creaked, he said, 'Is that you, Minnie?' and opened his eyes.

'Tis Hannah,' she told him. 'Minnie is gone to the Maying with Maria. She looked in on you before she went and thought you were asleep.'

'I may have dozed. Come in, Hannah. I did not see you yesterday and was anxious about you. Help me sit up a little and we can talk more easily. Ah, that's better.'

He looked at her face more closely, seeing the dark-rimmed eyes and the cheekbones that showed more prominently than they should.

'You do not sleep well?' he asked.

'I take my sleeping draught and I sleep,' she said flatly. 'But I wake early and cannot sleep again. And my dreams are fearful.'

'Your face grows peaky. You must eat, Hannah. You have the child to think of – Simon's child. Only two more months. You mustn't starve the little lad!' He smiled with an attempt at lightness, but they were neither of them deceived. Simon's death had proved the one disaster from which Luke would never really recover. The news had brought on a seizure which, though not severe, had slightly affected his vision. Occasionally, too, he would slur his words together and he grew tired quickly and slept longer.

'I beg you not to set your hopes too high,' she said uneasily, for it was a vexed question between them. 'It may be a girl.'

'Twill be a boy, I know it,' said Luke. 'I feel it in my heart and in my head. A beautiful boy with his father's good looks – and mayhap his mother's good sense too. Oh Simon, Simon! Why did he have to go with Wyatt?'

'Don't!' cried Hannah. 'I cannot bear to think on what might have been but for his stubborn pride. You Kendals are so arrogant. You will not listen to reason, but must always make grand gestures with no regard to the consequences.'

Luke remained silent, dismayed at her outburst, and she shook her head slowly.

'I'm sorry,' she said. 'I meant no disrespect to him. But

the waste appals me. He could be here, with us. He could see the child, hold it in his arms. Now there's nothing, and my joy is vanished with him. And all to what purpose? Mary is still Queen, and there are dead men hanging from every gibbet in London. In truth, I fear for this child I carry – this Kendal heir you crave. Will I rear him and love him, only to lose him in a senseless turmoil as soon as he is old enough to bear arms?'

She brushed away the tears, but more followed. Luke held out his arms to her.

'My legs may be useless, but my arms still serve me,' he said, and she clung to him, weeping, while he whispered comfortingly, rocking her as a mother rocks a child.

'Tis God's will,' he said. 'I truly do believe it, Hannah. We may not understand it, but there is a purpose, a reason – a plan, mayhap.'

Hannah made no answer, and he sighed heavily. 'You loved him, I know. I loved him, also.'

'He gambled with our love!' she cried suddenly. 'When he gambled with his life, he gambled with ours also. How could he do it? How dare he?'

'Dear Hannah, don't ask. Only God could answer such a question. You will find another love – later. There will be joy again, and peace. You will not stay alone.'

'I will not take another husband – unless you find me another Simon.'

Hannah did not see his face darken at her words. Luke's body might fail him, but his mind was as clear as ever, and one thought obsessed him – that if Hannah's child *was* a girl and Hannah remarried, the Kendal line at Heron would come to an end. To Luke such an eventuality was unthinkable. The Heron lands were Kendal lands, the Heron mine was the source of Kendal prosperity, the Heron wealth was for the Kendal family alone. His mother had been instrumental in restoring the failing Heron fortunes, and he could not, *would* not, let it fall into other hands.

Since Simon's death he had turned the problem over and

over in his mind, desperately considering what might be done to save the situation. Melissa was now wed to Thomas, and her son Oliver was a Benet. Matthew, Luke's stepbrother, had only one child, Sophie. Abigail's children were Jarmans. However he looked at it, he was faced with the unpalatable fact that the only remaining Kendal was Hugo. The knowledge that Hester's son was the sole Kendal with any claim to Heron was bitter indeed. Yet if Hannah produced a son and then wed elsewhere, did that guarantee the Kendal line? Reluctantly, he had to admit that it did not. A boy's chances of reaching manhood were not high. Plague, accident, war – the times were perilous. Luke himself had lost three sons. No. However distasteful the idea might be to him, Luke was secretly resolved that Hugo must move into Heron. He must be persuaded to wed Hannah and she must be persuaded to take him. They would have sons, but Simon's son would be heir. Only if he died would Hugo's sons inherit. He must bide his time until after the child was born. If it was a boy, there was less urgency. If it was a girl, he would speak to Hannah directly.

This conclusion had afforded him some small satisfaction, but now, as he turned it over again in his mind, a fresh and terrible thought struck him. Suppose he, Luke, were to die before the child was born – or before he could put forward the proposal to Hannah? A fearful coldness seized him and he shivered.

Hannah glanced up at him. 'Luke? Are you cold?'

'No, no.'

'You shivered, Luke. I felt it.' She looked at him with concern, her own grief temporarily forgotten. 'Let me make you a hot drink and mayhap a hot brick for your feet.'

'No, child. Tis nothing. I am warm enough.'

'But –'

'Hannah, I must talk to you. I must! Twill not be easy for me – nor you . . .' She looked at him in alarm as his agitation grew. 'You must forgive me. Must promise to forgive me for hurting you . . .'

'You don't hurt me, Luke. You are most kind. What is the matter? You speak so strangely. You are not yourself.'

He caught hold of her hands as she made to stand up, and his eyes held hers with an expression of great desperation. 'No, don't pull away from me, Hannah. Look, I am calm again. See?'

'Indeed you are *not* calm,' said Hannah. 'You look so pale. Shall I send for the physician? Are you –'

'I am distressed, that is all, and I shall not be calm again until I have spoken with you. I beg you, sit down again and listen patiently. When I have told you what is in my heart you will understand. Sit down, Hannah.'

Wonderingly, she sat down, fearing another seizure and watching him carefully for tell-tale signs.

'I will put it plainly,' he said after a moment's pause. 'If I prolong it, the resulting hurt will be no less. I want you to promise me that, come what may, you will wed Hugo. No, don't speak yet. Just hear me out. Simon was his friend; he would not think ill of the match. Hugo has some claim, and he is a Kendal. I may not live to see Simon's child but, boy or girl, Hugo will give you other sons and Kendals will remain at Heron. I will not listen to arguments, Hannah. Tis my last wish, and you must promise to obey it. I must have your word on it, so that if I die I can sleep easy in my grave.'

'Wed Hugo?' she whispered incredulously.

'Aye – Hugo,' he insisted. 'He is surely not unattractive. Many women would welcome him as a husband. Oh Hannah, I don't insist that you should dote on him. Only that you wed him. Don't look at me so – I tell you I haven't lost my wits. I am urging you to do this from the best of motives.'

'But *Hugo*? You have always scorned him, called him a hothead, and worse. You cannot be serious. Is he suddenly turned angel, then?'

'He may be reckless. Aye, he is reckless, I grant you. But so was Simon, and you could forgive him.'

'Could I?' she said quietly.

'Recklessness in a young man is not altogether bad. Oh, Hannah, think on it, I beg you. Tis true, Hugo was foolish, foolhardy even, but he is older now, and wiser. He has been exiled for his rashness and has lost a wife, which sobered him. You have lost a husband and must surely sympathise with him in his loss. You have that much in common, surely? Both have lost the one you held most dear . . .'

'He is a Papist.'

'Papist! Protestant! What does it matter now? He is a Kendal! That is what matters. Mary cannot reign forever. She is an ailing women and must relinquish the throne to Elizabeth, who has promised a fair church where all may worship unmolested. Elizabeth will keep her promise. The world changes. We all change . . . Hannah, what do you say? Do you begin to be persuaded?'

She sighed heavily. 'I begin to think on it,' she said. 'I can say no more than that.'

He let his hands fall limply on the coverlet and she saw that the exchange had exhausted him. Suddenly he looked at her, and his lips trembled. 'Have I betrayed him?' he whispered. 'Speaking like this – have I betrayed my son?'

Slowly she shook her head. 'You loved each other,' she said simply. 'I think he would understand.'

The maypole had been set up in the square and bedecked with bright ribbons, and the square itself was now crowded with young people, many in pairs but plenty more alone or in groups. The boys without partners eyed the girls who were still available, each boasting to the other that he could get the girl of his choice by doing no more than lifting a little finger. For their part, the girls put their heads together, giggling, and declared that no foolish lad would ever persuade them to take part in anything so childish as a maypole dance. A few older folk stood at the edge of the crowd and even more watched from the houses which overlooked the square, crammed five or six to a window, indifferent to their discomfort.

The nut man shouted his wares, and the smell of hot salted nuts sweetened the air and drew a crowd round his brazier, which stood at one end of the square. Beside him, his daughter sold toffee apples, and beyond them an elderly flower seller was doing a roaring trade in posies. The pedlar was there as usual, his bewhiskered face beaming, his wheezy voice chanting his familiar song. With his eye for a pretty face and his unashamed flattery he was selling a great many trinkets.

An awning of blue and white stripes had been erected and underneath sat three fiddlers and a drummer. Conveniently near, an ale wife had set up her trestle table and was finding the musicians even thirstier than she had expected.

Overhead, the sun shone warmly and Minnie, lifting her skirts 'to cool her legs', managed to reveal her skinny ankles to the drummer who, she fancied, was looking at her in a certain way.

'Here he comes!' Maria cried, and promptly looked in the opposite direction, so that Matt should not guess how anxious she had been for his arrival. Matt's hair was washed and combed as flat as it would go and shone silkily in the sunlight. His face and neck were clean and he was wearing his Sunday best clothes in honour of the occasion.

'I'm here, Maria,' he told her, and she turned in feigned surprise to greet him. 'How do I look?'

Maria looked at him carefully and was pleasantly surprised. He had nice hair and eyes, she decided, and a cheerful face. He was tall and well-built and his embarrassed smile was no worse than many others around her.

'You look very well,' she told him and saw his smile broaden into a grin. He flicked a speck of imaginary dust from his breeches and winked nervously at Minnie.

'Tisn't me you should be winking at,' she laughed. 'Tis Maria. And ain't you got anything to say to her – as to how *she* looks?'

'Oh! Aye!' He winked elaborately at Maria, opening his mouth wide as he did so. 'You look very well,' he said, adding 'and bonny' for good measure.

Maria smiled and said, 'Thank you kindly.'

Minnie leaned towards him and whispered, 'You must buy her a trinket. All the lads do.'

'A trinket?' He looked dismayed. 'I don't have no money.'

'What, none at all?' Minnie had been well primed on the ride down and knew exactly what Maria hoped for.

'Only enough for a sip of ale or a toffee apple,' he said.

Maria was pretending to be otherwise engaged, but listened now while Minne broke the bad news. Matt watched anxiously. Maria swallowed her disappointment and settled for half a coconut-full of nuts instead, so that they might all three enjoy them. They had just finished them when there was a roll on the drums and everyone rushed to claim a ribbon. With a delighted whoop, Matt put his head down and charged bull-like into the fray to emerge victorious with two ribbons. Mollified by his success, Maria took her place beside him, resplendent in an apricot taffeta gown with a circlet of flowers in her hair. The warm colour suited her, and she saw with secret satisfaction that Matt was not the only one to find her attractive. She lowered her eyes demurely and waited as the fiddlers struck up the first dance of the evening.

Those who had been unlucky would take their turn next, but for the moment they had to content themselves with looking on as the dancers swung out away from the pole and began to weave in and out, crossing and re-crossing the ribbons and drawing them tighter and tighter round the pole. The watchers stamped their feet and clapped their hands in time with the music, and Maria skipped and swayed, light as a feather, happy and excited. At intervals Maria passed Matt, who jumped and hopped with more enthusiasm than grace, and their eyes met and each broke into a smile. Faster and faster went the music, faster and faster went the dancers, until the ribbons were wrapped round the pole in the special Mayday pattern and the music faltered and the dancers found their partners at last for a celebratory hug and kiss.

Minnie rushed up to them, her black eyes gleaming. 'I was asked!' she cried. 'While you were dancing. I was asked to dance!'

Maria, breathless, put a hand to her heaving chest and said, 'Asked to dance. Who by then, Minnie?'

Minnie gave a shriek of laughter. 'The nut man!' she gasped. 'Tis true, I tell you. Don't look that way. Tis true! Would you believe it – and his own daughter sat beside him hearing every blessed word! Asked me right out, he did. Such impudence! I gave him a right sharp look, I can tell you. Aye, and a kick on the shins – for he wouldn't take no for an answer and tried to steal a kiss. Oh, dearie me! The nut man!' She burst into peals of laughter.

'Matt will dance with you, won't you, Matt?' said Maria. 'Just one dance – to please me.'

Matt hesitated, while Minnie held her breath. 'And you'll wait here for me?' he asked Maria, 'And not go dancing with no one else? Remember, I'm your proper partner 'cos of the May branch.'

Maria promised to be faithful, and Matt and Minnie whirled away to the next tune. She had no especial desire to dance with anyone else, but she *did* want to be asked. She stood with one hand on her hip, the other spread across her stomach. In fact, she was pushing up her breasts to make them look fuller, so that they curved out a little above the neckline of her gown. The hand that rested on her hip bunched up a little of her skirt, so that her neat foot could be seen tapping to the music. If only Hugo could see her, she thought. If only he could be with her as her partner. If only *he* had brought her the May branch. Oh Hugo, Hugo! Wait for me, I beg you, she urged silently. My breasts are swelling already and I am taller – an inch or more! And inside, my body is changing from child to woman. Not every month, but twice so far, and mama says I am well on the way. I will be a woman as soon as I can, Hugo, only wait for me!

'Will you dance with me?'

A young man was standing in front of her, dark-haired with large grey-green eyes.

'I'm promised,' she said, 'but thank you kindly.'

A moment later there was another one. 'Don't you recognise me?' he asked.

'Tis the saddler's son!' she cried.

'May I have the pleasure? Or failing that, a dance?' he asked cheekily. But laughing, she refused him also.

By the time Matt returned with a perspiring Minnie, she had received three invitations and her satisfaction had given way to triumph.

Luke's words had disturbed Hannah more than she cared to admit. The truth was that they had expressed a need within her that she had been reluctant to admit even to herself. Her reassurance to Luke that he had not betrayed Simon was welcome to her own ears. She shared Luke's fears: that plans for the future would appear callous and unfeeling to those who did not understand them. Yet she was lonely, with child, and very frightened. Only to herself would she admit that the terrors of childbirth haunted all her waking moments. Without Simon these fears had increased, until she no longer dared dwell on her approaching confinement, but must always turn her thoughts in other directions.

And she was lonely without a man in her life. She missed the warmth of his love and his physical presence, the support that he gave in so many ways – endorsing her decisions, praising her cooking, reinforcing her management of the servants, and recently, sharing the anxieties of Luke's condition. And she missed his body – the only one she had ever known. Their love-making had been so sweet, and his eagerness so exciting. A 'lusty gentleman' she had called him teasingly, and he had not denied it. Her own body had leaped into life as he took her, filling her body and drowning her senses. He had taught her to need a man – and then he had deserted her. Would any man ever again bring her to such heights? Would Hugo? Could she bear to have unfamiliar hands caressing her body or another man's voice whispering to her in the darkness? The answer was a sad one. Any other man would be a poor second to her beloved Simon.

Suddenly she knew that she must be near him again and made up her mind to ride down to the churchyard. She called hurriedly for Jack to saddle her mare, promising to ride side-saddle and take it very slowly. But Jack insisted on accompanying her and she had no heart for an argument.

When they reached the churchyard, he lifted her gently from her horse.

'I'll wait here, ma'am,' he told her. 'If you need me, just call; I'll hear you. And mind you go careful, for there's brambles and all sorts as could trip a lady in your state.'

She nodded, only half-listening, and began to walk along the path, ducking her head under the sombre yew trees that cast patches of shade across the unkempt grass. She walked slowly, her head down, wrapped up in her thoughts, and so did not see the figure kneeling at Simon's graveside until she almost stumbled over her. Guiltily, the woman scrambled to her feet, and Hannah saw the countless red-edged daisies scattered over the newly laid turf. Perplexed, she looked from the woman to the long mound that was Simon's grave. Something that Adam had told her came into her mind.

'Was it you?' she said. 'That sat with him? Adam said there was a woman –' The woman nodded, her eyes on Hannah's rounded belly. Hannah, seeing this, said, 'This is his child.'

'I envy you.'

'Were you with him when he died?'

'No,' said Maggie. 'It grieved me that he died alone.'

Both women wondered how to react to the other.

126

'All these daisies . . .' said Hannah.

The woman glanced at them and looked up with a hint of defiance in her eyes. 'They're in remembrance,' she said, 'of times long past.'

'Are you Maggie – the baker's wife? Melissa spoke of her.'

'The baker's daughter,' Maggie corrected. 'Aye, Simon worked for us before his father acknowledged him.'

'And did you love him?' asked Hannah curiously, and without hostility.

'I did and I still do, but he was not meant for me.' Her voice was low and flat, but she kept her eyes full on Hannah's face. 'I saw him the day before he died. We met by chance. I gave him a daisy as a battle favour, to bring him luck!' She glanced away to hide the pain in her eyes. 'I was with another man,' she added. 'Our lad also must up and off to join the rebellion. Men are such fools.'

'Did your lad die?'

Maggie shook her head.

'I begged him not to go,' said Hannah, 'for the child's sake and my own. So we have both lost him.' She sighed heavily, then straightened her shoulders with a gesture of resignation. 'They die, and we are left with the business of living . . . How was he, that last night? Was he in good spirits?'

'I think they were afeared,' said Maggie, frowning slightly. 'He was with friends, and they joked and laughed too heartily to keep their courage up. My lad did also.'

Hannah twisted her fingers nervously together. 'Did he speak of me?' she asked.

'Aye, and sweetly. The babe also. He was very proud of you both. He said he counted himself most fortunate.'

'He promised to return,' said Hannah bleakly.

'They never expect to die.'

There was a silence.

'I must go,' said Maggie, but suddenly Hannah was reluctant to be alone and searched for a way to delay her.

127

'Have you been here before today?' she asked. 'To his grave?'

'I come most days.'

'I've seen you before today – at the funeral, maybe? Were you there?' Maggie nodded. Hannah knelt suddenly and taking up one of the daisies, twirled it between her fingers. 'When I first came to Heron, I was very young,' she said. 'I loved another, but it was not to be. I did not want to wed the bastard son of Luke Kendal, and I was determined not to love him. We rode from Sussex – a long, uncomfortable journey – and I arrived sick at heart and very weary. I had quarrelled with Gregory, my brother, and was near to tears.' She laughed softly. 'I can see myself now, so cold and disgruntled, desperately trying to hide my misery. Then I saw Simon –' she looked up at Maggie '– and all my anger melted away. The cold, the quarrel, the weariness. Nothing mattered any more. And now he's dead.'

'You have his child,' said Maggie. 'That's something to live for.'

'Aye.'

'There's a time for mourning,' said Maggie. 'Try to think joyfully for the child's sake. Wed again if you must. Every child needs a father. Now – I must go. I wish you a safe delivery.'

'Pray for me,' said Hannah. Maggie nodded and turned to go.

'Wait!' cried Hannah. 'I have to ask it. That night, before the battle. Did you lie with Simon? The truth, I beg you.'

Maggie gave a slight nod. 'A man needs comforting before a battle,' she said simply. Suddenly Hannah held out her arms and the two women clung together until Jack, growing anxious, came in search of Hannah and took her home.

CHAPTER EIGHT

At first Maria read the letter from London without fully comprehending the contents. But a second reading filled her with a deep dismay, and the third a sense of outrage. She crumpled it up, then tore it into shreds and flung them into the air, leaving them to flutter down like snow and settle around her feet on the gravel path.

'I *will* not,' she whispered, and bowing her head, she covered her face with her two clenched fists. 'Never, never! I will not marry anyone but Hugo. They cannot make me. Sweet heaven help me, but I will never marry this Harold Cummins!'

Her mother's letter had been very calm and matter-of-fact. Maria would be pleased to hear, she wrote, that a betrothal had been arranged with a certain Harold Cummins, a second cousin. The financial details had been concluded to the satisfaction of both parties.

Harold Cummins was twice widowed and his second wife had died in childbirth. He was forty-seven years old and reasonably wealthy, owning a small farm and a comfortable home on the outskirts of Romney Marsh in Kent. His elderly sister lived with him and had acted as housekeeper since his wife's death. There was a married son by his first wife, but he lived in Calais. As soon as Hannah was safely delivered and could spare Maria, she was to come home, where preparations were already in hand for her removal to Romney House.

Maria stamped all over the fragments of the letter and ground her teeth in an agony of frustration. She would not marry him. She would not say the words. They could threaten, starve and bully her – they could beat her! She would marry Hugo and no one else. Another year and he might see her differently. He would see her as a young woman. A sudden gleam of hope shone in her eyes. If he knew about Harold Cummins, surely he would realise she was old enough to be betrothed. He might even be jealous! The idea gave her a moment's pleasure, but it quickly gave way to a dark despair.

'Maria! Maria! Come quick.'

Minnie had come racing into the garden, her skirts held indecorously high in an effort not to trip. She beckoned imperiously and Maria obeyed, her letter forgotten. 'Is it Hannah's time?' she cried.

'Hannah's time?' Minnie shrieked with laughter. 'No, they're killing the pig!' And she raced back towards the stable yard, followed closely by Maria.

They scrambled onto the gate. Maria perched herself on the top rail, while Minnie stood on the bottom one and rested her arms and chin on the top. Jack and Jon were still chasing the pig, which was dodging them, squealing with panic and moving with surprising agility for such a heavy animal. Urged on by the jeers of their audience, Jon and Jack redoubled their efforts and finally managed to corner the animal and slip a rope round its neck.

'What a racket!' cried Minnie.

Jon looked up, grinning. 'Sound like the racket you made when you had your first bath!' he reminded her, and she snatched up a clod of earth and threw it at him. Jack grumbled for Jon to pay attention as he tried to silence the pig with a loop of rope round its jaw. The animal still struggled frantically, kicking and writhing on the dusty ground and the two dogs watched from a respectful distance, whining excitedly in their throats.

They dragged the pig under a tree and tossed the rope up and over the lowest, firmest bough. One moment the pig was on the ground, the next a quick jerk on the rope had swung him into the air, trotters dangling. With one slash of the knife Jack cut its throat, and Marie and Minnie watched speechlessly as Jack and Jon sprang back to avoid the sudden gush of blood from the severed artery. The pig's legs moved convulsively, and then it was still. At once Jack stepped in again and threw the rope round its hind legs, and cut the head free, so that it tumbled head downward and turned slowly, blood spurting, dripping off the snout on to the ground.

At that moment Beth appeared and shouted to Minnie to fetch in the dry linen from the orchard. Minnie pulled a face and said 'God's teeth!' and waited for Maria to offer to help her. Maria, however, was deep in her own thoughts.

'How long till you scrape it?' Minnie asked Jack.

'A half hour or so,' he said. 'You'll be back by then.'

'If she don't find me another little errand,' grumbled Minnie, and off she went with a bad grace, casting a reproachful look at Maria's unsuspecting back.

Jack glanced across at Maria. 'That's all there is to see for a bit.' But Maria said, 'I'll wait. I've matters to think on,' and sat watching the dead pig turning, turning, its warm blood now reduced to a trickle, attracting the flies.

Maria watched, but her thoughts reverted to the prospect of Harold Cummins. She wondered what he looked like. Forty-seven was old, so he was probably skinny as a bean pole, or fat as a bladder of lard, and his hair would be thin and straggly – if he had any hair at all. He would be set in his ways and would compare her endlessly with his other wives, who would doubtless have been paragons of virtue. But according to her mother, he *was* wealthy. Wealthy or rich? Or had she said only comfortable? Maria wished that the letter was still in one piece so that she could reassure herself on that point. Suppose he was rich and he soon died? She would be left a wealthy widow . . .

But no! By that time Hugo would most likely have taken another wife. She dared not risk it. She sighed again. She would have to sidestep this betrothal – feign illness, perhaps, so that her journey to Romney House could be delayed indefinitely. Or she might go to them and pretend madness, behaving so outrageously that they would gladly pay her mother to take her back.

Harold – what a boring name.

Her perch on top of the gate proving uncomfortable, she slid to the ground. The two dogs ran to her, hoping for some attention, but she shooed them away, still engrossed in her problem. What did an old man's body look like? she wondered. She had bathed young Oliver, but there her knowledge of the male form ended. Would an old man be able to give her a child? Presumably – for his last wife had died in childbirth. 'But I want Hugo's child,' she told herself. 'I want to be Mistress Kendal, not Mistress Cummins. I shall write to Mama this very night and tell her so.'

She kicked a loose stone which flew, unfortunately, at one of the dogs, which fell to yelping and ran off limping slightly. Maria felt a pang of guilt, but only a small one. What was a sore leg, compared with her own problems? She found herself walking in the direction of the orchard and decided to help Minnie after all. Between them they pulled and straightened the sheets and folded them back into the large wicker basket. While they worked, Maria told Minnie about Harold Cummins.

'There's no need to sweat,' Minnie told her. 'At forty-seven he'll not last long if you keep him on the boil. Beth's uncle wed at fifty, and his young bride never used to let him out of bed. Dead, he was, within four months, and she ups and weds a dancing tutor. Have you got a dancing tutor?'

Maria had to admit that she hadn't – but she had got Hugo.

'You mean you'd *like* to have him,' Minnie corrected her.

'I think he's waiting for me,' said Maria. It was her most frequent assessment of the situation. 'Else why hasn't he wed again?'

'I dunno,' said Minnie, 'but if you're set against poor Harold, you might put in a good word for me! I'd stir his stumps for him, I would! He may be old, but he's rich – I'd settle for that.' She staggered away with her basket, laughing uproariously, and Maria made her way back to the stable.

The scraping of the pig involved plunging the carcase into a bath of scalding hot water, after which all the bristles were scraped off. It was then divided up into the various cuts required, and the mass of meat dumped unceremoniously on to the kitchen table. Maria watched, only half aware, as the offal was pulled out for the 'frys' and Minnie broke and crushed the salt for the hams.

'You're quiet, Maria,' said Beth curiously. 'D'you want to try your hand at these sausages?'

Maria shook her head. 'I've seen enough dead flesh for one day, thank you,' she told her. 'It begins to sicken me.' She did, in fact, feel a little queasy. 'I shall walk over to Ladyford. The fresh air will do me good.'

So saying, she set off at once before she could change her mind. She had decided to reveal the contents of the letter to Melissa and ask her advice.

She had almost reached the gate when she heard hoof-beats behind her and saw that it was Jack who followed.

'Tis the Mistress started her pains,' he cried. 'I've come to fetch Melissa.' He slid off the horse's back, tossed the reins to Maria and ran past her into the house, returning a few moments later alone. 'She's not there,' he said in some agitation. 'Nor her husband.'

'Mayhap they've gone into Ashburton,' said Maria. 'Should you go and look?'

He hesitated. 'But she may *not* be gone there. I daresn't leave the Mistress too long. Beth's there, but she can't do nothing with her. In a real fright, she is. White as a sheet and trembling, Beth says. Should I ride down in search of a midwife?'

'Aye, do that, Jack, and I'll go straight back and help Beth.'

'I made up the fire and put them kettles on,' said Jack, 'but that's the sum of what I know!'

'Not one of us knows much more than that,' said Maria, 'but we won't help her by confessing it. You be off and I'll go straight back.'

Jack had not exaggerated. Hannah was terrified of the ordeal which was now upon her. Maria arrived to find her lying on the bed, her legs drawn up, her face hidden in a pillow, which did nothing to lessen the sounds of her distress. Beth was appalled to learn that Melissa had not been at home.

'Today of all days!' she whispered. 'But at least you're here. The Mistress won't heed me, not anything I say. Just screams when the pains come and cries out for Simon. Won't take a sip of wine, nor even let me wipe her face.'

'Don't fret, Beth,' said Maria as confidently as she could. 'I'm here now. I'll stay with her while you fetch a flagon of wine. Jack is gone for a midwife but he'll be back directly.'

Hannah turned towards her, lifting her pale tear-stained face and holding out her hands imploringly.

'Oh Maria! Sit with me, I beg you. I'm so afeared. The pains are so bad I think I shall die, Maria. I – Aah! Here it comes again – dear Heaven help me! Tis right here, cutting me like a knife –'

Maria fought back the memory of the pig with its throat cut, bleeding, bleeding. 'You will *not* die, Hannah!' she protested cheerfully. 'I shall not allow it. There, that pain is done with. Tis quite natural. Now sit up. Oh, what a sight! If your poor babe could see his mama, he would run back in again, I swear he would. Ah, you smiled. That's the way. Now sit up. You'll be more comfortable and you'll be able to take a sip of wine.'

Hannah began to protest that she wanted nothing, but Maria silenced her with a finger against her lips. 'If you will not be biddable, I shall go downstairs again,' she threatened. 'All this fuss over bringing a baby into the world. When the next pain comes, you take up this pillow and bite the corner, hard as you can. But no tears. Simon's babe waiting to be born – and you'd wash him away on a wave of tears.' She wiped Hannah's face with a damp flannel, removed her head-dress and gently brushed her hair, tying it back with a piece of lace.

The next contraction came and Hannah doubled up with the pain, but she had taken a little courage from Maria's words and cried out less grievously this time. Beth returned with the wine, and Maria persuaded her to drink it slowly, assuring her that it would relax her and ease the pains.

'Is there hot water?' Hannah asked. 'And towels? *Aah!* Oh, God in heaven help me! Spare me – Oh, tis worse each time, and my back aches so. Oh, Maria, there is something wrong, I know it. It shouldn't be this bad. There's something wrong with me. I'm going to die. I know it in my heart. I shan't live to see my child.'

Her eyes filled with tears again, but Maria guided the goblet of wine to her lips and made her drink. 'Why is Jack taking so long?' Hannah demanded. 'And where is the midwife? I fear they will not come in time. Oh Maria, Beth, stay with me, I implore you –'

Her voice rose to a scream, and Maria began to feel the first prickle of fear. Would Hannah die? And how would they deliver the child if the midwife was not to be found? She looked at Beth, who was praying earnestly, her eyes closed, her hands clasped in front of her face.

Time passed and the pains grew worse and closer together, and even to Maria's inexperienced eyes, it was evident that the labour had reached a new stage. A sudden rush of clear liquid soaked the bed, and Hannah's fears multiplied. Maria soothed her and assured her it was normal, and held her hands while Beth eased off her wet gown and shift and removed the soiled sheets.

'Put on your nightgown,' Maria urged Hannah. 'You'll be more at ease. Beth, do go to the window and look for sight of Jack and the midwife. They must come soon.'

Once the waters had broken, Hannah felt the need to bear down and could not resist the powerful urging of her body.

'I must push,' she whispered. 'I must! I must!'

'Push then,' said Maria, praying that it was indeed normal, as she hoped. 'Push Simon's baby out into the world.'

Beth held her shoulders to still her writhings, and Maria waited, heart racing, as the small head appeared. 'A tiny head,' she whispered. 'Oh, Hannah, the babe is nearly born. One more push. Try, Hannah, try! Just once more!'

The last convulsion pushed the baby, wet and slippery, into Maria's waiting hands. Carefully she cut and tied the cord. And just at that moment they heard the clatter of hooves and knew that help was on hand.

'Oh, Hannah, you were so brave,' whispered Maria tearfully. 'And see what Simon has given you – a little son, Hannah. A perfect little son – and listen to that! His first cry, and what a noise!'

Wrapping a towel round the baby, she put him into his mother's arms. Hannah, her face flushed, her eyes soft, forgot all her exhaustion as she held the wailing child close and looked down into the tiny, wrinkled face.

'Greetings, Simon's son,' she whispered, then to Maria and Beth: 'I can't find words to thank you.'

'You did all the work, ma'am,' laughed Beth tremulously. 'And you've a fine, healthy son to show for it.'

Hannah turned to Maria. 'Go tell Luke he has a grandson,' she whispered. 'Tell him the Kendals have a new, very noisy, heir!'

Minnie sulked for the rest of the week, seething with resentment at being left in the kitchen to salt the hams and prepare the frys – 'up to my arms in pig!' as she put it. But Beth was unrepentant.

'It was good experience for you,' she said. 'Someone had to do it, and that someone was you. Pork's got to be put down promptly this weather. You was best well occupied and out from under our feet.'

Minnie complained at length to Luke, but he was too happy with his new grandson to spare her much sympathy.

Minnie seethed with the injustice done her and wallowed in self-pity to such a degree that even Jon, usually tolerant of her tantrums, told her abruptly to 'stop griping'. Finally, she appealed to Maria.

'I hate salting ham,' she protested, 'and I hate chopping offal. Tis horrible messy work, and my hands are that sore! And everyone else was upstairs enjoying the excitement –'

'Enjoying it!' cried Maria incredulously. 'I was frightened half to death –'

'You could have done the pork, then,' said Minnie sullenly. 'I wouldn't have been frightened of a baby being born. What's to be frightened of? From what I hear it came by itself – just popped out into the world . . .'

'You don't understand,' said Maria. 'Or you don't want to understand. I've told you how it was –'

'Oh, aye! Everyone has told me how it was,' snapped Minnie, 'and said as I don't understand. If I'd been there, I'd *know* how it was and I *would* understand.'

Maria was hard put to it to keep her patience. 'Minnie, do stop grumbling and come and take a look at him,' she coaxed. 'When you see him you'll be that pleased you won't feel angry any more, I swear it.'

But Minnie refused. She now had two grievances. Firstly, she had been denied the thrills of Hannah's delivery. Secondly, the new baby was receiving an inordinate amount of attention which would previously have been paid to her. She now began to convince herself that the rest of the world was conspiring to cause her discomfiture, and she went out of her way to irritate everyone, preferring disapproval to an imagined indifference. In short, she made a thorough nuisance of herself. She was never where she was meant to be and took to hiding in corners, hoping to hear herself maligned. She tormented the dogs until one of them bit her and then sulked anew because Jon told her it was her own fault and that she needn't expect any sympathy from him.

'You haven't even seen the little lad,' said Jon. 'Everyone else has, and there's that many visitors coming to the house to pay their respects. And letters come from London and Rochester. They're naming him Allan – twas the old man's choosing. Allan Kendal. What d'you say to that?'

'Not much,' said Minnie. 'Tis just a name.'

'His hair is that fine and pale – tis like spun gold. Leastways, that's what Maria says and she's right, near enough. And so tiny – his little hands pounding the air and his eyes that blue, you wouldn't believe it! Like forget-me-nots, Maria says.'

Minnie regarded him sourly. 'Maria says! Maria says!' she mocked. 'I never thought to hear you droning on like an old woman about a bit of a baby. Seems to me everyone's gone soft in the head.' And she flounced off to brood anew on Maria's foolishness and her own unhappy state of mind.

It was while Maria was still out of favour that Minnie, lurking one day outside Luke's bedchamber, overheard a conversation between him and Hannah concerning Hugo. And as she listened, her mouth fell open with shock and then closed again into a hard line. So, she thought, the foolish, doting Maria was due for a bitter disappointment.

Impulsively, Minnie decided to be the bearer of the bad news. Before she could have a change of heart, she sped off in search of her erstwhile friend and confidante. She found Maria in the garden, sitting under the oak, with the two dogs who, seeing Minnie, growled warningly.

'Stop it, you two,' scolded Maria. 'Tis only Minnie.' She held up a square of fine linen to show her. 'I'm making him a pillow-case and sewing his initials in the corner. See? "A" for Allan is already done and the "K" –' She broke off, startled by the intensity of Minnie's expression. 'What is it, Minnie?'

Minnie searched her mind for the right words, her eyes narrowed with pent-up anger. 'Tis your fine Hannah,' she cried, 'and your fine Allan that you dote on. Since you love them so much you'll be glad to hear the news.'

'What news?' stammered Maria, alarmed by the maid's vehemence. Her small black eyes were glittering and her voice was shrill.

'Why, Hannah is to have a new husband,' cried Minnie, 'and little Allan a new father. Don't you want to know who it is?'

Maria's thoughts began to whirl.

'Tis Hugo! Oh, don't shake your head that way, ma'am. Tis true! I heard it with my own ears not five minutes ago – not a hundred yards from here.'

'Oh, no!' whispered Maria, and her hands fell idle, the sewing forgotten.

'Tis true, I tell you. I heard Luke and Hannah not a moment ago. "I will have him" she says. "I have thought on it and I will have Hugo". Those were her very words, and he says, "Tis wisely done".'

'*Hugo!*' whispered Maria. She tore her eyes from Minnie's face, unaware of her look of triumph, and stared blankly into the garden while her emotions churned black and despairing and all she could hear was her own voice whispering his name again and again. For minutes she sat still and silent, while the world around her lost shape and form, and the terrible pain within her heart became the only reality.

'Maria?' said Minnie.

But Maria did not hear. No, Hugo, her soul cried, don't do it, I beg you. Don't wed Hannah. Wait for me. Wait for me.

'Maria!'

She will not love you as I do. She never will, Hugo. I love you, remember me? Your funny little Maria? Don't do it, Hugo. Dear God, don't let him do it. Hannah will find another man. She will never love him. She never even *liked* him. Sweet Heaven, you know I speak the truth. Hugo, my dearest Hugo, how can this be come about?

139

Minnie watched her with mounting nervousness. She had not expected such a response to her news, and the girl's strange manner made her uneasy. She leaned forward to peer into Maria's face, trying to read her expression.

'Maria!' she cried, and shook her by the shoulders; but Maria's face remained frozen into a blank mask. Minnie was bewildered. She had anticipated a display of anguished tears or furious recriminations, and this cold withdrawal robbed her of the expected sweetness of revenge. Her own anger had dissolved and now she watched helplessly as Maria suffered.

'Maria,' she said hastily. 'Don't look so black. Mayhap I heard it wrong. The door was shut and I may have –' Her voice trailed into silence. Neither of them believed that she was mistaken.

The last of Minnie's anger vanished, leaving her contrite. 'I'm sorry, Maria,' she said. 'Truly I am. I never meant to listen – no, that's a lie. I did. But I never meant to hurt you – no, that's a lie also, 'cos I did. I was that wicked. Oh, Maria, say you're not angry with me – or I'll hang myself from a tree like that poor old pig and cut my own throat. I will, Maria!'

'Hugo,' Maria whispered. 'If he's to wed Hannah, then I've lost him forever.' She stood up slowly, and began to walk away. The square of linen fell to the ground unheeded. Minnie burst into tears, and the two dogs, after a baleful look in her direction, loped after Maria.

It was nearly an hour before Maria was missed, and another hour after that before Minnie was finally bullied into a full confession of what had taken place in the garden. For her share in the calamity she was locked in the cellar. Later she would be sent back to Ladyford. Meanwhile, Jack, Jon, Matt and Jacob from Ladyford were all despatched to search for Maria.

As the light began to fade, Dartmoor was bathed briefly in the red glow of the setting sun, softening the hard contours of the granite and warming the vegetation that clothed its inhospitable slopes. The yellow gorse was still in flower, raised above the moss and dark wortle berries that grew among the tufted cotton grass. The peaty marshes gave back some of the day's warmth in wisps of white vapour, and tall rushes stood motionless, betraying the mires, but Maria, her thoughts turned inwards, paid no heed to their warning. Finally, floundering through the edges of the springy turf, she tripped and fell sprawling into the water. Alarmed, the dogs began to bark, breaking the silence with their yelping, leaping to and fro and hindering Maria's efforts to regain a footing on firmer ground. Cursing them roundly, she managed to stand upright again, and only then did she pause to take stock of her surroundings.

She had run, walked and stumbled across the moor for hours, ever since leaving Minnie. Her shoes were long since broken and tossed aside, and her bare feet were scratched and bruised by the sharp granite stones that lay hidden in the grass. Her skirt was frayed, torn by brambles and torn by the dogs, who had sprung forward from time to time and tugged at the cloth, hoping for a game. Hitherto, Maria had been oblivious to everything, but now she was shocked into a sudden realisation of her predicament. She stared round, seeing no familiar landmark, and frowned. On the ridge to her left a heavy mist was rolling towards her and she felt the first stirrings of unease. To her right, the moor stretched as far as the eye could see, broken only by a few boulders and the occasional tree. The dogs watched her, their heads cocked inquisitively. A rabbit sprang suddenly from the grass ahead of her and scuttled erratically towards the comparative safety of its burrow. The dogs raced after it, and Maria watched them listlessly. Hungry, tired, defeated, she turned to look back the way she had come, and saw the tall patches of reed and darker green of the marshy areas. The sun had dipped lower now, half-vanished below the horizon, and the mist was closing in, cold, grey and clammy to her skin.

Still Maria hesitated, reluctant to admit that she was lost, afraid to admit her fear. She dared not try to find her way through the marshes in the dark, for the deep pools of peaty water were thick with weeds and and even in daylight the surface mosses were treacherous. In the failing light she would never pick her way safely between them. She marvelled that she had come safely through them thus far, considering the careless nature of her flight.

The dogs returned, disappointed, to await her displeasure, but she paid them no attention. At last she decided to move towards higher sloping ground, where there was less chance of standing water. The dogs followed close at her heels, as shivering, she slowly made her way through the darkening landscape. The mist deepened and with the disappearance of the sun, the air cooled rapidly.

Her very bones ached with the cold and her fear mounted as time passed and still she found no sign of habitation where she might ask for shelter. To stay out on the open moor would be to risk a severe chill or fever. She might die from exposure. With a shudder, she pushed such thoughts to the back of her mind. Could she light a fire? No – she had no tinder. Pausing, she listened, her ears tuned for the slightest sound that might help her. But not even a bird sang or, if it did, its song was muffled by the mist.

Faint with exhaustion and numb with cold, she was on the point of despair, when the dogs suddenly hurried forward whining eagerly. One of them was scratching at wood! Please God, she prayed, let it be a shelter of some kind, no matter how crude. Her prayer was answered. In the gloom she made out a door. It had been closed for many years and was swollen with the damp, but she finally forced it open and staggered thankfully inside, followed by the two dogs. As her eyes became accustomed to what little light remained, she saw that she had stumbled upon an old moor house – one of the simple temporary dwellings put up by tinners, who lived in them while they worked their lonely claims.

The ashes of a long dead fire reminded her how unutterably cold she was. In one corner she found a pile of dank-smelling hay and bracken, and an old sheepskin hung on a hook in the wall. Wearily she took down the sheepskin and throwing herself on to the hay, covered herself as best she could. Then she curled up and called the dogs to lie with her, so that the heat from their bodies might warm her own. And there she lay, wretched and uncomfortable, thinking of Hugo, until her exhaustion overcame her misery and she fell at last into a fitful sleep.

She was woken next morning by the excited yelping of the dogs, who stood at the door, their tails wagging furiously.

'Maria? Tis only I, Matt, out here. I'm coming in.'

'Matt?'

She was half-asleep, wondering where she was, but as soon as she tried to sit up her cramped limbs reminded her of the previous day and the painful memories came flooding back. Matt pushed open the door, thrusting back the dogs, who welcomed him deliriously.

'Shut your noise, you stupid animals!' he cried, but nothing could wipe the beaming smile from his face. He, Matt Cartright, had found Maria, his May girl. He stood looking down at her as she sat dishevelled and forlorn among the mildewed hay. Her face was pale and dirty, and her hair, free of its head-dress, hung tangled almost to her waist. Maria's stoicism vanished at the sight of him, so large and friendly – and capable. Tears of weakness suddenly filled her eyes and ran down her cheeks, and then Matt was beside her. She felt herself being lifted on to his lap and rocked, while she wept helplessly, bawling like a child, her head pressed against his proud chest.

'There, there,' he crooned. 'You cry if you want. Tears do be good for you. Aye, they washes away the hurt. That's what they say, and I dare say tis true . . . So this is where you hid yourself – in old Retter's moor house! And me riding all over the place and thinking you're eaten by wolves or drownded in a mire! That's it – you cry all you want, and

143

I'll just hold you. There, there. You're like my own babe as is crying with a sore knee or suchlike, and I'm your pa, as'll make it better. Hush now, little suck-a-thumb! My ma used to call me that, she did . . .'

So he prattled on, gentle and loving, until gradually her sobs lessened and then ceased. He pulled up the hem of her skirt and dabbed her eyes dry. She sniffed weakly and her breath jerked in and out as she strove to steady herself for the return journey.

'A fine old pother they all be in,' he told her. 'Folks scurrying in all directions, and that minx Minnie shut in the cellar with the rats for company. And Hannah there, one minute wringing her hands and wailing, the next promising to push you off home if ever you're found.'

'I want to go back to London,' said Maria. 'I can't stay there if – if he is coming to be Master of Heron. I'd as soon wed Harold Cummins as watch Hugo wed to Hannah.'

Matt was stricken at the thought that Maria would be going away, but he said nothing – only set her on her feet and whistled for the dogs. She stretched awkwardly and groaned as her body protested at the ill-treatment it had received. Once outside, she stood in the early morning sunshine and sighed deeply. The mist had lifted now, and birds sang in the heather; Matt's horse grazed nearby, nibbling the tender deer grass and flicking its tail at the flies.

Matt swung himself into the saddle and reached down to pull Maria up behind him. 'Hold on tight,' he told her. 'Put your arms round my waist and don't let go. I don't want you falling off.'

Maria obeyed and Matt put the horse into a canter. With the exhilaration of the ride, Maria felt much of her usual resilience return, and enjoyed the sensation of the horse moving rhythmically over the springy turf and her hair streamed behind her in the breeze. When they were nearly home, she said suddenly, 'Stop, Matt. Let's sit awhile. I want to talk to you.'

They dismounted and sat together in the lee of a rock

where the breeze could not reach them. Maria looked at him soberly.

'Matt,' she said. 'What would you say if I asked for you to come with me to Romney House? That's where I have to go – where I shall wed this Harold Cummins. How would it be if I could take you as my – my man?'

Matt frowned with concentration. 'You take me with you to – to this Harold? To be your man, like?'

'Aye. To ride with me if I went out alone, and care for my horse –'

'Chop your wood? Fetch water?' he cried. 'Run errands?'

She smiled faintly. 'Just be around, so that I know I have a friend. He has an elderly sister, and she'll not welcome me, I'm certain. And I've no maid of my own. They must let me take someone of my own.'

'What of Minnie?' he suggested fearfully.

'I'll not take her,' said Maria grimly. 'I'll take you or nobody. And if they refuse me, why then, I shall refuse to go.'

Matt's frown deepened. 'But you'll be wed to him,' he said. 'You'll sleep with him.'

'I must if we're wed,' she said gently. 'But you'd be my friend and protector and we'll laugh together when they can't hear us and ride out together sometimes, or go hawking. Oh, what d'you say, Matt? Will you leave Heron and come with me?' Seeing him hesitate, she went on: 'You'll never see me again else, for I shan't come back to Heron while *she* is wedded to Hugo.'

This gloomy prospect finally persuaded him, and they shook hands on it. Up he went into the saddle again and on they rode, down into Heron. Though her heart sank at the prospect of the homily she well deserved, Maria yet felt her spirits soar. Fate had dealt her an unkind cut, but she had found a way to meet it.

145

CHAPTER NINE

Luke lay back, eyes closed, listening with satisfaction to the sounds of merrymaking in the Hall below. A few latecomers were still arriving, and he could hear Jack greeting them before leading away the horses. Melissa had promised to come up as soon as everyone was seated and the wedding breakfast was under way. They had offered to hire a comfortable carriage to take him to the church, but he had refused. A wedding was a wedding; he had seen plenty already and had no desire to brave the rigours of a dull November day just to see one more. So they were wed. Hugo Kendal was Master of Heron, and little Allan was his heir. It was well done. All very satisfactory . . .

A knock at the door jerked him awake again. Seeing Hester come into the room, Luke groaned inwardly. No doubt come to crow over her victory – and looking every inch the part, he told himself, with her small black eyes and beak-like nose. He laughed wheezily and began to cough and cough, until the tears ran down his face and his face reddened. Hester looked at him anxiously.

'Are you recovered?' she asked. 'Should I fetch Melissa?'

'Of course I'm not recovered,' he said testily. 'I'm never likely to recover now. I'm an old man and you're an old woman, and we're neither of us going to recover from that!'

She smiled thinly, and he remembered why he had never liked her: she had no sense of humour. She was a dour woman. He tried to listen to what she was saying, frowning with the effort. She was dressed in dark grey, a colour which did not suit her. Perhaps a pigeon was more apt than a crow,

Luke thought. Aye, a skinny grey pigeon . . .

'I said, a very charming ceremony,' she repeated. 'Are you listening to me, Luke? A very nice ceremony. The new vicar has a most charming voice, clear as a bell. Everyone heard every word, they assured me so: every word. And Hannah looked charming, but no doubt you saw her earlier. Quite charming, I thought.'

'So it was all *charming*,' he said, with a suspicion of mockery in his voice which escaped her entirely. He sighed guiltily. He must try to be nice to Hester. He had promised Melissa. Hester went on.

'What a shame poor Luke isn't here to see it, I said, but if he can't leave his bed, he can't and that's all there is to it. It might come to any of us, I said.' She looked at him with a hint of malice in her eyes, but he was almost too tired to care. Almost, but not quite.

'And did Hugo look charming too?' he asked innocently.

'Hugo looked very well. He's a handsome man, Luke. You can be proud of your new son-in-law.'

'No doubt I will be,' said Luke. He closed his eyes, waiting for her to arrive at the reason for her presence here. It would have to come. He knew Hester.

'So,' she said loudly, forcing him to open his eyes reluctantly. 'So.'

'So?' he repeated, deliberately obtuse.

'So your clemency has brought its reward,' she said.

'My clemency?'

'To my son, not so long ago. Oh come, Luke, let's not bandy words. We are too old for such games. Confess you are finally content that you saved Hugo from the gallows – for now he ensures the Kendal succession on which you set such store. Say it, Luke. I'm his mother and you owe me that much.' Seeing that he made no answer, she moved a step nearer to the bed. 'Luke!' she said more sharply. 'I came to you then on bended knee and pleaded with you to save my son's life. First you refused me. I shall always remember.'

'And then I saved him,' said Luke. 'Will you remember that also?'

'Aye, I'll remember and be grateful.' Her eyes flashed. 'But the wheel has come full circle, Luke. You need my son. So confess that you are glad now, that twas wisely done. That –'

The door opened and Melissa came in with a small tray.

'Papa, I have come as I promised. I have brought you some cake and a glass of Madeira so that you may toast the bride and groom.' She smiled at Hester, pretending not to notice the tension between them. 'Hester, you are missing all the excitement,' she said. 'The conjuror has arrived and the children are open-mouthed, bless them.'

She set the tray beside the bed and winked surreptitiously at Luke. Hester hesitated a moment, then abruptly held out a hand.

'They are wed,' she said. 'Let us wish them every happiness.'

Luke nodded and took her hand briefly. She glanced at Melissa and walked unsmiling towards the door. Melissa looked at her father with an unspoken question in her eyes, and he sighed.

'Hester,' he called, 'I am glad on it. Indeed, I am most glad.'

Hester turned, and a radiant smile gave her hard face a sudden, transient warmth. Then she closed the door gently behind her, and they heard her footsteps as she went downstairs.

'That was well done, Papa,' said Melissa and kissed him approvingly. 'Was she very difficult? I thought I had best rescue you as soon as it was seemly.'

Luke shook his head. 'I've survived worse,' he said. He took the proffered glass and Melissa raised hers also. 'To Hugo and Hannah – and Allan,' he said.

'To Heron,' said Melissa, and their glasses touched.

'Everyone wants to come up and see you,' said Melissa, 'but I have said no. The physician says you must avoid too much excitement. Do you want to see anyone?'

'In truth I am happy just to lie here in peace and know they are all under my roof,' he said. 'Tell me again who is below, and I shall imagine it all.'

She settled herself on the edge of the bed and began to count them off on her fingers. 'There's Abby, of course, and Adam – you've seen them – and their three, and Hugo's stepsister Sarah. Jo and Louise Tucker are here – we shall miss them when they move.'

'When they move?'

'Aye, I told you, Papa. They are building a new house two miles east of Maudesley. With a slate roof!'

'Did you tell me? I forgot. So Maudesley will stand empty?'

'Aye, until such time as they might renovate it. Tis in a poor state, Papa. So damp – and the far wall is badly cracked, and there is rot in some of the roof beams.'

'A new tile roof, you say? Hmm. There's nothing wrong with a good thatch in my opinion . . .' He closed his eyes again and the wine glass tilted in his hand, spilling the pale liquid on to the coverlet.

'Papa!'

She mopped up the wine and he drank what was left, refusing any more. 'Do you want to sleep?' she asked him.

'No, no. Talk with me a while longer,' said Luke. 'Is Matthew there and Blanche?'

'Neither, Papa. Matt is crippled now with his arthritis and Blanche will not leave him. Sophie is come, though, and will be up to see you later. The others are on Hugo's side.'

'And Catherine?'

She looked at him sharply. 'She is dead, Papa, long since.'

'Dead, is she? Ah yes. I forget these things . . . And that young Maria?'

Melissa smiled ruefully. 'She would not come,' she told him. 'She's headstrong, that one, but I feel for her. Poor girl – there has never been anyone in her life but Hugo.'

'But she's to wed a Harold someone, surely?'

'Aye, but with a very bad grace!'

'Ah . . . There's a devil of a racket downstairs for so few people! And listen – that young Allan wailing, I'd know that sound anywhere. Too much attention, no doubt. They'll spoil the lad.' His face clouded and he sighed deeply. 'I wish Simon could have seen him . . .'

Melissa put a hand over his. 'It wasn't to be, Papa,' she said.

'No . . . Ah, my head swims so. I think I must sleep awhile – and then I must talk with Hugo. He knows nothing about mining, nothing at all.'

'Don't forget, Papa, that Simon knew nothing, if I recall, but he soon learnt. And Barlowe is a good man and will teach Hugo, also. Now you sleep. You look so tired and your eyes are dark. Should I fetch the physician?'

'Physician? Don't talk so wildly, Lissa. Do I need a physician to tell me I must take a nap? Save all this fussing for your young Oliver, bless him. He told me yesterday how he will learn to swim in the river when the summer comes. Jacob will teach him, he says . . .'

He lay down and allowed her to tuck in the sheets more firmly.

'I'll put another log on,' she told him, 'and Minnie shall come up in an hour's time and see if you are awake again.'

But suddenly he was struggling to sit up again, and his coughing started, shaking his thin frame.

'What is it, Papa?'

'The river –' he said, but before he could continue, another paroxysm seized him.

'The river? Oh no, don't try to talk. Wait, I'll fetch the linctus.'

She poured a spoonful of syrup into a spoon, and he managed to swallow it. Gradually, the coughing ceased, and she wiped his face.

'That cough,' she said. 'It will shake you to pieces. Are

you better? Then what is this about the river? Won't it wait until tomorrow?'

He shook his head weakly. 'The river,' he repeated. 'Tis all in the river. I have to tell you – the plate from the priory, Melissa. Tis all there. A golden crucifix, goblets, a silver chalice – all in the river . . .'

Melissa shook her head, confused. 'A silver chalice?' she said. 'And goblets? What are you saying, Papa? I don't understand –'

'From the priory,' he said. 'The priory . . . Brother Andrew . . .'

'What of it, papa? The priory is derelict. And Andrew is dead now. The priory is gone, Papa.'

He nodded, then shook his head. 'All the plate,' he said. 'All in the river –' Then he began to cough again, and she made him take more syrup.

'And there's to be no more talking,' she said firmly. 'All the plate is in the river. Aye, I heard you. We will talk more about it tomorrow. I must go downstairs, or they will send out a search party. And you are to sleep, Papa. No one will disturb you for an hour. I shall send for the physician tomorrow, whatever you say. That cough is no better – indeed, I think it grows worse.'

But he was already half asleep and made no answer. Gently, she kissed his forehead, made up the fire and tiptoed out of the room.

Hannah and Hugo lay side by side in the big four-poster bed with the drapes tied back. The air was scented with lavender, the fire crackled in the hearth and the leaping flames sent splashes of light across the new wall-hanging – a wedding gift from Hester.

'It looks well there,' said Hannah. 'It catches the firelight and will catch the early sunlight also.'

'Aye, so it will.'

It was nearly midnight and all the visitors had either

departed or retired to their makeshift beds, some in Heron, others in Ladyford. Next door they heard Luke coughing, and above them came the occasional creak as Beth or Minnie changed position in the wooden truckle beds.

'The orange cream turned out well,' said Hannah, 'but the brawn was a little salty, wouldn't you say?'

'I didn't think so. It was all good. Everyone was impressed.'

'Oh, I do hope so. Beth is very good.'

She fell silent.

'And the sun shone!' said Hugo. 'We were very fortunate. They say the sun shines on the righteous.'

She laughed dutifully. Somewhere Allan began to cry, and Hannah sat up, listening.

'The wet nurse is with him,' said Hugo. 'You need not go to him.'

She relaxed and was silent again turning over in her mind the events of the day, reassuring herself that all had gone as planned and that there was no fault to be found in her management of the celebrations. Somehow, though, she did not feel like a bride. It was as if the day's events had been in honour of someone else – as if another woman had stood at the church door vowing to love, honour and obey. Simon was her husband, but Hugo, his cousin, now lay next to her. He filled Simon's space in the bed, but not the space in her heart. Desperately she tried to concentrate – on the guests, on the breakfast, on the wedding gifts . . .

'I thought Abigail looked pale,' she said. 'But mayhap it was the colour of her gown. Dark green is not an easy colour to wear.'

Hugo said nothing. He was thinking of Margaret, who lay cold and straight in her coffin, the half-formed child cold and still within her belly. He had wanted Margaret and he had wanted Heron, but only one of those wishes had been granted. He had gained a wife he did not love, but he had made certain vows and would try to keep them. This woman beside him would satisfy his body and give him an heir, but he would never forget that it was Simon's child who would take Heron. Did that matter? he wondered, strangely resigned to this latest quirk of fate -- a fate which had used him so haphazardly over the last few years. He tried to visualise Simon as he had been all those years ago, when the two cousins had shared the dangers of the rebellion which swept the West Country. He had saved Simon's life, and now Simon's life was taken away and all that Simon had once owned, home, woman and child, was his. Was it design? Was it divine intervention? And if so, why did he feel no emotion, no elation, that these things had come to pass?

He tried to think about the woman lying beside him. He had a husband's duty to perform, and yet the thought gave him no pleasure, aroused almost no interest in his mind or body. He was dismayed by the admission.

'One of the geese was quite untouched,' said Hannah. 'I told Beth we would eat it tomorrow with some onions and a white sauce.'

'I cannot think on food!' laughed Hugo. 'I have eaten and drunk enough for two days!'

How can this be? thought Hannah in growing amazement, as time passed. Are we to lie here discussing such mundane matters on our wedding night? Does he feel as indifferent towards me as I do towards him? What is the matter with us? Guiltily, she tried to think of Hugo's body, trying to picture the curve of his chest and the line of his shoulders. He was shorter than Simon, and as dark as Simon was fair. This Hugo would give her dark-eyed children – if he gave her any at all.

She wondered if he was asleep, and hoped he was – and yet what a slight that would be. Tears of frustration pricked her eyelids. Sweet Heaven, don't let me cry, she thought. Hardly knowing what she did, she sat up suddenly, holding the sheet to cover her breasts, ashamed of her nakedness. She was trembling and tears had begun to well up in her eyes.

153

'I'm not Margaret,' she stammered. 'I never can be – and you are not Simon. Oh, we have done wrong, Hugo. I fear we have. I know it. Twas a mistake – no, don't touch me. Tis not your fault, nor mine. They have manoeuvred us. Oh God, let me be, Hugo. Let me weep. Tis all I'm fit for tonight.'

He sat up awkwardly beside her, afraid to put his arm around her, afraid to comfort her.

'You don't want me,' she wept. 'You never have, nor likely ever will. You still love Margaret. No, don't protest otherwise, for tis the truth and I've seen it in your eyes. And I bear no love for you. Simon is my husband still: Heron is his, Allan is his, I am his. Oh Hugo, what's to be done? How can we live together? How can we bear it?'

She looked at him, but hurt by her words, he merely shrugged, adding to her despair. She sobbed bitterly, her shoulders, shaking, both hands clutching her bowed head, her fingers entwined in her long, wavy hair.

Unable to watch her without touching her, Hugo slid out of bed and crossed to the fire, grateful for its comforting warmth. He resented her inference that he was not entitled to Heron, or had come by it unfairly.

'You agreed,' he said. 'You agreed to Luke's proposition. You consented before I was even approached.'

'I know, I know,' she cried. 'And I blame myself for it. And yet you agreed for your part. You don't deny that?'

'I don't.'

She looked at his stocky, muscular body, silhouetted against the firelight, his arms and back shadowed with dark hairs. His legs were thick, with well-shaped calves. His dark head sat on a short, powerful neck.

'I owed Luke a debt,' said Hugo. 'He saved my life.'

'But Simon owed his life to you!' cried Hannah. 'Tis such nonsense to talk this way. Oh, forgive me, Hugo. I don't mean to censure you. We are both to blame. We have both been rash. We have wed one another, we are tied in the eyes of God, and there's no undoing it. How shall we live

154

together, Hugo, after tonight?'

'I swear I cannot say,' he said turning to her. 'But I am weary and my head aches with too much wine. I am wretched and your weeping unnerves me. If I cannot comfort you, then I shall sleep here by the fire. A sheepskin will cover me well enough.'

But Hannah's tears were almost spent, and she held out her hand to him to beckon him back to the bed. He climbed in beside her and they knelt, facing one another. Gently he brushed the hair back from her tear-stained face.

'Mayhap one day you'll love me,' he said.

'And you might want me.'

He nodded.

'We are such fools,' she whispered.

He took up a strand of her hair and put it to his lips. 'There's no need for haste,' he said. 'We are joined till death do us part. We may yet find happiness together.'

'But for tonight?'

'Brother and sister!' he said. 'And tomorrow night if you wish it. But not forever.'

'To sleep, then,' said Hannah.

'Aye, and no more tears. How will we face the household tomorrow if you are red-eyed? They will think your new husband beats you!'

Hannah smiled faintly and snuggled into his arms and was soon asleep. Hugo, feeling her soft body relax in his arms, wondered if perhaps he might one day desire her. Was one woman very like another? But as he drifted into sleep, it was Maria's image that floated into his mind and he dreamed of her and woke with her name on his lips.

In the early hours of the morning, Luke woke up with a pain in his chest. He waited for it to pass, but it did not. It increased steadily and was like nothing else he had known. Finally, becoming seriously alarmed, he reached for the bell which usually stood on the coffer beside his bed, only to find it missing. Then he remembered: Oliver had played with it when he came up to say goodbye, just before Melissa and Thomas went home to Ladyford.

Young rascal, he thought fondly then clutched at his heart, as a new, fierce pain tore through him, taking his breath away and making him cry out. But the cry had no substance – he could make no sound. Perspiration broke out on his forehead, and a cold fear seized him: his heart was failing and he could not cry or ring for help! He tried to drum his fist against the pillars of the four-poster, but the sudden movements only doubled the pain in his chest, and he gave up, panting painfully. The constriction was now an agony. Cursing his useless legs and failing vocal cords, he decided to let himself fall out of the bed on to the rug; from there he would drag himself to the door and try to slam it. He leaned sideways and let himself down, his fall slowed by the bedding wrapped around his legs. Fresh waves of pain filled his body and threatened to overwhelm him. *He was dying.* Fear lent strength to his arms, and he began to pull himself along the floor on his elbows . . . Only three yards more – but a last, terrible pain closed round his heart, and he lost consciousness.

When he came to, he was aware of warmth and softness. He was in bed. There were voices. Women's voices, hushed with apprehension. And a man's voice. Simon's, perhaps. He tried to open his eyes, but his eyelids were heavy and would not move. He tried to speak and his lips remained still. More voices. And then he drifted away again into nothingness . . . Then more voices and fingers touching his face, holding his wrist, feeling his chest and abdomen. Warm water soothed and washed his tired flesh, and he heard weeping. A door closed. Dogs barked and there were footsteps and more voices.

'Mama!' he whispered. She was holding his hand, kissing it. 'Mama.'

Someone leaned over him, blotting out the light, and he heard the word 'Hannah', but it meant nothing. They were lifting his head, feeding him warm milk with a spoon, drop by drop. It trickled round his useless tongue and dribbled out of his mouth . . .

Then he was in the hospice, and Isobel was beside him. Poor mad Isobel. He fed her, holding the wine to her lips, and she drank greedily until it spilled down her chin and she looked over the rim at him with those poor, mad eyes.

'Don't look at me,' she begged. 'Don't, I beg you.' And she threw down the goblet and ran away across the grass and over the cliff, and as she fell her clothes billowed out like wings and she became a bird, a large crow, that turned and flew at him, pecking at his eyes. She was Marion Gillis, the witch woman . . . But no, for there she was swinging from the gibbet with her dog beside her, and little Alison calling the dog to her and patting it kindly.

'Alison!' He tried to warn her, but the word was no more than a croak. He heard the word 'Melissa' and made no sense of it.

And then the light faded and he opened his eyes and saw a candle burning and a woman sat beside him.

'Mama!' he whispered, but she shook her head and there were tears in her eyes as she kissed his forehead and straightened the sheets. A strange sound filled his brain – a sound of waves upon the sea – but the water lay gleaming in the sunlight with hardly a ripple, and there was no wind for the sails. Only the *Mary Rose* moved slowly ahead, turning across the bay. '*Mary,*' he whispered, but she too left him to slide under the grey water . . . A little later he opened his eyes and saw Melissa watching him. He smiled and gave a nod of his head and she jumped up and rang the bell suddenly and Hugo was there, smiling and talking, but Luke could not hear his voice. Hannah stood on his left, her eyes red-rimmed, and Little Oliver was held up to see his grandfather – or was it Jeffery – and where was little Abby?

'Oh, Papa,' said Melissa. And Luke, smiling, closed his eyes and died.

'What is that child doing?' asked Hannah irritably. Beth cast a guilty look at Minnie, who stood at the kitchen table. In spite of her puffed eyes and red-blotched face, she wore an earnest expression and now gave Hannah a defiant look. Her fingers were busy inside a small mixing bowl, and beside her was a collection of fruits, nuts and spices.

'She's making a soul cake,' said Beth, 'to take away the Master's sins, so she tells me. Never heard of such a tale, I told her, but she wouldn't budge from it. Leastways, I thought, it keeps her from under my feet and puts an end to her wailing –'

'A soul cake?' Hannah repeated, mystified.

Minnie added a few currants to the mixture in the bowl and said loudly, 'If twas right for my ma, then tis right for the Master.'

'I told you he didn't have no sins,' said Beth.

'We all have sins,' said Hannah wearily. 'We all make mistakes. Tell me about it Minnie, but quick, for there's much to be done with the funeral tomorrow. Ah, what a week!'

Beth looked at her pityingly. What a week, indeed! A wedding one day and a death the next. But Minnie was scowling.

'I don't want to tell you,' she protested. 'You'll laugh, like Beth did.'

'If you don't tell me,' said Hannah sharply, 'you'll go straight back to Ladyford and stay there. I've troubles enough without bothering with your tantrums. So speak up and make haste about it.'

Reluctantly, the girl stopped what she was doing, kicked the table leg twice, and then looked up at Hannah.

'The soul cake be laid on the departed's chest, and all the sins do go into it, and tis eaten, and the sins be gone into him as eats it, and the departed's soul goes clean up to heaven, and tis true enough for me grandmother made one when me ma died and she's not come back to haunt me.'

'I see,' said Hannah dubiously.

Beth whispered. 'I didn't reckon it could do no harm, ma'am, and she were that fretted this morning there was no reasoning with her.'

'Let her be,' said Hannah. 'As you say, it can do no harm. Now I must ride over to Ladyford. Melissa is coming with some black drapes, and Jack must fetch another cask of cider from the town. Little Allan is gone home with her for a few days. Tis a cheerless time and he's best out of it –'

And so she went off on her various errands, leaving Minnie to finish her soul cake. When it was done she shaped it, dough-like, and sat it beside the fire. Then she cleaned up the mess as she had promised, under pain of a clout if she should forget. Satisfied, she went outside to look for Jon.

He was chopping wood and was glad to pause for a moment and wipe his face on his sleeve.

'I've a favour to ask,' said Minnie, wondering how best to go about it.

'Ask away then,' said Jon.

'Tis Luke's soul cake,' said Minnie. 'I be making him a cake to take away his sins and –'

'Who said the Master had any?' Jon demanded.

'Hannah says we've all gotten sins and we all makes mistakes, so don't be so smart, Jon, for you don't know everything!'

'Never said I did.'

She sighed with exasperation and continued. 'When the sins be inside the cake, why then, someone has to eat them, so's the Master's soul can go straight to heaven and not dally on the way.'

'What's the favour, then?' asked Jon.

'Why, for you to eat the cake,' said Minnie.

'What about the sins?' asked Jon nervously.

'Them as well.'

Jon's nervousness deepened into suspicion. 'I don't want no more sins on me,' he said. 'I've got enough of me own! Ask Jack to do it.'

'I've asked him and he won't.'

'Then no more will I.'

'You're afeared!' Minnie taunted furiously. 'You're both afeared of a poor old man's sins!'

'Of course I am,' cried Jon. 'Any man would be. I don't know what he's done, do I? Might be something fearful – and then who'd eat my sins when I die? If you're so brave, then eat it yourself – tis you that's making it. Tis your idea. You'll not find anyone to eat it for you, I'll warrant. No disrespect on the Master, but we've all got sins of our own.'

He took up the axe and swung it into the log, which spat splinters of wood. Minnie went thoughtfully back to the kitchen. Would it count if she ate the soul cake herself? She had no qualms about Luke's sins. She was young and would lead a blameless life henceforward. That way she could atone for Luke's sins and maybe some of her own as well. But would it work?

The cake was finally baked to her satisfaction – a little burnt on one side, but fair enough. The skewer came out clean, and she put it on a dish and carried it up into the bedchamber where Luke was laid in his coffin, two candles at the head of it and one at the foot. The two dogs followed her in. She shooed them out, but they crept in again, hopefully following the smell of the soul cake. Minnie tiptoed up to the bed and looked into the coffin. Luke looked very peaceful in his white gown and cap, his hands clasped over a crucifix. His eyes were closed, but perhaps he would hear her.

'Tis only me – Minnie,' she began nervously. 'I dare say you'll remember me.' One of the dogs leaned lovingly against her legs, and she pushed it away without taking her eyes from Luke's face.

'I've brought you this soul cake,' she told him. 'Tis a mite burnt, but you won't have to eat it, my dear Master. I made it myself and put in all that I should – figs, currants, nutmeg and the like – and Beth let me do it and so did the Mistress. Oh, pardon me, a moment –' She slapped at the dogs, who had sidled closer again. 'So tis a fine cake, Luke, and I'm putting it here on your belly 'cos your hands is across your chest – there!'

She watched the cake anxiously, then looked at Luke's face. How long did the sins take to go into the cake? she wondered. 'I'll give it a few moments,' she told him. 'Meantime – well, there's a good many red eyes hereabouts with your passing, you can take my word on it. You'll be missed, and that's for certain. *I* miss you –' Her voice trembled slightly, but she controlled it with an effort, not wishing to distress him with her tears. 'I'm going to eat the soul cake for you, for there's none others willing. I do hope it works, Luke – I mean, Master.' She looked at the cake again, but it appeared unchanged. Gently, she moved plate and cake and was about to take the first bite, when one of the dogs whined eagerly. A gleam came into her eyes as a thought struck her. Could a dog eat sins? Would the dogs be willing? They had both adored Luke after all. Impulsively, she took one mouthful, then broke the remaining cake and tossed it to the dogs.

'We've shared your sins,' she told Luke. 'They're all gone and you may rest easy. Twas all very well done, Luke. Are you pleased?'

Just at that moment, one of the candles flickered, and she took this as an answer in the affirmative. Kissing two fingers, she laid them on his lips. Then, calling the dogs to follow, she tiptoed softly out of the room, a faint but satisfied smile on her small, plain face.

CHAPTER TEN
London – 1555

Maria woke with a feeling of panic. The ninth of February – her last day in London. Tomorrow she would set off with Matt, and together they would ride towards a new life in Romney House on the outskirts of Appledore. There she would learn the ways of the household from Ruth Cummins and would prepare herself for her eventual wedding to Harold. The prospect did not excite her.

'One last day!' she whispered. 'My last day of freedom.'

To everyone's surprise she had agreed to the betrothal without demur. Hugo's marriage to Hannah had shattered all her dreams and she now viewed the future with indifference. She accepted her mother's choice of a husband. Old, young, rich or poor – he was of no interest to her. She would share his bed, manage his home, bear his children. But she would not love him. They would not make her love him. She faced a loveless future – and tomorrow it would begin.

'My last day!' she said again, and slid out of bed to greet it.

A few hundred yards away, in the Tower ward of the Fleet prison, a man echoed her words in earnest. He knelt on a mattress of rotting straw which had served him as a bed for the past seventeen months, but would soon serve him no longer. His misery was almost at an end. The persistent squalor and neglect which had robbed him of his health would fall to the lot of the next unfortunate to languish there. John Hooper's last day had arrived. Sentence had been passed on him by the Queen's Chancellor, Stephen Gardiner, and he had been committed to death by burning.

Now he prayed in his own way, with his own prayers. He would not conform to Queen Mary's Catholicism. He would not accept that the Pope was spiritual head of all Christians, and he would not submit to Rome. Nor would he put aside the wife that Protestantism had allowed him to take. For all these 'heresies' he had been stripped of his bishopric and would soon pay the ultimate penalty. Two common criminals shared his cell, and they watched in awe as the once-great man prepared to meet his God.

Outside in the square the people began to gather, anxious not to miss the spectacle. Singly, in pairs, and in small groups they came, their motives various. Those who shared his faith came to support him in his hour of need, to offer their prayers and to will him the strength to bear his pain. Others came out of curiosity, to see how a man survives an ordeal. Others to learn how to die. Those that opposed him would come to watch the heretic burn and glory in the sight of justice being done. A few would come to jeer. Many would be there to make an honest living, selling refreshments and souvenirs. Pickpockets would swell the numbers, and jugglers and musicians would keep the crowd entertained while they waited for the main event. Already a stool had been set down in the middle of the square and the first few faggots laid against it. There was an excited murmur of anticipation from the crowd.

Maria looked at Matt in dismay. 'But I thought to go to Madelaine's,' she said, 'and then the Lane for my shoes. I have no mind to see a burning. Twould be a poor way to spend my last day. Oh, Matt, say you'll come with me to Madelaine's. I'll buy you a venison pasty if you will.'

Matt shuffled his feet. 'I don't care to go to Madelaine's. Tis no place for a man. I'll fetch your shoes for you, though, and see the burning on my way home.'

'Tis not a pretty sight,' she told him, 'to see a man burnt in the flames.'

'You've never seen it!' he cried triumphantly. 'You said so yesterday. How d'you know tis not a pretty sight? They say tis edifying to see a holy man give up his soul. And there's plenty that think so, to judge by all the folks flocking that way.'

Maria looked at him in exasperation, then turned to her mother. 'Tell him, Mama,' she said.

Her mother, who was in the middle of ironing, shrugged her shoulders. 'What can I tell him? I've no wish to hang about in the cold to see a man roast – but that's cos I've got better things to do with my time. There's your last bag to pack, a letter to write to Harold Cummins, and Lord knows what else to be done. The gloves must be got from Madelaine and the shoes collected – I've no time to spare. If you've a mind to see Hooper, then fetch the others after, or you'll have to go down to Kent without them. And no gadding off on your own, Maria. There's a sight too many rogues about on a day like this, so don't you go a yard without Matt. D'you hear that, Matt? Don't you let her out of your sight, Madelaine's or no Madelaine's.' So saying, she set the iron back on the fire and folded the sheet, pretending not to notice Maria's expression.

'But to watch a man burn!' said Maria.

Her mother took a pillowcase from the basket beside her and shook it before laying it across the board. 'Seems to me you're making a great pother about nothing. Twill all be over once the flames reach the powder, and that won't take long. One bang and he'll be dead and well out of his miseries, poor man. I saw a witch burned once, years ago, straightway up goes the powder and twas all over in the wink of an eye. Except for the dog.'

'Which dog?' said Matt.

'Hers, poor thing. It jumped in the fire after her. Didn't want to be parted from her, I reckon. They dragged it out, but it went in again, howling all the while, its fur all smouldering. That was a fearful sound, that dog howling. I can hear it now!'

Maria shuddered and turned to Matt. 'Why then,' she said, 'I'll come with you to see Hooper, if you'll come to Madelaine's after.'

And so it was finally agreed.

By the time they reached the square the crowd was already considerable.

Matt's face fell. 'We'll not see anything!' he grumbled. 'All that shilly-shallying.'

Maria, ignoring him, jumped up and down, trying to see over the heads of the crowd. But it was impossible. Children sat on their fathers' shoulders and some people stood on upturned tubs. A few on horseback watched from the rear.

'Is he there yet?' Matt asked a man beside him. 'Is Hooper brought out of the Fleet?'

'Aye. Brought out some minutes ago and stood on the stool. Walked by me, he did, and walked so straight and tall, for all that he looked so ill, poor man. Held his head up high and smiled so gently. England will lose a good man when he goes.'

An old woman turned to them, and Maria saw that she had tears in her eyes. 'Cruel, I call it, to stand him out there in this cold wind. The fire's not even built! And they say what faggots there are look damp and not likely to burn. How must his wife feel, poor soul, to see her husband treated so cruel?'

'His wife?' cried Maria. 'Oh, surely she isn't come to watch!'

'Why, not to watch,' said the old woman indignantly. 'But to share his last moments and pray for his departing soul. I'd be here if twas my old husband, bless him, but he's dead and buried these past four years, God rest his soul. Died peaceful in his bed, I'm happy to say, but – Ah, here comes the rest of the fire. And not before time!'

There was a disturbance behind Matt and Maria as two

165

men pushed through the crowd, carrying armfuls of reeds.

'Quick!' cried Matt, and grasping Maria's hand, he pulled her behind him in the wake of the reed-bearers. To Maria's intense dismay they found themselves in the forefront of the spectators. She glanced anxiously behind her but the crowd had closed its ranks again. There was no going back.

Immediately ahead of her was John Hooper, standing on a high stool above two bundles of faggots. His hands were clasped and his lips moved in prayer. He paused when the reeds arrived and taking a bundle in his arms lifted them up and kissed them, then tucked them under his arms.

'That's the way,' he told the man. 'Lay them in a circle about my legs.'

Another man stepped forward. 'Forgive me!' he said.

'I know of nothing to forgive.'

'Tis I shall light the fire!' he said.

'Why then, tis your job and you don't offend me,' said Hooper. 'God will forgive you your sins.'

All was ready. There was a murmur from the crowd as the burning torch was put to the faggots. Somewhere in the crowd a woman cried, 'John! John!' and another, 'God be with you, sir.' Voices shouted slogans against the Queen, assured of their anonymity by the size of the crowd. Maria crossed herself and nudged Matt to do the same.

'Taint going to burn,' said Matt. 'The faggots won't take the flames. D'you think tis a sign from God?'

'A sign of damp faggots, more likely,' said a woman on their left. 'That poor man. Why can't they do the job properly and put him out of his misery.'

Still the faggots refused to burn, merely belching forth smoke which was blown sideways into the crowd, making them splutter and curse. More faggots were brought, and the torch applied once more. This time the reeds caught alight and the flames leaped up to burn Hooper's hair, but he made no sound except to pray aloud, 'Oh Jesus, son of David, have mercy upon me and receive my soul!'

Maria was near enough to smell the scorched flesh, and her stomach churned. 'The gunpowder!' she cried. 'I see no gunpowder.'

'They've strapped it to his legs,' said the old woman. 'Any minute now twill explode. Just one spark will do it.'

The fire round the victim's legs was now burning fiercely, but still the gunpowder did not ignite. In a fearful agony Hooper cried out, 'For God's love, dear people, let me have more fire!'

Maria buried her face in Matt's jerkin, her hands over her ears, and he put an arm round her protectively. Yet his own eyes were drawn to the terrible scene and he watched as though hypnotised as yet another load of faggots were brought to the fire and a fresh torch applied to kindle them. Suddenly the gunpowder exploded, but at the same moment the wind gusted strongly and took the force of the explosion away from Hooper's body, leaving him very much alive and horribly conscious.

A horrified murmur broke out among the crowd.

'What is it?' cried Maria. 'Is he dead?'

'Don't look on it,' said Matt. 'The powder's missed him. He just burns and burns –'

'Oh dear God! I cannot bear it!' cried Maria. 'It sickens me! Take me away, Matt, I beg you. Take me away from here.'

But the crowd were so densely packed that there was no way of escape. The stench of burning flesh was blown on the wind, and the smoke rose from the spluttering blood and fat that dripped down from Hooper's body. Everywhere people wept and prayed aloud, and others shouted that something be done to put an end to the victim's suffering. Maria, panic-stricken, raised her head and stared wildly round at the nightmare scene unfolding before them. Then she gave a small moan and fell senseless into Matt's arms.

The party riding south the following day consisted of two young men on pilgrimage to Canterbury, an elderly widow and her maid, who were bound for Dover and thence to Calais to visit a daughter, and Maria and Matt. Maria was very quiet and she listened dully as Matt, explaining her reluctance to talk, described the previous day's event to their fellow-travellers. Unwilling to fan the memories, she allowed her horse to drop back a little so that she could compose herself as well as possible before they reached their destination.

'And he didn't die? Oh, that's too unkind!' exclaimed the widow. 'Too unkind! And all in the name of our dear Lord. Sweet Heaven, what is the world come to when a man must suffer so for his beliefs.' She sighed deeply. 'And the poor girl was distressed by it. And rightly so. Swooned away, you say? Tut, tut! But the pain of another is often harder to bear than one's own, wouldn't you say? My late husband, God rest his soul, always said so – and he was right. But to linger in such agony. And him such a saintly man! What bunglers to let such an unkind thing come about. Who will be next, I wonder? Is any one safe in these troubled times?'

Matt, unable to interrupt this monologue, cast a few glances in the direction of her maid, but the girl's stodgy features were set in a determined scowl; she had been reprimanded earlier for encouraging one of the other young men, and now maintained an aggrieved silence.

'. . . My dear husband used to say there are more sins committed in the name of religion than there are leaves on a tree – and he was right, wouldn't you say?'

Matt nodded vaguely, bored with the conversation. He glanced over his shoulder to see if Maria would extricate him, but she rode with her eyes downcast, deep in thought.

'Your sister, is she?'

'Eh?'

'Your sister – the young lady?'

'No – no!' said Matt, secretly flattered by her mistake. 'She's my Mistress. I'm escorting her to her betrothed,' he added in a loud voice, so that the maid and the two young men should be fully aware of his importance. 'I shall stay with her there as her protector.'

'Her protector?' The old woman peered at him suspiciously. 'Where's her maid, then?'

'She don't have no maid,' said Matt. 'There'll be maids enough at Romney House. She's got me instead.'

'Hmm.'

'Chose me herself, she did,' said Matt, lowering his voice confidingly. 'Said she'd need a strong right arm in case of danger or suchlike. They say the Marsh is a wild place with unruly people, but none shall harm a hair of her head while I've breath in me body!'

Whether the widow was convinced by this declaration Matt never knew, for at that moment one of the young men reined in his horse sharply and pointed ahead.

'Smoke up ahead,' he said, 'where there are no dwellings. We should go cautiously for fear of beggars.'

They all conferred as to what should be done. The highway along which they now rode was muddy with recent rains, but if they made a detour they would find the ground almost impossible and would make slower time. The days were short, and to ride in darkness would be to invite disaster. Matt, Maria and the widow intended to ride as far as Tonbridge and sleep overnight at the Chequers Inn. The young pilgrims would then leave the group at Sevenoaks and turn east towards Canterbury, to rendezvous with three friends in Maidstone.

'I propose we send the men ahead,' said the widow. 'We shall look fine fools if we lose the beaten track, and all for a solitary woodman or a harmless shepherd.'

The two young men showed little enthusiasm for the idea, but Matt was eager to prove himself.

'Wait, Matt!' cried Maria. 'And take heed before you go – you must try not to attract attention. Ride slow and keep your eyes skinned on either side of the track in case of ambush. At the first sign of hostility, ride back hallooing as loud as you can, and we will turn our horses and make ourselves scarce.'

Their precautions, though wise, proved unnecessary. Instead of robbers and brigands, Matt found a young beggar woman with a sickly husband, huddled under a makeshift shelter in the shade of a tree.

'He waves us on!' cried Maria thankfully, and they urged their horses forward.

The beggar woman stared at them with hard eyes as they drew up. The man beside her lay doubled up, wrapped in a threadbare blanket, his face half hidden. An iron pot hung over the fire, and the woman was stretching out bare hands to warm them by the blaze. The fire reminded Maria of John Hooper and she longed to look away, but something in the woman's eyes prevented her.

'Don't encourage them,' warned the widow. 'They are all counterfeits and as like as not, the man is as fit as we are. My husband used to say –'

The beggar woman stood up suddenly and held out a hand.

'Alms,' she said, her face expressionless. 'Alms, for pity's sake.'

'Ride on,' said the widow, taking hold of her maid's reins also. The two horses sprang forward, to wait a little further up the road. 'Don't heed her, I tell you,' she cried, seeing that the others hesitated. 'They are all idlers and good for nothing. The man is cup-shotten, I'll warrant. They will gull you out of the clothes you stand up in!'

The two young men each tossed a coin to the beggar woman and rode on, their consciences clear. Matt looked at Maria. She was still staring at the woman, who stood by the fire, the two coins clapsed to her chest, the other hand outstretched towards her.

'Alms,' she repeated tonelessly.

'What ails your husband?' Maria asked.

'The wasting sickness. He will die shortly.'

'And what will you do then?'

The woman shrugged. The man under the blanket moved and cried out as though in sleep, but the woman still stared at Maria.

Matt, uneasy, touched Maria's arm. 'The widow is right,' he whispered. 'We should ride on.'

But the sick man cried out again, and Maria turned to Matt. 'The cheese that was left from breakfast,' she said. 'Give it to her.'

Matt sighed noisily, but obeyed without argument. The woman took it calmly and stuffed it into the pocket of the tattered man's coat that she wore. 'Show me your hand,' she demanded, but Maria shook her head. 'A ring, then. Hand me a ring and I will tell your fortune.'

'She will not!' said Matt, sensing a trick.

She turned towards him and spat. Then she turned again to Maria.

'Then tell me your dreams.'

Still Maria shook her head. With an impatient toss of her head, the woman bent down and with her finger drew a circle in the mud and subdivided the circle into eight sections, each line passing through the middle of the circle. From another pocket she produced a handful of small, oddly-shaped pebbles. These she held out to Maria.

'Take them in your hand,' she said, 'then drop them altogether into the circle.'

By this time even Matt was intrigued and made no effort to stop Maria as she followed out the instructions. Three of the pebbles fell outside the circle. Seven fell inside it. Speaking in a monotone, the woman began to pick out the pebbles, interpreting the position of each one as she did so.

'You have few enemies, but your rash tongue brings trouble upon you . . . Your mind is heavy with an unexpected grief . . . Take care of your health. Avoid humid airs. I see a fall . . .' She picked up two which lay together, pursing her lips and frowning. 'I see a great change in your life within three years. A journey and a change. I hear bells ringing . . . Ah, there is a child, a son.' She tossed the pebble up. 'He is dark . . . And a quarrel . . .'

She looked up to see that Maria was listening, then picked up the three pebbles that lay outside the circle. 'These mean a wish come true.'

Further up the road, the widow was growing impatient. 'We shall ride on,' she said. 'You must catch up with us later.' But she still waited.

'A dark son,' repeated Maria. 'A wish come true.'

The woman stood up and held out her hand. 'Pay me,' she said.

Maria gave her a florin, and the lustreless eyes gleamed briefly. 'I speak only the truth,' she said, seeing the question in Maria's eyes, then she busied herself with the fire which was dying, adding a few more twigs and coaxing it back to life.

Maria and Matt cantered up to rejoin the others and the widow looked at her sourly. 'They are all deceivers,' she began. 'My dear late husband used to say –'

'Your late husband said a deal too much,' said Maria cheerfully. 'Ah, there's my rash tongue getting me into trouble. What do you say, Matt? Isn't that a good omen – that her predictions are come true so soon? Race with me to that stone bridge. I challenge you!' And she kicked her horse into a surprised gallop, leaving the others to stare at each other in astonishment.

'She also predicted a fall,' muttered Matt, and with a sigh of mock resignation, he whipped up his horse and went hallooing after her.

From the outside Romney House looked peaceful enough: a large, asymmetrical house, white and black under a thatched roof, the garden bordered on all sides with clipped hedges and shrubs growing against a red brick garden wall. Behind it, wooded ground sloped upwards towards a fine red sunset, a sure sign of fair weather the following day. The bees were silent in their wicker hives and the fish in the small pond swam sluggishly beneath a thin film of ice. Every dead leaf had been removed from the lawn and even the bird droppings had been scraped from the roof of the side porch. Harold Cummins was nothing if not thorough, and he was desperately keen to impress the young lady who was to be his third wife.

Ruth sat in the high-backed chair beside the fire and tried to concentrate on her stitching, while her brother Harold continued to pace up and down the length of the Hall on his long thin legs, as he had done for the past hour and a half.

'They're late,' he said again.

Ruth repressed a scream of irritation. 'The roads are wet,' she said. 'It will slow the horses. Don't distress yourself, Harold.'

'But mayhap she has delayed for other reasons. An accident, or an attack. The highways are no longer safe for honest folk. I wish I had ridden up to London to escort her home myself.'

'She did not wish it,' Ruth reminded him tartly. She had tried to make him insist on accompanying his young bride-to-be, and had taken umbrage when he gave in to what she considered to be Maria's whim on the matter. 'You have only yourself to blame,' she went on. 'You should have showed the girl right from the start that you are master.'

'She is only young,' he protested. 'I don't want to oppress the child.'

'She's not a child,' said Ruth. 'She's a young woman. Don't go pandering to her every wish, or you'll spoil her temperament. I warned you when you wed your first wife, and I warned you again with the second. You chose to ignore me – and look what happened!'

'I think they were happy,' he said timidly.

'Happy? Indeed they were!' cried Ruth. 'A sight *too* happy in my opinion. The first rode roughshod over all your needs and desires, and the second wasted your money. Oh, they were happy as pigs in muck, Harold Cummins, but were you?'

'I think I was,' he said mildly, pausing to stare hopefully out of the window.

'Well, I was *not*,' she retorted. 'And I don't intend to stand by and see you making the same mistakes a third time. I'm your sister, Harold, and –'

'I think I hear them –' he interrupted her, '– but no. I imagined it. I am so eager for her to arrive.'

'So eager to start making a fool of yourself, you mean. I know you, Harold. I've watched you grow up from a shy, foolish boy to a shy, foolish old man and I'm not –'

'Not old, dear,' he reproached her. 'Fifty-four is hardly old, is it? Indeed, I hope not. So young a girl will not relish an *old* man.'

'She'll relish a comfortable home and security, whatever age you are.'

'I do so want her to be happy here.'

Ruth gave up the pretence of stitching and threw down the sleeve she was working on. 'Harold Cummins!' she cried. 'I tell you, she'll be well pleased. Tis a fair match, considering her dowry. Her family are well-respected but – whatever is it, Meg?'

The maid had knocked at the door and now rushed straight in, her words tumbling out in her excitement.

'Jem says he sees them coming. He's been up to the top of the hill, and they're not a mile away. And cook says, should she bring in the vittals yet? And am I to curtsey?'

'Dear Lord,' grumbled Ruth, successfully hiding her own excitement. 'Tis not Queen Mary on a royal progress, child, tis only the Master's new bride. Calm yourself at once. No, we do not want the food until they are in the house – I'll send word. And you'll curtsey to Maria, but *not* to her lad. He is no more than Jem and should be treated accordingly.

The maid hurried out again. Ruth tucked up a wisp of grey hair that had somehow escaped her eagle eye.

'How do I look, dear?' asked Harold, swallowing nervously.

'You look the way you always look,' she told him. 'Very proper. Now stop fretting. I hear them at the gate. Give me your arm, Harold. We shall walk slowly to the door – together.'

Ten minutes later, the greetings over, Maria stood in her room, her hands over her face.

'He's *old*,' she whispered again and again. 'He's an old man! Holy St. Katharine, his hair is nearly silver and his shoulders hug his chest. Oh, that kiss! How could Mama do this? Did she know? So old! So – so *thin* and spare like a reed.'

Yesterday she had been indifferent to her fate, but the beggar woman's prediction had awakened her to better prospects. The woman had promised her a child – a *dark* child. How could that be Harold's child? His eyes were a faded blue, his eyebrows sandy. Harold Cummins was fair. So she would one day have another husband – one who would give her a dark-haired child. *It must be Hugo!* She had thought of nothing else since that chance meeting on the way to Tonbridge. How matters would resolve themselves she could not begin to imagine, and yet the idea haunted her, filling her with new hope. Her indifference had given way to a new awareness of herself and new ideas to conjure with. The woman had foretold changes – within three years. She had vowed to herself that she would suffer Harold Cummins, come what may, since fate had marked her down for a more glorious future. Mayhap the next three years were her testing time. If so, she would do her best to be dutiful. She would earn her remission.

But so old, dear God! Had her disappointment shown in her eyes? She hoped not. Harold Cummins had trembled as he kissed her. His bony arms had held her briefly to the narrow chest, and she had fought against her revulsion. He was not to blame for his ageing body, old age came to everyone who survived long enough. And he was kindly and seemed well-intentioned towards her. Thankfully, she glanced at the single bed. It would be hers for a year and a half. After that she would have to share Harold's bed. But she chose not to dwell on that fact. She was almost Mistress of this large household, and that state must offer some delights. Meg was to be her maid, and she had brought her own manservant with her. With Matt on hand she need never feel isolated among so many strangers. He would be there to greet her each day with his familiar moon-faced grin, an ally in a strange camp.

She splashed warm water over her cold face, and decided to reserve judgement on Ruth. If Harold's sister intended to dominate her, then there would be battles. If she only intended to guide, then there would be fewer of them. Maria could go no further. Both Hannah and Melissa had told her; be Mistress in your own house. She intended to be just that.

As she went in to supper, she was still chilled from the journey, but wore a favourite gown of deep, red velvet, which gave colour to her face. Her head-dress was edged with crisp white braid, which contrasted with her dark eyes and finely curved brows. Harold was enchanted, and throughout the meal his eyes never left her. He sat at the end of the long table, and Ruth and Maria sat on either side.

'We don't allow the servants to share a table with us,' said Ruth, 'except on special occasions. Many families do these days, but I believe it breeds familiarity – and Harold agrees with me.' This last was added quickly, so that Maria should see them united in their policies. Maria nodded without answering and Harold, absorbed in her, appeared not to have heard.

Beetroot soup was served with bread, and they ate in silence for a while. Maria was too tired to eat much and she was wondering how Matt was faring. Although she was aware of his limitations, she could not bear the thought that others might mock him or take advantage of his simplicity. She would question him on the matter, and woe betide any that did so. Just then she became aware that Ruth was leaning across the table, rapping on it for her attention.

'I beg your pardon,' said Maria.

'The journey,' Ruth repeated. 'You were late arriving. We thought some mishap must have befallen you.'

'Oh no. Twas my fault. The springs at Tunbridge Wells were so near, I couldn't resist a visit. I drank three bowls of the water. Very strange, it tasted.'

'You are not unwell, I hope,' said Harold.

'Not at all. But tis said to protect whoever drinks it from a great many ailments.' She ticked them off on her fingers. 'Gout, smallpox, the palsy, dropsy, fevers –'

'Fiddle faddle!' said Ruth. 'I have never swallowed a mouthful of the stuff, and I am never sick or ailing. I wear a nutmeg round my neck at all times and that serves me excellently. The claims for the wells are quite ill-founded in my opinion, but no doubt they earn a handsome reward for whoever puts them about. It ought to be stopped, don't you agree Harold?'

Harold hesitated, aware that he was being manipulated. Quickly Maria said, 'But I met an old man there who was cured of an ulcer – he told me so. He said that the old King Henry might have found relief there for his leg, if he had but known.'

Ruth snorted. 'If the King's leg could have been cured there, then doubtless his physician would have advised a visit. The fact that he didn't –'

'Mayhap his physician –' began Maria, but Ruth was not accustomed to argument.

'Mayhap nothing!' she snapped. 'I have told you, tis all nonsense. You may take my word on it.' She clapped her hands loudly, and Meg appeared to remove the soup bowls. 'Harold, have you remembered your pill?' she asked briskly, to signal that the subject of Tunbridge Wells was now closed.

Harold looked embarrassed and avoided Maria's eye. 'I have taken it,' he said in a low voice. 'I don't think –'

'Harold has a stone,' said Ruth, 'but hopefully he'll not have need of surgery. He takes one pill in the morning and one before supper. If I didn't remember it, he would forget nine times out of ten.'

Harold laughed nervously. Maria was beginning to dislike Ruth. With a gleam in her eye, she turned to Harold. 'I do believe the spring at Tunbridge Wells is recommended against the stone,' she told him innocently. 'Mayhap you and I could visit it together one day.'

He opened his mouth to answer, but Ruth was quicker.

'Harold doesn't ride these days,' she said. 'He suffers from a shortness of breath –'

Maria clapped her hands delightedly. 'But the water counteracts a shortness of breath,' she said. 'Oh, how fortunate that I have discovered such a place, Harold. You cannot fail to benefit from its healing properties! We must ride out –'

'The weather is far too inclement,' cried Ruth, her voice rising slightly so that Meg, startled, paused in serving the stew and dropped a piece of carrot on to the table. 'Oh, now look what you've done, you careless girl. Fetch a cloth at once and tell cook I'm not at all pleased with your progress.'

The girl withdrew hurriedly, and Ruth glared at Maria and Harold in turn. Maria, ignoring the little drama, turned to Harold, smiling. 'So that is agreed,' she said. 'We will ride to the Wells together as soon as the weather improves, and I shall prove all that I have told you beyond a shadow of a doubt – and I shall have the healthiest husband in all Kent. Do say tis agreed, Harold for I am *so* looking forward to it?'

Touched by her concern for his well-being and overwhelmed by her youthful enthusiasm, Harold was willing to agree to anything. 'I do agree, Maria,' he stammered, quite oblivious of Ruth's meaningful look. 'Indeed, I agree most heartily. We will ride together, as you suggest. That will be most pleasant.'

Meg returned, wiped away the offending carrot and

served three generous helpings of savoury mutton stew. Maria, snatching a quick glance at Ruth, saw that the older woman bit her lip in vexation at the outcome of the conversation, and she suddenly regretted her small victory. It would never do to antagonise Ruth if they were to live together under the same roof. She searched her mind for something to say to heal the small breach, but nothing suitable occurred to her.

Ruth, however, was rapidly recovering from her discomfiture. 'Tomorrow we will look through some accounts,' she told Maria. 'I expect your mother has given you some instructions in household management, but they will doubtless have gone in one ear and out of the other. In my experience, young women are willing enough to apply their evenings to dancing and playing the virginals, but not to more serious matters. Do you sing?'

'A little,' said Maria cautiously.

Harold smiled eagerly. 'I shall hope to hear you sing before too long,' he said, but Ruth immediately broke in with, 'I thought so. And dance, no doubt?'

'A little – but I accompany myself on the lute when I sing.'

'Huh!' cried Ruth triumphantly. 'Singing and dancing. What did I say? Tis all young women are good for these days. What do you understand of provisioning? Or disciplining the servants? Very little, I suspect.'

Maria considered before she spoke. 'My mother was at great pains to teach me all she could,' she said, 'but I am eager to learn more. I shall take it most kindly if you will help me.'

Ruth, taken aback by this sudden humility, could only nod. But Harold raised his glass. 'A charming answer,' he said. 'A toast to the three of us. I am sure we are all going to get along quite splendidly.'

Maria raised her glass and hoped most fervently that he was right.

CHAPTER ELEVEN

The hoped-for rapport did not develop, and as weeks slid into months various minor irritations became major, and two major ones became almost intolerable. At last Maria wrote a long letter to her mother and sent Matt to London to deliver it. In it she outlined her miserable existence at Romney House and begged to be allowed home.

'I envy Matt his glimpse of London,' she wrote, 'and would I were in his shoes. Romney House is so quiet and orderly that I am driven to whisper so as not to disturb its great peace. Romney Marsh is quiet and flat and covered in grazing sheep, which I cannot abide, for they are senseless creatures at best. Ruth rails at me constantly and I cannot please her, no matter what I do; nor does she like Matt, but must always call him Matthew to provoke him, and complains of him to Harold. He is old and weak and dotes upon me like an old woman upon a lap dog.'

In fact, Maria was homesick for the familiar faces of friends and family, and the noisy bustle of London. Ruth did not 'rail at her constantly', merely tried to bring her out of her melancholy mood with brisk words and a variety of tasks intended to occupy her time. But Harold did indeed 'dote' upon her. For the first time in his life he was in love, and felt for Maria a genuine and desperate passion which he was quite unable to hide. Ruth, meanwhile, was forced to stand by helplessly as he struggled unsuccessfully with his emotions and 'made a fool of himself over the girl'.

Matt, too, had his share of problems. The other servants found it difficult to reconcile his special position in Maria's eyes with his simple mind, nor could they speak easily in front of him, for fear he might report their words to Maria. The extent of his 'learning' was negligible: he could not read or write, and all but the simplest financial transactions were quite beyond him. Over twenty years old, he was six foot tall and broad-shouldered, but he had the mind of an adolescent and his boyish tricks and irresponsibility did not readily endear him to his fellows, who found him clumsy, awkward and unpredictable. As a result, Maria was constantly called upon to defend him.

Meg was jealous of him too, for if Maria rode into Ashford or Tenterden, it was Matt who went with her, while she was left behind sulking at the loss of an excursion which should rightfully have been hers. It was not that Maria disliked the maid. She would have taken her along as well as Matt, but the rides out were her only opportunity to give vent to her emotions, and she could hardly air her many grievances about Romney House and its inhabitants if Meg was with them.

Maria's main complaint however, was one she could not divulge even to Matt. Harold's feelings for her aroused a deep distaste which bordered on revulsion. His mere physical presence provoked in her a nervous reaction which was painfully obvious to anyone who saw it; her body grew tense, her face paled, and she flinched visibly if he approached within a yard of her. Her whole being shrank from contact with him, and if her hand accidentally brushed his across the dining table, she would immediately snatch it away. The knowledge of his desire for her dismayed her, and the thought of one day sharing his bed so appalled her that she thrust it from her whenever it entered her mind. Nor could Maria respond to his timid advances or return his endearments. In fact, she could not take one step or make one loving gesture towards the man who was to be her husband. Her wretchedness affected her appetite and her face grew thinner, and Harold watched, anguished, as her vivacity and love of life gave way to a growing despair.

'Where is Matthew?' demanded Ruth, coming upon

Maria by the linen chest. 'No one has seen him today, and Jem needs a hand with the far gate. Tis half off its hinges, but very heavy, and one man alone will never manage it.'

'He's gone to London,' said Maria.

'To London?' Ruth stared at her blankly. 'Matthew has gone to London?'

'Aye.'

'*You* have sent him to London? For what reason, may I ask?'

Maria saw Ruth's expression change from disbelief to incredulity, and finally to anger.

'To fetch my taffeta gown. Now the weather is milder –' It was half the truth. Maria hoped that the sin of omission was less heinous than a downright lie.

'To – to fetch a gown! You sent him all that way to –' She stuttered to a halt, speechless, her chest heaving, and looked at Maria furiously. 'I don't believe you,' she said. 'Tis quite preposterous to send the boy all that way to fetch a gown. There must be another reason.' Maria stared back, her eyes cold, but *her* heart, too, beat uncomfortably fast. 'Answer me, Maria. Is there not another reason?'

Maria remained silent, but now it was fear that held her tongue.

'Maria! Answer me, I say, and I want no lies.'

'I don't lie,' said Maria.

'Then tell me why you sent Matthew to –'

'*Matt! Matt!*' screamed Maria suddenly. 'His name is Matt! I sent him to London to fetch my gown and take a letter to my mother. Is it a sin to write to my mother?'

'Aha! So that's it! A letter to your mother. Saying what?'

'That's for her eyes alone. The letter was a private one from a daughter to her mother.'

Ruth gasped at the girl's sarcastic tone. 'Saying what?' she demanded again. 'Saying that we beat you? Is that what you have said? Saying that we starve you and treat you unkindly? Is that what you tell her? Lies, Maria! All lies!' She was trembling with emotion, white with rage, but before Maria could answer, Harold had entered and now stood aghast. Ruth rounded on him hysterically. 'This girl – this wanton, ungrateful girl – dares to write to her mother saying God knows what – that we use her ill, no doubt.'

'A letter?' stammered Harold.

'Aye, she has sent Matthew with a letter –'

Maria shouted, 'His name is Matt. And why should I not write a letter? Mama desires to know how I am and if I am happy. I am *not* happy. Should I lie and say I am?'

Harold cried, 'Maria! Oh, do not say you are unhappy –'

'But I am!' screamed Maria, quite helpless to stem the flow of her own words. 'I hate it here. I hate you – all of you. I hate this house, this wild, bare, quiet country –' Her voice broke and she began to sob, but as Harold moved towards her she sprang back, hands outstretched to keep him at a distance, saying, 'Don't touch me! Don't come near me! I don't love you and I never will. I want to go home and never see you – any of you – again.' And she threw herself on to the floor, rested her arms on the linen chest, and sobbed despairingly – an ugly sound which tore at Harold's heart and ended Ruth's hysteria.

'Oh, Maria –' he whispered. 'Child – don't weep so, I beg you.' He looked helplessly at Ruth and saw to his horror that tears trembled in her eyes.

'We have not ill-used her,' quavered Ruth. 'We have done all that could be done. She is a wicked girl to pretend otherwise. Tis best she should go –'

'Oh no!' cried Harold. 'Not go – not Maria. Oh, don't say she should go, Ruth, I could not bear it.'

Ruth looked down at Maria, then at her brother. 'Then send the lad away,' she said. 'Send Matthew back to London for good. He and Maria, they make mock of us when they ride out – Oh, don't trouble to deny it, Maria,' she cried, seeing that Maria opened her mouth to speak. 'I've seen them everywhere together, their heads close. I've heard them whisper and laugh. Send the lad back to

London, Harold. He should never have come. I warned you of it, but you paid no heed. He has no place here, Harold. He can't even write his name and is little more than a simpleton –' She broke off, as Maria scrambled to her feet, her eyes blazing.

'So you'd send him back to London, would you?' she said. 'A simpleton, you call him? Simple he may be, but he has a loyal and loving heart and he is worth two of either of you. Aye, we whisper and laugh together – to raise our spirits in this dreary place! So you'd send my lad back to London, would you? Then we shall go – but I'll go also. We came together, Matt and I, and that's the way we'll go.' And she stepped over the discarded linen and ran along the passage and out of sight.

The large leather hold-all stood open on the bed, and Maria rolled up her clothes and squashed them into it, weeping silently as she moved about the room, her tears falling onto the pomander which Harold had made for her the day before and onto the small silver mirror he had brought back for her from a visit to Rye. With fumbling fingers she unfastened the locket he had given her as a welcome gift, and laid it on the pillow. She would take nothing of his. A small prayer-book in a red leather case lay under the pillow. She would leave that also.

'Maria!' Harold was standing in the doorway, white and shaken, but she could not bring herself to look at him.

'Don't ask it,' she whispered. 'Let me go. Just let me go.'

'Maria, dear little Maria, I must ask it,' he pleaded. 'Don't leave me. Your Matt shall stay, indeed he is most welcome. You are both welcome. You will both be loved –'

'Don't!'

'Let us try again, Maria, I beseech you. Can we not try once more? To be friends and live in peace? I need you, Maria –'

'You don't need me. Don't say it. Don't ask it,' she cried, struggling to close the hold-all.

'I love you, Maria. I know you don't love me, but mayhap

you will one day. I won't touch you, Maria. I won't speak of love. Anything you ask I will do gladly, only don't go, Maria.'

She seized the hold-all, and staggering under its weight, tried to carry it to the door of the chamber. Harold stepped forward, arms outstretched sideways to bar her exit.

'No, Maria –'

'Let me pass, I beg you.'

He grasped the bag and tried to take it from her, his eyes haggard and his lips moving soundlessly. Suddenly as they struggled for possession of the bag, he gave a choking cry and released his hold, so that Maria, thrown off balance, stumbled and fell. When she got to her feet she saw Harold doubled up on his knees, clutching his heart.

'Harold! What ails you?' she cried. 'Oh, dear God! Speak to me, if you can.'

He shook his head, gave a loud moan and collapsed sideways on to the floor. His mouth fell open, his eyes stared vacantly into space and his limbs sprawled.

'Oh, sweet Heaven, don't let him die!' she whispered. 'Harold, forgive me.' She watched his chest rise and fall. He was still breathing. Swiftly she snatched up his hand and kissed it. Then she ran from the room, shouting to Ruth for help.

Matt sat on the grass with a small board propped against his knees. The board supported a slate, over which his slate pencil crawled laboriously with many a painful squeak. Harold closed his eyes and tried not to mind them. He lay back on a makeshift bed in the June sunshine, well wrapped in furs. He was too weak to walk and his appetite was still poor, but he thought himself the happiest, most fortunate man in Kent: Maria was still with him.

'Up, down to a point, up and down, that's "M". Down, down and a bit in the middle, and that's an "A". Down and across the top, tis a "T", and one more – that spells MATT, and tis my own name! I've done it again! I've writ my own name.' Proudly he held up the slate for Harold's approval. 'What d'you truly think on it?' he asked anxiously. 'Will Maria be pleased?'

'Aye, she'll be well pleased,' said Harold. 'They are good, neat letters. You've done well, Matt. She'll be back directly and you can show her.'

Matt held the slate at arm's length and studied his work with a satisfied smile, nodding his head as though to affirm Harold's verdict. His eye lit on the 'M' and frowned slightly. 'That "M" is a mite wobbly,' he said. 'Shall I try once more?'

Harold shook his head. 'Script is never perfect,' he told him. 'My own hand leaves much to be desired. But if you are keen to work on, I'll show you another letter – no, I'll show you two more letters and you shall make the name Maria. That will please her.'

'Twill please me, too,' said Matt. 'Twill be a surprise for her.'

'Letter "R"' said Harold, taking the pencil and demonstrating as he spoke. 'It goes down, round and out – so. And "I" is easy. Come, try the "R" and then you can try the whole word.'

Matt took the slate pencil and bent his head industriously, tongue out and brows knit in intense concentration. *Squeak, squeak.* Harold sighed and closed his eyes, letting his mind dwell momentarily on that terrible day when he had thought Maria would leave him. He had never known such panic as when he had found her packing her clothes. His first two wives had died without any sense of agonising loss, yet Maria was different. She had been at Romney House such a short time; they were not even man and wife – indeed, she was little more than a house guest at that time. But somehow she had burned a bright image in the dim recesses of his mind, so that now – now that she was staying – the very sound of her name was enough to set the greyest day alive with colour. *Maria.* The name –

'That's a "R" then, and there's the "I" next to it,' Matt announced gleefully. 'So how do it become MARIA?'

Patiently Harold explained the word, and Matt bent over his task once more. Harold considered him. He was not intelligent and he would never make a scholar, but Harold could not fault him for enthusiasm and persistence. Every day, when Harold sat out in the sun, Matt would appear clutching his slate and smiling in his trusting, child-like way, willing to learn and so eager to please. Maria was right. The lad had many good qualities. He closed his eyes and sighed happily as he raised his favourite vision of Maria holding one of the suck-lambs in her arms, her eyes soft with a new tenderness. One day she would hold a child in her arms – his child. The thought thrilled him exquisitely. After all, he was not too old for fatherhood. This was no more than a temporary weakness – by the time they wed, he would be fit again. A man of his age was not old. Older men had given their wives children. He would put that worry aside for the present and concern himself with regaining his health and vigour. Then – Ah, then! What a handsome couple they would make as they rode into Tenterden together to buy silk for a new gown, or fine hose for her slim young legs . . .

Hearing the swish of a hem brushing the grass, he opened his eyes. But it was Ruth who came, a spoon and bottle in her hands.

'Your medicine, Harold,' she scolded. 'You forgot again. How will it do you good if it remains in the bottle? And the physician will blame *me* if you are not making good progress.'

'But I *am*,' he said, struggling to sit up a little higher.

'And Jem's looking for you, Matthew,' said Ruth. 'He has one of the horses lame and would like you to lead it to the smithy. Are you finished with your lesson?'

Matt hesitated, torn between the two choices. If he stayed he would see Maria and show her his writing. If he went he would enjoy the adventure. He had not been entrusted with such a task before and was vaguely aware that an honour was being conferred on him.

'I'll go,' he said at last, scrambling to his feet. 'I'll write the name again tomorrow, tell her. I'll most likely write it better.' And tossing down the slate, he was off, lumbering across the grass towards the stable.

'He broke a mallet this morning,' said Ruth, sighing. 'He is so clumsy – he doesn't know his own strength. Jem says he hit the fence post such a blow the head snapped off straightways.'

'He means well, dear,' said Harold. 'And he tries to please. See that slate there –'

Ruth glanced down at it with a disparaging sniff. 'But they are all misformed,' she said. 'A child could do better.'

'He *is* a child, Ruth, despite his large frame. You must remember that.'

'Must I, indeed?' she said. 'Now, open your mouth –'

Harold swallowed the medicine and coughed weakly. 'Where is Maria? She said she would join me directly.'

'She is practising on the lute,' said Ruth. 'A song she has written herself to surprise you on your birthday tomorrow.'

'A surprise for my birthday? But, Ruth, you have told me of it now!'

'So I have,' said Ruth. 'How foolish of me. You had best forget I mentioned it.'

Harold reached up and took her hand. 'Ruth, have you still not forgiven her? I have assured you the seizure was not her fault. I had felt unwell earlier. I have explained it to you, but you seem to persist in fixing the blame on Maria.'

'I don't wish to speak of it,' said Ruth. 'You know my feelings.'

'I do,' he said, sighing heavily. 'And I have prayed that God will soften your heart. She is only a child.'

'Oh, Harold, Harold,' she wailed. 'To you they are both children. To me he is a – a clumsy, feckless oaf, and Maria is –'

'No, Ruth,' cried Harold. 'I forbid it. I forbid you to miscall her. She is so dear to me, and one day she will be Mistress of Romney House and my wife. Be patient, I beg you, for my sake.' His face lit up. 'Look, here she comes.'

'And I must be off. I have much to do,' said Ruth quickly, and hurried away, passing Maria halfway across the grass.

'Why, where is Matt?' said Maria. 'He should be practising his letters.'

Harold smiled. 'He has worked hard – see there on the slate. He is gone to the smithy with one of the horses.'

Maria looked at the clumsy letters. 'He needs more practice,' she said, disappointed by his slow progress. 'Do you think he will ever learn? His reading is no better. He stumbles along, guessing at the words if he doesn't know them. I dare not laugh for fear of offending him, but oft times I'm hard put to keep back a smile. He makes such a nonsense of it.'

He indicated the grass beside him and she sat down, resting her head against the furs. He longed to touch her and for a moment his hand hovered over her hair; but then he recalled his rash promise, and without any prompting on her part, he kept his word.

'Don't fret, Maria,' he told her. 'Such things take time. He is still young enough. For such as Matt any progress is a triumph.'

'And what of you today?' she asked, shading her eyes from the sunlight as she turned her head to look at him. 'Ruth says you are feeling much stronger.'

'I am indeed. I shall soon be on my feet again and dancing a jig.'

They both laughed, and it seemed to Harold most pleasant and natural that they should be sitting together in the sunlight. Suddenly, for the first time, he began to believe that the matter of their betrothal could turn out well and that they might indeed marry and live happily as man and wife. He was not a selfish man and he prized Maria's happiness above his own. *Somehow* he would make her happy, would make her love him.

Her eyes caught his, and in her teasing expression he seemed to glimpse the beginning of affection. Impulsively, he took a lock of her hair in his fingers, and although she saw what he did, her expression remained the same. It was the first gesture of love he had made since his illness, and yet Maria did not repulse him. The hair lay across the palm of his hand like a strand of brown silk, and he watched it glimmer in the sunshine. Silently, he uttered a prayer of thanks to God for his infinite mercy and he closed his eyes and let the joy sweep through him.

The following day there was much activity for it was Harold's birthday and despite his protests, Maria was determined they would celebrate the occasion with a grand 'diversion'. A rich cherry cake was made, covered in almond paste and decorated with paste flowers, a special flagon of Madeira was brought up from the cellar, and a new ham was started. Maria prepared the table herself, covering the board with a red cloth topped by a smaller cloth in white damask edged with lace. Rose-heads floated in a shallow silver bowl and strands of honeysuckle ran from one end to the other, twining round the various dishes of nuts and sweetmeats set out upon it. The best goblets were set round and brightly coloured ribbons hung from the candelabra overhead, fluttering gently.

It was nearly eight o'clock before Maria was satisfied and Meg was sent running through the house with a tambourine to signal the start of the entertainment. Jem and Matt carried Harold downstairs and helped him into his chair at the head of the table. When he was settled there, Meg beat a rhythm on the tambourine and Ruth appeared bearing the cake, while everyone clapped and cheered and cried 'Blessings on your birthday'.

Harold smiled with pleasure. 'What a fine cake!'

'Tis Ruth's doing,' said Maria. 'She made it all in one day, and I watched her so that I might learn all her secrets.'

Ruth smiled, pleased by the compliment implicit in Maria's remark. 'But first the ham and beetroot,' she said, and they all sat down, including the servants.

'Oh, the cook,' cried Maria. 'She mustn't miss the fun. Go fetch her, Jem, there's a dear. Today we must be one big family. And afterwards, Harold, you shall have your presents.'

They all laughed and without ceremony began to help themselves to the food and wine, whereupon Meg returned with a message that the cook asked to be excused the feast, as she had a mouthful of troublesome teeth. 'She says she eats but slowly, and only slops, and –' The recital threatened to continue until Ruth said hastily, 'That will do. Sit down and eat your own food before tis all gone. She can come in later and watch the performance.'

There was a great clatter of knives, and much cheerful teasing. Harold was persuaded to try a little of everything and thoroughly enjoyed himself, while Ruth nibbled delicately, frequently wiping her mouth on her handkerchief. Matt chomped steadily saying little and Jem kept them amused with jokes and riddles and made it his task to refill the goblets, so that before long Meg was giggling helplessly and Maria's eyes sparkled vivaciously.

'And now,' said Maria, when all that remained was the cake, 'I have a surprise for you. My Lord Cummins will cut the first slice of cake, but first –' She signalled to Jem and Matt, who rose and went to stand on either side of Harold's chair, while Ruth stared, uncomprehending. They then picked up the chair with Harold still in it, and moved it back three yards. Maria set the cake beside Harold's platter and then moved to him, her hands outstretched.

'– My Lord Cummins will *walk* to the table,' she said, 'with the help of My Lady Maria.'

Ruth rose from her seat, agitated, and Harold looked at Maria in dismay. He had not walked since his seizure.

'Oh, my dear,' he stammered. 'I doubt I can do it. I doubt my legs will –'

'Do it for me,' said Maria softly.

'No,' cried Ruth. 'He is not fit, Maria. Whatever are you about?'

'I think he is,' said Maria quietly.

'But the physician is most insistent –'

'The physician is an old fool,' said Maria, her eyes still on Harold's face. 'Legs grow useless when they are propped in a bed all day. Come, Harold, will you take a few steps – to please me?'

'Do have a try, Master,' cried Meg, and there was a chorus of encouragement from Jem and Matt.

'I don't know –'

'Just a few steps – I will help you,' said Maria. 'And Matt and Jem shall be on either side to see you don't fall.'

Seeing that he still hesitated and fearful of Ruth's influence, she whispered to him, 'Will you be carried to the church on our wedding day? Twill be a poor occasion if you do . . .'

He laughed in spite of himself at the suggestive tone of Maria's voice and the wink she gave him. 'I'll try it,' he said, and a cheer went up. Ruth turned aside, distressed and anxious as Harold took Maria's hands and was slowly pulled to his feet.

'You are like a feather,' Maria told him. 'We must fatten you up, that's for certain, or you'll blow away in the first strong wind when autumn comes! Now, steadily – that's the way – look straight ahead, not down at your feet –'

With an effort, Harold lifted his left leg and pushed it forward. Losing his balance, he swayed, but Jem supported him and eased him upright again. The right foot went forward and again he swayed, but this time it was Matt's turn to help him. He clung to Maria's hands, his eyes on hers, willing himself to do as she asked, willing his feeble legs to move.

'You're doing splendidly,' cried Maria. 'Oh, Ruth, do

look. He *can* do it, you see! Our Harold is on the mend. Now the right, and you have nearly done it. One step more . . . Bravo!'

Quickly Jem and Matt brought the chair forward again and Harold sank down into it with a groan that was half relief, half triumph. Another cheer went up, and Matt threw his cap up into the air where it fell into the candelabra and Meg, being smallest and lightest, was lifted up screeching delightedly to retrieve it. The gaiety was infectious, and even Ruth relaxed into a smile and turned a blind eye to the exuberant behaviour.

'A toast!' cried Maria. 'All glasses raised for the Master's recovery. Why, he will be walking unaided within a few weeks!'

'If I can learn to read, the Master can learn to walk,' cried Matt, and Meg tried to box his ears for his cheek, but couldn't reach. At last the cake was cut and pieces apportioned, and much to Ruth's gratification it was rated 'beyond excellence'. Then it was time to call in the cook for the diversion proper was about to begin.

Maria threw back a last goblet of wine and hurried out on an undisclosed errand, and the cook, whose name was Amy, put in an appearance, declaring that if anything could take her mind from her teeth, twould be a holy miracle sent from God, and she would go to church on Sunday and tell Him so. She was a small, dumpy woman with a gloomy nature, who enjoyed a variety of ailments; but she was also a good cook and sober in her habits, and she and Ruth understood one another.

Jem produced a small kettledrum from its hiding-place in the far corner of the room and beat a tattoo on it. The door opened and in came Maria, dressed as a gipsy in tattered but colourful robes, much adorned with ribbons and scarves. Jem played the tune on his pipes and Meg filled in with the tambourine as Maria swirled into her dance. She had a natural grace and a keen sense of rhythm and she sang as she moved, snapping her fingers in time to the music. Her eyes flashed and her hair fanned out, and as she spun laughing into the climax of her dance every eye was upon her. She ended with a great leap and a shout and then sank into a deep curtsey, while the applause rolled round the darkening Hall.

'Well done, Maria. That was beautiful, beautiful,' cried Harold.

'And now my present to you,' she said, and gave him a tooled leather inkwell.

Ruth gave him a small carved coffer, and Matt had worked day and night to finish a wall ornament made from a slice of tree trunk, sanded and polished, which bore the words 'God rest ye', burned into the wood with a hot poker. ''Twas Maria wrote the letters with a charcoal, but twas I burned them,' he confided, and Harold thanked him with a genuine emotion. The servants had combined their slender resources to buy him a tortoiseshell comb, which they now presented to him. 'Precisely what I need,' he exclaimed – and then it was time for the rest of the entertainment. It was growing dark and Harold was looking tired.

Meg recited a cheerless poem about a lovelorn shepherd; Jem surprised even Maria by walking around the room on stilts, and Matt gave a noisy and inept demonstration of the art of drumming. ''Tis a wonder he doesn't drum right through the skins,' cried Ruth, her hands over her ears; but mercifully Matt's performance was brief.

'The finale,' Maria announced. 'A song I have written and set to music – for Harold.' And she sang softly in a thin, clear voice, accompanying herself on the lute:

'The way through life
Be some days hard
And some ways drear
And some days long
Yet with a love
To light the way
The way be like
A sad sweet song'

Maria kept her eyes down as she sang, so that no one should read there the misery she had hidden all day – ever since the letter from Heron that arrived that morning. In it Hannah had written cheerfully of Melissa and family, all of whom were thriving. The mine, too, was prospering, despite continuing frictions among the men. Hugo sent his kind wishes to her, and as for herself – she was pregnant, but so far had suffered no sickness. She asked Maria to pray for her. Hugo's first child would be born in January.

The cool autumn winds, when they did arrive, did not blow Harold away but did tend to seek out and aggravate the weaknesses in his body. His breathing became laboured and he developed a rough, wheezy sound which worried Maria and Ruth, although the physician insisted it was nothing to be alarmed about. He made slow progress with his walking and although his appetite returned to normal he still failed to gain weight and felt the cold more keenly than he had done before. His eyesight, too, began to deteriorate and he could no longer amuse himself by reading. Spring came and went and there was little improvement in his condition. A slight relapse in March set him back again, and for a while he was depressed and frustrated. His farm would inevitably have suffered, but fortunately he had two good shepherds who maintained the flocks in his absence. Meanwhile, Maria and Ruth were thrown into each other's company more than they might have chosen, but a grudging respect developed between them and a truce was tacitly observed.

Maria helped in every way that she could, and as the year went on she even learned to shear the sheep, a task which she tackled with great enthusiasm and commendable results. Occasionally, she would ride with Ruth to visit Harold's friends who lived in the neighbourhood, or entertain them to supper at Romney House. Harold, meanwhile, was content without the company of others. While he had Maria, he had everything he wanted in the world, and she was never far from his thoughts. If she rode into Tenterden, he imagined her attacked by highway robbers; if she went hawking, then surely she would be thrown from her horse. He waited daily for some disaster to take her from him, and was only really at ease when she sat speaking with him in the evenings, or reading to him from the large Bible. She also learned to play chess and would sit beside the bed until the candle burned low and it was time for bed.

Hannah wrote frequently, inviting her down to Heron to see the new baby, a girl whom they had named Beatrice. Maria always intended to accept the invitation, but at the last minute found an excuse not to go. Whenever she allowed herself to think about it, she grew jealous and unhappy. It seemed now that not only would she never wed Hugo, but she would never wed Harold either. And even if she did, she secretly doubted that their relationship could be other than platonic. She tried to resign herself to remaining childless, but the idea caused her so much anguish she could not accept the finality of it. Yet, the beggar woman had told her she would have a dark-haired son, and Maria clung to that small shred of comfort. She would trust in Fate.

A year later Hannah was expecting Hugo's second child, and England was expecting war with France. Philip of Spain had, as predicted, involved them in his own dispute with Henri II, and on June the seventh, war was declared. By December Calais, for centuries part of England, was under seige and by January 1558 it was in French hands. This crushing blow shocked and angered the people of England, and the Queen's announcement that she was expecting Philip's child was not received with the rapturous enthusiasm for which she had hoped. While Maria lived quietly in Kent, England seethed at the disastrous outcome of the Queen's marriage to Philip, and when the pregnancy proved false, the Queen's reputation sank irretrievably.

Philip had cost England dearly, and would never visit her shores again. Queen Mary lived out her remaining days sick, reviled and alone, and died on the morning of the seventeenth of November. The people of England found new hope as the bells peeled all over London to ring in the young Elizabeth as the country's new Queen.

CHAPTER TWELVE

'They may call Elizabeth "bastard" or what they will,' said Abby, 'but she cannot make a worse Queen than her sister, and might well make a better!'

'She's prettier than Mary,' said Matt.

Melissa laughed. 'You cannot rule a kingdom with a pretty face. Tis what's in here that matters,' she said, tapping her head.

At that moment the waggon, falling into another rut, threw them into a grumbling heap on the floor and they were too busy for a while examining their bumps and bruises to continue the discussion.

'Hugo will insist that Mary was much maligned,' said Melissa, as soon as she was satisfied that no bones were broken. She took her seat again on the wooden bench running along the side of the waggon, which Adam had hired to take the women, with Matt as escort, to the new Queen's coronation.

'Hugo must say so,' said Abby. 'He knows which side his bread is buttered, and had it not –'

'*Was* buttered!' said Abby. 'If he is wise, he'll temper his remarks. They have landed him in trouble before now.'

'At least they cannot exile him again,' said Maria, quick to spring to his defence. 'We are at war with France now.'

'They would simply send him elsewhere,' said Melissa. 'But I think he is older and wiser now.'

'And has a family to consider,' Abby said righteously. Melissa looked at her fondly: she was still the same, in spite of her six children. A little fatter, perhaps, but her nature was as sweet as ever it had been. Life for Abby obviously revolved round her family – a warm, close-knit family, which in turn revolved round the flourishing boatyard which had belonged to the Jarmans for generations. Melissa and Thomas, Hugo and Hannah, Maria and Harold had all been offered hospitality as a base for this trip to London. Harold, Thomas, Hugo and Hannah had all declined for various reasons, and the three women had therefore decided to take Matt with them.

All the children had been left behind after a warning by Abby that the streets of London at such a time were not the safest place to be. She spoke from first-hand experience, for when she and Adam had gone up to watch Queen Mary's funeral procession, there had been drunken men, gangs of prentices, rogues and confidence tricksters everywhere, and the general lawlessness had eventually erupted in a disgraceful scene within the chapel of Westminster Abbey. While the Queen's body lay in its grave, the people had ransacked the chapel, stealing banners, standards and wall-hangings, which were fought over and torn to shreds by souvenir-hunters. Even the effigy of the Queen was destroyed. For allowing such a scandalous thing to happen, the Bishop responsible was placed under house arrest and informed in the strongest terms of Elizabeth's displeasure.

'How is Hugo faring?' asked Maria as casually as she could, taking advantage of the fact that someone else had brought his name into the conversation.

Melissa considered. 'Well, I think – but he's changed.'

'Changed? In what way? I haven't seen him for several years now.'

'Oh, he is more sober and laughs less than he did,' said Melissa. 'I think Margaret was the woman for him, and Hannah cannot quite replace her. He spends more time at the mine than he does at home, but Thomas says who can blame him? Hannah is engrossed with the children, and – Ah! Has this driver supped too well?'

They all braced themselves against the erratic swaying of

the waggon and Matt, lifting the leather curtain, shouted to the driver to go with greater caution or he would reach London with a waggon-load of cripples. Then, pleased with his own audacity, he withdrew his head and said cheerfully, 'I reckon that'll make him mend his ways.'

Just then, however, there was another great lurch, and amid screams of genuine panic, they were all flung into the air as the waggon tilted alarmingly. They heard the driver roar and the horses neigh in fright, as with a last shuddering jolt, the waggon settled on to its side and they crashed painfully on to each other in a welter of sprawling arms and legs.

'Dear God, we've overturned!' cried Melissa.

Confusion reigned for a moment or two as the passengers struggled upright and regarded each other fearfully.

'I am in one piece,' exclaimed Maria, 'though dreadfully shaken. What about you Melissa? Is your eye hurt?'

Melissa nodded, one hand clasped over her left eye. 'Not serious, thank the Lord, but a knee or an elbow went into it. Oh, Abby! You're hurt!'

Matt was helping Abby, who, white and trembling, clutched at her right arm, her lips trembling with shock and pain. As Melissa crawled awkwardly towards her, the window flat, which was now above them, opened and the driver put his head in to stare down in concern. Blood trickled down his face from a gash on his head.

'Are you folks still alive?' he asked shakily. 'I hardly dares look in, and that's the truth!'

'Barely,' cried Abby, 'and no thanks to you! Are you blind, that you cannot see the ruts in this God-forsaken highway?' She eyed him furiously, her pain lending sharpness to her tone. 'My arm is broke, I'm certain, and my sister's eye badly bruised –'

'Tain't the road, ma'am,' he interrupted, 'tis the waggon. The wheel's come off. You can't blame me for that, now.'

Abby groaned and shook her head despairingly. If only

Adam had come with them, she thought, blaming herself for their predicament.

'We certainly can!' snapped Melissa. 'You should keep your vehicle in better repair. Putting folks' lives at risk because –'

'Taint *my* waggon,' he said sullenly. 'I'm only the driver. Tis my Master you should be ranting at.'

'Oh, we will be, don't you fret,' she answered. 'But that won't help us now. What's best to do? If we go outside we shall freeze to death.'

The man suddenly seemed to become aware of the blood dripping down his face and wiped it away with a sweep of his arm. 'The horses be nettled,' he said. 'They was thrown, too, and there's one lame by the look on it.'

'Damnation!' cried Melissa. 'Oh, I'm sorry, Abby, but tis so trying. We cannot be far from London, yet we'll never see the Queen now. And if we had been nearer home we might have – Whatever ails you, Matt? You are pale as a ghost.'

Matt tried to smile, but it was more of a grimace. 'Tis my back,' he said. 'Tis hurting most cruel. I must have twisted it, or else it got a clout and me not even noticed it.'

'Lordy,' said Maria. 'What a pickle we are in. If Harold could see us –!' She left the sentence unfinished, laughing ruefully. They looked at each other woefully and then broke into half-hearted laughter at their dishevelled appearance.

'We must look like a waggon-load of scarecrows,' laughed Melissa. 'But what is to be done? We must think sensibly. We can't stay here, that's for certain. The driver must go for help and bring men to set the waggon right-side up and put the wheel back on.'

'We shall be here for hours,' groaned Abby.

'And poor Matt,' whispered Maria. 'He looks quite green. We cannot let him lift or pull the waggon if his back is hurt.'

The man above them grumbled. 'Well, what's to be done

then? I can't hang in this window much longer. My backside's fair freezing.

Maria giggled, and Melissa and Abby tried to hide their amusement. 'But he's right,' said Maria, 'we're wasting time.' She turned to look up at him. 'Unhitch the horses,' she told him, 'and tie one of them to a tree or post. You had best take the other and ride on towards London. Ask for help as soon as you find someone suitable.' She glanced down for general approval, and they all agreed. 'A smithy would be helpful,' she told him, 'and a physician. But they'll doubtless all be gallivanting off like us to see the coronation.'

'I'll be off then,' said the driver. 'You ladies huddle up close and keep warm. I'll be back soon as I've found help – and remember: taint my fault the wheel's come off, so you mustn't go blaming me. I've a wife and babes to keep, and I've no mind to lose my job.'

'We'll remember,' said Maria. 'And ride with all care. If you fall off and break your neck we shall all be worse off.'

The man withdrew his head. As Maria sat down again, Matt made an effort to get to his feet but gave a loud gasp of agony and sank down, ashen-faced, clutching his back.

'I thought to go with him,' he said sheepishly, 'but my back's that sore I doubt I could sit a horse.'

'You stay here with us,' said Abby. 'You can't leave three women alone on the highway. We must do as he says, huddle together and keep ourselves warm. Thank the Lord we are not on the way home, for if twas dark *and* cold we'd be in a far sorrier state.'

Gingerly, nursing their bruises, they shuffled closer together, and covered themselves with the sheepskins. Matt, at one end, said, 'Tis like four babies in one big bed,' and the three women laughed at the picture they made.

'Well,' said Abby, 'if we are doomed to sit here for hours we can at least amuse ourselves by putting the world to rights and exchanging gossip. That will surely help to pass the time.'

'We are fortunate,' said Melissa, suddenly serious. 'We might well have been more seriously hurt – or even killed. We should thank God for our delivery.'

Guiltily, they all agreed and bowed their heads to give silent thanks.

Then Matt said, 'I be getting hungry.'

Suddenly the same thought was in all their minds: the basket of food they had packed for their lunch.

'Oh, Matt, how clever of you!' cried Maria. 'We can have a picnic while we wait.'

To their relief, the food was not spoiled, although the basket had been flung to the furthermost corner of the waggon and had come to rest upside down. The wine packed in straw had also survived, and they were soon enjoying the cold mutton pasties, rich cherry cake and dried figs that Abby had provided for them. Abby's arm, although very painful, did not appear to be broken and Melissa's sight was unimpaired, although as time went on the swelling developed until her eye became a mere slit.

'Thomas will think I've been fighting,' she giggled.

Now that the worst of their fright was over and they were warm and well-fed, they began to make the best of the situation and their spirits revived.

'Since we cannot see the coronation,' said Melissa, 'Abby shall tell us about Mary's funeral, or else we shall know nothing about either.'

'Or shall I sing a song?' said Matt, who had no interest in the late Queen's funeral. 'No, better still I'll tell you a naughty tale I heard in a ale house. There was this old widow woman –'

'No, Matt,' cried Maria hastily.

'– and she had a he-donkey,' he went on, 'with a big long –'

With a shriek Melissa clapped a hand over his mouth, and they all burst out laughing.

'I was only going to say "tail",' he protested, grinning wickedly.

'They want to hear about the funeral,' said Abby primly, sounding to Melissa exactly like the little girl she had once been, reprimanding their brothers Jeffery and Paul, for some outlandish prank. Those boys were dead now. There was no Jeffery and no Paul – just two sisters, side by side in a broken-down waggon. Melissa reached suddenly for her hand and squeezed it gently.

'Tell us about the funeral,' she said. 'Matt will behave himself.'

'Shall I sing my song then?' he suggested, but Maria said 'Later – if there is time.'

'They took her from St. James's Palace to Westminster,' Abby began, 'and we waited halfway, sat up on a bench which cost Adam a tidy sum for all of us. A scandal, he called it, and ought to be stopped – but that's by the way.' She laughed, a little embarrassed now that she held their entire attention. 'First, a large number of mourners, and then all her servants – hundreds of them – in long black gowns. So sombre, it tore at your heart strings. All two by two, they were, with men riding alongside on horseback to keep the line straight. Then gentlemen mourners and gold banners. And the heralds carrying the Queen's royal ornaments –'

'What's a royal ornament?' asked Matt.

'Crest and mantle and suchlike,' she told him, 'and her sword. Then came the coffin covered with her effigy. So life-like it was, some folks wept to see it, but others – Oh, twas pitiful to hear! They shouted "Treacherous Mary" and "Calais" and "Murderess". There were scuffles in the crowd, and even fighting! The children were frightened and, I confess, I was also.' She sighed. 'Not that I approved of what she did – all those poor wretches burned or hanged – but at a funeral . . . twas so undignified.'

'Matt and I saw Hooper burned,' said Maria with a shudder. 'Twas a cruel sight. I try to forget it, but I can't. The memory haunts me. I can still see him –'

'I can smell the hot flesh,' cried Matt, wide-eyed, but

Melissa cried, 'Oh hush, Matt. Don't, I beg you,' and Abby hastily continued her account.

When she had finished, Matt was allowed to sing his song, and then they talked desultorily about Rochester and the current state of the boat-building industry; about Ladyford, Thomas and Oliver; about Romney House, Harold, Ruth and sheep. Then they talked about Heron and mining, and Matt's reading and writing, and the coronation they were missing; and finally returned to the funeral of Queen Mary.

At last they fell silent.

'We have talked in a circle,' said Maria.

'We have talked for a long time,' said Melissa. 'What has become of our driver? And why has no one come to our aid?'

'I'd best have a look outside,' said Matt, but as soon as he tried to move, the pain in his back returned, and Maria forbade him to go anywhere.

'I'm the only whole person here, she said. 'I'll go outside and see if there is anyone in sight. Don't worry, I shan't go far,' she added, seeing Abby begin to protest. 'I'm still well and the exercise will be good for me.'

She clambered to the end of the waggon and climbed out. Within minutes she was back, with nothing to report.

They looked at each other anxiously. 'He wouldn't just abandon us, would he?' said Melissa.

'He might,' said Matt. 'I reckon so. He had funny eyes, close together. Gone off to see the Queen, most likely. We should all have gone with him.'

'With only two horses?' said Abby sharply.

They began to wonder how they would get home if the driver had indeed abandoned them. It was January and the sun would set early and the air would cool to near freezing. The few sheepskins would be quite insufficient to keep them warm during the night. The alternatives were either to set off walking in the direction of Rochester, which was quite impracticable with Matt's back trouble and all the women wearing the flimsiest of shoes, or to send one of them home on the remaining horse to fetch help, or simply to hope for a passing waggon to carry them all home.

Time passed and no one spoke. Abby's elbow was hurting her, and she had now given up any pretence to the contrary. Matt was ashamed of being incapacitated when, as sole male, he should have been of use to the others, and grew taciturn and despondent. All topics of conversation had been exhausted, and although no one mentioned the risk of attack by highway robbers, it was in all their minds. Their anxiety gave way to unexpressed fear, and as time passed their desperation mounted.

Suddenly Matt cried, 'I hear horses. I swear I do.'

'Horses?'

Abby looked at Melissa and whispered, 'Friend or foe?' and Melissa cried, 'Don't let them see you, Maria, until you see what manner of people they are.' But she was already halfway out.

'Sweet Heaven,' prayed Abby, 'let them come in peace.'

'There are five or more,' Maria informed them. 'They look well-dressed and – Aye, the driver is with them! We're saved – I'm certain on it.'

Her optimism turned out to be justified. The driver had finally overtaken four young men returning to London from pilgrimage who were quite content to miss the coronation. They had then searched for a smithy and having found one, persuaded him after much argument to accompany them.

'So here we are, good people,' said the driver, 'but the smithy here must first be assured of payment, for he says he's missing much passing trade on such a day, and has been dragged out here with no sight of a coin, for I've no money.'

The smith, a burly, sullen-looking man, studied the faces peering out from the disabled waggon.

'You shall have your money,' said Abby. 'I shall pay you myself and then deduct it from the cost of the waggon hire. Here's a florin on account, and have no doubt you shall get the rest. Now, help us down for pity's sake. We are all cold and cramped –'

'– and well pleased to see you,' said Melissa. 'And most grateful to you, young sirs.'

The four men, whose ages ranged from eighteen to twenty-four, introduced themselves and proceeded to assist the passengers to climb down on to the road-side, where they eased their legs and tried to keep warm, shaking their arms and stamping their feet as they watched the rescue operation.

The waggon, although not large, was heavy and cumbersome, and it was some time before the efforts of the six men succeeded in righting it. This achievement was met with loud cheers, and Abby offered the four young men a small payment for their time and trouble. Gallantly they refused it, saying it had been a pleasure to serve three such charming ladies. They then rode back towards London, leaving the smith to replace the wheel and check over the condition of the other three. That took the best part of another hour, but then, at last, the waggon was roadworthy and the time had come to go home.

'What a day!' Melissa lamented when the smith had been paid and they were once more ensconced in the rugs and rolling homewards. 'I hope Elizabeth's reign will prove less disastrous to us than her coronation has done. By now she is Queen and we have missed it all. Yet I swear I shall remember her coronation day for the rest of my life!'

They all cried 'Amen' to that and settled themselves as comfortably as they could for the journey home.

The outcome of their adventure was to prove less serious than had seemed likely. Although Melissa developed a badly discoloured eye, her sight remained unimpaired and Abby's elbow turned out to be sprained, not broken. Matt's back was severely strained and he was not allowed to walk for several weeks, but he revelled in the attention and made a total recovery within the month. As Melissa had predicted, Queen Elizabeth's coronation would be etched on their memories forever.

The second child that Hannah bore Hugo caused her a great deal of discomfort and misery. When April, the eighth month, arrived she was already very weak. The vomiting had persisted, and she could keep down very little food, existing solely on barley water enriched with honey and calvesfoot jelly. She worried constantly in case the unborn baby suffered from this meagre diet, and grew morose and irritable. Beatrice and Allan were more than she could cope with and to her relief, Melissa had visited Heron daily throughout March with Oliver, to care for them all. By April she herself was showing signs of fatigue and Thomas insisted that it was too much for her and that she would ruin her own health if it continued. It was decided that Maria should be approached, and a letter was duly despatched by Hannah.

When Maria read it, her face went white and then flushed in confusion. She bent her head so that Harold should not see the expressions racing across her face – shock, joy, fear and love. Could she do it? she wondered frantically. Could she nurse Hannah and watch her give birth to Hugo's child? They should not ask it – it was too cruel . . . And yet, the urge to see Hugo was as strong as ever, and this was a Heaven-sent opportunity to be near him and share his life, if only for a few weeks.

'What does she say?' Harold asked.

'Oh – she is unwell and asks me if I would care for her until the child arrives. I don't know –'

Harold's face fell, but he tried not to let Maria see the extent of his dismay. 'How long would that be?' he asked.

'A month or more.' Maria could not bring herself to look at him, knowing the expression she would see in the faded blue eyes, and hating to hurt him.

'So long! Twill seem like forever. But you must go.' He smiled faintly. 'You may have to ask her to return the favour one day.'

She nodded absent-mindedly, still uncertain whether to go or stay. It would be Heaven and Hell: to be with him, and yet apart from him. To see him with Beatrice, whom she still had never seen . . .

'She is still sickly, you say,' said Harold. 'I dare say the tumble she took in the waggon brought it about. A woman with child should not –'

'Hannah wasn't with us, dear,' Maria reminded him. 'It was just Melissa, Abby and myself – and Matt, of course.'

His memory was getting worse. And he looked so frail. Was it fair to leave him? Maybe he needed her more than Hannah. Sighing, she re-read the letter aloud for Harold's benefit, and then Ruth came in with an apron-full of fresh herbs. When told of the information she was adamant that Maria should accept. The prospect of having Romney House and Harold to herself appealed immensely. She was devoted to her brother, and it wasn't easy for her to take a secondary role in his affections.

'We shall manage well enough for a few weeks,' she said briskly. ''Tis about time you went down to Heron. I expect Hannah will find you very much changed – very grown up and decorous. Oh, she'll see quite a change, won't she, Harold?'

'She will indeed,' said Harold.

'You'd best take Matthew with you,' Ruth suggested. 'We can manage here with Jem and Meg, not to mention cook. You go and enjoy it. We can manage, can't we, Harold?' She spoke as though the matter were already settled.

'I dare say,' said Harold.

Still Maria dared not look at him. She knew how much he missed her if she so much as rode out for a day's shopping. A month would be an eternity to him. He would pine, she knew, like a dog parted from a beloved master.

'That's that, then,' said Ruth, sensing Maria's doubt and Harold's wretchedness. She scattered the lavender over the floor with an expert flick of her wrist. 'You must send word as soon as possible. Poor Hannah! Such an unhappy time!

But there, the Lord sends these trials to test us. Will you care for the children also?'

'No,' said Maria. 'If I decide to go to Heron, Melissa will take them to live at Ladyford.'

'*If?*' cried Ruth. 'There's no "if" about it, is there, Harold? She must go where she's needed, and your old Ruth will look after you until she comes back.'

At last, when she had bustled out again, Maria looked up at Harold. He reached out a trembling hand for hers, and there were tears glistening in his eyes.

'Dear Harold,' said Maria. 'Don't look so forlorn. I cannot bear to see tears in those kindly eyes. Tell me to stay, and I will do so. I *am* in two minds, whatever Ruth may say. You are my dearest husband-to-be and I cannot leave you if you are unwilling.'

He sighed deeply and shook his head. 'I want you with me every moment of every day and night,' he confessed with a shaky laugh, 'but that is so selfish. I have no right to dominate your young life. The journey and the visit will make a change for you – and you will have some young company for a change. You must go, Maria – but promise you will come back safely.'

'I promise,' she said. 'Romney House is my home and I am happy here.'

Hannah was asleep when Minnie peeped into the room. Nodding with satisfaction she sped off downstairs and out of the main door, half crouching so as not to be spotted. She arrived panting in the stable yard and found Jon raking out the straw from one of the stables.

'*Borrow a horse?*' he repeated. 'No, you cannot borrow a horse. It's more than my life's worth to let you borrow anything from this yard. Jack's got eyes like a hawk's and he'll have my head on a platter!'

'Only for an hour or so,' she wheedled. 'I'd bring it back with all its legs, I swear it.'

He looked at her curiously. 'Why d'you want a horse? – Ah, I see it. You want to ride out and meet them. Well, you can't. And don't give me that look. I'm used to your scowls, so it don't scare me a bit. You can't have a horse and there's no more to be said – and mind your feet, or I'll be raking you next.'

Minnie continued to glower at him, but avoided his rake by leaping onto the open half-door. Suddenly she beamed.

'I'll let you kiss me . . .' she offered. 'If you let me have a horse, I'll let you kiss me twice – once on my lips and once anywhere you please. How's that?'

'*Ugh!* Twould put me off my supper,' he said. 'Now hop it. Jack'll be back and he'll –'

'He won't be back just yet,' said Minnie. 'I've seen him – he's with Beth.' This was a downright lie, but Minnie had few scruples. 'They're a-kissing while you're out here raking out the stable.' She laughed shrilly. 'Seems like you've got the mucky end of the stick.'

He whistled in astonishment, and the rake was suddenly still. 'Him and Beth!' he said. 'Well, damn me.'

'I saw them, but they didn't see me,' Minnie elaborated. 'Poor old Jon – you don't get to kiss nobody, do you?'

He looked at her suspiciously. 'You telling it straight?'

'Cross my heart and fingers. But you can kiss me and all that other if you let me borrow one of the horses.'

'All that other?' he laughed. 'What d'you know about "all that other"? Not much, I'll warrant.'

'I know enough,' said Minnie indignantly. 'I've got eyes in me head, and I spy on people.'

'I warrant you do too, you horrible baggage.'

She smiled in what she hoped was a winning way. 'I'm quite pretty, Jon,' she told him. 'Mayhap you've never looked at me proper.'

'Well, I have – and you're not, so come down off that gate before I wallop you with this rake. You *can't* take one of the horses, and that's flat.' He reached forward to renew raking, but quick as a flash Minnie sprang off the gate and flung her arms round his neck, planting a flurry of kisses on his face. He was caught off-balance and unable to dislodge her arms from his neck, fell over, taking her down with him.

'Oh, Jon!' she shrieked, giggling. 'What are you doing to me? Let go of me!' She flailed her legs and managed to roll Jon over on top of her, her arms still tightly clasped round his neck. They rolled through the soiled straw and she felt the damp of it oozing through the thin stuff of her gown. Still she clung on, until suddenly Jon relaxed his efforts to escape and to her utter amazement was returning her kisses.

Immediately she began to try and wriggle out from beneath him, turning her head away to avoid his lips, but his hand took up a handful of her hair and turned her face towards him. He kissed her slowly, then rolled over and then stood up, brushing his clothes down and keeping his eyes on her face. For a moment she lay breathless and speechless; then she scrambled to her feet, staring at him, confused.

'You – you –' She searched for the right words, but without success.

'So now *I've* had some kisses,' he remarked, trying to hide his own feelings. 'Thank you kindly, ma'am.'

'You – That was a rotten thing –' she began, then stopped again.

'Don't you like kissing, then?' he said. 'I thought you did. You was on about it so.'

'That kiss –' she said. 'I never meant that sort of kiss. You shouldn't have, Jon – leastways, not without asking.'

He shrugged. 'Too late now,' he grinned. 'Did you like it?'

'I'm not saying,' she said. 'I'm not saying unless you lend me one of the horses. Just for half an hour, Jon, to ride out and surprise them. They'd be that astonished to see me riding along.'

'No,' said Jon. 'But you did like it, didn't you?'

A small sigh escaped her and she hesitated.

'You did!' he prompted.

'I don't know,' said Minnie. 'Twas so long ago I've forgotten.' Her small face glowed with suppressed excitement. 'Mayhap you'd better –'

Not waiting for her to finish, he pulled her gently into his arms and kissed her again. As he did so, he opened his eyes and saw the black lashes against her skin and the dark line of her brows. She no longer looked plain, but appealing and somehow vulnerable. He released her slowly, and she said unsteadily, 'I remember now – I did like it.' So he kissed her again, and it was thus left to Beth to welcome Matt and Maria when, tired and hungry, they eventually reached Heron.

Hugo left the accounts he was studying and went out to add his own greetings to those of the servants. The dogs were leaping around the newcomers, their tails wagging ecstatically, and Hugo scolded them.

'Quiet, you monsters! You'll have Maria over. Down, I say! Back!'

They obeyed instantly, backing away and then sitting down in an agony of frustration, their eyes pleading for attention. 'Maria! Is it Maria? My dear child, you are grown so tall and –' He shook his head, amazed at the change in her.

'Two years or more,' said Maria, her eyes absorbed by the familiar face. 'I think I must have grown up.' She laughed lightly and bent to fondle one of the dogs, to hide her nervousness.

'I think so too,' he said.

To Maria's eyes, Hugo looked tired and there was something lacking in his face that disturbed her. When she raised her head again, she searched his eyes to discover what it was. An absence of joy, perhaps? She was not certain. But some of his former arrogance had gone and there was a guardedness about him – almost a cautiousness – that she

213

did not recognise. He kissed her lightly on both cheeks, a habit he had acquired during his stay in France, and held her at arm's length.

'Indeed, you have grown up,' he repeated, and this time Maria was able to laugh more naturally.

'You do not say for better or for worse!'

'Oh, for better.'

'Thank you, Hugo.' She couldn't resist saying his name; it was always a delight to her. 'I'm afraid I don't look my best – I'm tired and dirty, and last night's bedding scratched me to pieces. I think the mattress was stuffed with thistles. But I'm so glad to be here and to see you again.'

He smiled, and then with an effort turned his attention to Beth and Matt, who were already exchanging gossip. Jack unloaded the baggage and Matt took it upstairs while the horses were led away to the stable. Beth was sent into the kitchen to fetch ale and provisions. When Maria and Hugo were alone, neither knew how to break the silence. Then they both spoke together, stopped again and laughed.

'Hannah is so grateful that you could come,' said Hugo. 'She is in very poor health and spirits, and your company will cheer her. She misses the little ones, but Melissa will bring them over each day if the weather permits. Hannah fears to lose touch with them, and yet their constant noise and chatter fatigue her.'

'I will help all I can.'

'We've missed you, Maria. You have been away too long.'

Was she imagining the expression in his eyes?

'I confess it. I'm sorry, Hugo –' She faltered and stopped.

'I understand the reason,' he said softly. 'Now you have a home of your own – and soon a husband of your own. I do most earnestly hope you'll be happy, Maria. You deserve to be.'

Try as she might, she could not answer him, but looked away.

'You haven't seen our little Beatrice yet,' he said, and seeing that she remained silent, added, 'She's a roly-poly of a child with her mother's colouring. We're hoping for another son this time.'

'And Allan, bless him?'

'Very robust. A true boy,' said Hugo proudly. 'Never happy unless I wrestle with him, toss him in the air or chase him.'

Maria nodded as they walked together up the stairs. 'I thought Minnie might be here,' she said. 'Is she at Ladyford?'

'No, here,' said Hugo, puzzled, 'but where I can't say. We couldn't keep her away. I thought she would trample us all in her haste to greet you. No doubt she'll be along presently to tire you with her chatter.'

Matt passed them at the chamber door. 'The bags is all in there,' he told her, 'and I'm to go down to the kitchen for a bite to eat – Beth's orders, if tis agreeable with you.'

Maria nodded and he rushed away, taking the stairs two at a time in his eagerness to eat.

'He has been a most conscientious escort,' said Maria. 'He's strong and willing –'

'And devoted to you,' added Hugo. 'He's most fortunate.'

By this time they were both standing inside the bedchamber with its newly panelled walls and the familiar four-poster bed.

'New drapes, you see,' he said. 'We had the upholsterer in a few months before Hannah knew she was with child again. And the walls. It must be two years ago. You will find the room warmer for them.'

'And very handsome,' said Maria, crossing to the window and looking down. 'It's as beautiful as ever,' she said. 'Heron is like a second home to me – it's somehow comfortable, like an old, favourite gown.'

But he seemed not to have heard the remark, for when she turned he was staring at her intently. 'Are you happy?'

he asked abruptly. 'Tis no business of mine, I know but –'
He shrugged. 'I would like to think you are.'

Maria looked at him and tried to reply that, indeed, she
was. But she could not say it. If anyone had asked her that
question a week ago she would have answered quite readily
in the affirmative. Now she could say nothing. Her feelings
for him were suddenly so acute that she could scarcely
breathe, and her thoughts whirled with a fierce excitement,
flooding her body with sensations which had lain dormant
for the past two years. All she could do was stare into his
eyes and shake her head, as though her lack of words
somehow lessened the betrayal.

For a moment neither spoke. Maria's conscious mind
told her she should never have come, should never have
placed herself in this dangerous situation. And yet she
rejoiced to be here, near him once more.

'Tell me –' she began, not knowing how to follow it, but
desperate to break the tension before she was forced to fly
helpless into his arms. 'Tell me about – the mine. Aye, the
mine.'

He looked at her, uncomprehending, then took his lead
from her. 'The mine,' he said, nodding. 'It prospers satis-
factorily – considering.' Now it was her turn to nod. He
went on. 'The new Jupiter drift is yielding as much as we
hoped, but we've reached a division in the vein – and that's
disappointing. We might have to look elsewhere. We've
made the link with the Venus shaft. Nearly three fathoms,
that one, but there were problems – the cost was too high.'
He spoke mechanically, and she listened without understanding – in fact, without hearing anything except the
beating of her own heart, as she struggled to keep her
composure amid the whirlpool of her emotions.

'Two men died recently. One slipped on the ladder
coming up from night shift. The icy weather had made it
treacherous. He was a good man – he fell into the sump at
the bottom of the shaft and was drowned. He left a widow
and seven children.'

'That's terrible!' She was jerked into awareness by the tragedy. 'And the other man?'

'Old Dick Leggatt died of the dust in his lungs. His face had turned quite grey, and he could hardly breathe. Couldn't lie down, not even to sleep. He slept sitting upright against the wall. I saw him two days before he died. It was horrible. We must find a way to keep down the dust . . . I asked you if you were happy, Maria?'

'Harold loves me. He's kind and gentle. Ruth is competent and a good teacher. I'm learning a great deal. Poor Harold is almost bed-ridden, though.'

'Will he ever recover?'

'He believes he will, but the physician says there is little hope. But he loves me, and I have a good home, servants, Matt is with me —'

'Maria —'

She saw the sudden irony of the moment. Hugo was looking at her just as she had always hoped he would, and now she was finally old enough to marry. But it was too late: he was married to Hannah, and she must wed Harold. He took a step towards her, but she shook her head in despair.

If you touch me, Hugo, I shall be lost! she thought. Her eyes travelled slowly round the room, as though searching for strength. 'So the mine prospers,' she said.

'Aye.'

'Good. That's good news. The accidents — you must not blame yourself.'

'No.'

'And the quality of the ore? Is that still high?'

He nodded. 'The oblique vein is very high and smelts cleanly.'

'Hugo, you ask if *I* am happy,' she said, 'but what of you? Are you happy? You look so strangely I cannot find the word for it. Tell me you are happy.'

'Fortunate,' he said carefully. 'I have Heron and the children, and Hannah is a good wife. I am fortunate.'

'Fortunate is not happy,' she said. 'A sheep with a rich

pasture is fortunate. A beggar with a crust of bread is fortunate.'

His smile was sad. 'My funny little Maria. We are both fortunate compared with many others.'

'And less fortunate compared with some – those that have love.' Her voice ended in a whisper and he had to lean forward to catch the words. With a cry Maria turned and walked quickly to the far side of the room, putting a distance between them.

'I must wash, and change my clothes,' she said, her voice unnaturally bright. 'I'm hungry and thirsty, and no doubt Beth –'

There was a shout of '*Maria!*' from below, and Minnie came clattering up the stairs and flew into the room, straight into Maria's arms. They hugged each other while Hugo looked on.

'I'll leave you two to your gossiping,' he said, and with a last intent look at Maria over Minnie's unsuspecting head, he strode out of the chamber and the door closed behind him.

CHAPTER THIRTEEN

The bedchamber was dark, for Maria had partially closed
the shutters to keep out the bright sunlight. The door was
propped wide open and Hannah was lying on the bed,
fanning herself with a large lily leaf which Allan had
brought her earlier. Her long hair had been woven in two
plaits, which Maria was now trying to fix on top of her head.

'Is that cooler?' she asked.

Hannah nodded. Her face gleamed with perspiration and
she wore only a long, loose shift. A few more weeks and she
would give birth to her third child, but now her swollen
body lay on top of the coverlet. Her small, neat feet were
bare, and she wriggled her toes.

'Simon used to be so proud of my feet,' she told Maria.
'He liked to stroke them. Like little birds' wings – he used
to say that one day I'd flap them and fly away.' She sighed.
'Instead he was the one that flew away. And now no one pets
these poor little feet. They are quite neglected. Oh, Simon!'
Tears brimmed in her eyes and she blinked rapidly. Maria
tied a ribbon through the braids to bind them together and
nodded approvingly.

'There!' she said. 'With your hair off your face you will
feel better, and as for your feet, they are truly worthy of
note. Draw Hugo's attention to them and he'll admire them
for you.'

'No,' said Hannah. 'I'm not admirable in his eyes, I know
that. When we were first wed, he thought only of his poor
dead Margaret. How could I compare with a beloved
ghost?'

'You mustn't think that way,' Maria reproved her.

'But tis the truth, no more, no less. How can anyone blame him for being loyal to the woman he loved? I'm equally at fault,' she sighed. 'Simon was *my* dear one . . .'

Two tears trickled down her cheeks, and Maria brushed them away with a small towel. 'The physician has told you not to dwell on such things,' she said. 'The past is over, and you mustn't let it spoil the present. Now then, not one more tear, d'you hear me, Mistress Hannah? Think of that poor babe inside you. He doesn't deserve a tearful mother. You must banish all these gloomy thoughts for his sake as well as your own.'

'I'm hot,' said Hannah, ignoring Maria's homily. 'Will you open the shutters again? Mayhap the air will blow through the room then.'

'There *is* no air,' said Maria, but she opened the shutters just the same, filling the room with beams of bright sunlight in which motes of dust danced giddily, stirred up by the swish of Maria's gown. She looked round to see if the open shutters had made her more comfortable, but Hannah's eyes were shut, and she was fanning again. Suddenly, with a faint snap, the main stem of the leaf broke. With a gesture of irritation, Hannah threw it onto the bed and placed her left hand over her abdomen.

'Stop kicking, little man,' she said. 'I sometimes fancy I have twins in here, for tis more like fighting than kicking. Or mayʰap a wrestling match.'

'Are you comfortable now?' asked Maria. 'If so, I'll go downstairs and –'

'No –' Her eyes snapped open. 'Don't go. I have something to ask you. Something that has bothered me for some time now. Will you answer me truly, Maria?'

Maria felt herself go hot and cold, but she could only nod. She longed to answer 'No', or tell Hannah to withhold the inevitable question, for she was convinced her love for Hugo was written large in her eyes and it was only a matter of time before everyone read it there. As a child she had boasted often of her passion for him and had even told Hugo himself. But now she was ashamed to have it known that she was helpless to put him out of her mind. She did not want their pity.

'Tis Allan,' said Hannah. 'Is he – do you think he is –'

'Allan?' Maria was taken aback. It was *not* the question she had expected after all.

Hannah studied her fingers. 'Do you think him strange or wild at all? Different in any way?'

Maria stared at her in surprise. 'Different? I don't understand.'

Hannah frowned. 'Mayhap I'm imagining it,' she said slowly. 'I hope I am. Melissa can see no difference, but now and then I think – his temper is so strong and sometimes his eyes burn like spots of fire. His tantrums are so fierce, he seems to lose control of himself. I've never seen such anger in a child before. It frightens me, Maria.' She sat up, the heat and discomfort forgotten. 'Have you seen it, Maria, this wildness?'

'No, Hannah, I haven't. But even if he is as you say, he will learn to master his rage when he is older – they all do. Give him time, he is only young.'

'No – tis more than the rages,' said Hannah, still averting her eyes. 'I see sometimes a look in his eyes as though he is wise beyond his years. *Too* wise.'

Maria thought hard. 'I've only seen Allan briefly each day,' she said, 'when Melissa brings them to see you. But I've noticed nothing untoward.'

'The truth is,' blurted out Hannah, 'I can't rid my mind of the Gillises. His grandmother, Isobel, was daughter to a witch! Did you know that, Maria? Allan has Gillis blood in him, you see, and that frightens me. Suppose – suppose he had Isobel's madness in his blood, or the witchwoman's evil! I'm so fearful for him! Now that I do not sleep well of nights, I lie here in the darkness and the idea torments me.'

She began to sob, weakly, making no effort to control her tears, abandoning herself to despair. Maria sat beside her and pulled her close.

221

'Weep away,' she said gently. 'Let all the tears out, all of them, that's the way. Cry away your fears, Hannah, for I swear to you, tis your condition has put this dreadful idea into your head. There is no truth in it, none at all. He is a normal boy with a temper, that's all. Believe me, you are fretting to no purpose and will make yourself ill just when you should be at your strongest and best . . . That's better. Now listen to me, Hannah. Listen calmly. Your time is nearly due. You are not so sickly and you eat better. These are all good omens that your child will be born safely and that all will be well. Shut out such morbid thoughts and think only of your new little son. Your Allan is a bonny child – you have nothing to fear.' She held Hannah away from her and wiped her face gently. 'Now I shall bring up the cards, and we will play whatever you choose, and you will have no time to think on those other matters.'

But in spite of these cheerful words, she was full of misgivings for the little boy as she hurried out of the room. Only the previous day Minnie had spoken to her along the same lines. Please God, let it not be so! she prayed. She determined to burn a candle for him in the church on Sunday, and ask God's special blessing upon him. On the way back upstairs with the cards in her hand, she changed her mind and decided she would burn two.

Wash day started early at Ladyford. Minnie rose as soon as it was light, and went down to the kitchen to light the fire, topping handfuls of dry leaves and straw with kindling wood and standing a selection of larger pieces alongside. Once the fire was well alight, she filled three large iron pots with water and hung them above the flames.

'Now don't you go out the moment my back's turned,' she admonished, and ran back upstairs to give her teeth, face and hands a hasty wash. She moved quietly, for Melissa had warned her on no account to waken the three children so early. Then, she roused Melissa and went back down-

222

stairs again to find the fire roaring healthily. Dipping a finger into the water, she found it already warm.

In the large tub, the badly-soiled clothes were steeping in an overnight solution of water and mild soap, and she rolled up her sleeves and set about them, giving the bad marks a vigorous rubbing in preparation for the main wash. Still only half awake, she sighed at the prospect ahead – an all-day wash session had little appeal in the summer, and she would have much prefered to be at Heron with Maria and Hannah in the hope that this time she would be allowed to share in the excitement of the delivery. The baby was two days late already, and the strain was beginning to tell in occasional bursts of irritation on Maria's part and tears from Hannah.

Melissa appeared, a large apron round her waist, and with a brief smile began to sort through the dry stuff in the basket – the children's woollen clothes, which had to be washed carefully by hand, the bedding, the towels, the delicate lace collars, cuffs and sleeves, Thomas's shirts, and plenty more. It would take the best part of the day. Melissa fervently hoped that Hannah's child would not choose today to make his entry into the world. They had delayed the wash a week already and it could wait no longer.

The two women worked on in silence, each thinking her own thoughts, for it was too early in the day for conversation. Melissa mentally checked and rechecked the preparations for the baby's delivery, mortally afraid of overlooking something vital: linens, towels, bowls, vinegar, crib, ointments, soothing draughts, shears, mirror, the birthing stool – she nodded to herself, reassured. Minnie, meanwhile, thought of Jon's mouth and his kisses and the feel of his fingers on her nipples, wondering how long it would be before she knew all his body, and he hers. Her stolen moments alone with him, though few and far between, gave her days a new sparkle and filled her nights with imaginings. Then she thought about Maria and wondered whether she had known all of a man – she thought it unlikely. What if she, Minnie, should discover it all first! She sighed rapturously at the idea and then, not looking where she was stepping, tripped and spilled soapy water into her shoe.

'Hell's blood!' she muttered, then glanced anxiously at Melissa to see if she had heard, for Melissa frowned on cursing, for fear of Oliver learning bad ways. But no – her slip had gone unnoticed and she bent down thankfully to mop her foot.

An hour later Thomas was up and about upstairs, and soon the children would waken. Now the kitchen was full of steam, piles of wet and dry laundry, bowls, baskets, tongs and soap. The monthly wash at Ladyford was well under way.

The orchard was full of sunlight filtering through the leaves and speckling the two beehives which were Thomas's pride and joy. Opposite one of the hives Allan stood watching. He was naked and his eyes were sleepy, but he was not sleep-walking. He had woken early and wandered out of the house and now stood in the orchard, enjoying the warm sun against his skin and the sensual feel of the grass under his feet. Outside the hive, a number of bees hummed and hovered to alert their queen. The boy stood motionless as singly, then in twos and threes, the bees began to come out of the hive, not flying, but crawling onto the platform and over the outside of the straw skep. They came in tens and then in hundreds, piled up in folds like glossy brown fur, thousand upon thousands of bees preparing to swarm.

Allan watched, absorbed, as the bees' excitement mounted and they began to fly round and round the hive in ever-increasing numbers. The sound of their flight was ominous, almost threatening, until suddenly they were all on the wing, an amorphous grey cloud following their queen. Allan stood entranced as one or two bees settled inquisitively on his bare shoulders and back and others ventured into his hair. He paid them little heed, his eyes fixed on the drama that was being played out before him, as the whirling cloud of bees began to condense into a darker mass and they swooped in the air, constantly changing direction.

As Melissa came into the orchard in search of him, she saw them pass right over Allan and she stood rooted to the spot in horror, a scream rising in her throat at the sight of the child standing like a statue, wreathed in a dark, vaporous mass of bees. She choked back the scream, terrified to cry out lest he make a sudden movement and alarm the swarm, and was forced to stand helplessly by. But Allan showed no fear as their furry bodies explored him, their tiny feet whispering over his skin from his eyes, now closed, to his toes, which curled upwards in a kind of ecstasy. Hannah's words came back to Melissa and, fascinated, she noted the expression on his face. His head was tilted back very slightly and the corners of his mouth were raised in the suggestion of a smile. Incredulously, she saw that he was completely at one with them.

Then the queen bee swung upwards and the rest of them lifted after her. She searched the air briefly, then settled on the lower branch of one of the apple trees; more followed. Melissa ventured nearer, and she and Allan watched breathlessly as the clustering bees settled around their queen, until the living black mass hung on the tree like a dark pumpkin. Without speaking, Melissa took hold of Allan's hand and he gave a long shuddering sigh as he prepared to leave them.

'They will nest there now for a day or so,' Melissa whispered. 'We'll go and tell Thomas and he will hive them later. Are you coming back to the house with me, little one?'

He nodded slowly and trotted along beside her, his expression serious. Suddenly, as they reached the front step, he turned a radiant face up to Melissa and said simply, 'Bees!'

When Melissa recounted the story to Maria later in the day they both became anxious, and when they went separately to their beds that night, they crossed themselves.

Early the following morning, Hannah started her labour pains; but by late afternoon they had stopped again. After several hours sleep she woke once more, her hands clutching her abdomen, and declared that the pains were back now, and much stronger. This time there was plenty of time to send for the midwife. Hannah's labour lasted nearly three days and culminated in the painful, difficult birth of a seven-pound boy who was born dead.

The shock and the grief that she then experienced gave way to a fever, and the whole of Heron went on tiptoe, whispering.

The physician's face was grave. 'We can pray for her,' he told Hugo. 'If the stars are propitious there may be some hope, but her strength is failing rapidly and she has no will to fight for life. The loss of her child has taken it away. I will bleed her again tomorrow if there is no improvement, but in the meantime make haste and send for those prescriptions I have given you. They will refresh her mind and purge away morbid thoughts.'

Hugo made sure his instructions were carried out to the letter, but still Hannah did not improve. However, as her condition did not deteriorate either, everyone became more hopeful that she would eventually recover.

Allan and Beatrice remained at Ladyford. Hugo, heartbroken at the death of his first son, threw himself into his work at the mine and was rarely seen, and it was left to Maria to attend Hannah and nurse her slowly back to health. The fever at last subsided, but Hannah was left feeling weak and wretched. Her round face was haggard, and there were dark circles under her eyes. She had lost all interest in herself or those around her, and even the sight of Beatrice and Allan aroused no enthusiasm in her. She resisted fretfully whenever Maria made to wash her or brush her hair, and turned her head away when food was offered to her. She could not be persuaded to read or sew and conversation with her was a very one-sided affair. When Hugo visited her she frequently wept, apologising over and over again for the death of their little boy, as though she was personally responsible for it. Nothing he said reassured her, and his visits seemed to cause her such anguish that he gradually shortened them to no more than a brief kiss and a greeting. As the weeks dragged on, still there was no change for the better. Maria was powerless to mend matters.

One day a messenger arrived with a brief letter from Ruth, who wrote that Harold had had a minor setback – 'a recurrence of his ailment' – and that he fretted daily for Maria's return. She reminded Maria that she had been at Heron for more than six weeks now and wished to know when she planned to return. Maria went through it carefully a second time, trying to read between the lines of neat, regular script. That Harold fretted for her she had no doubt; but could Harold's condition be worse than Ruth implied? It occurred to her that even if it was, Ruth would possibly still prefer to have the sole nursing of him and therefore might minimise the gravity of his condition when writing to Maria. But then why write at all? Or maybe Harold was well enough, but Ruth resented Maria's extended stay at Heron, feeling that her duty lay at Romney House . . . The wording of the letter was unemotional, almost indifferent, and after much deliberation Maria found it impossible to gain any insight into the writer's mind or motive for writing. She decided to say nothing to Hannah until she had spoken to Hugo on the matter.

That afternoon, Hannah slept, while outside the sun shone brilliantly. On an impulse Maria decided to ride down to the mine and speak there with Hugo. She had been tied to the house for weeks and the prospect of a ride and a brief taste of freedom appealed to her. Jon saddled the sorrel for her and helped her mount. She had left word with Beth that she had ridden out 'to blow away the cobwebs', so that no one would worry if she was not back too promptly.

As Maria walked the horse out of the grounds she looked back at the house, sprawling among its grass and trees, the windows reflecting the sunlight under its mellowed thatch, and a deep sigh escaped her. She followed the line of the roof ridge to the tall chimneys and down the pale walls to the windows with their wooden shutters and the large, stout door. It was a sizeable house, but not modern, and with no pretensions to grandeur: just a large, comfortable home. And that was how it always felt to Maria – home. Why, she did not know, but ever since she could remember, her arrivals at Heron had filled her with contentment and her departures with sorrow. It was this which caused her to sigh so painfully. The prospect of leaving it yet again brought a feeling of desolation that she never experienced anywhere else. And yet it had never been a true home to her, and never would.

She sighed again, turned the horse abruptly, urged it into a trot, then a canter, and her spirits rose as she felt the hooves pounding beneath her and the air lifting her hair and streaming it out behind her. With a sensation of real freedom at last, she felt suddenly that she could ride and ride, never stopping, never losing her freedom, until she and the horse fell exhausted and sank into oblivion. Then she laughed at herself for such foolishness. Of course she had responsibilities like everyone else, and she had to attend to them. But as she rode, her spirit soared rebelliously and the idea persisted. Finally she gave herself up to the luxury of her imagination and rode over the moor, free as air, free as the lark that rose suddenly, trilling, from the roadside at her approach, free as the coney that darted away, zigzagging erratically ahead of the horse, its white bob-tail signalling danger to its fellows even as it fled.

At last she turned off the highway and slowed the horse to a walk, the better to appreciate the contours of the landscape. Dartmoor unrolled before her, purple with heather and splashed with yellow gorse. Shading her eyes from the sun, she drank in the beauty which surrounded Heron as the sea wraps an island. In the winter it looked stark and bare with a harshness that was awesome; now, softened by the colours of the flowering plants, it lay hazy under a blue sky. A few stunted, wind-bowed trees stood out from the smooth carpet of moss and heather that clung tenaciously to the meagre soil. Here and there large boulders jutted out and the skyline was broken by granite escarpments, rich with precious ores hidden within the rock, not yet stolen from it by the labour of men. She saw, too, the darker patches where tall green reeds betrayed the presence of the ever-deadly mires and bogs, where a horse or cow could vanish in less time than it takes to tell, with only a few bubbles and a swirl of peaty water to mark the spot. Men, too, she thought, and shuddered suddenly.

In the far distance she saw a small herd of grazing animals, deer perhaps, or the small but sturdy ponies that roamed wild across the moor. The sun warmed her, and her taut nerves began to relax as she rode slowly on, watching butterflies and bees, her ears and eyes sharpened to a new awareness, so that even the crushing of lichens under the horse's hooves was audible to her. The whole of the moor, it seemed, was hers alone. Briefly, rarely, Maria was at peace with herself and the world – and God.

At the mine, it was a different story. The morning shift was coming up and the afternoon shift preparing to go down. The minehead was full of tinners, and everywhere was bustle and activity.

Maria stood to one side, fascinated, watching unremarked by the queue of men waiting at the small stone building that served as a store for all their equipment, where the men coming off duty handed in their picks and shovels and surrendered the remaining oil in their lamps.

The foreman checked each man, ticking the names on a list and making various entries in his big ledger. The men's faces and hands were black, but their legs and feet were protected by leather boots and they wore caps over their hair. Some coughed painfully from the dust in their lungs, others tried to straighten bent and aching limbs, some spat. A few grumbled, some whistled, the rest remained silent, wearily waiting to go home to a well-earned rest. Over the shaft itself, two men toiled at a windlass, winching up the men one at a time in a large leather bucket, which scraped and swung precariously on the end of a rope.

Further over still, small wooden trucks stood filled with lumps of ore which would be sorted and graded later by women in another hut. Some of these now came out of the hut, shouting and waving their farewells and preparing to go home. A few waited for their menfolk; the rest went off in groups of two or three, chattering desultorily with their friends. One carried a small child slung across her back in a wicker pannier, and Maria watched with a kind of envy as a man joined her, put his arm round her, and kissed the child. These women, she thought, marry whom they please and their children are love children. Maria Lessor must wed poor, kindly Harold and never have a child.

When the last of the morning shift had been brought up, the waiting line of men moved forward. Each was allotted a certain task and issued with the necessary tools for the job. His lamp was filled, and he moved over the shafthead and climbed into the bucket with the practised agility of years. Then he was lowered out of sight, and the next man moved up to take his place.

Maria waited patiently, reluctant to disrupt them at such a busy time, but when the last man had gone down, and the bells sounded above and below ground to signal the start of the afternoon shift, she dismounted and leading her horse, went towards the store to enquire after Hugo's whereabouts and ask whether she could speak with him.

'He's coming up shortly,' the foreman told her, a large, powerfully built man with a heavily pock-marked face. 'He went down to inspect the new drainage.'

'Does he often go below ground?' Maria asked.

The man shrugged. 'Now and then. It's good for the men to see the Master sharing the hazards now and again – else they think that all he does is spend the profits.' He looked at her curiously. 'Not bad news, is it?'

'No, but I have to talk with him.'

'How's his wife, poor soul?' he asked. 'They say she might never be right again, losing her babe like that. That's hard on a woman, that is. My old girl lost three in a row that way. Never breathed, poor little souls. Never even opened their eyes to the light of day.'

'And did your wife survive?'

'Aye, she did, but she was different after. Kind of mournful. Then she died of a fever in childbed with our seventh. Seven boys we had, three dead, four lived. Now the oldest of them's dead.' He rubbed his eyes tiredly with a huge forearm. 'Choked to death on a chunk of bone nigh on two year ago. Good job my old girl never lived to see it. Worshipped that one, she did. He was sickly, see, with his chest. Couldn't breathe, even as a little 'un.' He gave a vivid demonstration, sucking in breath in loud, rasping gasps, and Maria nodded sympathetically. 'The other three's down the mine. Ah, here he comes,' he said, as the windlass creaked and Hugo was brought up to the light once more. He looked drawn and he gave Maria only the barest nod, before addressing himself to the foreman.

'Something must be done about it,' he said, and Maria noticed a ring of authority in his voice that she had not heard before. 'There's standing water in four places and tis sluggish in others. You say that Dawlish is responsible? The new man?'

'Aye. He reckoned he was up to it and spoke knowingly at the time, but I don't rate him very high. All mouth, that one.'

'Give him his money and get rid of him,' said Hugo brusquely. 'Who else have you got?'

'None I'd trust.'

'And when is Franks like to return?'

'Not for a week or more. He can scarcely stand, so his old girl says.'

'Then deal with it yourself at the weekend. I've set another man on baling. This seepage is a damnable nuisance. I'll be glad if this drift *is* run out. We'd be better to sink a new shaft if the oblique stringer proves a sound one.' He glanced towards Maria and allowed himself a brief smile. 'I'm not good company,' he said, 'but come into the store. Ted is going home now. Oh –' He turned back to the foreman. 'Any move from our awkward neighbours?'

'Another letter, threatening court action this time. Tis on your desk.'

'I'll read it,' he said, sighing heavily. Motioning Maria to join him, he ducked his head and went into the storeroom which doubled as an office.

Maria sat herself down on the end of a bench, having first wiped a portion clear of dust. 'I was surprised to see so many people about,' she said. 'As I came across the moor it seemed deserted.'

'They come from miles around,' said Hugo, picking up a letter and scanning it quickly. A frown creased his face.

'What is their complaint?' asked Maria with genuine interest.

'The usual,' he said heavily. 'Our washings sully the river. They say we're killing the fish.'

'Your washings?'

He explained quickly. 'Forgive me – we take out the ore and it has to be crushed and washed in strakes to separate the grains of tin ore from the soil and other deposits. All the fine-ground rock and sand is carried back into the river and downstream. They claim that we pollute the water and silt up the river farther downstream. Add to that lazy tinners – a few, not most – a man who cannot dig a drainage run, and high wages. I sometimes think the tin would be best left in the ground.'

Maria laughed gently. 'You don't mean that.'

'Don't I?' He looked at her, and suddenly she glimpsed the depth of his present despair.

'Forgive me,' she said. 'I do understand how tis with you.'

'And now poor Hannah!'

Seeing him look so utterly defeated, Maria felt her heart go out to him and longed to take him in her arms and comfort him. 'I think Hannah is on the mend,' she said with as much conviction as she could muster. 'She took a little gruel yesterday and this morning ate an egg beaten in wine.'

'You are so good with her,' he said. 'What would I do without you?' He sensed her sudden stillness and looked at her sharply. 'What is it?'

She shook her head, finding it so difficult to put into words the news that she must leave Heron.

'Maria? Dear God – Harold has written. Is that it? He wants you with him. Aye, I see it in your face.' He sat down heavily at the table, facing her, and put his head in his hands. 'I dreaded it, but of course you must go. You owe us no allegiance. Harold is your betrothed.'

He said the last four words bitterly, as though they were hurtful to him, and Maria's heart raced uncomfortably.

'Hugo, I'm sorry,' she stammered. ''Tis from Ruth, the letter. Harold is unwell. He is worse and asks for me.'

He nodded.

'I must go,' she faltered.

'Go then!'

She stared at the dark, bowed head, hurt by his tone, and stood up, agitatedly. 'I truly am sorry,' she said in a low voice. 'I swear I would rather stay. I love Heron,' she added defensively.

'You love Heron.'

'Aye.'

She crossed to him and put a hand on his shoulder, but he shook it off. 'Go then,' he said again and raising his head, looked round at her. 'Go home to Harold, Maria. I think tis best – for him, for you, for all of us.'

'Hugo?'

'Except for Hannah, of course,' he said. ''Tis hardly best for her. But you have commitments elsewhere, and we must manage without you. My sympathies are with Harold. If I

233

were in his shoes –' his tone was suddenly softer, '– I would want you with me.'

She could not answer him, although she knew he waited for her reply.

'Maria –' His expression changed once more. 'Forgive me. You must go, of course. We will hire a woman from Ashburton. She will act under the physician's instructions. Hannah will be well cared for. I shouldn't have spoken so. We are in your debt already, and –'

'No, Hugo. You owe me nothing. I have been glad to help. I don't want to go.'

'Poor Maria,' he said. 'What a dilemma. Harold wants you to go, and Hannah wants you to stay.' He took her hands in his. 'And what does Maria want to do?' he asked, the intense expression in his dark eyes belying the lightness of his words.

Suddenly Maria dropped to her knees, hardly knowing what she did, and laid her head across his knee. Although she was silent, he understood and sat stroking her hair, murmuring her name.

'Don't!' she whispered, and looked up into his eyes. 'Don't call me your sweet Maria. I am not yours and never can be.' She stood up and ran to the door, then seeing the windlass man eye her curiously, she closed it and leaned back against it, feeling the rough-hewn wood with fingers that tingled, as did the rest of her body, with a heightened awareness of her own vulnerability.

'Don't make me say it,' she begged.

He rose to his feet and she saw in his face a look which she recognised as the dawn of hope. A hope that she dared not nourish. They could never be together. *Never.*

'Maria!' he whispered.

They stood facing each other, only a few yards separating them.

'I love you,' he said.

'No!'

'I love you, Maria. I must say it. I must know that you

234

know it.' She stared at him speechlessly. 'Say it, Maria,' he said gently.

She shook her head. She was Harold's bride-to-be, and he was Hannah's lawful wedded husband.

'Say it.'

Maria closed her eyes. If only she could reconcile her conscience, she could answer him. Was there a way? Could she justify a confession of her true feelings? Suddenly it came into her mind that by telling him of her love she could make him happier. He was weary, and he had married for convenience, as she soon would. Apart from his children there was no real love in his life. She had the power to change that. Perhaps a secret love was better than no love at all.

'I love you, Hugo!' she cried. 'I have always loved you, always, you know that. And being here with you has reaffirmed that love. We can never belong to each other, but we can still love each other, can we not?'

Nodding, he held out his arms, and she ran to him and was held close against his heart, which beat as loud as her own. Then his mouth was on hers in a passionate kiss and his hands were feeling the soft curves of her body wonderingly, as though, with his eyes closed, he was committing her shape to his memory.

A wild excitement surged through her and she gave herself up to the glory of feeling his body close to hers, his fingers entwined in her hair, hearing his voice whispering her name.

'Oh, Hugo, what are we to do?' she cried. 'I cannot bear to leave you. How can I go? How can I stay? Both will be an agony for me.'

'For me also.'

'I'll write to Ruth or to Harold. I'll say that Hannah is no better. That's true enough. I'll stay one more week – But no, I dare not. My love for you will show in my eyes and Hannah will see it.'

'Maria, I beg you. One week more. If you send a message

tomorrow, by the time it reaches Harold the week will be up and you will be on your way. To speak of love and to lose you within a few hours – I cannot bear that.'

'Nor I. But I am so afraid. Hannah –'

'She doesn't love me, Maria. She will not grieve for herself, but only for you – and me. She's fond of me, but her heart will always be Simon's. She has never pretended otherwise and I have accepted it.'

'And Margaret?' said Maria suddenly. 'You loved Margaret. I was so jealous. So racked with jealousy I couldn't bear to see you together. Do you remember?'

'A terrible child!' he agreed, laughing.

'And Margaret?' she asked again, gently.

He nodded slowly. 'I loved Margaret. Aye, I did love her. The way a callow youth loves a maid. But – my Maria! Ah, that's different.' She laughed, and he touched the tip of her nose lightly with his finger. 'Maria – her I love as a man loves a woman. Her I love forever.'

'Oh Hugo! I love you, my dearest. Heart, body and soul – What is it?'

He had paused suddenly and was pulling off one of his rings.

'Let me give you this ring,' he said urgently. 'Let us make our vows with this ring. No one need ever know.'

She looked at the ring he held out to her – a square garnet mounted in gold.

'My stepfather gave it to me,' he told her. 'Take it even if you don't wear it. Look at it when you are wretched and think of my love for you. Mayhap twill cheer you.'

He slipped it on to the middle finger of her left hand, because it was too big for the others. Then he put it to his lips and kissed it and held it for her to do likewise.

'I, Hugo, take thee, Maria, to love until death do us part,' he whispered.

'I, Maria, take thee, Hugo, to –' her eyes shone with tears, but she blinked them back, '– love until death do us part.'

236

They both said 'Amen' and kissed again.

'I would cherish you if I could,' said Maria.

'And I, you.'

She sighed tremulously and looked around her, aware again of the store in which they stood, with its tools and buckets and table littered with papers. Outside, her horse whinnied and she looked at Hugo, startled.

'How long have I been here? They'll be alarmed –'

'Not that long.'

'But I must go.'

'I'll ride home with you. I cannot let you out of my sight.'

She slipped off the ring and put it in the purse that hung at her belt. Hugo gathered up some papers to take with him and then fetched his own horse.

As they left, Maria fancied the windlass man eyed them curiously. Did their love shine in their eyes? she wondered. Did the man notice the change in his master's farewell? Let them, she thought recklessly. Just for today she would not care. She would revel in their newly-acknowledged love and let it fill her being with joy. One week more, and they must part. Time enough then for heartache.

She caught Hugo's eye and smiled brilliantly, letting her eyes take their fill of him while they might. Faintly from the shaft there came the sound of distant picks on shadowed granite rocks as they turned their backs on the mine and rode out together across the sunlit moor.

CHAPTER FOURTEEN

Throughout the journey home to Kent, Maria was so thoughtful that even Matt noticed a change in her. Even while they had shared the road with other travellers, she had said very little and by the time they were within five miles of Appledore, Matt's curiosity proved too much for him. As the two of them now rode alone he eyed her surreptitiously for a time, before putting his thoughts into words.

'You be mighty quiet,' he said at last.

She turned her head and looked surprised to see him. 'I beg your pardon,' she said. 'I didn't –'

'I said that you be mighty quiet.'

'Quiet?'

'I mean you say little and don't sing or whistle.'

'You mean I am poor company?' she said. 'I confess I am. I'm sorry, Matt. I have matters to think on.'

'Bad or sad matters?'

'Most likely both.' She sighed deeply.

'Hannah's not going to die,' he assured her.

'I know it.'

'Nor poor old Harold – I mean, the Master. He'll not die neither. He'll make old bones, you'll see.'

She rode without speaking for another mile or so, and Matt did not venture further comment. Suddenly she said, 'How d'you like it at Romney House, Matt?'

''Tis fair enough, though Heron is more to my liking.'

And mine, she thought mournfully. Choosing her words carefully, she went on. 'If at any time I were to leave Romney House, would you care to stay on?'

His blue eyes opened and his jaw dropped. 'Leave Romney House? You be going to leave Romney House and poor old – the Master and sharp old Ruth?'

'I didn't say that,' Maria said hastily. 'I said *if* I was to leave –'

'But why, ma'am? Why are you going to leave Romney House and the Master and –'

'Matt! Don't ramble on so. Your tongue runs away with you. *If*, I said! I don't say I *am* going to leave.'

'But where will you go?' His face wore the pained expression of a child who cannot understand his tutor. 'Will you go back to Heron? Is that it?'

'No, that's *not* it, Matt,' she said irritably, 'nor shall I tell you again not to assume so much. If you cannot give me a simple answer, then there's no more to be said on the matter.'

He glanced sideways at her face and was put out to see by her expression that he had somehow earned her displeasure. He sighed moodily. Women were not always easy to understand, and his Mistress was no exception.

'I've forgot the question,' he said suddenly. 'I would answer it, but I've forgot what tis.'

It was Maria's turn to sigh. 'If I were no longer at Romney House, would you wish to stay on there and make it your home?'

'No, I wouldn't,' said Matt. 'I'd rather come with you – else who'd protect you?'

She smiled faintly and nodded.

'I'd rather come with you,' he went on rashly, 'even if you went to – to –' He searched his memory for some remote place which would involve him in great personal sacrifice, if not actual danger, but nothing came to mind, so he said 'Scotland.'

'Thank you, Matt.'

After a long pause he said firmly, 'Ruth don't care for me overmuch. I'd not stay with her.'

'*Mistress* Ruth.'

'Mistress Ruth, then. But she don't.'

'The Master is fond of you,' said Maria. 'He teaches you to write and is well pleased with you.'

'I be a good scholar,' said Matt proudly.

'Aye . . .'

She relapsed once again into a reverie, and his efforts to revive the conversation met with no response, so he resumed his whistling and watched the marsh, in its autumnal glory, stretching away in all directions, the flat, green fields dotted with grazing sheep and edged with yellowing aspen, elm trees and the occasional horse chestnut. The village of Appledore sprawled before them, and Maria reined in her horse suddenly.

'Matt, you must make me a solemn promise, do you understand? A most solemn promise.'

'Aye.'

'That you will not speak to anyone of what I said on leaving Romney House.'

'Aye.'

'Then say it, Matt, with your hand on your heart.'

He put a large hand over his heart, frowned with concentration and repeated, 'Aye.'

'Tut! That's not enough,' said Maria. 'You must say the words. Repeat after me: I, Matt Cartright . . .'

'I, Matt Cartright –'

'Do solemnly swear never to tell –'

'Do solemnly swear never to tell –'

'The matter of which Maria spoke.'

'The matter of which Maria spoke. Should I say Amen?'

'If you wish.'

'Amen.'

'Thank you, Matt.'

'And you won't leave me with sharp old Ruth?'

Maria sighed. 'I won't leave you,' she told him, 'and now there's no more to be said.'

It did not require any more. Maria would not leave him, and with that he was content.

240

When they reached Romney House she found Harold in bed, propped up with pillows, a book lying open on the bed before him. His head lolled to one side, his eyes were closed, and he was breathing with apparent effort, the saliva gurgling in his throat. Maria, shocked, was immediately contrite about her delayed return. She stared at him, and with an effort repressed a shudder. He had grown so old while she had been away.

Ruth, beside her, noted her reaction and said, 'He looks better when he's awake, of course. Folk always do. But his breathing is very difficult and one side of his mouth droops. He is embarrassed by it.'

'And will he ever recover?' asked Maria, her voice low.

'The physician thinks it unlikely – poor Harold!' She turned away suddenly, and flung her apron up over her face to hide her emotion. Awkwardly, Maria put an arm round her.

'He has lived for your return, Maria,' said Ruth. 'This last week he has been so fretful, he would scarcely eat. He grows so thin. When I think what he was like as a boy!' She lowered the apron and said eagerly, 'Oh, you should have seen him then, Maria. So tall and slim and so agile. He would outrun anyone – man or boy. And jump! He would jump the stream in the far meadow with no effort. He used to wager with the other boys that he couldn't do it, so they'd find the widest part of the stream and he'd look suddenly doubtful – and how they'd gloat!' Her eyes sparkled at the memory, and Maria saw suddenly that she must have been beautiful in her youth. 'They were so certain then that he'd fall in they'd double the wager and he'd take it reluctantly, glancing at me in such dismay. And then he'd do it! No one could outjump Harold; or outrun him. I'd laugh so much at the look on their faces! And always he'd buy me some trinket out of his winnings when next the pedlar came by. A comb, once, I recall, and another time a ring with a pearl in it. He was so generous.'

Ruth's mention of the ring reminded Maria of Hugo's

ring, hidden in her purse, and she flushed guiltily. To hide her confusion she said, 'I wish I had known him then.'

'He was so brave, too,' Ruth continued. 'Once a wild dog came into the village, driven mad with pain from a wound in the head. It well-nigh killed one of the children, and no one would touch it. They threw stones and sticks to drive it away, but it grew more crazed than ever and hurled itself about in a frenzy at those who baited it and savaged one of the men about the arms and face. Harold fetched a blanket, cast it over the poor beast and threw himself on to it. He was only fourteen then. Only fourteen . . .'

'No wonder you are so proud of him,' said Maria gently.

Ruth stared at the old man in the bed. 'And look at him now,' she said wonderingly. 'He looks older than me.' Maria could not deny it. 'But what am I thinking of,' said Ruth. 'You must be weary and hungry. We'll let him sleep and you can talk with him later.'

Maria sat at the table in solitary splendour with a jug of milk, bread and soft cheese. Ruth sat by the window, spinning in the failing light. Neither spoke. Mechanically, Maria cut bread and spread cheese and ate it without tasting it, washing it down with mouthfuls of milk. There was a dish of plums, and she ate several. There was a sultana tart, and she cut and ate a slice. All the time she was trying to marshal her thoughts and, despite her hunger, it left her no time for the appreciation of food and drink.

Maria knew now that she could never marry Harold Cummins. There were two reasons. One was her love for Hugo, hopeless though it was, and the other was Harold's present condition. The pathetic sight of him had repelled her, and her flesh had recoiled. She was angry with herself, but the strength of her reaction convinced her that even with the best of intentions, she could never sleep with him. The very thought of his feeble caresses made her shrink inwardly. But she would never let him know of it.

Harold had changed so drastically in so short a time. And yet before she left for Heron, they had been loving and affectionate towards each other, like two good friends. The idea of marriage had not appalled her as it did now. She sighed and finished the milk, unaware that Ruth's gaze was on her while the woollen thread twisted and twirled in her fingers.

Maria shook her head helplessly. She did not have a clear choice between the two men. That would have been difficult enough. To deny the man she loved in favour of the one to whom she was betrothed – even that would have been possible; others had done it before her, she did not doubt. Or to abandon the man to whom she was betrothed in favour of the man she loved. That would be cruel, but also possible. Yet that was not the choice before her. Hugo was not offering marriage. No – her choice lay between marrying without love or remaining alone. Before, she could have married without love, but now – how could she bear to hurt Harold by revealing her true feelings? If she wed him he would see it in her eyes and be humiliated and ashamed. She would have to give another reason: one which he would accept, but which, although it would hurt him, did not rob him of his self-respect. She sighed again.

'He even has to be fed now,' Ruth said suddenly. 'These last four days his hands tremble so much that he can't hold a cup or bowl and cannot cut his own food.' Maria stared at her. 'He cried when he thought of you and how you would find him.'

'Oh no!' whispered Maria.

'The doctor spoke honestly with him, telling him that his heart is very weak and any undue exertion – do you understand, child?'

Maria nodded slowly.

'Harold knows all this,' said Ruth, 'but he will never tell you. We talked at great length and I said I would tell you.'

'I see.'

Ruth wound the wool and laid aside the spindle, then stood up and walked to the table, resting her hands on it for support. 'He knows he cannot marry you now. He says it would be a mockery. Poor Harold –' Her voice shook and Maria reached forward and gave her her hand.

Ruth went on. 'He will release you from your betrothal if you wish it, but if you choose you can remain here until such times as your mother makes another match. That is for you to decide. He loves you, Maria.'

'I know he does.'

'Could you marry him?'

Maria shook her head.

'I thought not,' said Ruth. 'I saw it in your face.'

'I wish it could be otherwise –' Maria faltered. 'I have no wish to hurt him. Oh Ruth, help me. What is best for him? If I stay –'

Ruth sighed. 'You must talk with him.'

'But you know him better than anyone else,' Maria pleaded. 'What would you have me do?'

'You must go,' said Ruth bluntly. 'Leave him his memories of you, then he need never see your –'

'Don't say it!' cried Maria. 'It hurts me.'

'Don't blame yourself,' said Ruth. 'You are young and must marry and have children. I shall love him and care for him as I have always done. We will be happy together and he will live out his last years peacefully and without regrets.'

'This is all so sad,' cried Maria desperately.

Ruth looked at her strangely. 'What will you do?' she asked. 'Go home to your mother?'

'Not at once, but I will write to her tonight. I shall go first to Canterbury and pray for guidance.'

'To Canterbury? But –'

'I cannot explain,' said Maria, 'but I must go.'

'And Matthew?' said Ruth.

'Oh, he'll come with me wherever I go,' she added with the hint of a smile. 'And now I must wash and change my clothes. Harold will be waking soon, I don't doubt, and will be eager to see me.' Reaching the doorway, she turned impulsively. 'I could not leave him in any hands but yours,' she said simply. And Ruth gave the slightest nod.

Maria went upstairs with very mixed feelings. Relief, that the decision had been taken out of her hands and that she no longer had to hurt Harold. Compassion, for the frail, helpless man who was to have been her husband and who loved her so passionately. She felt a great longing to reach Canterbury, where she would ask God to strengthen her resolve.

On the way home from Heron, Maria had decided to enter a nunnery. She would take her dowry to pay for her place and might even take holy orders. The prospect was a daunting one, and yet she could see no other way out for her. If she could not marry the man she loved, she could at least remain faithful to him. She would renounce wordly life and spend her days in prayer and care of the sick and needy. No doubt her mother would scorn the idea, but she would put up less resistance when she learned that Maria would not consider another betrothal.

Sighing, Maria called Meg to help her out of her travelling clothes and then, after washing, allowed her to choose which gown she should wear – a task which gave the little maid much pleasure.

'I think the blue damask, ma'am,' she said when she had finally made her selection, 'with the lace head-dress. And I'll brush your hair to take out all the dust. The Master's missed you – he will be pleased to see you home.' And so she chattered on, unaware of her Mistress's nervousness. Maria was grateful that she did not need to talk.

'Thank you, Meg,' she said finally, wondering how the girl would receive the news of her departure. Meg had been eagerly awaiting the wedding, and Maria had no doubt she would be sorely disappointed.

'There, ma'am, you look rare bonny!' cried Meg, and began to tidy away the discarded garments while Maria made her way reluctantly to Harold's bedchamber.

He was awake when she went in and held his arms out to her with a look of such joy in his eyes that Maria felt a sudden doubt as to whether she would be able to leave him.

Perhaps she should stay with him until he died?

'My dearest Maria!' he cried, and as she bent to kiss him, she saw tears in his eyes. 'I've so longed to see you. You'd be very vain if you knew how impatient I've been for you to come home.'

'I'm sorry I was away so long,' said Maria. 'Poor Hannah –'

'Ah, poor Hannah. How is she? You have left one invalid to come home to another, it seems. Poor Maria, we should say. So much nursing. Ruth told me you looked tired, and so you do – but still so beautiful. Sit beside me and tell me about Heron and all your adventures, for I have led a very boring life confined to bed all this while. Ruth, bless her, has worn a groove in the stairs with so much running up and down. And did Matt behave himself and do you credit? Did he astonish them with his writing?'

Maria sat beside him, holding his hand, waiting for him to stop. He was talking, she knew, to hide his wretchedness and to delay the moment when they must talk about her departure. She smiled and laughed with him, and told him about the children and their pranks, and then about the death of Hannah's child.

'That must have been a great sorrow,' he said simply. 'I felt for her when your letter came.'

Then he told her how one of the dogs had gone missing and turned up a week later none the worse for his escapade, and how a gipsy had tricked an old friend of his out of all the gold he had in the house. After that neither could think of any more to say and they looked at each other despairingly.

'I know, Maria,' he stammered suddenly. 'I know. You must go, tis only right. I am grown suddenly old and frail. No, let me finish. We must be honest with each other, however much it hurts. We owe each other that, don't you think?' She nodded dumbly. 'You will one day be a beautiful woman, Maria, and you deserve a young husband to give you – give you all that a woman needs.'

'No, Harold,' she began, 'I shall never –'

'Don't say it, Maria. It would give me no pleasure to think that I had come between you and the joys of a happy and fulfilled marriage. I knew those joys with my own dear Sylvia, God rest her soul. You must find a soul mate, Maria, and then you must write to me and tell me how happy you are, and give me news of the children –'

'But –'

He put a finger to her lips and gently motioned her to silence. 'For days I have practised my little speech,' he told her, 'and you must hear me out. Where was I? Ah yes, news of the children . . . And I will send them gifts and letters and be like a grandfather to them. Mayhap you will visit me and cheer up my lonely days –' He looked at her and saw that her own lips trembled. 'What is it, Maria?' he said gently. 'Is that not a happy picture I've painted for us both? You must not grieve. Tis God's will, Maria, I do believe that.'

Maria looked into the gentle, sensitive face. 'Dear Harold, I have a terrible secret,' she said, 'which I long to tell you to ease my own burden. But fear to, lest it makes your own less easy to bear.'

'A secret, Maria?' He was disconcerted.

'May I confide in you, Harold – as one who loves me? Will you forgive me if it hurts you? Mayhap I should remain silent. Mayhap tis selfish of me to –'

'Tell your secret, Maria, and let me help.'

'No one can help me, Harold,' she said, and then, summoning up all her courage, 'Tis Hugo Kendal of Heron. We love each other!'

'Hugo Kendal? Hannah's husband? You love him?'

She nodded, her eyes dark with pain. 'I have always loved him,' she said, 'ever since I was a child. I will never love anyone else in that way – and he is married to Hannah.'

'But –but you were prepared to wed me, Maria. I don't understand.'

'Hugo has never loved me until now. He spoke of it –'

'Ah – I see. Poor Maria.'

'Poor Maria,' she began to cry. 'And poor Hugo, and Hannah, and you. Why is life so difficult, Harold? Why can't we make one another happy instead of wretched? I don't understand.'

'Come into my arms, little Maria, and cry if you must.'

She sobbed against his shoulder until at last she felt calmer, and he teased her that his nightshirt was damp and likely to give him a chill if she didn't cease her tears.

'So I shall go into a nunnery,' she told him.

'Oh no, Maria!'

But she nodded, and talking with great seriousness, finally persuaded him that she was in earnest.

'Then you must do as you think best and as the Lord guides you,' he said. 'But I beg you, write to me occasionally if tis allowed, and burn a candle for my sins. Mayhap later you will change your mind, but if not – well, you will be safe and comfortable and among friends. We cannot ask much more in this old world!'

So they parted for the night, closer than they had ever been before. And Maria went to bed much easier in her mind than for the past eight days, and fell immediately into a relaxed and dreamless sleep.

The final leave-taking, a week later, was a sad affair. Matt made his farewells and was given a quill pen and a pewter inkwell by Harold so that he should be encouraged to continue his writing lessons. To Maria, he gave a miniature of himself as a young man, which touched her deeply, and in exchange she cut off a lock of her hair and stitched it on to velvet with flowers and her name embroidered around the edge. Harold was unable to see them off with the rest of the household, so they parted tearfully in his bed-chamber, with each of them trying to smile and master their sorrow.

Maria and Matt rode away from the house at mid-day, later than intended, and turned at the gate to give a last wave to the small knot of people who stood on the steps to see them go. For all her protestations of regret, Maria had a suspicion that Ruth was probably pleased to have her beloved brother in her sole care once more, but she could not begrudge her that. Finally Romney House dwindled behind them and was lost to view by a bend in the highway.

Maria felt an unexpected lightening of spirit, and was almost ashamed, but pulled herself up sharply. She had acted as honourably as she could, and at Canterbury she would do her penance. Without a word, she took Hugo's ring from her pocket and slipped it on to her finger, uttering a private vow never to take it off.

'That be a very handsome ring,' said Matt. 'Did the Master give it to you?'

'No,' said Maria.

'Ruth then?'

'Not Ruth either.'

'And you won't say?'

'No.'

He relapsed into an injured silence, but only briefly. His was a sunny disposition, and here he was, riding towards adventure in Canterbury with his mistress beside him. Happily, he thought of all the envious glances that would come his way as her escort.

'I'm hungry,' he remarked after a while.

'Maria laughed. 'We have scarcely left the house and cook said you ate a breakfast large enough for four men. You cannot be hungry, Matt.'

'My belly's rumbling.'

''Tis most likely indigestion. You have eaten too well, not too little.'

He patted the horse's neck and urged on the pack horse with Maria's belongings which followed them on a longer rein. 'Meg kissed me,' he said, blushing fiercely at the memory.

'Did she indeed!'

'Aye. She said she'd miss me.'

'I'm certain she will.'

'Do we be going to Canterbury?'

'Aye.'

'Will we see the sea? I've never seen the sea. They do say tis mighty big.'

'I fear not, Matt. We shall ride cross country to Ashford and then follow the river to Canterbury. There will be plenty of travellers going our way once we reach Ashford.'

'Meg says the sea goes up and down like this –' He gave a demonstration of wave motion. 'Meg's brother was a sailor 'fore he was drowned, and he told her. But Meg, she says you can walk in it and along the edge, for the water's very flat and thin there, not like the river. And no weed in it, she says. Not along the edge, that is. Take the mistress to the sea, she says, she'll like it.'

Maria hid a smile. 'Did she? How thoughtful of her.'

He looked at her hopefully. 'Oh, Meg told me special, like,' he said. 'If the mistress hasn't seen the sea, you must take her and she must walk along the edge of it in her bare feet and feel the sand under her toes. There's sand, Meg says, and it be real soft to your feet.'

'Matt, I've already seen the sea,' said Maria, 'and I've walked in it.'

'Ah!' His face fell, comically.

'But if you like, when we leave Canterbury we could ride west of Whitstable where Abby takes her children, and you shall see the sea there – if the weather is fine still.'

A broad smile lit his face. 'I'd like that real well, ma'am,' he said, and looked up into the sky. 'And I do believe the weather will hold, don't you?'

'I do, Matt,' she said, then paused, wondering how best to broach the subject. 'Matt, I've something to tell you. Tis only fair you should know and have time to think on it. After Canterbury – and Whitstable – we go to London to see my mother. She will not be pleased that I leave Romney House, and I doubt if we shall stay long with her.'

'But where shall we go next?'

250

'I – I shall go to a nunnery, Matt, and I shall live there for the rest of my days. Don't ask me why. Tis my own affair and no need for you to know.'

'A nunnery! With all those old crows!'

'They are not crows, Matt,' she said, trying to keep a straight face. 'They are holy and good women who have renounced wordly ways. I shall live with them – at Arnsville, most likely. If you think you can bear to live there also, I will try and have them take you on as groom or handyman. If you cannot bear it and my mother has no need of you, you must go back to Heron, where you will be most welcome, I know.'

Matt made a tremendous effort to come to terms with this startling news. He put his head on one side and contorted his face into the awful grimace that, for him, signified deep concentration.

'But they be all in black!' he protested.

'They are still good women.'

'And wordly ways is fun!'

Maria had no answer to that.

'Black crows!' he muttered rebelliously under his breath.

'What did you say?' said Maria sharply.

'Naught.' He rode on in a gloomy silence, wrestling with his thoughts, tugging the unfortunate pack horse irritably when there was no real need. 'Couldn't you find another husband?' he asked. 'You be handsome enough.'

'I've no wish to wed. But think on it, Matt. You can give me your answer when we reach London. There is plenty of time.'

On reaching the tiny hamlet of Ham Street, they halted briefly for wine, bread and meat, then rode on through Bromley Green to Ashford. There, as Maria had predicted, they fell in with a large crowd of pilgrims and continued with them, although keeping a little apart; most of them were men, and the conversation grew bawdy as the wine flagons gew lighter. As they sang and joked in loud voices Matt looked on enviously.

'Laughing, now –' he said to Maria. 'Is laughing holy?'

''Tis not unholy.'

'And singing?'

'That depends on the song. Holy people sing hymns and psalms.'

'Oh . . . and lewd jokes?'

'Not holy.'

'Ah, but you like to sing and laugh, ma'am, indeed you do. I've heard you singing and laughing too.'

She shrugged. 'You can still have all that at Heron,' she said. 'I shan't think ill of you if you decide to return there.' *In fact I shall envy you*, she thought, *for you will be near Hugo*. She fingered the ring, then lifted it to her lips and kissed it. She wondered how Hannah was faring, and Beatrice and Allan. And Ladyford, with Melissa and the gentle Thomas and Oliver –he was a handsome boy. Yes, she would envy Matt if he went back. She fell to thinking about the mine, her brief visit there had intrigued her. How was it done? How did the men persuade the rock to give up its treasures? To her surprise the mine had rather captured her imagination, and several times since it had come back into her mind. And Hugo, poor loveless Hugo, who had channelled so much of his energies into its development.

'Is kissing holy?' asked Matt.

'I dare say,' she said. 'If wedlock is a blessed state, then kissing must be blessed. I'm not certain. I can't know all the answers to your questions, Matt.'

'Will you be all in black too, ma'am?'

'Not necessarily, but I shall dress soberly.'

'You'll hate it, ma'am!' he burst out. 'No singing or kissing or pretty clothes. Why, you'll be that miserable! Don't go, ma'am, I beg you.'

'I mean to come to terms with it, Matt,' she said. 'There's no other way for me.'

'Then I can't come with you, for I'm not at all holy and those black women with their holy ways will nag at me

252

and –' A thought suddenly struck him and he asked, 'Is nagging holy?'

Maria laughed. 'I doubt it, Matt, I want to think now. You ride on and join the merrymaking up ahead. We've a long ride yet and twill pass the time for you.'

The path was rising now as they began to cross the North Downs and Maria began to relax a little as the beauty of the rolling countryside soothed her troubled mind. Her thoughts wandered to the past and to the future, but Hugo featured largely. Hugo as she first remembered him, tossing her up into the air and laughing at her screams; Hugo returned from France with his Margaret; Hugo distraught and feverish after her death; Hugo dangling Beatrice on his knee, or showing Allan how to feed grass to the horses without getting his fingers nipped. Always the memory of his swarthy face and broad, white smile brought an answering smile to her own face. More than one woman traveller, glancing back curiously at her, correctly deduced that she was in love.

As they passed Boughton Aluph and Godmersham, the sun began to drop lower in the sky. A kind of peace came to Maria as the hours passed and she felt that she had made the right decision. As Matt had said, she did enjoy wordly life, but she was also young enough to learn new ways. The knowledge that Hugo loved her in return would sustain her through all the difficulties and hardships. She would cling to that.

As the sun touched the rim of the far hills, they reached the outskirts of the city and rode in, weary but triumphant, at the West Gate. The party of travellers then split up into its various groups, for some had ridden ahead to reserve rooms at the various hostelries, and the two priests would be sure of a welcome at Poor Priests' Hospital.

Maria had planned to stay overnight at the Chequers, a large hostel at the end of the Mercery, but was reluctantly turned away by the landlord. There had been a great wedding at the Cathedral, he told her, and so many guests had flooded into the town, reserving all the beds in advance, that pilgrims and others were out of luck. So they made their way along the lane toward the cathedral and Maria bought two cloth badges of St. Thomas and two small bottles, which they would later fill at St. Thomas's well.

'The holy water still flows pink with the saint's blood,' Maria told an awed Matt as they made their way through the market and through a gate into the cathedral precincts. Matt gasped at the impressive grey building towering skywards, its huge arched door and pinnacled towers silhouetted against the sky and touched with the red-gold rays of the setting sun.

'Tomorrow we will take a look inside,' Maria promised, 'but first we must find a roof for the night.'

They tried every hostel and even the less salubrious lodging houses, but all without success.

'You can sleep in the cathedral,' the last landlord told them. 'Plenty of folks do, though the priests will turn you out at the crack of dawn to get ready for early mass. Still, tis dry, and you could do a lot worse.'

For lack of any alternative, they decided to do as he recommended; but first they bought pies and wine and sat on the grass outside, picnic-style, huddled into their clothes, for the sun had gone down now and the air had cooled noticeably. When it grew dark they made their way into the cathedral itself, where they found others in a similar plight. Many of them were ordinary travellers unable to find shelter, but many were genuine pilgrims, for Queen Elizabeth had so far proved liberal-minded with regard to religion, and people felt freer to worship in their own way without fear of persecution.

'Not like it used to be, though,' an elderly man told them as they greeted him and Maria made desultory conversation, remarking on the number of people settling themselves for the night's rest. 'My grandfather once told how it was in his father's day – you couldn't move in the city on special days. Folks sleeping anywhere – in the streets even.

Can you imagine that? Pandemonium, he called it, and rogues making a rich living off gullible strangers. A hundred thousand people came in one year, can you believe that? A hundred thousand! Jubilee Year, that was. Fourteen-twenty – and my grandfather could recall that. A tanner, he was, and my brother after him.'

'And you?' said Maria, spreading a blanket.

'Not now. Quarrelled with my elder brother and went to sea.' He laughed wheezily. 'Never regretted it, although he's a wealthy man now and I'm a poor one.'

All around them blankets and furs were spread out on the stone floor and wine and foodstuffs were produced, along with devotional books and packs of cards according to the various inclinations. Some even played chess, while others played instruments and sang songs, some religious, some distinctly irreligious. But for the most part people talked to one another and friendships, however temporary, were forged. Maria sent Matt outside to check that the horses were safe and that the old man paid to guard them had not so far absconded with them. Soon he returned with news that all was well, and the two of them settled down for the night. The high interior of the cathedral with its fine windows and graceful columns and roof was lit by the many devotional candles burning at the altar and elsewhere, and in this weirdly shadowed setting, Maria, weary in mind and body, finally fell asleep.

The next morning, as they had been warned, they were roused early from their sleep and hustled outside to fend for themselves; but despite the hard stone floor, Maria had slept well and was in high spirits. They sent the old man to buy bread and ale and they paid him well for his trouble. Then, having eaten and drunk their fill, they slowly explored the town, admiring the many fine churches and houses and loitering over the various stalls, crammed with souvenirs and mementoes of the town and its famous saint.

When the mass was over, they returned to the cathedral, where Maria left Matt with the horses while she prepared for her reason to visit Canterbury. Barefoot and on her knees, she made her way the length of the aisle and then prayed to the saints for forgiveness of any wrong she had done and for any wrong thoughts she had harboured. In particular, she prayed that her love for Hugo would be pardoned, explaining earnestly that she would never cause Hannah a moment's grief by it and vowing to spend the rest of her days in prayer and holy works in atonement for it.

She rose, then, and walked backwards to the door and out into the sunshine, where she put on her hose and shoes again.

'You should pray, Matt,' she said. 'This is a very holy place.'

But Matt said he 'daresn't'. Then they made the rounds of tombs and relics and holy places and finally visited the Well of St. Thomas, where they filled the tiny bottles which an old woman, for a few groats, then stitched on to their clothes, along with the badges purchased the previous evening.

Matt drew a deep breath when they were once more outside and announced that holy places made him sweat and that if a nunnery was a holy place like a cathedral then he couldn't abide it and would go to Heron.

'So be it, then,' said Maria, as lightly as she could, for the prospect of parting with him distressed her. After all, he would have been the one link with her former life. But maybe without such a reminder she would find it easier to cast off the outside world in favour of the cloistered one she would soon be entering.

'Tis decided,' she said. 'Now we need to talk about it no more. We'll ask directions for Whitstable and you shall see the sea.'

Within the half hour they were leaving Canterbury, skirting Harbledown and heading for Blean and Honey Hill.

The beach gave Maria one last glorious hour of pleasure-loving worldliness, and she was to look back on it with unfading joy in the years that followed. Matt, too, enjoyed every moment, from the first glimpse of the wide blue-green bay and the soft brown curve of the shoreline. The tide was out and, surprisingly, few people were about. It was a magic time for both of them – a time in which they surrendered themselves entirely to the delights of the moment and banished all thoughts of past and future.

At first they walked side by side, discovering shells and seaweeds, popping the bladderwrack, and exclaiming over the long strands of thong weed. They found corks, driftwood, a sodden leather bottle and many other oddments which the tide had rejected. Then they threw stones into the sea, watching them arc upwards, black dots against the clear sky and played at jumping the pools left behind by the retreating tide; then, out of breath, they searched the same pools for the tiny sea creatures and delicate purple and green weeds that grew in the cool depths.

'Look at me! I'm a dog!' cried Matt suddenly, and began scooping up sand at a great pace and hurling it backwards between his legs.

'What sort of dog?'

'A poodle!'

She shrieked with laughter. 'Then you shall go on show in the next fair, for you must be the largest poodle in the world!'

'A mastiff, then. No, I'm a Great Dane.'

'Then I shall call you – Danny! Here Danny! Good dog.'

Matt abandoned his digging and lumbered over and sat up, begging while Maria, laughing, popped an imaginary sweetmeat into his mouth.

'Let's see you catch a coney then,' she teased, and laughed again as he raced away, barking furiously. He returned exhausted, carrying a piece of stick in his mouth and, kneeling down, laid it at Maria's feet.

'A mighty thin coney,' she remarked.

'But a coney nonetheless,' said Matt. 'Aren't you going to pat my head and call me good dog?'

She patted the two-coloured mop he called his hair.

'And some mistresses,' he said slyly, 'kiss their pets.'

'I'm not so foolish!' laughed Maria. 'Enough of your impudence. Some mistresses kick their dogs too, and treat them most cruelly, so get up on your feet lest I give you the toe of my shoe! That's better. Did all that running wear you out?'

'No,' he said indignantly. 'I was short of breath, that's all. Shall we walk in the water's edge?'

Maria hesitated. Looking round, she saw that no one was near so she nodded mischievously and pulling off shoes and hose, sprang into the water, screaming as it splashed up over her legs and lapped coldly around her ankles.

'Slow coach!' she taunted. 'Hurry up, Matt, or I shall be out before you are in! Tis *so* cold – but quite delicious.'

He ran in beside her, clumsily kicking up more spray, so that her skirt was wetted. Bending down, she splashed him in retaliation.

'Catch me if you can!' roared Matt, his eyes sparkling with excitement. 'But you won't,' he shouted back over his shoulder, 'because I be a fast runner!'

And to prove it, he ran off, splashing through the foaming water and shouting with glee. Maria picked up her skirts and followed, but she was soon far behind him.

'Wait for me!' she shouted breathelessly. 'I grant you're the fastest – only *wait* for me.'

He turned at once and waited, watching the slim figure running towards him in a flurry of glistening spray, her long dark hair tossing behind her. As she drew near she stumbled and almost fell, then, regaining her balance, flung herself into his waiting arms, panting and laughing. As she clung to him, she felt his heart beating fast like her own, and the strength of his arms as they held her.

'Oh Matt,' she cried. 'Don't leave me!'

He looked down with a kind of wonder at the young woman in his arms and saw the passionate entreaty in the dark eyes.

'I don't reckon I could,' he said.

CHAPTER FIFTEEN

Melissa read the letter right through and then sat for a moment in thought, trying to visualise the writer. She considered the impression the letter had left on her, the reader, and she frowned slightly, unable to fasten on anything tangible, but aware of a vague disquiet. Was it a happy letter? An unhappy letter? On the face of it, it was neither – and that was what troubled her. It was a guarded letter, neither one thing nor the other.

Maria had never been one to write guardedly, but perhaps her letters had to be read by one of the other nuns before approval was given. She looked at it again, by-passing the greeting.

'I have been here for three weeks now and the strangeness is less than at first. I think with time I shall understand this new way of life and find the peace of mind I seek. My little room is quite bare of ornament apart from the wall-hanging which my poor Harold gave me and the bed he sent me so that I may, at least, sleep in a familiar place. My window is high up in the wall, so that I may not concern myself with matters outside and am able to think more readily of spiritual things. I have not seen my dear Matt since we parted on first arriving at the door, but the cellaress spoke with him twice and tells me he is well and in good spirits.'

Melissa wondered whether this was by design or accident. Possibly the division between the religious and secular members of the community was actually discouraged.

'. . . The nuns are kind to me . . .' Not *very* kind, thought Melissa, '. . . and there is a novice whose name is Katharine who is my own age – a bastard, but highly born,

259

and she smiles most readily. Our food is simple, but well prepared, and I am always hungry – as you will no doubt recall! We eat in the frater most days where no meat is served, but on one occasion in the misericord we had pork.

'I take some instructions with the two novices from Dame Augusta, who is at pains to instil in me the virtues necessary for this life. I hope I make some progress, but I confess I am often bewildered and not always ready with my answers when I should be. And yet I try.

'We are a small house and not wealthy, so my dowry was most welcome. The thatcher is to come and repair the creamery roof and the cellaress believes Matt will carry the straw for him. I shall watch out for a sight of him if that be so. The cellaress is very large and jolly and is often reproved for her unseemliness, but says she cannot change her ways.

'We pray often and sing psalms, at one time kneeling, another standing, and I have many to learn by heart, which I fear will take me forever, for what I learn one day is lost by the next . . .'

Just then Thomas came into the room and she turned to him, holding out the letter. 'Tis from Maria,' she said. 'Do read it, Thomas. I confess it bothers me a little. I think she is unhappy. I wonder if she made the right decision.'

'It was her own choice, and she was quite adamant about it,' said Thomas. 'You must not disturb yourself on her account. She has been there such a short time, she is no doubt homesick. Take that frown from your face. You will wrinkle that pretty forehead!' He sat down and patted the bench beside him.

'Read it aloud,' she said, and he did so with frequent interruptions from Melissa who, despite his good-natured teasing, continued to wear a worried frown. He went on:

'. . . I also am assigned for one month to assist the chambress with the wardrobe, and this week did sew a bolster and the week before darned three worn mantles. This week I am to make a cushion for the guest-room, for my sewing is greatly admired . . .'

Thomas laughed. 'I never thought to hear Maria boast of her sewing. She was always reluctant to put thread to needle. They must have wrought a miracle, these nuns!'

Melissa smiled at him, then said, 'But do you think she is content?'

'Let me finish it first, Lissa – *when* you have done frowning!'

With an effort she relaxed her expression, and he kissed the tip of her nose approvingly and continued:

'. . . I walk in the cloisters four times a day and greatly enjoy the fresh air and exercise, and there is a table of food for the birds which pleases me also. I have heard a dog bark on many occasions but have never seen it. Mayhap it belongs to one of the servants, for we may not keep pets for fear they distract us from our devotions, which they would most certainly do. Yet the Dame Agnes, that is the cellaress, has a tame jackdaw, and there was a dovecot, but tis fallen into disrepair and not yet restored.

'Now my paper is full and I can say no more than God be with you all and think of me often. Remember me to those that love me. Your loving friend, Maria.'

'Well?' demanded Melissa. 'Is she content, do you think?'

Slowly Thomas put the letter down. 'I would not say so,' he said carefully, 'but wait. Let me finish. Tis early days, remember, and she is very young, very headstrong –'

'Very passionate!'

'Aye, very passionate and not the stuff that nuns are made of. Yet she has not vowed to become a nun, only to live with them and share their lives. She is not totally committed and, if desperate, will no doubt admit to an error of judgement. She has a mind of her own –'

'But supposing they change her, make her more docile –'

'Then she will conform to the new life and all will be well.'

'But she won't be Maria if she is docile.'

He laughed at the look of dismay on her face. 'She will not

live there long if she is *not* docile! She is young enough to learn new tricks if she chooses to – and she has chosen just that. She has chosen to shut herself away from the trials and tribulations of the world –'

'But she –'

'But she must give herself time to discover new outlooks and new behaviour. She does not say she is unhappy, though I grant you she may be homesick. It won't be easy for her – but less than a month! Tis no time at all! Now, write to her cheerfully and assure her all is well. We must help her all we can, so do not paint too rosy a picture of life at Ladyford –'

'Is it rosy for you, Thomas?'

'Aye, my little Lissa. For me tis as rosy as I could wish. I'm well satisfied with my Lissa and my beloved Oliver. And is Ladyford rosy for you?'

'Indeed it is, Master Benet. Most rosy, and I am most fortunate in all I have. I love you, Thomas, you know that, and Oliver adores you. You can do no wrong in his eyes or mine – except perhaps that you won't be cossetted and will ride out in all weathers and come home with damp clothes.'

'You fuss over me. I am not an old man yet.'

'Nor ever will be in my eyes,' she declared, and kissed him.

'Where is Oliver?' asked Thomas.

'Out riding with Jacob. He wanted to ride with you, but you were so late home I sent him to ask Jacob.'

'Who jumped at the chance, no doubt.' He stretched his arms tiredly above his head. 'I'm sorry I was late, but there is more unrest at the mine. Hugo was delayed and I had to see him there instead of at Heron.'

'Serious trouble, do you think?'

He shrugged. 'A run of ill luck, mayhap. Who can tell if these things be accident or malice? Hugo sacked a man who was incompetent and the man's cousin took it ill. A truck was set loose and overturned, injuring another man, but none can prove how it happened. Some men now will not work the same shift as the cousin, and so it goes.'

'Poor Hugo.'

'Aye, and Hannah still not right again since the death of her son. Hugo says the physician fears a severe melancholy. She weeps still and will not eat, and scarce looks at Allan or little Beatrice.'

'Poor little souls. Oh dear, I wish I could put the world to rights for those I love.'

He laughed again and held her close. 'Your concern is with your Lord and Master, meaning myself. So when may I expect to fill my belly?'

'Oh!' she jumped up guiltily. 'Forgive me, Lord and Master! I was so concerned with Maria's letter! Change out of your clothes, my love, and I will have food on the table in an instant. Hot spiced sausage and beans, with damson tart to follow. How will that suit?'

'Most excellently. I will be down again directly – and no more frowning. Our Maria will survive. Never fear.'

Matt, as Maria had predicted, was attached temporarily as assistant to the thatcher, his own boy being sick of a fever which refused to break. Matt revelled in the work, not least because it gave him the chance to talk to another man. In a world of women, that was luxury indeed. Not that there was a lot of time for talking, for the thatcher spent most of his time at the top of a ladder, and Matt remained at the bottom, at least while the old dark reeds were tugged loose from their frame and dropped down to the ground. Matt had offered to assist, but the thatcher had laughingly refused.

'You're a strapping lad,' he said, 'and I've had strapping lads afore. Rip, tear – they go at it like crazy, and before you know it, they've pulled off half the roof as well. You'd be just such a one, I can see it in your eyes. No, lad, you bide your time and tidy away the old reed, so's Dame Agatha don't sharpen her tongue on us again. Real fierce that one is when she's put out. I mind how she was last year when I was doing the stable roof. Sweep up the old stuff and pile it over there, in the far corner of the yard. We'll burn it when it's dry enough.'

Thus relegated to terra firma, Matt did as he was told and worked enthusiastically until the cellaress put her head out of the adjacent kitchen window.

'You'd best curb that whistling when Dame Agatha's around,' she warned him. 'She can't abide whistling.'

'Oh.' He looked crestfallen. 'Can you abide it?'

'Me? Oh, I like a bit of a whistle, I do,' she said. 'Reminds me of my husband. God rest his soul.'

'Your husband?'

'Aye. Don't look so shocked. I'm a widow and have been these last twelve years. We had no family, so his brother inherited – and here I am. Snug as a bug.' She shrugged resignedly.

Matt looked at her curiously. 'Do you like it here?' he asked.

'Aye, why not?'

'Will Maria like it?'

'In time she might.' The cellaress put her hands on her hips and considered. 'Maybe not,' she said at last. 'Some never do. But I'm fed and clothed, and I like my work.'

A slow grin spread over Matt's face suddenly. 'You shouldn't be talking to me,' he said. 'You'll be saying a few Hail Mary's if you're caught talking to me, 'cos I'm a man.'

At that moment another bale of decayed reed came slithering off the roof, and the cellaress gave a little scream and slammed the door to keep out the dust. But she laughed to herself at Matt's words. Big old baby! But she liked him well enough and decided to keep back the best of the scraps from dinner for him. The rest would go to the poor.

Outside, Matt raked with a will, looking forward to the bonfire. From time to time, when he thought the thatcher was not looking, he darted round the corner and stared hopefully up at the small window which the cellaress had pointed out to him. That was Maria's window, and he longed for a glimpse of her! This time he waved his arms above his head and gave a piercing whistle, but still no face appeared and he was forced to go back to his work disappointed.

The thatcher was provided with meals as part of his fee, and he and Matt sat down together on a bench outside the kitchen door with a bowl of vegetable broth and a hunk of bread apiece.

The old man broke up the bread and dropped it into the bowl. 'Dry old stuff,' he grumbled. 'Never get decent bread here. Always stale.'

'We get buns, though,' said Matt, through a mouthful of bread. 'And fritters we had last Sunday. Twas a Saint's day, last Sunday was, so we got fritters. Four, I had. No one else had four, but the kitchener, she says I'm the biggest, and there's more of me to fill up than those wizened old nuns. Two each was all they got.'

'Seems like you're a bit of a favourite, then.'

'I might be,' said Matt. 'I dunno.'

The old man looked at him from beneath bushy white eybrows. 'Where d'you keep popping off to?' he demanded. 'When you reckon as I don't see you. Off round the corner –'

Matt blushed. 'Oh, tis nothing.'

'Taint nothing.'

'Tis!'

'You go looking for someone. Now who is it?'

'Oh – tis just my old mistress as I'm hoping to see,' Matt confided somewhat reluctantly. 'Only you mustn't say nothing, for tis against the rules, see, for me and her to talk. Her being all holy now and me being a man.'

'Ah. Your mistress, is it?'

'Aye. Tis Maria. I been her lad for years, and she couldn't bear to come here without I come too. But she's never looking out of her window.'

'I heard you whistle.'

'Oh.'

'Reckon everyone did. You want to be careful.'

'Aye.'

The old man leaned towards him. 'You want to chuck a stone through the window. That'll make her look.'

Matt stared at him, wide-eyed with admiration. 'A stone! Of course!' he cried, and abandoning the spoon, he lifted the bowl to his lips, drained the rest of his broth noisily, and stood up.

'Aren't you goint to wait for your pasty?' said the old man. 'There's a mutton pasty still to come.'

'I'll be back for it,' cried Matt, and dashed off.

Finding a smallish pebble, he threw it towards Maria's window. His aim was good and it missed only by inches and bounced back. The second one went in, and he waited breathlessly. Almost immediately a face appeared at the window, and he ran forward throwing caution to the winds, as he shouted Maria's name. Suddenly there she was, looking down at him in amazed delight.

'Oh Matt, Matt! Are you well? I'm so glad to see you!'

He stared up at her, grinning broadly. 'Aye, well enough. Ah, ma'am! I've been that eager to see you. And are you well, ma'am? Do they treat you proper?'

'*Ssh!* Matt! Take care. Someone will hear us. Come closer and then we need not shout. That's better. Oh, Matt. I wish I could meet you just for five minutes, just to talk. Oh – Matt, someone is coming!'

She disappeared from view and he waited anxiously, but there were no raised voices. Nor did Maria reappear. He considered tossing in another pebble, but decided not to in case one of the nuns was in the room with her. He waited a while longer, then went back to the kitchen, where the old man was pushing the last mouthful of pasty into his mouth.

'I was going to eat yours,' he joked, 'if you didn't come back. Well, did you see your mistress?'

Between mouthfuls Matt recounted what had happened.

'Wants to meet you, does she?' said the old man, with a

266

chuckle that was mainly a wheeze. 'Well, you can think on that while you're working. I want you to fetch the other ladder from me waggon and prop it alongside mine. Then you're to fetch an armful of reeds, bring it up and hand it over. You'd better have a head for heights, that's all I hope.' And he chuckled again. 'On your feet, lad, and let's get on with it while there's no breeze. Plays havoc, the wind does, and that there weathercock's veering.'

The next afternoon, Maria sat with Katharine, the young novice, listening half-heartedly to the Mistress of the Novices, who was speaking to them about the importance of confession, while the other half of her heart and mind toyed with the message the cellaress had given her from Matt. He said that he would wait for her in the orchard after Compline, the last religious office of the day. After that, the nuns would retire to the communal dorter to sleep until two o'clock the next morning, when the bell would wake them for Matins and Lauds. Maria was determined to see Matt on just this one occasion, and she had made up her mind to tell him it must not happen again. The question was, how was she to avoid going to bed with the others?

'Maria! You don't answer me,' snapped Dame Augusta. Maria coloured. 'I asked you to tell me how many good reasons there are for our confession and what they are.'

Maria hesitated. She had heard the beginning of the discourse, but missed most of the rest.

'I'm waiting for an answer.'

'There are six reasons.'

'Six powers. Go on.'

Frantically Maria racked her brain in an effort to recall what the nun had been saying. It clears away sins and –'

Katharine, in an effort to help, was mouthing something which Maria could not interpret.

'You were not paying proper attention, Maria. I shall say it again. The six powers of confession are to confound the Devil, to free ourselves from impure thoughts, words and deeds, and to make us children of God. Confession must be practised in a certain way so as to accuse ourselves and not others of the faults we confess; to cause us to feel sorrow and bitterness at our failure; to be made willingly and without duress, to cause us to feel shame, but to make us hopeful that we can do better. Confession should be made truthfully and without restraint, and as the result of long deliberation and from a true repentance of the fault . . .'

Maria propped her chin in her hand, so that her face could be directed towards the Sister while her mind was busy elsewhere, but Dame Augusta frowned and signalled with a flick of her finger that Maria should resume her previous position with her hands held in her lap.

'And straighten your back,' she added. 'You also, Katharine. Our bodies should be attentive to God's words as well as our minds. Bodies attentive. Minds retentive. Where was I?

'Repentance of our faults,' said Katharine promptly. Maria envied her the apparent interest with which she followed the nun's words.

'Aha – confession must be entire. It must cover every fault from small to great, and it must tell in detail how it was made, when and to whom, in which manner and circumstance . . .'

Perhaps, thought Maria, she could ask to be allowed to stay on alone in the chapel to pray for guidance and strength of purpose. But what if the request were refused? Or another nun was directed to wait with her? Or perhaps she could pretend she had lost something and had to go searching for it – something of value. Or pretend a faintness and run out for air? But someone would most certainly run after her.

'Maria! Repeat what I have just said.'

Maria stared at the irate face of the nun opposite and hoped her resentment did not show in her eyes.

'Forgive me. My thoughts wandered and I did not hear it,' she said quietly. ''Twas a grievous fault and I repent willingly and most sorrowfully, with shame, humility, a desire to make amends and after deliberation.'

There was a long silence. Katharine gasped and Dame Augusta's eyes narrowed. Maria waited for the rebuke she knew she deserved, but there was silence while the nun tried desperately to decide if Maria's little speech was truly intended as an affront. The moment lengthened, and still she did not know. Katharine looked nervous, but Maria looked at the nun steadily, aware that she had taken a terrible chance and already regretting it. Dame Augusta swallowed hard.

'I see you have learnt more than I thought,' she said levelly. 'In that case you will probably know also that true confession is always followed by penance.'

Maria nodded, while her heart hammered in her breast.

'You will fast and remain in your room, seeing no one until tomorrow noon.'

Maria nodded again.

'You will also pray and ask forgiveness for your inattentive ways and ask for more steadfast attention to your studies in the future. You will also stay behind after Compline and pray alone for one hour. Katharine, where had I got to?'

Katharine stammered out a reply which satisfied Dame Augusta, and Maria, hiding her exultation, made a determined effort to concentrate. The old nun, having played so innocently into her hands, at least deserved her undivided attention for the rest of the study period.

'O Lady, St. Mary, since thou had great delight within thee, when Jesus took flesh and blood in thee, receive my prayer . . .'

The litany continued, followed by the rest of the office, until at last the kneeling nuns rose stiffly to their feet and made their way in twos past Maria, who was left kneeling alone in the chapel. When the shuffling footsteps had faded, Maria turned her head and looked around her. But a sixth sense warned her to remain on her knees, just in case Dame Augusta returned to see that she was still there. It was as well she did, for after a short interval had elapsed, the old nun appeared beside her, looking as stern as ever. 'An hour, Maria – and I shall return later. Be devout and humble and think carefully on all that passed between us, that you may ask forgiveness if your intentions were not honourable.'

This last barb went home, and Maria's face flamed, but fortunately it went unnoticed in the dim light of the one remaining torch ensconced on the wall above her. As Dame Augusta moved silently away, Maria felt instinctively that she was bluffing. Why should the nun delay her own slumber just in order to supervise a penance? But she could not be certain. It was a risk she would have to take. She whispered Ave Maria, several Paternosters, then added a prayer of her own asking God's forgiveness for her present deceit. Then, gathering her courage, she stood up, rubbing her knees, which were sore from prolonged contact with the stone floor, and slowly turned. There was no sign of anyone, so she took off her sandals and walked slowly up the aisle to the door, not daring to close it in case its creaking hinges betrayed her early departure.

Outside, in the shadowy cloisters, Maria put on her sandals and tiptoed across the flagged courtyard, her ears pricked for any sound. A nightjar called; from beyond the dairy she heard the occasional lowing of the cows, and from somewhere above her the sleepy crooning of the few doves that remained in the derelict dovecot. Once across the courtyard she let herself out by the kitchen gate and ran round through the garden and into the orchard beyond.

Thin moonlight glancing through the apple trees cast weird shadows, and in the distance a fox barked, harsh and plaintive. At first she thought the orchard was empty – there was no sound or movement. But as soon as she called 'Matt!' a figure rose up from beside one of the trees on the furthest side. 'Oh Matt!' she cried, and ran forward to meet him. Flinging her arms round his neck she embraced him, and he returned it until she winced under the strength of his arms and protested that it was like being hugged by a bear.

'Maria,' he repeated again and again. 'You look so – so –' He shrugged, lost for words, while Maria looked down at the dark grey tunic and sandalled feet.

'Your hair,' he said. 'Have they cut off your hair?'

'Not all of it,' she told him. ''Tis tucked up under the veil. Now tell me, quickly, how things are with you, Matt. Are you happy? I didn't think we would be parted like this. Are you fretting? Tell me, for I dare not stay out too long.'

'I'm well enough.'

'Where do you live? And sleep? I never catch a glimpse of you.'

'Over the stable, I sleep. 'Tis warm and dry, and the horse is company. I daresn't come into the cloisters on pain of most dreadful punishment.'

'Most dreadful?'

'Aye, no dinner! But Dame Agnes likes me. She gives me a mighty fine plateful of leftovers before she feeds the poor. That's extra, that is.'

'I never see the poor.'

'Why there's three of them come daily with their bowls while you're all muttering away in the chapel. Two youngish women and a rheumaticky old man. Sometimes more. They talk to me, they do.'

'And what do you do all day, when you're not thatching?'

'Bits and bobs,' he said vaguely. 'Some days I help Sam Gittings, the man as looks after the animals. He comes in each day. And sometimes I dig or chop wood.'

'Are you happy, Matt?'

'I dunno. Are you, ma'am?'

Maria hesitated. 'I dunno!' she said.

They both laughed.

'Matt, if you want to go back to Heron you must send me word –'

'And you'll come too?'

'Oh no, Matt. I must stay here.'

'All that chanting and praying!'

'Aye,' she said. 'I had a letter from Harold. Ruth wrote it down for him. And I'm hoping for one also from Melissa. We may not write above one a week, nor receive more than that.'

'Do they be kind to you?' Matt asked. 'If not, I'll –'

'They mean well, I am certain. Oh, Matt –'

He waited, but she did not finish, merely sighed deeply.

'The thatcher be a kindly man,' said Matt. 'I like thatching. I hump the reed up the ladder. I'm strong, see, and he be old and weakly. He says I'm a strapping lad.'

'So you are, Matt – Matt, I miss you.'

'Aye. I wanted to see you, but they said twas a temptation and a snare of the Devil. I was afeared then.'

'Poor Matt. You needn't be.'

'But I don't want no messing with Devils and suchlike.'

'No, but you are quite safe.'

He looked round nervously and Maria also cast a hurried glance behind her to satisfy herself that they were still unobserved. 'We'd best go now,' she said. 'If you need me at all, if you are in trouble or unhappy, send me word by the cellaress and I'll try and come here the same night. I can't promise, but I'll do my utmost. Now you must go. Think on me kindly, Matt.'

'Aye.'

'I'll pray for you,' she said.

'I'd like that,' he said, and with a last clumsy hug, he ambled off into the darkness, leaving Maria to retrace her steps.

Quietly, she let herself in at the kitchen gate and hurried to the deserted chapel. Had an hour passed? Most likely not. She returned to her former place and knelt down and said an earnest, if unconventional, prayer to God that her escapade might remain undetected. Hardly had she finished it, when footsteps sounded behind her and Dame Augusta stood beside her, still fully dressed.

'That is enough,' she said. 'You may go to your rest.'

272

Maria crossed herself and stood up. 'I thank you,' she said. But it was not for the remission of penance that she expressed her thanks; it was for the opportunity of seeing Matt.

As Maria turned to go, Dame Augusta caught the trace of a smile on her face and wondered anew what kind of girl this was. Would they ever reconcile her proud spirit to a life of piety and self-denial?

Harold Cummins died almost three months to the day after Maria's departure. In spite of the physician's verdict of death by 'a sudden failure of the heart', Maria blamed herself, privately diagnosing a broken heart, and applied to the Prioress for leave of absence to attend the funeral. To her surprise her petition was granted on condition that one of the older nuns accompanied her, and Matt was allowed to escort them. The dour Dame Agatha was chosen as her chaperone, which might have dismayed Maria, had she not been genuinely grief-stricken by Harold's death. Since Matt did not possess a black suit, the Chambress produced a length of fine black silk ribbon with which to adorn the sleeves of his best clothes. And so, with Matt looking quite the gentleman, the three of them set off early on the Thursday morning to ride the twenty-one miles to Appledore.

Maria, red-eyed and deep in thought, sat her horse silently and took little notice of the wintry landscape unfolding around her. She could take no pleasure in her brief freedom from the restricted life of Arnsville, but was engulfed by despair. If only she had stayed on at Romney House, she thought. She might have prolonged his life! Does a happy man live longer than a wretched man? She had made him happy by her presence, so surely by her absence she had made him wretched? Did Ruth blame her? she wondered unhappily. Would she be met by reproaches? If so, she must bear them with humility. Her own grief would be her penance. Should she confess her faults when she returned to Arnsville and ask forgiveness for them? She tried to assess her situation in the light of her newly-acquired knowledge, but she was still inexperienced and confused, and could not reach a solution that afforded her any peace of mind.

As she wrestled silently with her problems, she was unaware of the nun beside her. Dame Agatha sat awkwardly in the saddle, unused to riding, and her thin lips moved in constant prayer. She kept her eyes steadfastly forward, ignoring the temptations of secular life which surrounded them. Men, ale houses, women in fashionable dress – all were met with a blank indifference. Dame Agatha was a tall, spare woman who delighted in the rigours of self-denial and found true joy in the disciplines of monastic life. For her the journey was a perilous adventure to be borne with fortitude, and she intended to deal severely with any manifestations of the Devil which might come their way on the journey. Her strength of character and purpose lay in her beliefs, and those beliefs she would uphold to the utmost. Glancing at Maria, she saw that she rode carelessly, her eyes blinded by tears.

'Pray, child,' she said. 'You weep only for yourself and not for the deceased. You should delight in his triumph, for his soul is on its way to Heaven. Pray for the safe passage of his soul and for forgiveness of his sins –'

'He had none,' said Maria. 'He was a virtuous man.'

'We all sin,' said Dame Agatha sharply. 'Even the most virtuous among us. There are many kinds of sin – sins of the mind, and of the body –'

As her voice droned on, Matt glanced past her to take a look at Maria. The old nun had been instructed to ride between them, but not to obstruct communication between them.

'Don't fret, ma'am,' he said timidly. Maria nodded without replying.

Matt's private opinion was that the nun had no right to

speak ill of the dead. To his knowledge, the old man had committed no sins. He was too feeble by far to commit any worth bothering about, he thought. He was a kindly old man, and so-called holy people should mind their manners and keep their opinions to themselves. He allowed his horse to drop back a little and scowled at the prim back. He considered putting out his tongue, but aware of Heavenly eyes above him, reluctantly decided against it. Instead he looked at Maria's slim form, slumped dejectedly in the saddle; he wanted to comfort her – but how to do it with the hawk-eyed Dame Agatha watching his every move?

'Keep up!' she commanded suddenly, as though reading his thoughts, and he was forced to nudge his horse forward and ride abreast once more.

They stopped at lunchtime in a small village and Matt was sent into the only inn to see what hospitality they offered. He came out trying to hide his satisfaction. The landlord, a large, corpulent man, followed him out, smiling broadly and wiping his hands on his apron.

'Good morrow, gentle people,' he boomed. 'And how can I serve you? Best ale this side of London, that's our boast – and tis no idle one. Cheeses? A capon, or a fresh rabbit stew? Mind, when I say fresh, my son snared it only yesterday, so can't be no fresher. Or fish, if tis a holy day for you two ladies? Let me help you down.'

Dame Agatha ignored his upstretched hands. 'Does he have a private room?' she asked Matt.

'Not very private, no,' said the landlord, 'but not very public neither, if you take my meaning. Tis early and we've no customers. The room's empty, the fire's blazing and the food's waiting to be ate!'

Dame Agatha hesitated. She was stiff from the unaccustomed ride and cold from the crisp air, but this man with his twinkling eyes and engaging grin must surely be a temptation sent direct to try her.

'We shall ride on to the next inn,' she said firmly.

'You'll have a longish ride then, ma'am,' he told her.

'The next inn is five miles further and closed, for old Simmons' daughter is be married today and they're all gone to Portsmouth.'

Matt meanwhile had helped Maria down from her horse, and she was stamping her feet and rubbing her hands to restore the circulation. 'Rabbit stew?' cried Matt, as heartily as he dared. 'I could eat a dish of that! Very warming stuff, rabbit. What say you, Maria?'

She looked at him vaguely and opened her mouth to say she had no appetite and could eat nothing, but saw the longing in his eyes. 'Mayhap we should eat,' she said meekly. 'I feel a faintness and should not care to be taken ill upon the journey.' She resisted the urge to labour the point with a fictitious account of such a calamity happening to an erstwhile friend, but seeing the older nun hesitate she almost regretted her newly-acquired conscience.

The landlord, however, had no such qualms. 'Why bless you,' he said, ''tis happening all the time. A lady was carried in here only last week, faint and sick with an empty belly – er, stomach, begging your pardon. Had to stay the night, she did, *and* shared the only bedchamber with four men. That was a riotous night, I'll warrant!' He laughed heartily and winked at Matt.

'We shall eat here,' said the nun hastily, 'but with all speed. We must be gone before your regular customers arrive.'

Matt was then allowed to help her down, and the horses were led away by a boy. They followed the landlord into the inn, which was simply furnished but warmed by a huge log fire. In a small back room they were given water to wash, and when all their needs were attended to they reassembled in front of the fire, holding out their hands to its welcome warmth.

The food, when it came, was delicious, and even Dame Agatha could find no cause for complaint. The stew was hot and thick with meat and vegetables, and a jug of good ale and a large newly-baked loaf completed the feast. The two women sat at one end of the table while the landlord's wife bustled in and out, pitying the beautiful but sad-faced young girl with her drab garments and stern companion. Matt, banished by Dame Agatha to the other end of the table, enjoyed it all immensely, and laughed and joked uproariously, intoxicated by his unexpected freedom, eating and drinking everything set before him with a noisy appreciation which appalled Dame Agatha and called forth several reprimands, none of which he heeded in the slightest, for the ale had gone to his head and given him courage. Watching him, Maria's own spirits revived a little, though she noted two bright spots appear in Dame Agatha's cheeks as the men's light-hearted banter shocked her delicacy of feeling. Perhaps, thought Maria, she regretted his banishment – without which there would have been no opportunity for their lively exchange.

To Dame Agatha's great relief, they finished their meal at last and were remounting their horses before the next customers arrived – a small party of merchants travelling towards London. They thanked their host, and, cheered outwardly as well as inwardly, were soon back on the highway, heading once more towards Appledore.

The funeral was a simple one, as Harold had requested in his will. Six poor men, all in black, were hired to walk in front of the coffin, and six more to carry it. Ruth followed with Maria and Dame Agatha, and Matt walked a few paces behind them. Then came his friends, nearly twenty of them, mostly local people, and lastly the servants. Leading them all was a single fiddler playing mournfully, and the sound of his music, flung into the grey air by a cold east wind, affected even the hired mourners who had never known Harold Cummins.

One of them, Davey, a gaunt man in his middle years, wondered that a gentleman should choose so mean a funeral procession – not that he cared. He was 'between work' with a wife and seven children to feed, and was glad enough to don the black suit provided for the occasion and put his left shoulder to the coffin, which, though long, was lighter than many he had borne. He considered himself something of an expert at 'weeping', as some called it. He had attended no less than thirty-two funerals in his time – five in one week years back, when a brief but violent outbreak of plague had hit the village.

The man in front of him stumbled suddenly, and Davey cursed him as the coffin tilted and the hard wooden edge bit into his shoulder. If a man couldn't stay on his feet, he had no business taking folks' money. He prided himself on never putting a step out of place, nor making a false move. He had never sneezed during the service, nor shown disrespect for any of the guests. It paid to do the job properly, for sometimes an extra coin of two had come his way and more than once he had successfully begged a bag of leavings from the funeral feast. He wondered if there was any chance of that today. There'd be such excitement if he went home with a few tit-bits! They'd have a party maybe, and light the lamp for an hour or so, and tell stories and sing all the ballads they knew. It would cheer up his wife, whose own mother had died not five weeks ago; she was still apt to break out weeping and was irritable with the little ones – and another on the way! He sighed. Please God, let there be some leavings! If God was attending to the matter of Harold Cummins' soul, surely he might also find time to attend to that small request? Time would tell, he thought philosophically, and put his mind to the matter in hand, which was easing the coffin off their shoulders and onto the frosty grass.

Ruth began to sob and Maria took her hand, and pressed it comfortingly, although tears blurred her eyes and her own lips trembled. As the service proceeded, Maria glanced round at the sombre scene, hoping it would have met with Harold's approval. Dear Harold, with his frail body and gentle ways! Now that death had stilled his shaking hands and quavering voice forever, she did not know whether to be glad or sorry. Why did she weep? And for whom? Harold was at rest and his soul was on its way to Heaven. Death should be a time of rejoicing. So did she weep for Ruth's loss or for her own grief? Opposite her, on the far side of the grave, Dame Agatha stood erect, hands clasped in fervent prayer, eyes closed. Matt stood nearby, embarrassed by the formality of the occasion, and kept his eyes on the newly dug grave. Or do I grieve for myself? thought Maria. Does it frighten me to know that one day I shall lie in a straight coffin, shut off from my fellows in fearful isolation, separated from all I know and love by a wooden lid? She shuddered.

'. . . And Harold Cummins, who was a model to us all,' went on the voice, 'has reached his final resting place, and his soul, freed from mortality, shall find its way towards that eternal peace that passeth man's understanding. He was greatly loved and will be greatly missed. He leaves no sons to carry on his name, but he will not be forgotten. We mourn with Ruth, his loving sister, and all his many friends . . .'

Maria wondered if the preacher knew of her defection and blamed her; ashamed, she could not meet his eyes.

'. . . His good deeds were many and his misdeeds few. He was a good master to his servants, a steadfast brother to his sister and a loving husband to his two wives . . .'

Maria was suddenly curious about the other two women in Harold's life. Now she would never know. The wind dropped and the dark clouds lowered ominously. A flash of lightning surprised and dismayed them, and above the low growl of thunder the oration was hurriedly concluded. A few large drops of rain fell, spattering onto the coffin lid like the drumroll that signals the finale of a performance. Was that all it was? thought Maria; then pushed such heretical thoughts aside. She would ask Dame Agatha to instruct her on the significance of life, for the need to know had suddenly overwhelmed her. Yet the nuns had taught her that life was a preparation for death and a life thereafter. At least when her own turn came, Harold would be there to greet her, a familiar loving spirit in the great unknown. That thought finally comforted her.

Later, when the will was read out, she learned to her utter astonishment that Harold had left Romney House and all else that he owned to her, with the proviso that Ruth be allowed to continue there in all comfort and honour until her death.

Stunned by the news, she was a prey to conflicting emotions as she rode away the next morning, and the journey back to Arnsville Priory was passed in a long discourse from Dame Agatha which she had requested on the relationship between life before and after death, to which she paid scant attention. This brought her several well-deserved reprimands from her austere companion, and Matt was heartily relieved when three young men joined up with them and he could drop back and enjoy more lively company.

CHAPTER SIXTEEN
DEVON

Five fathoms underground, the afternoon shift toiled in the flickering light of their oil lamps, which cast large shadows of men across the rock walls and roof. Half an hour earlier they had taken their last look at daylight before being lowered down the steep shaft, sitting on a stick at the end of a rope which was winched down inch by inch. Now they worked at their allotted tasks, some strengthening the timbers that supported roof and walls, others at the tail, levering fragments from the face of the rock and tossing them into a small wooden truck. Later the rock face would be 'fired' to soften it, and by Monday the work of the miners would be a little easier.

Above them, Hugo sat in the store-cum-office and chattered with Melissa, who stood at the window, looking out somewhat impatiently. Between them sat little Allan and Oliver. Oliver was now a boy of ten with his father's serious grey eyes; Allan a plump child still, with Simon's fair hair and blue eyes, who looked with a strange intensity on the world around him. They were all waiting for Jed Retter who, characteristically, was already nearly an hour late.

'I suppose he *is* coming,' said Melissa doubtfully, and the two boys exchanged dismayed looks at her words.

'I think he will,' said Hugo, 'but I did warn you how unpredictable he *is*. Give him a while longer. Tis worth the wait if he does come, but if he doesn't I shan't rail, just count myself lucky that he's still around to come at all. Men of his kind are rare enough.'

'And if he doesn't find any?' said Melissa.

Hugo shook his head, at once serious. 'Ah, then we must go on with our underground explorations. But I confess we are baffled: the oblique stringer has come to nothing – vanished and without trace. Most likely a rock fault or movement has lifted it, but we might spend precious time tunnelling in all directions –'

'What is a stringer?' said Allan.

Oliver said at once, 'Why, a vein of ore, you ninny,' and received a sharp nudge in the ribs from Allan and a warning look from his mother.

Fortunately, before further blows could be exchanged Melissa cried, 'Someone is coming – an old man. Is Jed related to Will Retter? The one who worked the mine years since for John Kendal?'

'Tis possible. Through a cousin, mayhap. Will's own family died in an accident – a fire, I believe. Come in, Jed. I'm pleased you could make the journey.

The old man did not reply, but stood outlined in the doorway, looking from one to the other. He was very small, shrunken almost, and his wild grey hair was long and straggled over his shoulders. His beard was long, too. Piercing dark eyes looked out of a wrinkled face, and his nose seemed not to have shrunk with the rest of his face, giving it a large, beak-like effect.

Allan gasped and opened his mouth, but Oliver returned the nudge he had received earlier and the small boy bit back the words. But they all knew what he meant to say – that old Jed Retter looked exactly like a wizard.

'Are you ready, then?' he asked abruptly. His voice belied his appearance, being strong and forceful. Melissa nodded hastily and the children scrambled off the bench, apparently hypnotised by the strange man who had suddenly appeared before them. Without another word, the old man turned on his heel and strode out across the yard to where his horse was tethered. Melissa hesitated, looking at Hugo for reassurance, but the two boys had already gone hurrying after the old man.

'And you will follow?' asked Melissa nervously. 'You'll catch us up?'

'Aye, as soon as I can.'

'Hugo, what shall I call him? Master Retter?'

Hugo smiled. 'Everyone calls him Jed,' he said. 'Twill give no offence.'

'The boys also?'

'Aye. Now off you go, or they'll be gone without you.'

Melissa ran after the boys, who were already mounting their ponies. It was a rare adventure for them and for her also. Jed Retter did not take kindly to being watched while he was prospecting, but Hugo Kendal was master of one of the biggest mines on Dartmoor and not a man to be denied lightly.

They rode in silence for nearly a mile. The old man seemed disinclined to talk and Melissa delayed her first remark for so long that it seemed an intrusion, and died on her lips. The two boys rode behind them and she glanced round from time to time.

'Let them be,' said Jed suddenly. 'A boy is a man and must think he fends for himself.'

Abashed, she could think of no answer and accepted the reproof with a meek nod of her head. Abruptly, the old man reined in his horse and slid to the ground, tossing the reins over a nearby bush. Then he lay down with his ear to the ground. Excitedly the others dismounted also, Allan nearly falling off in his haste to copy the old man. Melissa was left to secure the horses, for by now the two boys were spreadeagled on the ground, which was still white from the night's frost.

'I can *hear* the tin!' cried Allan. 'I can!'

The old man chuckled and raising his head, winked at Melissa who, seeing signs of humanity in him, relaxed a little and laughed. 'What *are* you listening for? she asked.

'Sounds of the miners,' he told her. 'Tis less a sound and more a vibration.'

He stood up and surveyed the ground critically. The boys scrambled up and stared also.

'You have to know a metal,' said Jed musingly. 'You have to love it.'

'Do you love tin?' asked Oliver.

'Aye, I do that. And see what it's done for me – made me a rich man with fine clothes. See!'

He spread out his arms and stood scarecrow-like, laughing at the bewildered looks on the boys' faces. 'Ah, tis fickle stuff, tin ore.' His eyes narrowed suddenly and he glanced at the bush to which the horses were tethered. He began to talk, half to himself.

'. . . Mind you, they're all the same – silver ore, lead, copper. Fickle as a jude, they are. Here one minute and gone the next, when you're mining it. The earth plays tricks on man. She doesn't give up her treasures too easy . . . Man can search for clues week after week, month after month, and still have no luck. Then by chance twill show itself. Sometimes a fire'll do it. They do say that a forest fire in Freiburg heated the earth so that the silver ore melted and ran on the surface and was thus discovered –' He broke off again and, moving to the left, pulled and tugged at a few small rocks to reveal a tiny trickle of spring water, which surfaced and disappeared again. He put some to his lips and nodded.

'It has a taste of tin,' he said. 'There's sulphur there, and maybe alum. I'm not certain, but –' He stood for a moment, deep in thought, while the boys, having sampled the water, watched him in awed silence. 'Aye,' he muttered. 'Tis fickle stuff.' Then he began to walk, apparently aimlessly, studying the grass and lichens underfoot.

'You can sometimes see the line of it,' he said, '– a line of damp grass in a frosted area. Keeps in the heat, you see, and gives it back at night, warming the soil above it so the frost don't bite so. Oft times it dwarfs the plants above it if it be an excessive hot vein. Now then, you lads, you'll step on my heels if you tag much closer. Go each your own way and search for a strip of grass as shows no frost. Let's see whose eyes are the sharpest.' He pursed his lips, lost in thought once more.

'Should I search also?' asked Melissa.

'No, ma'am. You bide by me.' He smiled. 'I may be old, but I can still enjoy a pretty face – Ah, that brought the colour to your cheeks. Oh, don't mind me . . .'

'We thought you might use a divining rod,' said Melissa hastily.

'I might yet, but I'm feeling me way, so to speak. Now if there was trees near abouts they might give us a clue.'

'Trees?'

'Aye, the leaves grow different colours according to what's beneath the roots – sometimes a blueish tinge or even black. But there's no trees hereabouts, so there's no joy to be had that way.'

Time passed, and they covered a surprisingly large area of ground before Hugo arrived to see how matters were progressing. He conferred with Jed while the other three waited hopefully. At last the old man went back to his horse and returned with a hazel twig.

'Now, you two lads shall help me,' he told them. 'Listen carefully while I show you how a rod is best held, for if you don't hold it right, twill tell you nothing. You could be standing on a vein of purest tin and the twig'll deceive you. Twill lay as dead in your hands. Right, you first, lad. Take it in your hands, so –' Oliver obeyed. 'Twig won't bite you. Now, turn your fists so the fingers is uppermost and the joined ends of the twig face the sky. A twig mustn't be too large, or the force of the metal can't move it. Nor must you hold it too light, nor too tight. Ah, I reckon you've got that about right.'

They all watched fascinated while Oliver wandered about, his eyes intent on the hazel rod.

'Tis my turn!' cried Allan, hopping up and down with excitement. 'Tis my turn now, Oliver. Give me the rod and I shall find the tin. I know it.'

'You know no such thing, Allan,' Hugo chided. 'So hush. You shall have the rod later.'

'But Oliver cannot find it and I *can*!'

Eventually Oliver admitted defeat and it was Allan's turn. Unlike Oliver, he took the twig in his hands quite naturally and set off at a steady pace, ignoring the others. The expression in his eyes reminded Melissa of the day the bees swarmed: an inward look, as though he listened to a voice within him. They made to follow him, but the old man beckoned them back.

'Give him his way,' he muttered. 'Let him be. We'll follow at a distance, but quiet, like.'

Ahead of them the small figure trotted on, now weaving to the left and now to the right, head slightly on one side. Hugo and Melissa looked at each other and the same thought was in each of their minds: this was Simon's son. Jed kept his eyes on the small boy ahead of them, but said nothing. For a while it seemed as though, in spite of his boasts, Allan's search would be as unproductive as Oliver's. Then suddenly he gave a cry and stopped. Instinctively Melissa put a hand up to cross herself, then dropped it hastily, ashamed of her superstitious reaction.

'By God!' muttered Jed. 'By the 'oly mother of God! I reckon he's there!'

Oliver slipped his hand from Melissa's and ran forward.

'You really think so?' gasped Melissa, but the old man was already hurrying towards Allan and she and Hugo followed. The twig in Allan's hand had twisted itself downward and pointed towards the earth. It seemed to tremble in his hands as though possessing a life of its own.

Melissa stared around her. 'But Oliver walked here,' she said. 'He covered the same ground!'

Jed looked at her with sly triumph. ''Tis not so much the forked twig, as who wields it,' he told her. 'Some folks has a peculiarity in them that hinders the force from the metal. Others don't.'

At the old man's words Oliver turned away and Melissa

286

sensed his disappointment. Her heart ached for him. But Allan looked up at Hugo, his eyes gleaming.

'I found it! I knew I would.'

'Is it tin?' asked Hugo.

Jed shrugged. 'Possibly,' he said, 'but it could be water. A spring.' Gently he took the hazel from Allan's hand. But in his own fists the twig doubled over once more to point earthwards.

'Hard to say,' he said, 'but if it's water, then the ore will likely be nearby. They run alongside sometimes. A bit of digging will soon tell you.'

He knelt down and snatched away the foliage, pulled up a few pebbles, glanced at them keenly, then handed them to Hugo.

'Tis possible,' said Hugo.

'A sight more than possible,' the old man corrected him. 'There's certainly water here – and not too far under. Mayhap only a fathom or two.'

Melissa clapped her hands with excitement as Jed's confidence in the find grew. Now that the first thrill had past, Allan returned to a boulder and sat there alone, wearing an expression of quiet satisfaction that was strangely at odds with his youthful face.

Hugo and Jed marked the place with stones and sticks and noted its position in relation to their surroundings. On Monday he would bring out several miners and begin a preliminary shaft. Meanwhile Jed decided to work over the surrounding area again alone, so that he could concentrate more fully. They thanked him for his time. If a vein of tin *was* discovered, he would be paid handsomely, but he would receive a smaller payment whether it was or not.

Hugo, Melissa and the boys rode back in high spirits. Hugo would remain at the mine until the next shift was due, so Melissa left him there and took the children back towards Heron to deliver Allan to his mother. Oliver and Allan rode ahead of her in earnest conversation, their voices shrill with the day's excitement. She saw with pleasure how quickly

Oliver had recovered his composure and good humour. He had his father's generous nature, she thought fondly. But as for Allan – what had he inherited from that ill-fated family? Time alone would tell.

The two boys rode on ahead as soon as Heron came in sight and Melissa let them go, knowing that they wanted to be the bearers of the good news. By the time she reached the house, they were already with Hannah in the main bed-chamber, where she sat on a stool having her hair brushed by the maid. When Melissa entered the room she took the brush from her and sent her away.

'So you have had an exciting time,' she said. 'These two scamps have told me all about it.'

Melissa agreed, wondering that Hannah showed no real interest in the news that the longed-for breakthrough might be imminent. 'Jed was very hopeful,' she said. 'He's an extraordinary man, Jed Retter. Have you met him?'

'No.' Again she seemed indifferent. 'The boys have told me all about it,' she said, as though to forestall any further details.

'I hope for Hugo's sake that tin *is* found. He has looked so worried of late. For one not reared to mining, it must be a grave burden.'

Hannah nodded and picked up the brush. She began to pull it through her hair with long, slow strokes. 'I would have ridden with you, but my head hurts,' she said wearily. 'And I feel the cold so.'

Always an excuse, thought Melissa sadly. She is still wrapped up in her private grief and seems almost unwilling to relinquish it.

'I have heard from Maria,' Melissa said, hoping to arouse more interest. 'She asks to be remembered to you.'

'She never writes to us,' said Hannah peevishly.

'Do you write to her?'

'No, I confess tis my fault. Letter-writing wearies me and

I rarely answer letters. I dare say she has despaired of me.'

'She seems content. She has been there over two years and –'

'Is it so long? Where does the time go to?' She laid down the brush and stared unseeingly ahead. 'Then Simon died three years ago? Tis not possible. Three years!' She sighed.

'Maria had a visitor – Ruth Cummins. Apparently she takes great interest in her welfare. Maria says she entertained her in the guest-room and they had baked heron. That must have been a very rare treat for Maria.'

'I don't know why she stays there,' said Hannah. 'She has Romney House. She could live there in comfort with Ruth as companion. She could eat baked heron every day of the week if she wished. She's not suited to that life, and no one can convince me otherwise.'

'Yet she stays.'

'All this nonsense about Hugo! Oh, I know why she's there and I have no time for such foolishness. She could wed elsewhere and have a family of her own. There is no shortage of suitable husbands, and after all, she is a wealthy woman now.'

Melissa bit back a sharp answer. It annoyed her when Hannah spoke that way, but she was so often sharp-tongued that to take issue on every occasion would mean constant friction.

The two boys began to wrestle half-heartedly, and Hannah sent them out into the garden. She spoke irritably, and they cast reproachful looks in her direction, for they had done nothing to deserve such sharpness. When they had gone, Hannah hid her face in her hands and Melissa waited, wondering.

'Let me brush your hair,' she suggested gently. 'Twill ease your head.'

Hannah nodded gratefully, tilting her head back and giving herself up to the luxury of the soothing movement. 'And is Matt still with her?' she asked at last.

'He is, and seems more settled. He works hard on the

farm or about the stables. There was some trouble a few weeks since, but it has blown over. He was teased by a man who delivered logs and they fought. The man was half-killed, Maria says. He is so strong, Matt, for all his childishness.'

'And the authorities took no action? He was most fortunate.'

'The man taunted him. One of the nuns was witness to it.'

''Tis no place for a man such as Matt – nor Maria, either. But I repeat myself to no avail. No one will listen or take heed. Maria cannot be happy there. She could always return to Heron and help me with the children if she does not care to live at Appledore.'

'But her regard for Hugo!'

'Childish fantasy!' said Hannah. 'Two years in a nunnery will have cured her of that. Hugo laughs if I speak of it – Ah!'

'I'm sorry. A tangle – there, tis gone.'

Abruptly, Hannah sat up and helped herself to a sweet-meat from the dish beside her. 'Take one,' she said to Melissa. 'They are Beth's speciality. I should not eat so many. I grow fat.'

She sighed heavily. She had put on a great deal of weight since the loss of her little son, and her face, which had once been described as 'homely', was now puffy and plain. Her figure had been neglected too. Too many sweetmeats and too little exercise had thickened her waist and stomach, and she had lost all interest in clothes.

'Hugo wants another son,' she said suddenly. 'He will not be satisfied until he has a son of his own. I tell him Allan will inherit Heron, but he is adamant.'

''Tis natural enough,' said Melissa, sitting down on the bed. She saw Hannah's fingers twisting in her lap.

'His persistence is not natural,' she shrugged helplessly. 'What can I do if my body refuses? I cannot order my womb to produce a son. I would if twere possible. He will not let the matter rest – his cautious enquiries each month are a constant reproach. Tis all I can do at times not to scream at him! He has an heir and a daughter –'

'Allan is Simon's heir.'

'And his also. Don't take his part, Melissa, for pity's sake. I cannot bear much more.'

'Have you spoken with the physician?'

'Aye, three of them. One says the stars are ill-placed, another that the fault is in my mind, that I'm afeared to have another child.'

'Is that possible?'

'Who knows? They are all fools. The third tells me to drink this and that and burn candles in church. I thought we were done with such Popish tricks, I told him, and he looked offended and would not come again. I'm weary of potions and draughts. I'm weary of everything! Oh Melissa, what am I to do?'

She burst into tears, but when Melissa tried to comfort her, pushed her away saying, 'You take his part. I know it. You all do. No one understands. Oh Simon, Simon!' And her tears fell even faster.

Melissa hovered uncertainly, unable to offer consolation, but soon withdrew, leaving her to her grief, and went slowly downstairs, her own heart heavy. Hannah mourning still for Simon, Maria possibly still yearning for Hugo – and Hugo? What did Hugo feel? Did he still grieve for Margaret? She did not know.

Her thoughts depressed her, but she made an effort to think cheerfully, resolving not to go home to Thomas with a long face, and thinking how fortunate she was to have the man she loved. Their own relationship had gradually ripened into a perfect union, enriched with deep love and spiced with a gentle passion. She never ceased to thank God for her husband and son, and it distressed her to know of another's heartache.

Beth was in the kitchen chopping oranges and Melissa told her to prepare a tisane and take it up to her mistress.

'And tell her I will take Allan home with me,' she said.

'He can stay the night, and Jacob shall ride back with him in the morning.'

After collecting the two boys, she rode eagerly back towards Ladyford. The prospect of the warm, loving atmosphere which prevailed there dispelled the last of her gloom. Sighing contentedly, she slapped the horse and urged it into a canter.

The find was later confirmed as tin, and immediately plans were drawn up for a new shaft to be sunk. Hugo was now inspired to look for new labour and to investigate the quickest method of reaching the vein and bringing the tin to the surface. He had been dissatisfied for some time with their production methods and felt sure that new machinery, driven either by water or horse-power, could be devised. He had heard that the large silver and lead mines on the continent used methods far in advance of those in England, and while not all of them would be suitable, he was sure the machinery could be adapted. However, before considering a journey abroad, he decided to visit one or two of the Kentish coal mines and see what could be learned from them, and consequently wrote to obtain permission.

Thus, three weeks later, Hugo rode towards Kent with Jon as companion. Reluctantly, he left his foreman behind as the murmurs of unrest, still present among the miners, made it inadvisable to leave them to their own devices. Four days later, his visits done, and well pleased with what he had learned, he and Jon rode to Rochester to spend a few days with Abby and her husband, taking with him small gifts that Melissa had made for the children and a long letter she had written to her sister.

Abby, to everyone's surprise, was pregnant again, but in good health and spirits, and Hugo and Jon were made very welcome by the whole family. Adam's mother had died the previous year, so Abby was now Mistress in her house and thoroughly enjoying her position. She managed the servants with a firm but kindly manner, and husband, father-in-law and children all adored her.

'I think I got a bargain with my little Abby,' Adam teased as they sat at supper the first evening. 'Seven children – and twill soon be eight, God willing. *And* she can cook.'

'Indeed she can' said Hugo. 'This pie is delicious. Aye, a good bargain, Adam.'

Abby laughed easily. 'You won't make me blush,' she said. 'For I got a good bargain also. Adam has given me a pleasant home and I have as much mud on the floors as any woman could wish for –'

Adam gave a roar of laughter and the three older boys grinned sheepishly. The amount of mud trodden into the house from the nearby boatyard was a constant bone of contention.

'Think on it, Hugo,' said Abby. 'A husband, a father-in-law and four sons, all with large feet, tramping in and out like a herd of elephants. No sooner has Ellen scrubbed the kitchen floor than tis dirty again.'

'I've told you,' said Adam. 'Put down sawdust and –'

'*Sawdust!*' She rose to the bait. 'And have my kitchens look like an ale house? Never, Adam Jarman.'

'I'm only a small elephant,' said Richard, the youngest boy. He was six and the image of his father.

'Even small elephants have big feet,' said Abby.

The two youngest children were in bed and asleep by now, but the others ate with them. Hugo, glancing round the table, was impressed with the air of contentment and good health, their cheerful faces, and hearty appetites. Unwillingly, for a moment, he compared the family with his own, but then guiltily put the comparison aside.

Abby was eager to hear all the news about Heron and Ladyford, and Hugo was hard put to it to answer all her questions. Then Adam and his father talked about the boatyard, which was flourishing.

'And will go on flourishing,' said Adam, 'if the new Queen keeps her promise. She has strong views on England's sea power and means to develop a fleet that will make this island impregnable. And not before time, in my humble opinion.'

Abby smiled. 'You never had a *humble* opinion in your life, Adam Jarman,' she said. 'With you an opinion is utter conviction!'

'And why not?' he protested. 'I'm always right. Have you ever known me to be wrong?'

This pretended conceit drew forth howls of protest from the entire family, who clamoured to remind him of many such occasions, all of which he denied categorically amid much laughter. The meal grew progressively noiser. Jon, eating in the kitchen with the servants, heard the racket and smiled to himself, glad that his master was enjoying himself for once.

Later the candles were lit and the children and Adam's father retired to bed. But Hugo, Abby and Adam sat on, talking in low voices, reluctant to relinquish an evening which had proved so enjoyable.

'I thought to visit Arnsville,' Hugo said suddenly, 'tomorrow morning, mayhap. Will they allow me to see Maria, do you think?'

Abby, who had been half dozing, opened her eyes and looked at him kennly. 'Maria?' she said.

'Hannah is anxious about her,' he lied. 'I said I might find time –'

'They will let you see her,' said Abby. 'She is not a professed nun, nor ever will be. A lay-nun, you might call her, though subject to the same rules. Tis short notice, though – unless you have written to them of your intention.'

'No.'

'She will welcome a visit from you,' said Adam, 'but you will find her changed.'

'In what way?'

'Abby saw her a few months since.'

'Aye,' said Abby. 'Her mother was visiting Arnsville and asked if I would ride down with her. Maria seemed –' she searched for the right words '– resigned, mayhap. No, that is too harsh a word. And yet content is wrong also. *Passive*. Aye, that's it, strangely passive. We both thought so. So unlike the old Maria, full of fire and so impetuous. Aye, you'll see a change in her, but she'll be pleased to see you.' She sighed. 'Poor Maria –'

'Why poor Maria?' asked Adam. 'She went there willingly. She might well resent our pity. But Hugo will see for himself. Now, for my part, I can scarce keep my eyes open –'

There was a chorus of agreement and a very pleasant evening was finally brought to an end.

Maria looked up at Dame Elinor in astonishment, her finger still marking the page which her young student was reading.

'A visitor? For me?'

'For you,' said the elderly nun excitedly. 'And a fine-looking gentleman he is, too. So make haste and don't keep him waiting.'

Maria's heart missed a beat and then steadied itself. 'Who is it?' she asked.

'Campbell, I think he said, but my hearing's not what it was.'

'Campbell? Not Kendal?'

Dame Elinor looked at her vaguely. 'Kendal? Campbell? Mayhap. You'll find out for yourself.'

Maria stood up on legs grown suddenly weak. 'Read on, Jennet,' she began, 'I'll return before long –' But the older nun laughed.

'I doubt it most heartily,' she said. 'Your lesson is at an end, Jennet. Be off with you. Shoo!'

Jennet needed no second bidding, but closed her book and departed gratefully. Maria followed the nun through the cloisters in an agony of despair and hope, unable to believe that it *was* Hugo who awaited her, yet aglow with the hope of seeing him again. And frightened, also, of what the sight of him might do to her fragile self-control. She must behave with dignity at all costs.

In all probability Dame Elinor would chaperone them. It would be easier if she did. Dame Elinor remembered her own youth and recalled it as a heady time. She had taken her vows in middle age and knew the world and its ways.

'In you go,' she said when they reached the guest-room. 'I'll sit outside the door if you've no objection. All that chitter-chatter will distract me from my contemplation!'

And with a kindly smile, she settled herself on the bench and Maria pushed open the oak door and went inside. Hugo stood at the far end of the room, examining one of the wall-hangings. He turned slowly as the door creaked on its hinges. For a moment they simply stood and stared, their eyes devouring each other: Maria, sombre in her dark tunic, her hair hidden by a black veil which partly covered her forehead, accentuating the perfect oval of her face with the large dark-lashed eyes. Hugo, brilliant by comparison in gold and brown slashed with red.

'Maria!'

'Hugo – welcome.' The words came out huskily, and Maria cleared her throat. 'Such a surprise! I couldn't believe it.'

'You didn't object?'

'No. I'm delighted. Tis always pleasant to receive a visitor. Sit down, please.'

She gestured with a trembling hand and he obeyed, sitting beside the empty hearth in one of the tall, straight-backed chairs. Maria sat opposite him. Unspoken, a message leapt between them – *I love you still* – and for a moment neither spoke, nor wished to. They could read in each other's eyes all they needed to know.

Then, aware of the nun outside and the lengthening silence, Maria said hastily, 'I hope your journey was uneventful.'

'Indeed, it was most enjoyable. This part of Kent is very beautiful.'

'We are most fortunate.'

He lowered his voice. 'Maria, are you happy?'

'Content –,' she amended, then mouthed the word 'now!' and he smiled.

'Did I interrupt your prayers?' he asked.

'I was teaching a child to read.'

He looked surprised.

'We have two boarders,' she explained. 'We are a poor community and the fee is welcome – even necessary. But how is Hannah and little Beatrice and Allan? And Melissa and –' She broke off, suddenly aware that he was not listening. Instead he was looking at her intently, and with the heightened perception that love brings, she saw in his eyes desire conflicting with guilt. She recognised it instantly, for it precisely matched her own emotion. Both felt desire. The guilt on his part was for feeling thus towards a woman embraced by the church. On her part, it was guilt at the knowledge of all that she had renounced by her presence within the world of the cloister. Neither dared speak what was in their hearts.

'Hugo,' she prompted. 'I asked for news of all at Heron and Ladyford.'

'All are well,' he said, his voice controlled and even. 'All. And Abby – she sends her love. They all do. I have come from there and will return when I leave you. Tomorrow we shall ride back to Devon.'

'Who rides with you?'

'Jon.'

'Jon! And Jack – and what of funny little Minnie?'

'She mellows with the years,' he said, 'or so I'm told. I see no change in her, but Hannah says she is improved.'

'And Hannah?'

'What can I say? She cannot fully shake off the melancholy.'

'I feel for her,' said Maria, '– and for you . . . And the mine?'

'Ah, the mine. Problems as ever, but we still search out

the ore and prise it from the rock. Melissa wrote to you of the new find, I think.'

'Allan and the divining rod! Aye, Melissa wrote in great detail . . . Hugo, you look tired. Are you well?'

'Tired, nothing more. You look – I cannot find the words.'

'My mind is changed, but –' she lowered her voice, '– not my heart.'

'Maria.' He stood up and took a step towards her, but she stiffened in her chair and he checked himself and sat down again, his eyes never leaving her face.

'Forgive me,' he whispered, and she nodded.

'Tell me about your life here,' he said finally.

She shrugged lightly. 'I pray and I study. I teach Jennet two mornings a week. I eat fish on Fridays and Wednesdays. I sew with the Chambress. The discipline –' She hesitated '– the discipline helps me. There are compensations: a peaceful, well-ordered routine, time to think on God, and prepare my soul for the life hereafter . . .'

He had the feeling she was repeating a lesson learned by rote.

'We should all do so,' he agreed, and then murmured, 'I miss you, Maria!' She gasped and glanced fearfully towards the door, which stood ajar.

'Forgive me!' His voice had sunk to a whisper again. 'I did not intend – I should have stayed away.'

She threw him a beseeching look, a finger to her lips. Then, in great agitation, she stood up and crossed to the table and stood beside it, running the tips of her fingers over its well-polished surface, her eyes downcast. Suddenly he stood beside her, his voice urgent.

'Come back to Heron, Maria. Give up this life and come back to us before they break your spirit. Come for the children and Hannah. We need you, Maria.'

White-faced, she turned to him. 'Don't ask me, Hugo, to give up what little peace of mind I have. At Heron I should be forced to see you as Hannah's husband. How can I do that? I still love you, Hugo. Aye, if that's what you wish to hear from me then you have heard it.' The words now came in a rush. 'To know that you lie with her – how am I to bear that, loving you the way I do? *That* would break my spirit. And if Hannah should bear you another child, what then, Hugo? Twas hard for me last time, knowing that I loved you. But now I know you love *me* also – have you no thought for *my* feelings? What you ask is too cruel –'

'Maria, I –'

'No, Hugo, I beg you. Don't ask it for I cannot refuse you, for certainly your pleadings would prevail over my better judgement. I cannot live at Heron and watch you daily with another woman as your wife. What am I to do? I cannot love any other man. What else is left to me, but to live out my days here with what little peace of mind I can salvage? Oh Hugo, you torment me! If you love me at all, leave me, for God's sake!'

He whispered, ashen-faced, 'What have I done to you? Maria, say you forgive me and I'll take my leave, if that is what you wish.'

The eyes that she finally raised to his were anguished, but she spoke quietly. 'I love you, Hugo, and there is nothing to forgive. You meant me no harm. Seeing you again –' She stopped, biting her lips. 'I must say no more. I think it best if you go now.'

'And I will see you again?'

'Mayhap. But not soon, Hugo. I need time to reconcile myself again. Remember me to everyone and say – say that I think of you often. All of you. And Hugo, think on me kindly.'

'I swear it. I could not do otherwise. God bless you, my dearest Maria.' And he was gone.

'So tell me,' cried Minnie. 'Tell me about Maria and then I'll give you what I've made for you.'

'For me?' said Jon.

'Aye. Tis something to eat, but I'll not give it to you until I've heard it all. How did she look? And did she pray out loud?'

'Maria?'

Minnie paused in her work and looked at him as though he had lost his wits. In front of her stood a large tub filled with steamy water, and a variety of pots and pans; beside her, a pot of sand, into which she dipped a damp cloth from time to time, applying it to the worst of the grease.

'Who else?' she said scornfully. 'Has the trip addled your brains?'

Thoughtfully, Jon looked at her and wondered uneasily, not for the first time, at the change in her. She was putting on weight, and her face had lost its peaky look and seemed to bloom.

'I know nothing about Maria,' he confessed. 'Twas the master went to visit her, not me.'

'But what did he tell you?'

'Nothing.' She stared at him in disbelief. 'Tis true!' he insisted. 'He came back with a face as long as a pikestaff and said she was "well enough".'

'Well enough? And that's all?' She gave an indignant snort. 'We knew she was "well enough" from her letters. Was she all in black?'

'I tell you, I don't know. What have you made me, then?'

'A custard, if you must know, but tis hid. I made it while Melissa was out hawking with Oliver. I put three eggs in it.'

'What if she counts them that's left?'

'I'll say I dropped 'em. If you're going to hang about here you might as well do something useful. There's a cloth. You can wipe the pans.'

'What about my custard?'

She grinned at him mischievously. 'You haven't told me nothing yet. You must have overhead something. Didn't you ask about her as you came home?'

'Oh, aye, I dare say I did.'

Seeing him screw up his face, thinking hard, she slapped a pan into one of his hands and a cloth into the other. 'Work while you're talking,' she told him, and began to sand the kettle. 'And what of Matt? Did you ask about him?'

'Ah, Matt. Aye. He saw Matt as he left. He was wearing a long black gown with a veil over his face and – *ouch!*'

Minnie swung at him with the kettle and he ducked, laughing uproariously.

'I had you wondering there for a while,' he chuckled, retreating to the far side of the table. 'Now don't throw anything. Oh, the look on your face!'

She glanced at him, hands on hips. 'I'm glad you think it so funny. I shall laugh myself – while I'm eating the custard.'

'You never would. You made that for me.'

'Tell me it all, then, or they'll be back from Heron and I'll get no chance.'

'I swear I know next to nothing,' said Jon. 'Real quiet he was when he came back from Arnsville, and on the way home twas hard to get a word out of him. He'd nod, shake his head or shrug his shoulders. Is she happy, I asked. Nod. Does she seem changed? Shrug. Did she send a message for Minnie?'

He invented this last question. Minnie's eyes widened admiringly. 'You asked him that?' she said.

'Aye, but a shake of the head was all I got. So give me another kiss and find that custard for me.'

Minnie went to the shelf and lifting the lid off one of the pans, brought out the pot of custard. 'You can find yourself a spoon,' she said.

'What's all this on the top?' asked Jon innocently. 'Looks like rust.'

'That's nutmeg, you ungrateful wretch. I couldn't find the grater so I scraped it with a knife – that's why the bits are on the big side. If you don't like it, I'll give it to Jacob.'

'Oh, I like it, Minnie,' he said hastily. 'I was only teasing. So what news since I been gone?'

'None,' siad Minnie, returning to the pans.

'Did you miss me?' he said, his mouth full of custard.

'I did and I didn't. Twas nice to sleep at nights without you snoring fit to –'

'Hush!' spluttered Jon, glancing anxiously towards the door. 'Don't talk that way! Someone might hear you.'

'I think I might like to be a nun,' said Minnie dreamily. 'I'd like to sleep in my own little room and –'

'Then you'd be disappointed,' said Jon. 'They sleep all together in the dorter.'

'So you *do* know something!'

'Only what they said in the kitchen. I heard nothing from the Master. I wager those toothless old nuns make a fair old racket, snoring and mumbling in their sleep!'

'And I wager they don't. Nuns is holy, and don't you forget it.' She sighed wistfully. 'I'd like to be a nun and have a handsome gentleman come a-visiting me. I think I'd look bonny in black –'

'Like a crow, and with that nose for a beak –' He scraped away at the last of the custard before she could snatch it back, but Minnie was wrapped in her imagination and ignored him.

'I'd smile very sweet,' she said, 'and say "God's blessing upon you, sir." And you'd have tears in your eyes –'

'Me? Leave me out of it!' he protested. 'I'm no gentleman!'

'*That's* true enough,' said Minnie promptly. 'What did you think on the custard, then?'

'Terrible.'

'Why d'you eat it, then?'

'To please you.'

Minnie snatched the dish away. 'I don't know what I see in you,' she remarked.

'*I* do,' he said cheekily. 'You've seen it often enough. You can't have forgot!'

And he dodged out of the kitchen, grinning hugely, as the dripping cloth flew through the air after him.

CHAPTER SEVENTEEN

Hannah sat by the fire, spinning. Beside her on the sheepskin rug, Allan played with a pair of dice, shouting triumphantly each time the numbers thrown matched up.

'Two fives!' He beamed at Hannah and she smiled absentmindedly, her eyes on the wool between her fingers, her thoughts elsewhere.

'Two threes!' he roared a short time later. 'I win again, Mama. 'D'you see that? I win again. Do you hear, Mama?'

'I hear,' she said, without turning her head. He snatched up the dice and showed them to her to prove his claim. 'See, two threes, and before that twas two fives, and before that two ones.'

She looked at him, amused by his eagerness. 'And you don't cheat?' she asked him.

While he was protesting his innocence, Beth knocked at the door and came into the room looking agitated, a frown on her plump kindly face.

'What is it, Beth?'

To Hannah's surprise she stood beside her, twisting the edge of her apron.

''Tis very awkward, ma'am,' she stammered, 'and I don't care to talk out of place, but I don't know what to do for the best and that's a fact.'

'For the best? About what?' Hannah's fingers slowed and the spinning came to a halt.

'About Minnie, ma'am.'

'Minnie? What's the child been up to now?'

Beth glanced nervously towards Allan, but the boy was engrossed in his play.

'That's just it, ma'am,' she said. 'She's not a child any more. She's a grown woman, for all her puny size.'

'How old *is* she?' asked Hannah.

'No one knows for sure,' said Beth, 'but she's sitting in the kitchen bawling her eyes out right now and reckons she's with child.'

The bold words were like a slap to Hannah. She rose to her feet, white-faced, letting the spindle fall to the rushes unnoticed. 'With child,' she whispered, her desperate envy robbing her voice of its power. 'With child, you say?'

'Pardon, ma'am?' Beth could hardly make out the words.

'You say she is with child? Minnie?'

'Aye, ma'am.'

'Does Melissa know of this?'

'No, ma'am. It seems that no one knows. She wouldn't believe it herself, but the wise woman in the village has told her it must be so. She's – she's missed these last five months, so she says.'

'Five months. Dear God!' With an effort Hannah steadied her voice. 'And whose child is it?'

'She won't say, ma'am. Just shakes her head the more and goes on bawling. I don't want to cause no trouble, but I thought twas best someone should know.'

'You did right, Beth. My thanks to you.' Hannah began to feel calmer. 'Send Minnie to me, and take Allan with you to the kitchen for a while.'

'Oh, that I will, ma'am.' Beth's frown faded. Allan was her pet and could do no wrong in her eyes. She held out a hand to him, smiling fondly. 'Are you coming with Beth, then, to help me make the mincemeat? I need a big strong lad to weigh up the currants and such.'

The prospect of the kitchen and all its excitements persuaded Allan, and he followed her willingly out of the room.

When they had gone, Hannah put up a hand to her face and stood, head bowed, breathing deeply, struggling to stay calm. The girl was not her servant, but Melissa's. But five months gone? It was preposterous. She was angry with herself for not realising. Angry also with Melissa, who was responsible for the girl. But who was the father? If it was not Jacob, it might well be one of her own servants, in which case she shared responsibility and must accept part of the blame for the girl's misfortune.

There was a clatter of footsteps and then Minnie burst into the room. Hannah, startled, looked at her in dismay. Her face was blotched and her eyes swollen, and the sullen expression, for so long absent from the plain face, had returned together with a new wildness in her manner.

'I shan't tell!' she cried defiantly, before Hannah could utter a word. 'You may tear me apart, but I shan't say nothing. He loves me. He wouldn't give me a child without I wanted one. And you shall all rant as much as ever you will, I'll say nothing. Nothing at all. You may beat me till I'm black and blue –'

'Hush, child,' cried Hannah. 'You must tell us. We shan't –'

'Don't you hush me! If I'm with child, then tis not my doing, for I didn't mean to have one. No more did he. Twas just the kissing and suchlike. I've no wish to have one, and I shan't have one – so there. Leave me be and –'

'Hush, I tell you!' shouted Hannah angrily, all her good resolutions gone. 'How dare you speak so. I insist you tell me –'

'And I tell you I won't!' Minnie stamped her foot. Suddenly her anger focused on the child's father. 'He's no right to give me a child if I don't say so. Howl all night, they do, and me with no husband and no money. He's no right!'

Then her face crumpled up and she began to give vent to loud, raucous sobs that made her face ugly. She fell to her knees in an agony of despair, even snatching up handfuls of rushes and flinging them around her in an attempt to express and relieve her frustration. She looked like a small, crazed animal, her anger replaced by fear and desolation.

'Minnie, don't –' begged Hannah, afraid to touch her,

yet unable to watch her. 'Get up, child.'

'Does a child have a child, then?' Minnie raged.

'I beg you to get up, Minnie. Get up, I say!' Hannah's voice rose and she fought back a rising hysteria. This awful uncontrolled snippet of a servant girl was with child without even trying; yet she, the Mistress of Heron, couldn't give her husband an heir. Mortified, she bit back the harsh words she longed to utter and her fingernails dug into her clenched fists.

'Minnie, you *must* tell us who is the father and we will –'

'I shan't. And I shan't have his child!'

'Oh, don't speak so foolishly!' snapped Hannah. 'Are you certain you know who tis?'

'Oh, I know,' said Minnie. She squatted back on her haunches, her hands still full of rushes. 'He said he loved me,' she said bitterly, tears trickling steadily down her cheeks. 'And I believed him. And now he's given me a child I don't care to have. I'd kill him if I could.'

'Don't say such a thing!' Hannah was shocked. 'Give me your hand and let me help you up.'

'No!' screamed Minnie, striking out at the hand held out to her, and scrambled to her feet and rushed out of the door.

Hannah blinked and breathed deeply. The short interview had exhausted her. Where had the girl gone? Who had she fled to? Slowly she became aware of the wool and spindle on the floor and picked them up. Then she straightened her back and reluctantly went out to try and find her.

Minnie was nowhere to be found at Heron, so Hannah rode over to Ladyford, expecting to find her there. If the father was not at Heron, then presumably it *must* be Jacob. Melissa had not seen her and received the news of Minnie's pregnancy with astonishment.

'I can't believe it,' she gasped. 'Five months gone and not a word. She *must* have known what was happening – and yet she hasn't had a moment's sickness, nor complained of a stray twinge. Can the wise woman be wrong, do you think?'

'She might,' said Hannah, 'but from the way the girl speaks, she has lain with someone, so I think tis likely true.'

'And she will not say who?'

'No.'

'Tis my fault,' said Melissa. 'I should have known – or guessed. But surely Jacob cannot be the father? I've never seen them together after dark, or seeming to dote on each other. I *cannot* ask him. I'll ask Thomas to deal with the matter when he comes home, but for the moment I shall send Jacob in search of her and not give the reason.'

On being told to search for Minnie, Jacob did not appear unduly concerned, nor even apprehensive. He hurried off, apparently pleased to be released from his wood-chopping, even if only for a short time. Hannah returned to Heron and Melissa was left to handle the situation as best she could. Oliver was also sent to look for her, but eventually both he and Jacob returned alone.

'No sight nor sound of her,' said Jacob, mystified. 'What's she up to? Another tantrum?'

'Aye,' said Melissa, 'in a way, and yet – oh, poor Minnie! I wish Thomas would come home. Take one of the horses, Jacob, and ride to the mine and tell him I have need of his advice most urgently.'

Thomas came home quickly, to find Minnie still missing and Melissa in a state of great alarm. He listened to the sad little tale, then shook his head.

'If we have searched Heron and Ladyford, where else can she be?' He thought for a moment. 'Has anyone searched Maudesly? Tis empty and close-shuttered, but she might find a shelter there somewhere.'

Jacob was despatched immediately, for dusk was falling. Another hour or so and it would be dark and the search would have to be postponed. They ate their supper without enthusiasm and had almost finished when Jon arrived.

'Jon?' said Thomas.

'Aye – they tell me Minnie's run away –'

307

'Oh, we hope not, Jon,' said Melissa. 'She's probably hiding somewhere. She must be hiding.' She looked appealingly at Thomas.

'I hope so,' he said. 'Why have *you* come, Jon?'

Jon shuffled his feet shamefacedly. 'The babe,' he said. 'If tis true, then the babe is mine.'

'Oh, Jon!' cried Melissa. 'How could we have allowed this to happen? Forgive me, I have neglected Minnie.'

'Don't blame yourself,' said Thomas. 'What's done is done. First we must find her. Poor Minnie must be very frightened, and if she stays out all night in this weather, twill do her no good – nor the babe. Five months!' He sighed heavily. 'We must search on until she's found.' He turned to Jon. 'Issue torches and ask Hugo if any of the tinners would help to look for her. We'll pay them for their pains . . .'

Seven miners volunteered to help, and the search was extended in all directions. Hugo and Thomas also rode out, and the countryside glittered with the light of more than a dozen flickering torches. At midnight they abandoned the operation and the men went wearily back to bed. Next day they resumed the search and the next day also, but met with no success. Of Minnie there was no trace whatsoever. She seemed to have vanished into the mists.

The proper authorities in the town were now notified, and a reward was offered for information leading to her discovery. The constables were alerted to look out for a small, dark-eyed maid, and there were three reported sightings, but each proved mistaken. The unspoken fear in every heart was that she had come to some harm, and as the days passed, it came to seem increasingly probable.

'If she's blundered into one of those bogs,' groaned Jon, 'we'll never know – and we'll never see her again. Damnation! I'm a selfish wretch. Poor little lass! I can't bear to think on it. Why didn't she tell me? I'm not an ogre, am I? Oh Minnie! I'd give my right arm to see her cheeky little face again.'

A week passed, and the search was abandoned, and all hope with it.

'Just to disappear so completely,' wailed Melissa, who suffered agonies of remorse. Nothing Thomas could say could alleviate her feelings of guilt, and a gloom settled on Ladyford as well as Heron. 'Not to know what has become of her . . . I lie awake at night, imagining her in some fearful place, hoping for us to find her and bring her home. Or else I see her poor little body stretched out on the moor in some god-forsaken corner where no one will ever discover it. If only Papa were still alive, he'd tell me what to do.'

'We have done everything possible,' Thomas protested. 'Followed every clue, acted on every suggestion, searched every moor-house and cave within miles. Someone must have taken her away – that's my guess.'

'– Or she is drowned in the river. Oh, Thomas, what else can we do? I can't bear this uncertainty – this not knowing if she is alive or dead.'

'I'm sorry,' he said. ''Tis a bad business and a lesson not to be lightly forgot. But I think we have done all we can. She is in God's hands now.'

'If only she knew we are not angry with her? And knew that Jon will wed her and all will be well. Do you think mayhap some kindly soul's taken her in and is caring for her?'

Thomas, who thought no such thing, declared it 'very possible', and with that small crumb of hope, Melissa had to be content.

Weeks passed, and months also. Thomas resigned himself to never seeing Minnie again and suggested as diplomatically as possible that Melissa should engage a new girl in her place. The idea distressed her and at first she refused, but eventually she too gave up hope, and enquiries were made in the village. A young girl by the name of Susan Watts was finally taken into the household at Ladyford and after a difficult first week, was grudgingly accepted by Jacob and later by the staff at Heron. Jon, however, could not bring himself to talk to her unless it was absolutely necessary, feeling that by so doing he was betraying Minnie's memory. Knowing the background – her father, a tinner, had helped in the search – Susan bore his coldness philosophically and being of a sunny disposition made the best of it and bore him no ill-will.

Minnie's disappearance affected Hannah in a subtle adverse way which Hugo did not fully understand. She mentioned her only rarely and then in scathing tones, apparently implying that the girl had behaved maliciously and with intent to injure all those who had formerly cared for her. As time went by, she made no kindly reference to her memory, but rather attacked the little ghost as ungrateful and inconsiderate. There was no compassion in her for the girl's plight and she seemed to accept her possible demise with near indifference. Hugo failed to fathom her reasoning, but accepted that it was best not to refer to Minnie in Hannah's presence.

Meanwhile life went on and spring bloomed across the moor, and the broad sweeps of grey-green land were softened with purple heather and dotted with yellow gorse.

One night, Hannah lay beside Hugo in the darkness, wide-eyed and far from the merciful oblivion of sleep. She stared at the end of the bed, where the drapes were parted slightly, revealing a bedchamber lit by bright moonlight. In the distance a fox barked and an early lamb bleated in terror. Suddenly the dogs began to bark. Beside her, Hugo stirred restlessly but did not waken. She had often declared that he would sleep through Judgement Day, so soundly did he slumber. His head reached the pillow and within minutes he was beyond the day's cares, whereas Hannah, a poor sleeper, shared the bed enviously, tossing and turning for hours, her fevered mind a prey to real and imagined fears.

Now, with an effort, Hannah put aside unhappy thoughts, remembering instead happier times. She saw herself as a child of nine or ten, chasing across the meadow while her adored brother, net in hand, waved her to silence, fearing that her voice might alert the small blue butterfly which danced in the air before him . . . And younger still, sitting on her father's knee and laughing up into his handsome face, feeling the roughness of his doublet against her cheek. She had been his favourite . . . Then, in her mind's eye she saw Simon smile at her so vividly that she almost gasped with the joy that leaped within her at his memory. Simon teasing her, pressing his forefinger to the top of her nose; calling to her as he slid from his horse when he came home each evening; Simon in earnest consultation with the mine manager, or running his smooth hand over her swelling belly, exhilarated by the fact that his child lay within. She saw his face glowing with pleasure as he departed to Figeac to bring Hugo and his wife home to England. Now Simon was dead and she lay beside Hugo, and *he* was Master of Heron. She sighed. Outside the dogs persisted in their barking, and she cursed them. They would rouse the whole house! 'You've heard foxes before,' she muttered. 'Be still, you stupid animals!'

Hugo turned abruptly onto his back and his outflung arm landed heavily across her chest. She pushed it away irritably, wondering why she could not love him as he deserved. She let her thoughts drift backwards once more and saw Simon's slim fingers and well-shaped nails pressing cloves into the pungent skin of an orange. He had once made a pomander for young Oliver and Melissa had hung it by his bed to sweeten the air. Poor Melissa; she had loved Simon once, long ago. But why 'poor'? She had Thomas now and was content. No doubt *she* slept well enough at nights, Hannah thought with the bitterness that was becoming a part of her nature. She recognised it and regretted it, but could do nothing to overcome it.

Cursing the dogs again, she slipped under the sheets, trying to close her ears to their clamour. The warmth and the darkness claimed her at last and she began to doze, and then to dream. She was floating, high in the air, aware of the passing breeze which ruffled her clothing and lifted her hair – hovering over a broad fertile valley. She saw, as a bird might see, the narrow river winding along like a curling silver thread below her. Then she was falling towards it, a soundless scream in her throat and the silver thread grew closer and larger, until suddenly it was a silver snake wriggling ahead of her in the grass as she made small ineffectual attempts to take hold of it . . . And it slithered into a cave and was lost in the darkness, and she blundered on in the darkness, groping her way forward towards a point of light at the far end of the cave – a cave which grew lower and narrower, so that she was forced to go down on her hands and knees. Then there came a rushing sound like a torrent of water, which blotted out the pinpoint of light and came pouring towards her, trapping her in its path. She began to scream – to scream the way a baby screams, in hunger and frustration, a lusty, despairing cry – and then she was wide awake and the crying was no longer a dream, but reality. After one moment of disbelief, Hannah scrambled out of bed and without waiting to find a shawl, ran out of the bedchamber and downstairs, her feet bare, her hair flying.

The dogs' frenzied barking was rousing the household – she could hear movements from all directions and footsteps following her down the stairs. But it was Hannah who unbolted and flung open the door and snatched the child from the step, and cradling it to her breast, soothed the passionate sobbing with murmuring kisses until her own tears ran down her face and fell on the small silver-blond head.

No one doubted that it was Minnie's child. Briefly, Hannah blamed herself for not waking earlier, or for not recognising that the dogs were alerting her to a familiar footstep. But she did not waste her energies in prolonged regret, because now they were required elsewhere. She took over the care of the small blue-eyed boy with a passionate zeal which astonished those around her. Gone was the indifference, and gone, too, the self-absorption. Minnie's abandoned baby gave her a new interest in life and a focus for all the frustrated maternal instincts, which, repressed since the death of her own son, had been poisoning her mind.

A wet-nurse was engaged to suckle the child, but Hannah insisted that the girl live in at Heron, for she steadfastly refused to let the child out of her sight. All the clothes prepared for her own baby were passed to him, and every attention was lavished on him.

'She'll kill him with kindness!' Jon protested, at once proud and self-conscious at the unexpected turn of events which had plunged him into the sudden limelight of fatherhood.

Hannah had demanded that he name the boy, but when he confessed himself unable to think of a single name, she suggested Benjamin, which met with his approval and was immediately shortened to Ben.

Ben flourished in the midst of so much love, and rapidly grew from a puny, wailing infant to a plump, contented little boy. He was a beautiful child with large blue eyes, long white lashes and silver-white hair which curled softly over his small, well-shaped head. His skin was smooth and his cheeks were rosy and wreathed for the most part in smiles. No one knew for certain how old he was when he arrived, but they guessed at between four and five months.

'At least we know now that Minnie didn't die,' said Melissa thankfully, a great weight lifted from her mind. 'She was obviously alive and well when she brought him to Heron. The mystery is how she hid from us all for so long.'

'And where she is now,' added Hannah, leaning down and putting her finger to the baby's hand, which closed over it at once. As she wriggled her finger, Ben laughed, a delighted gurgling sound which never failed to enchant its hearers. 'Where is your mama?' Hannah asked him. 'And what would she think of you now? Grown so plump like a little fat puppy.'

'Poor Minnie,' said Melissa. 'Maybe she will come back one day.' She leaned over the crib and clucked at Ben lovingly. 'You'll see her one day, little man, never fear. See how he clings to your finger as though he will never let go.'

Melissa looked at Hannah's glowing face as she played with the baby and marvelled anew at the change in her. She had lost a little weight, and she now sang and hummed cheerfully as she went about the business of managing Heron. Allan and Beatrice also benefited from her new-found happiness and took pleasure in the addition to their family, arguing over who should rock his crib when he cried – which was rarely – and sharing the small excitements of his daily routine. They played with him and chattered over him, brought him daisy-chains and made him a pomander to keep away evil humours. They tried to teach him to say 'papa', sang songs to him and counted his toes and fingers. In short, Benjamin was greatly loved by all and thoroughly spoiled.

'He's just like you, Jon,' said Beth in pretended dismay. 'The spitting image, poor little mite. Tis to be hoped he don't grow up so ugly.'

Jon grinned good-naturedly. He enjoyed his new role and was grateful to Hannah for her wholehearted acceptance of Ben into the family circle. But never expressed was his very real concern over Minnie's welfare. With the baby's arrival at Heron, there had been renewed attempts to find her, but as before, the intensive search merely produced one or two false rumours which led nowhere. No one seemed to have seen a dark-eyed girl begging, and no one answering to Minnie's description had been seen asking for work in the area. Jon wondered uneasily if she were being held somewhere against her will, unable to contact her friends. But if so, how did she contrive to bring the baby to Heron, and why had she not made her presence known? Unable to answer any of these questions, he was forced to admit defeat, taking comfort in the thought that she was presumably still alive and hopefully well. One day, indeed, she might return – but it seemed unlikely. At least he had his baby son, and for the present that must content him.

Hugo took the addition to the household philosophically, pleased that Hannah had a new interest in life, for he had problems of his own which demanded a great deal of his attention. The mining of the new shaft was proving a slower and more difficult undertaking than at first anticipated. There was still feuding between the two brothers and he had been forced to allot them different shifts and threaten them with instant dismissal if there was further friction. Drainage continued to be unsatisfactory, although the introduction of a simple water-pump was now almost completed and would solve that particular problem. Most disturbing was the case now being brought against them in the courts by a farmer lower down the river, who alleged that the water had been polluted by the waste products produced by the mining process. All mining concerns lived under the continual threat of such legislation, and Heron was no exception. It was also the case that the large amounts of soil and grit carried away by the water had to be deposited somewhere; and if that somewhere was a river mouth, silting of the river bed would affect navigation and cause more trouble.

Another matter which concerned him was the depletion of stocks of their own trees suitable for timbering within the mine. When the wooded area of Heron land failed to meet their requirements, they would be forced to buy outside in competition with other mines, and prices would be considerable. All of these matters were no more than the hazards of the industry, but Hugo could never recall having had to face them all at the same time.

He spent much time in consultation with Barlowe, and a great deal more in anxious discussion with other Dartmoor mine-owners at the tinners' parliament at Crocken Tor, which met to consider the worsening situation. Hugo, it turned out, was not alone in his difficulties.

It was hardly surprising, then, that the illegitimate child of one of the servants could arouse little interest in him. The child was well and being cared for: Heron had shouldered the responsibility, as was proper – beyond that, the child's presence hardly impinged at all on his thoughts. He was relieved to learn that Minnie was probably alive, but he intended to waste no more time over a recalcitrant servant. He had more important matters to attend to, and as far as he was concerned the incident was closed.

Melissa and Oliver dismounted and Oliver helped Allan down. They tied their horses to the rail and went in through the creaking gate to the churchyard. The sun shone and small flies danced in a cloud under the dark trees. Melissa took Allan's hand, but he pulled it free again and ran ahead to walk with Oliver. A grave-digger was busy in one corner, heaping red-brown earth beside him, and a young woman crouched beside a newly-filled grave, rocking on her heels and weeping.

'Why does that woman weep?' Allan demanded in his clear, piping voice. Oliver hushed him quickly.

'But *why* does she?'

'I don't know,' said Oliver.

'Is her husband dead?'

'Hush now!'

'But is he?'

'Mayhap.' Oliver looked appealingly towards his mother, and Melissa went forward to walk with them.

'Look there!' she cried, to distract him. 'A bumble bee! See, Allan?'

'I like bees,' said Allan, and Oliver gave his mother a thankful glance. They crossed to the corner of the grave-yard that was reserved for the Kendals, and Melissa stood with bowed head, eyes closed, and whispered a prayer for each departed soul.

'Where's papa?' asked Allan.

'Under the grass,' said Oliver.

'And who else?'

316

Oliver grinned. Allan loved to listen to the catalogue of Kendals who were or were not buried there – it was a small ritual which his strange young mind seemed to relish.

'Uncle Jeffery was drowned in the *Mary Rose*, but Uncle Paul –'

'I didn't know them.'

'No, you didn't . . . Uncle Paul is there, who was killed by bad men, and grandpapa whose heart failed him, and –'

'There's Maggie from the pie shop!' Allan interrupted him, and ran along the path towards a small, dumpy woman, who hesitated to come closer.

Melissa opened her eyes abruptly at the name. The two women had never met, although Melissa knew of her existence. Their eyes met and Melissa, first to regain her composure, said, 'Do come near. My prayers are done.'

Slowly Maggie walked towards them, with Allan tugging at her skirt to hurry her along.

'Maggie makes the best pies!' cried Allan. 'She does!'

Maggie smiled faintly. 'So I tell them all,' she said, and Melissa smiled and held out her hand.

'Where do the years go?' said Maggie wonderingly. 'You were only a girl when I first knew your brother.'

Melissa looked at the round, worn face. The curly hair was generously flecked with grey now, but her eyes were still warm and humorous. 'You recognise me, then?'

'Aye. I know all the Kendals. I come uninvited to weddings and funerals.'

'She makes the very best pies!' cried Allan again.

Maggie looked at Allan with a certain softness of expression. 'He's so like Simon,' she said.

Melissa nodded. 'He is that.'

'Your husband brings the boys into the bakery on occasions. I give them pies or a tart as a small treat. Allan is all we have left.'

'Aye. And you, Maggie. Are you happy?'

'I dare say I am. I never think on it,' she said. 'The shop keeps me busy now my parents are dead. It keeps me out of

317

mischief and keeps me clad and fed, but tis hard for a woman alone.'

'I can imagine.'

'But you have a fine husband, so kindly spoken and patient with the boys. I like a man as loves his children.'

'We're happy,' said Melissa simply. 'But will you always run the shop?'

Maggie shrugged. 'I dare say. While I can keep the lads working and keep my wits. When I'm old – ah, well, the Lord will provide.'

Melissa hesitated. '. . . If ever you want to work as a cook – in our household, I mean – Thomas always promises me a cook, but –' She broke off, embarrassed.

'Are you offering me the post of cook?' said Maggie, astonished.

'I suppose I am.' Melissa laughed awkwardly. 'I only meant that – if you were ever in need of a good home . . . Twas foolish of me. Of course, you have your own home.'

'But if ever my luck runs out – is that what you mean? Then I take it most kindly, and won't forget it.'

Melissa looked at the gravestones and sighed, 'All my brothers,' she said. 'All gone.'

'Wars!' said Maggie and spat on the ground derisively. 'Rebellions! They rob us of our menfolk and leave us their children so that they may grow to manhood and be ripe for plucking again.'

'Oh, don't say so!' cried Melissa fearfully. 'When will they call a halt?'

'Your young Oliver is a fine lad. I envy you.'

Then Maggie dropped onto Simon's grave the handful of petals she had brought and stood for a moment in silent prayer. She swallowed suddenly, and opening her eyes, faced Melissa. 'We've never said this before,' she whispered, 'but I regret the harm I did you. I was so jealous.'

'Twas so long ago,' said Melissa. 'And besides, all came out for the best. We never could have wed. We both loved and lost him. Then poor Hannah lost him also.'

'She has Allan.'

'Aye, she's fortunate in that.'

Maggie sighed. 'I must go home,' she said, 'and check the ovens, send the lad to the mill for more flour and prepare the mutton for the pasties.'

Allan threw a handful of daisies onto the grave. 'Maggie makes the very best pies,' he said again, and laughing, she ruffled his hair.

'Maggie saw Uncle Simon at the war,' said Oliver. 'He fought bravely.'

'He did indeed,' said Maggie. 'But now I must leave you. I'll remember your offer,' she told Melissa. 'Who knows? One day, mayhap . . .'

She shrugged, bade them farewell and made her way back along the path.

'We must go too,' said Melissa, and walking with a boy on either side, pitied Maggie her lonely state.

Hugo and Barlowe stood together at the trestle table, their heads bent over a sketch which Hugo was drawing.

'See here,' said Hugo, pointing. 'Two or three pipes laid the length of the tunnel and connected to double bellows here – we must raise it all a foot or two from the ground – and the bellows are worked by foot pedal. One man will be all we need. A blow hole in each bellows covered by a flap lets out the noxious air, which is then dispersed upwards. A narrow shaft at the tail end, quickly dug, will allow fresh air to be drawn in to replace what is drawn out at the end here.'

Barlowe scratched his head. 'No reason why not,' he said somewhat doubtfully. 'Quite a drain on the timber supply, though, piping the whole length of that tunnel.'

Hugo shrugged. 'The men cannot work it otherwise,' he reminded him. 'Old Matt could have died. We were most fortunate. Next time we might not be. Another fatality, and I think we'll have a mutiny on our hands!'

'Aye. The men are in a strange mood: restless and quick

to argue. I think they fear the Queen's talk of foreign miners.'

'Ah, they fear any change. They will no doubt distrust this scheme –' he tapped the sketch '– until they see it proven. The Queen is right. We need new ideas, a breath of fresh life, in the industry. If the foreigners can teach us anything, then let us welcome them with open arms, I say.'

Barlowe laughed. 'The men may not agree.'

Hugo shrugged. 'Those that cannot accept new ideas will have to go,' he said grimly. 'Closed minds hinder progress.' He glanced at the table clock on the shelf. Barlowe nodded and went outside and struck a gong, which boomed out the change of shift. Hearing it, a man at the shaft bottom kicked at the timbering, and the vibration travelled to the nearest miner, who struck the wall with his pick and sent the message echoing through the rock wall until it had reached all the men. Now miners and shovellers all made their way back along the tunnel, some pulling trucks loaded with ore, others carrying only their own tools, and all lit by the waning light of the almost empty lamps.

One by one they were hoisted up to the light of day, their bodies aching with fatigue, their eyes half closed against the glare of daylight, and queued to sign off as others queued to sign on.

As Hannah rode up, she saw the latecomers converging on the mine from all directions across the moors: a few on horseback, most running or walking, threading their ways along familiar paths worn down by the feet of their fathers and grandfathers before them. But today she had no eye for the pattern of moving men against the background of the moor. Her heart was too full and her mind too eager with news of her own that could not wait: she was with child.

'Hannah? What brings you here?'

Hugo had come to the door of the hut and stood smiling up at her. She smiled back, a brilliant smile, and saw the curiosity in his face flicker into something akin to hope. He held her as she slid to the ground.

'Not here,' she said.

The hope shone in his eyes. 'Hannah?' he whispered, but she shook her head, reluctant to share her news with anyone but her husband.

'Not here,' she said again. 'Walk with me a little way, out of this bustle and din.'

He took her hand and led her along a path which rose steeply, until soon they were looking down on the busy scene from across the broad expanse of moorland.

'So tell,' he said. 'You torment me with your silence.'

'Tis a child, Hugo!' she cried, watching his face light up with joy, just as she had known it would. 'I waited so that there could be no mistake. Twill be a son, I know it. I *feel* it is a boy, and the physician is of the same conviction. My stars are well placed and all aspects harmonious. Oh, Hugo, this time all will be well.'

Hugo took her in his arms, aware of what the news meant to her. 'My clever little Hannah. He kissed her gently and then held her close without speaking, confused by his own reaction.

Hannah was his wife, and he had always longed for a son. His pleasure at the news was dimmed only by the knowledge that the wrong woman was to bear his first boy. He thought instantly of Maria, imagining how the news would distress her. Or would it? She wrote to Melissa occasionally and her letters seemed calm and resigned – almost placid. Perhaps she had accepted her chosen role in life. He had not seen her for so long – a year, maybe two. Abby said she had changed. He sighed, forcing himself to consider what Hannah was saying.

'– only five months away. No doubt Melissa will loan us Susan when the time comes, and Annie will still be with us. She has all but weaned Ben – in time to suckle the new babe. Oh Hugo! I can scarce believe it. After so long a wait – I had given up hope, I confess it.'

'Every man should have a son,' laughed Hugo. 'I shall be as proud as a peacock. A brother for Beatrice and Allan.

Quite a little family – with young Benjamin also.'

She smiled, pleased by this last reference. Though she never spoke of her feelings to Hugo, she looked on Ben as her own, even though he could never inherit, nor become a legal member of the family. Allan was the Kendal heir, and now this new son would be next in line; but to Hannah, Ben was as dear as her own children and she prayed secretly and earnestly that Minnie would never return to claim him.

'And what shall we call our new son?' Hugo asked.

Hannah threw back her head, looking into the cloudy sky for inspiration. 'Gareth, mayhap – or Martin? Or Stephen, after your father?'

'Or Horace after yours!'

'Horace? Oh no! Tis a dreadful name. We could not be so cruel.'

They laughed together, then hugged again.

'So you are pleased with my news?' she asked.

'Most pleased. Now I have something to brag about, and the problems here –' he waved a hand towards the mine '– pale into insignificance. You are a most dutiful and clever wife!'

'Then I shall ride home and leave you to begin your boasting.'

'Ride carefully,' he said as they retraced their steps.

'Oh, I will,' she assured him. 'I shall take great care of our new son.'

And pausing, they kissed again.

CHAPTER EIGHTEEN

Minnie stood at the door of the ale house, slumped against the wall, with an air of deep misery which was genuine enough. The rest of her act was not.

'Spare a coin for a poor dumb woman,' cried her elderly companion. 'A poor dumb creature as can tell your fortune as soon as glimpse your palm, be it ever so grimy!' He bellowed with laughter. 'A true daughter of the moon, she is, and famous throughout the West Country till her sad affliction. Now not a word can she speak –'

'How can she tell fortunes if she can't speak?'

The crowd of merchants roared with approval at this remark and turned mocking eyes towards Minnie, who scowled and spat. Her companion gave her a spiteful jab with his elbow and hissed, 'Smile, you stupid baggage.' Then he turned towards his questioner with an innocent smile.

'Quite simply, your Lordship, sir.' The others sniggered at this veiled jibe. 'She tells me in sign language, and I translate. Quite a sight to see, I assure you. You'll not see the like of it elsewhere I'll warrant – and so accurate, she is! Twill astound you. Twill frighten you if you have secrets, for she'll ferret them out before you can write –'

'Daughter of the moon, you say? What is she, then – a gipsy?'

'Half gipsy, half as English as you and me.'

One of the men snorted in disbelief and pushed past into the ale house.

Another stared at Minnie curiously. 'Aye, she has gipsy

eyes,' he said. 'Dark as sloe berries. Never trust a gipsy, my mother used to say, they're all the same – liars and cheats. Stole all the washing from the front hedge, they did, while she was giving them bread at the back door. That's gipsies for you. Don't trust them further than you can kick them!'

A loud burst of laughter greeted this sally, and two more of the party went inside, leaving one man still fiddling with a badly adjusted saddle. After a sharp kick on the ankle, Minnie levered herself off the wall and approached him silently. She held out a hand for his, and he glanced at her with distaste. Her feet were bare and covered in sores, her clothes tattered and dirty, and her face and arms were covered in flea-bites.

'Oh – I –' He hesitated, aware suddenly that the rest of his party had left him. Minnie's partner moved closer, and there was a hint of menace in his shifty eyes which the merchant, a small, timid man, did not care for. Again Minnie thrust out a hand.

'And what was it made her dumb?' he asked, delaying the moment when he must surrender his well-manicured hand to this disreputable-looking wench.

'Lost both her parents in a fearful accident,' said her companion with a chastened expression. 'Mother and father burnt to death in a fire. Give her your hand. You won't regret it. You'll be so delighted with her powers of perception you'll run inside and beg your fellows to come out and share your good fortune. Give her your hand. She's dirty, I grant you, but she won't bite!'

The small man smiled nervously and looked round for an ally, but the courtyard was temporarily deserted. From inside the building, roars of laughter rang out temptingly and he longed to join his friends and be done with this wretched pair. The woman wore a surly expression and the old man stank of stale urine and garlic.

Slowly he held out his hand, and Minnie took it in one of hers, turning it this way and that and peering at it intently. Then she began to trace the various lines that crossed his palm. Shaking her head, she pursed her lips, then shook her head again.

The merchant looked anxiously towards the old man. 'What's wrong?' he asked. 'Why does she do that? Why does she shake her head?'

Minnie's fingers drew a figure of eight in the air, and the old man said, 'Eight years.'

'Eight years? What of it?'

Minnie sighed deeply and made a small tutting sound.

'What?' cried the merchant. 'Why do you look so grave? What does it mean, eight years?'

The old man held out his own hand. 'Payment first,' he said smoothly. ''Tis a rule we live by, for we have been cheated so many times. Folks hear their fortunes then will not pay. A silver shilling, if you please.'

'A – a *shilling!* 'Tis monstrous!'

Minnie let his hand fall, still shaking her head mournfully, and the man hesitated.

'I – I'll give you half a shilling,' he said rashly, and fumbled in his purse for it. 'There now, and you've been paid handsomely. So tell me – this eight years. What does it mean?'

Minnie resumed her examination of his hand and her finger traced out a variety of geometric shapes for her companion to interpret.

'Eight years –' murmured the old man. 'Why, you will lose a member of your family eight years from this very day. A brother, mayhap, or a father?' He waited for corroboration, and it came quickly.

'My father – his health is not good. His spleen –'

Minnie's fingers danced again, and the old man raised his eyebrows.

'Why, there's a piece of good news. It seems a fortune is coming your way by this dying – Oh, a considerable fortune. Let me congratulate you, sir.'

'A fortune? But I am not the oldest son. I'm –'

'Yet it comes to you. There is some mystery here,

mayhap, but she cannot see clearly yet . . . Ah, your health, sir – now *there's* a vital piece of information!' He watched Minnie's fingers as they executed a complicated movement. 'A little trouble with a stone, mayhap? Ah, then soon, mark my words. Before the month is out. A little discomfort, but no need for surgery –'

'Surgery?'

'She says *no* need, sir. Don't fret about it. And later a little fading of the eyes – nothing exceptional in that. Apart from that, why a clean bill of health, sir. That alone is worth half a shilling, surely? And now the heart, sir. Oh, the affairs of the heart. Ah, she grows tired.'

Minnie put a hand to her head and swayed obediently. The merchant looked disappointed.

'She is weak, sir, still weak from the loss of her parents. Such a disaster. To lose one's parents and one's speech all in a day.'

'The affairs of the heart . . .?' prompted the merchant eagerly.

At that moment one of his fellow-travellers leaned out of the doorway and whistled.

'Come, Daniel. Don't bandy words with them, they're not worth a groat. There's a little lady here as'll sing for us, and wearing mighty little above the waist! Tis a sight not to be missed – freckles in the most amazing places!'

'I'll be with you directly!' called the merchant.

Minnie was slumped once more against the wall, her eyes blank with exhaustion and indifference. The old man shook her by the arm.

'Now stir yourself, my dear,' he said grimly. 'This nice gentleman would know what's due to him pertaining to matters of the heart – isn't that so, sir? I thought so. Then another half shilling, sir, and she'll tell all.' So saying, he grabbed the man's arm and leered up into his face, forcing the merchant to recoil from his foul breath and fumble in his purse resignedly for the rest of the money.

'There!' he said. 'Now make haste, woman.'

326

The pantomime was repeated. The merchant was promised a new wife more handsome than the first, within the year, and also a mistress of wondrous youth and vitality – 'a sewing maiden, mayhap' – who would pander to his every-whim and bear him a handsome son. Lastly a warning.

'But beware the man born under a waning star who speaks to you with friendship in his voice and plots your downfall behind your back. August is the month to guard against. Deception, it holds for you.'

Another shout from the doorway and the sound of a fiddle proved too much, and the merchant, muttering his thanks, hurried inside.

'Right,' said Minnie. 'My share if you please.'

'You'll get it later.'

'I want it now,' she said, her voice rising. 'I want my rightful share. Yesterday you cheated me, *and* the day before – aye, and the day before *that*. Ah!'

She ducked as his fist swung out. Missing her, he stumbled, still clutching the coins in his gnarled and dirty hand.

'If I don't get my fair share, I'll go in there and tell them as you're a fraud!' cried Minnie desperately. 'In the stocks, that's where they'll put you. So hand over my share *and* what you owe me.'

'You cussed little vixen!' he snarled. 'Is that the thanks I get for taking you along? Is it? You'd put me in the stocks? God's blood, you're tighter than a tick, you are. Rightful share, my eye. You'll get your rightful share of my fist if I catch you!'

'I don't owe you naught!' screamed Minnie. 'Why should I thank you, you cheating bastard! You wouldn't earn any money at all if twasn't for me. You had nothing when I met you, except a so-called ulcer on your leg that wouldn't fool a one-eyed idiot.' She spat at him again, and again he lunged towards her. Then, changing his mind suddenly, he lurched in the direction of the ale house door. Minnie gave a squeal of rage.

'Oh no, you don't!' she cried, and flew after him. 'You'll

not fritter my money on sour ale to be thrown up in an hour's time. Give me my share, I say!'

'Hush your din! D'you want them to hear you? Dumb, you are, and just remember it.'

Minnie caught at his arm and tugged him back with all the strength she could muster. 'You give me my money,' she cried, raising her voice. 'Give me my money! Swindler! Cheat!'

He tried to thrust her away, but she clung on tenaciously like a small terrier at a bear-baiting. Just then a small wagon appeared and rolled to a halt beside them. An elegant lady lifted the leather window-flat and peered at them anxiously.

'He's a cheat,' roared Minnie. 'He's gotten my money and he won't part with it.'

She began to kick and pummel the old man, but with a last final effort he swung her off her feet and threw her backwards against the wall. Banging her head she slid half conscious to the ground, while the old man, muttering furiously, made his way up the steps to the ale house.

The driver sprang down from the waggon and opening the door, helped the lady and a gentleman to alight. Minnie looked up at them through blurred eyes that refused to focus. The lady paused, listening to the raucous sounds from within.

'If they have no private accommodation we must travel on. Such a noise! And look at this wretch.' She indicated Minnie with the toe of her grey satin shoe.

'Spare me a coin or two,' said Minnie, fighting back tears of wretchedness. 'I haven't eaten since daybreak.'

The woman looked at her husband. 'How disgusting,' she said. 'They are more like animals than people.'

'An animal has more dignity,' said the man, and Minnie spat at him. He raised his cane threateningly, and Minnie snatched at it, tugging furiously. Taken by surprise, he lost hold of it and in a flash she was up and off, pushing a way through the bramble hedge before the driver could catch her, and then over the fields to the shelter of a nearby wood.

As the sounds of their pursuit faded, she came down from the tree where she had taken refuge. She looked at the cane and saw it had a silver top. It might fetch a shilling or two if she could sell it – but she must take care; the theft might be reported, and she could easily be whipped if discovered. Still, if she could find a buyer who would ask no questions, it would at least mean a bite of food and a mug of ale. Keeping away from the highway but in view of it at all times, she set off towards the next town and whatever might befall her there.

As soon as the nuns had left the frater, Ellen went in to clear the table and prepare it for the next morning's breakfast. She gathered up the wooden trenchers and stacked them, emptying the remaining scraps of fish and bread into a large basket. The knives, spoons, trenchers and mugs went into a bucket of hot water which stood on the floor. The linen napkins were each shaken, refolded and slipped back into their respective rings – the bone one for Dame Agatha, the chased silver for the Prioress, the carved wood for Dame la Retta.

Ellen hummed cheerfully as she worked, looking forward to the evening ahead, when Matt would come into the kitchen to share the last hour of the fire with them, while the nuns, Compline over, would retire to the dorter and snatch as much sleep as they could before the bell summoned them again to early morning prayers. She liked the hour while they slept and ordinary folk could enjoy themselves with a handful of stolen currants and the glowing embers of the fire.

The table cleared, she wiped it over with a wet cloth, rubbed it dry and put out the napkins in their appropriate places. Dame la Retta liked to face the window, the Prioress sat at the head and the new one, Dame Isobel, had to sit away from the door, as she had a wheezy chest and was susceptible to draughts. Fussy old biddies, she thought without rancour. First, she began to wash and dry trenchers and mugs, and then the cutlery; next, straighten the benches and close the windows for the night. All done, she told herself, and took the bucket outside and flung the contents over the grass. Collecting the cloth and the basket of scraps she hurried back to the kitchen.

Maria was checking the accounts in a big ledger and she glanced up at Ellen.

'Not much tonight,' said the girl. ''Twas a tasty bit of fish and easy on their poor old teeth. I'll see how many we've got outside.'

The poor sat on benches beside the creamery, their faces turned eagerly towards her. She counted quickly. The usual, except for blind Annie, and two she didn't recognise. She smiled at them briefly and went inside again.

'There's five of 'em so far,' she told Maria. 'Blind Annie's not here yet –'

'Then she won't come today,' said Maria. 'She's always early.'

'Bill's here and Old Barnaby and the foolish woman, and there's two I've never seen before – a woman and a man with an eye-patch. Horrible, he looks.'

Maria stood up and glancing into the basket of scraps, said, 'There's nothing there for five hungry mouths. Fetch out the last of yesterday's pasty and a loaf.'

'Shall I put another log on the fire?' said Ellen hopefully, afraid it might not last the evening.

'Just one then,' said Maria, and Ellen hurried outside to find the largest one she could.

Maria made a note in the ledger that she fed five poor, then sanded it and closed the book. She took the basket outside and crossed the grass towards the creamery. Five faces turned hopefully towards her and five pairs of hands reached out, ready cupped. She gave bread, pie and scraps to each and made a point of speaking kindly to each one, aware that in most cases it would be the only friendly words they heard.

'Your name, please?' she asked the man with the eye-patch. His reply was unintelligible, so she repeated the question. By way of answer he snatched a chunk of bread and pie and ran off with it. They all watched him go, and Maria sighed resignedly and turned to the woman, who was waiting, hands outstretched, head well down.

'And your name, please?' said Maria. The fingers closed over the food, but the woman made no answer.

'Tell me your name,' said Maria. 'I must make a note –' She paused, seeing something in the shape of the woman's head – something in the set of her head on the short neck and narrow shoulders . . . 'Your name, please?' she repeated.

''Tis I, ma'am.' The head remained bent, the face hidden – but the voice! Maria dropped the basket and took the woman's head in her hands, turning the face towards her.

'*Minnie!* Sweet heaven! Minnie, and in such a sad . . .' She dropped her hands, but continued to stare at the bedraggled woman before her.

'Don't look on me!' cried Minnie, turning away and stuffing the food into her mouth like a starving animal, choking and spluttering in her haste to fill the painful emptiness that had racked her for nearly three days.

'Don't, I say!' she mumbled, struggling to eat the mass of food in her mouth and snatching frantically at any morsel that fell out again. Clasping her stomach, she threw back her head and closed her eyes, overwhelmed by the satisfaction of a filling belly. 'Oh God!' she murmured. 'Oh God, in heaven, thank you!'

She swallowed the last of it as Maria watched her, shocked into silence. 'How –' began Maria. 'I cannot believe my eyes. How did you come by *this* place? Did you know –'

'I knew,' said Minnie defiantly. 'I remembered.'

'We thought you dead.'

'Not me.'

A voice interrupted, demanding when the ale was coming. For a moment Maria stared at the man blankly.

'Oh, the ale! I'm forgetting it,' Maria apologised. 'Wait. You shall have it. Ellen!' The girl came running, and Maria asked her to pour them their usual half pint. 'And you are to come with me,' she said firmly, leading Minnie into the kitchen, where they could talk freely, away from prying eyes and flapping ears.

She poured Minnie a glass of ale, and then another, and waited patiently until she had finished and was wiping her mouth with her tattered sleeve.

'We all thought you dead,' she repeated, 'until the baby arrived at Heron. Twas your baby, Minnie? Speak honestly.'

Minnie's look of concern was proof enough that the baby was in fact hers.

'I wanted it to be cared for decent,' she mumbled, the familiar sullen look settling over her features. The skin was stretched over her cheekbones and her dark button eyes were sunk in their sockets. Against the pallor of her skin they seemed darker and larger than ever, giving her face the look of a skull. A poor diet and the vagaries of the weather had chapped her lips, leaving them broken and scarred, and her hair was matted.

Maria was appalled by her appearance, but tried to hide her feelings, if only to spare the woman's pride – if any remained. Minnie stared down into her empty mug and said nothing. She was defeated, dully waiting for the inevitable reproaches and punishment. Too exhausted to fight any longer, she gave herself up to apathy and oblivion and closed her eyes.

Maria's voice came faintly to her ears. 'He is well and greatly loved, Minnie, your little boy. They write that he is thriving. Hannah has named him Ben.'

'Ben?' said Minnie vaguely.

'Aye. Oh, Minnie, Minnie!' The reproach she had tried so hard to hold back now spilled from her lips. 'How could you leave in that way? How could you trust them so little?

332

And poor Jon! Minnie, twas a terrible thing you did. Do you realise that?'

Minnie shook her head wearily, wishing Maria would stop. Wishing she could fall asleep and sleep on forever, secure in the knowledge that rough hands would not drag her back to wakefulness and make demands upon her which she had no strength to meet. She swayed and nearly fell, and Maria suddenly realised the extent of her exhaustion.

'Come with me,' she said, and led her to the Prioress.

Briefly she explained, and the older woman nodded gently.

'She can sleep in the dorter for tonight,' she said. 'We shall make other arrangements later. There is a spare bed, I believe, but first wash her well.'

With Ellen's help, Minnie was given a quick but thorough bath, and her hair was treated for lice. The hot, soapy water and vigorous scrubbing refreshed and renewed her temporarily, and Matt, coming unaware into the kitchen for that blissful hour with the currants, was dumbfounded to see her alive and well and not so very different from the last time they met. Maria, however, decided that he and Ellen should have their precious hour of relaxation undisturbed, and took Minnie with her to the small cell-like room that was hers by day. She had been granted a dispensation by the Prioress to miss Compline, and so the two of them sat on opposite sides of the table while Maria tried to encourage Minnie to tell her story. Minnie, fed and bathed and wearing a spare tunic begged from the Chambress, began to talk, reluctantly at first.

'I was angry with Jon for what he'd done to me,' she said, 'and hid to frighten him. I went along the old tunnel in the mine.'

Maria's jaw dropped. 'You went down the mine?' she gasped. 'But how? And in the dark?'

'Twas the old drift that's not used any more, except to store oil and rope and suchlike. I'd been down once years before, when I was sent to look for Luke – I mean, the

Master – so I knew my way. Then I heard scratchings and suchlike in the night, and I thought twas the knockers, the little demons, coming to get me. So I ran further in and got lost. Tis like a warren in those tunnels. I found myself where the big fall was in the old man's day –'

'John Kendal?'

'Aye, him. Where the water brought the tunnel down – all rocks and boulders and the drip, drip, dripping of the water. *Ugh!*' She shuddered at the memory.

'How long were you down there?'

'I don't know. Couldn't tell, 'cos twas dark all the time. I thought I'd starve to death and be gnawed by the rats. I kept sleeping and wandering and sleeping again. At last, I found the way out, but I never knew where I was, nor how long I'd been there. I thought as how they'd have looked for me –'

'Twas a massive hunt!' said Maria. 'I heard all about it.'

'I reckoned on how angry they'd be and how I'd be punished. I felt sick with the babe, and hungry, and that shamed!'

'Poor Minnie,' said Maria gently.

'I thought to hide out for a while and let them calm down, and then I'd go back and tell 'em I was sorry, and they'd be pleased to see me still alive and maybe wouldn't punish me so harsh. Then in the town I heard folk say the constables were after me –'

'Not after you, Minnie. Just looking for you.'

'Tis the same thing! I didn't want to go to prison. I didn't want the babe born in a gaol. I stole some food 'cos I was hungry, and then I thought I'd likely get whipped for that . . .' She gave a shuddering sigh.

'They thought you'd run off across the moors,' said Maria, 'and were most likely drowned in one of the mires or set on by cut-throats. Poor Jon was grieving terribly and blaming himself.'

'Twas his fault!' cried Minnie.

'Twas the fault of you both,' said Maria in a quiet tone, for she would not lecture the girl.

'Then it got near my time,' said Minnie, her eyes darkening as she recalled her fears. 'I didn't want to be all alone. I thought to get rid of it, but didn't know how – and besides, I had no money. Then I remembered the plate in the river.'

Maria looked at her blankly.

'The silver plate that Luke threw into the river at the end of the garden.'

'Silver plate?' Maria echoed foolishly. 'I don't know what you mean.'

'Twas always rumoured so,' said Minnie. 'They said the King gave him silver goblets and the like when he helped them and the Mistress –'

'When Luke attended the investigation of Harben Priory? Is that what you're saying? That the King rewarded Luke?'

'Tis true enough,' said Minnie. 'They said the Mistress made him throw it all away as cursed. Threw it in the river, so they said. And twas all still there.' Minnie faltered.

'Go on,' prompted Maria.

'Why then, I thought I'd look for it –'

'After all these years?'

'Aye. And I found one. A silver goblet, it was, and all stained from the mud. But I polished it up and – and meant to sell it, and then pay the wise woman to help me at the birthing.'

'Oh, Minnie. You foolish girl! If only you had gone back to Heron.' Maria sighed heavily and then, regretting her outburst, waited for Minnie to continue.

'I asked a man in the market if he'd give me five shillings, but he said no. Then he snatched it from me and rode off with it. Thieving Jessy! If ever I meet with him again –'

Maria hid a smile and refrained from pointing out that Minnie had stolen it also. 'So you had nothing once more,' she said.

'Aye. And when the babe was born, twas that sudden I never had time to ask for help. In the middle of the wood, I

335

was, and night coming on. I found a charcoal burner's hut and the old fellow let me bide there. I reckon he liked the company. He was a strange old man – not right in the head. He caught rabbits and he had a catapault. He could hit a bird with it – on a branch, that is, not on the wing.'

Maria nodded.

'We ate everything: pigeons, duck, rabbit, hedgehogs – but he was odd. Talked to himself all the time, never listened if I answered him. Then the babe started to cry a lot and he didn't like that. He didn't care for so much bawling, so he turned me out, and that's when I took the babe to Heron. Oh, how those dogs did bark! I thought I'd be caught. I almost wanted it . . .' She shrugged. 'I went away then, and met this old man who said we could go along together. I'd pretend to be dumb and tell fortunes with sign language.'

Maria shook her head, amazed.

'– But he was a cheat,' said Minnie bitterly. 'Scum – that's all you can call the likes of him. Never gave me my rightful share of the money, so we went our separate ways. I stole a cane with a silver top and sold it, but the man reported me to the constables and I had to run again. I didn't know where to go and didn't know where I was. I asked someone if they'd heard of Arnsville and they said it was nearby . . .' She shrugged again.

'So here you are,' said Maria. 'I am so thankful you are safe. But as soon as it can be arranged, I shall take you home. No arguments, Minnie. Heron is your home, and your son and Jon are there. I shall not rest until you are back where you belong.'

They rode back to Devon with a group from Cornwall, who were returning from a wedding and in high spirits. Matt rode with them, but on this occasion none of the nuns accompanied them, since the only ones considered suitable were either too old or infirm and the Prioress feared that the younger ones might be too vulnerable to temptation along the way.

As Minnie rode along on her borrowed mare, her mood veered between apprehension and eager anticipation. Inwardly she trembled at the thought of what lay before her – the reproaches, the difficult decisions that would have to be made about her future welfare. Most of all, she dreaded the meeting with Jon and her son, and the loss of their good regard for her. She rode for the most part in silence, much to Matt's disappointment, for he had looked forward to a journey enlivened by an account of Minnie's adventures. Minnie, however, had revealed it all, or nearly all, to Maria, and had no desire to repeat the painful process for Matt's benefit. In the fullness of time another full account would have to be given to Hugo and Hannah, and the prospect daunted her.

Maria was also in a reflective mood, with no desire for conversation. Normally, her life was a communal affair and her only periods of solitude taken up by prayer, reading and contemplation of spiritual matters. She did not indulge in reminiscences, nor in reveries about the future. Her new-found serenity had been achieved by firm self-control and a determination to abide by the rules of the house, even though she had taken no vows. In all other respects she was one of the nuns, and had learned the rewards that came with a life of self-denial and prayer. Now, though, she was no longer shielded from the outside world, and found it as loud and boisterous as ever it was. Fearful of its effect on her, she turned her mind towards prayer and contemplation and was content to find that by these means she could keep the world at bay. 'Take Minnie, and ride on with the others,' she told Matt. They needed no second telling.

And so they proceeded, with Maria riding a few yards behind the main party, aware of their worldliness, but thankfully untouched by it.

When they were only a few miles from Ashburton, Maria called Matt back to her. 'You had best go on ahead and tell

337

them we are coming,' she told him. 'That will give Hannah time to prepare herself. Tis going to be a difficult reunion, and she is far gone with child.'

Matt rode away in a cloud of dust, eager to reach Heron and revelling in his role as the bearer of such exciting news. Maria had written a letter to Hannah, but no messenger had been available at the time, and so it had never been despatched. Matt's departure brought home to Minnie the fact that they were nearing Heron and her courage began to fail her. She dropped back and rode silently beside Maria, dark-eyed with despair.

'Don't look so stricken!' Maria chided. 'The sooner we arrive, the sooner twill all be done with, and you will see Jon and your son again!'

'They may not welcome me,' said Minnie.

'I think they will. We shall soon find out. Make no mistake, twill not be easy – but that is only just. You did them a grievous wrong, and God in His infinite wisdom brings all sinners to account. Look on it as a settlement of an account long overdue, and pay up as cheerfully as may be. When tis over, your slate will be clean again and the past done with. Now ride quietly, think on what I've said, and pray to God to give you humility – which was never your strong point!'

She gave Minnie a smile to soften the last remark, and received a faint smile in return. And so they rode on, until suddenly one of the Cornishmen called, 'A rider approaches in haste,' and several of the men drew their swords or set their hands against their daggers in case the lone horseman intended them ill.

Maria shaded her eyes and recognised Hugo.

'Tis a friend,' she told the others. 'Have no fear.'

Hugo drew alongside amid cheerful greetings, and Maria found herself once more looking on the features of the man she loved.

'Maria,' he said levelly. 'Greetings. Tis good to see you again.'

338

'I thank you.'

His eyes said more; but Maria remained calm, apart from a small fluttering of her heart.

'And Minnie,' he said, turning to her. 'The news came as a great shock, but we are all pleased to know you are still alive.' He eyed her with pleasure, but his tone was cool. Minnie's place at Ladyford had been filled; Hannah had accepted her child. Life had resumed its even tenor – and now it was to be disrupted again. But the servant had been instrumental in bringing Maria to him once more, and for that he was grateful to her.

'Ride on ahead,' he told her curtly, and with an anxious glance at Maria, she did as she was bid. 'Matt is riding on to Ladyford,' he told Maria. 'Twas fortunate I was at home. Hannah was badly shaken by the news.'

'I can well imagine,' said Maria. 'I wrote at length, but there was no means of getting the letter to you and Minnie's presence was disruptive to our quietly ordered life.'

'I can well imagine!' he said.

'It seemed fairest to remove her with all speed. Also I feared that she might easily disappear again, and I shrank from such a disaster. I'm sorry to add to your problems.'

He shrugged lightly. 'My shoulders are broad,' he said. 'We are all looking forward to seeing you, and Hannah is most anxious that you should stay as long as possible. The child is due in two weeks' time and she is prey to all manner of morbid fancies.'

He kept his face averted from her, and Maria knew it was as much for her sake as for his own. The brief exchange of love in their eyes was enough. He had glanced at her hands and had seen his ring. Suddenly Maria slipped it off and put it into her purse. It would never do for Hannah to see it on her finger. He nodded to show that he understood the reasons for her action.

'Minnie has much to tell,' said Maria. ''Tis a miracle she has survived so much. She is sadder and much wiser.'

'We all are,' said Hugo, somewhat grimly, Maria thought.

339

'Hannah dotes so on the child. I fear this news has distressed her.'

'Poor Hannah – and at such a time. But you will have your own son, God willing.'

'Aye. You seem much changed,' said Hugo. 'Last time we met you were – like a taut bowstring. Now you have a peace about you, a quietness of spirit.'

'I have found my way at last. God has been merciful to his poor confused daughter.'

'I'm glad on it.'

'And I.' She hesitated. 'May I speak frankly, Hugo? I would like to lodge at Ladyford while I –'

'At Ladyford?' the pain in his voice was evident.

'Aye. Twill only be for a few days, then I must return to Arnsville. Hannah is with child, Hugo. That is not easy for me. Please say you understand.'

'I do. Of course, it must be Ladyford, but Hannah will be sorry – she likes your company.'

'I think, too, that Heron may be stormy for a while. Minnie's return from the dead will bring its share of problems. I am unused to such upheavals. Our cloisters are protected from such excesses.' She laughed. 'At Ladyford I can keep my silences and prayers – provided Melissa will take me in for a few days.'

'You know she will be delighted. Maria –' She looked at him. 'Give me your hand.' He took it and put it to his lips. 'Sweet lady, I salute you,' he said, and then he released it again. 'And now we part from the rest of the party.'

They had reached the parting of the ways and the farewells were said. Hugo, Maria and Minnie rode on, but no one spoke. Then Jon and Jack came galloping out to meet them, waving their caps in the air and shouting greetings. Maria had, as always, the fleeting but strong feeling she had come home.

340

Minnie sat on the sawn-off bole of a pear tree and studied the results of Jon's efforts critically. The shape of the house was there for all to see, laid out in the rubble underpinning, which rose a foot above the ground in a neat rectangle. Mentally she tried to arrange the furniture they had been promised – a bed from Ladyford, a trestle and bench from Heron. Jon would put up several shelves. The crib would go beside the bed. Fondly, she glanced down at the child on her lap.

'Is he sleeping?' Jon asked, and she nodded, almost unable to believe her good fortune. She was married and held her own son on her lap – and it had all happened in the space of a week! And here was her husband building them a house, and maybe by the autumn, they'd be living in it.

'Will it dry out by September?' she asked. 'What d'you think, Jon?'

He paused for a moment. 'Wouldn't care to promise,' he said. 'Cob's funny stuff – takes a fair while to dry right out. But we could maybe reckon on October . . .'

'I'd like that,' said Minnie, rocking Ben gently, although there was no need, for he slept soundly.

'I wish he wasn't called Ben,' she said suddenly. 'I'd 'a chose a better name if I'd been here.'

'Well, you wasn't,' Jon reminded her sharply, and she relapsed into a hurt silence. He turned over the mixture of broken clay and sand, sprinkled on more water and straw, and trod it all in together.

'I'd have called him Simon,' said Minnie defiantly.

'Then I'm glad you didn't,' said Jon, 'cos I like Ben.'

He added a bucketful of small stones and stirred and trod again. Then he fetched a piece of timber and laid it down carefully.

'That's the windowsill,' he told her proudly. 'And I might set a few slates over it when tis done, to keep the rain out the wood.'

Minnie was impressed in spite of herself. This was a new Jon she had come back to, a Jon who had grown from a boy

341

to a man in her absence. Jack had even hinted that Susan at Ladyford had fancied him, telling her she had come home 'just in time'.

Minnie was properly grateful, at least for most of the time. She watched Jon as he shovelled up the cob and slapped it onto the foundation, treading it well down and compacting it into a neat slab. He was sturdy and fair, and not bad-looking – and he'd stood up for her when Hannah was at her most shrill. And that Susan was pretty enough, with her dimpled chin and those creamy breasts of hers – why, she pushed them up so high, twas a wonder they didn't fall out of the top of her bodice. Minnie had little to offer in the way of looks, but the child was hers and she and Jon had lain together for a long time. She sighed contentedly, recalling the expression on Susan's face after the wedding.

'I was only teasing about the name,' she said contritely. 'I do like Ben. He looks like a Ben.'

'Aye, that's what most folks say.'

'He's got your nose,' said Minnie, 'and your colouring. There's nothing of me in him at all.'

Jon shovelled up more of his mixture and grinned at her cheekily. 'Mayhap the next one will,' he said.

'The way you're carrying on of nights, it won't be so long neither,' cried Minnie proudly. 'You get worse as you get older.'

'I've some catching up to do,' said Jon.

Minnie laughed and peeped into Ben's face. She liked it best when he was awake, for then he was getting to know her; his sleeping moments were so much lost time. He had cried at first when Hannah left them alone and the memory of his tears haunted her. She too had some catching up to do.

But Ben slumbered on, his mouth slightly open to reveal his first four teeth. For a moment she peered at them closely.

'I wish I'd seen his first teeth come through,' she said.

Jon laughed. 'You'll see all the rest, and share the sleepless nights. Real crotchety he was, and nothing would soothe him. The Mistress tried to –'

'She'll have her own son shortly,' said Minnie quickly. 'All the signs are favourable. Twill certainly be a son.'

'I hope so.'

'Jon! What are you doing there? You said twas the window, but you're filling it in!'

'I'll cut it out after. Tis stronger that way.'

'Ah.'

'You think you could build it better?'

'No, no!'

'Then give me credit for a bit of sense.' Less sharply he asked, 'When's Maria going back?'

'I don't know. I don't reckon she does, either. I wish she'd stay, but she seems content at Arnsville.'

'I can't imagine it.'

'Hannah begs her to stay on. She's had bad pains and cramps these past two days and thinks the babe may come early.'

'Maria should have wed,' said Jon, wiping his forehead.

'She never will now,' said Minnie with conviction. 'She thinks like a nun. I never thought she could, but she does.'

Minnie sighed contentedly, thinking herself a very fortunate woman. Jon had been given a small plot of land beyond the Heron stables and a week off to start work on their home. In the evenings, Jack, and Jacob sometimes came to lend a hand. The walls would be dried out by the autumn, and the thatch would be set over it before the winter arrived. By next spring, they should be able to move in. She would have lots more sons to please Jon, and a couple of daughters to keep her company; then they could sit and spin together in the evenings and laugh about the menfolk. She would learn to cook, and she would sew . . .

'You've a rent in that jerkin,' she said. 'I'll mend it for you later.'

343

'Is that a threat or a promise?' he teased. Her laughter shook the baby awake, and happily she turned her attention to renewing her acquaintance with her new-found son.

CHAPTER NINETEEN

Hannah's son was born safe and well after a mercifully short labour, and the entire household rejoiced.

'Tis a boy! A son!'

Hannah, flushed and excited, received their congratulations and gazed with adoring eyes on Hugo's first son. Hugo kissed and hugged her, and the midwife departed, paid more than generously for her efforts, to recount that 'they was all at sixes and sevens and fairly drunk with joy!'.

Melissa brought Oliver to see his new cousin, and Maria accompanied them to add her own good wishes. She had been prevailed upon to stay until the baby's arrival, and now she was glad she had done so. The sight of Hugo with his wife and son hurt her less than she had expected, and she realised that she could, after all, live at peace, knowing that the man she loved had a family and life of his own in which she could have no part. Instead, she would content herself with the love they had declared for each other.

'He has your small feet and hands,' said Maria, 'but his father's dark eyes.'

Hannah kissed the dark downy head. 'We are going to call him Martin,' she said. 'I think it has a fine ring to it.'

'Martin – aye, I like it,' Maria agreed. 'And how do you like your new brother, Allan?'

'I don't care for him' said the little boy with unnerving honesty. 'I like Ben. I would like Ben to be my brother.'

Maria smiled. 'But Ben is your friend,' she said. 'Now you have a brother *and* a friend.'

'And a sister,' said Beatrice.

'And a sister – why, of course. How could we forget little

Bea. Now, say goodbye to your mama and little Martin, and we'll see what Beth has made for 'four hours'. I think she spoke of cherry tarts.'

The children hurried out of the room, and Hannah closed her eyes wearily. 'Twas over so quickly,' she said, 'and yet I feel so tired. Last time I –' She stopped abruptly as the picture of her stillborn son flashed before her.

'Don't think on it,' urged Melissa. 'Twas God's will, Hannah, and now in his mercy he has given you another beautiful son. Sleep awhile. We will take the children to Ladyford to sleep until the wet nurse is installed. Heron must be becoming a second home to Annie.'

Hannah arranged her body more comfortably on the bed and closed her eyes. The weariness troubled her vaguely, seeming so disproportionate; but after all, she was getting older, and child-bearing was a tiring business. Tomorrow she would be better. Her breathing changed imperceptibly and she gradually fell asleep and slipped into a dream.

Large black crows hovered above her, their wings beating urgently. In the dream she whispered that it was a sign of death and waved her arms to frighten them away, but they perched instead on the arms of a scarecrow and sat watching her with their black, beady eyes. Why do you wait on me? she asked them, and they opened their beaks and cackled and cawed and looked at each other knowingly. Maria was in the dream, scattering corn from an apron filled with grain, and she, Hannah, followed behind her, begging for a handful of corn. Maria turned, laughing at her, and threw the apron of corn up into the air, where it floated for a moment, then fell to earth as drops of rain, pattering down – like raindrops – like teardrops – falling like tears, while the crows watched, cawing, and Maria laughed . . .

'What does it mean, Beth?' she asked next morning. 'Crows in a dream – what does it mean?'

'Crows, ma'am? Why, tis a sign of – that is to say, I don't know, ma'am,' she answered clumsily.

'You *do* know, Beth. Is it a bad sign?'

346

'I don't know, ma'am,' Beth lied. 'But just you sit up now and eat this egg. I've boiled it with a solf yolk, just how you like it. Shall I fetch a shawl to put round your shoulders?'

'No, Beth. I'm too hot already.'

'Hot, ma'am?'

'Aye. Tis this room. It faces the sun.'

'There's no sun this morning, ma'am,' said Beth, laying a cloth over the bedspread and setting down the tray. 'Tis a raw old morning. But it might be fine later.'

She hurried away, leaving Hannah to ponder the omens of her dream. The egg in its wooden pot looked tempting enough, but she had no appetite. Fumbling with the ribbons, she unfastened the neck of her bed-gown and wished she had asked Beth to open the windows. She pressed a palm to her burning forehead and was surprised to see it gleam damply with perspiration. There was a knock at the door and Annie entered.

'Heaven smiled on you, ma'am,' she said delightedly. 'A son, I hear. Where is the little lad?'

'Nextdoor,' said Hannah. 'He cried in the night and they thought he would wake me, so –'

'And he did, I'll wager.'

'No. I slept right through it. I feel so weak. I have slept all night – I had horrid dreams – and now here I am, half asleep again. Go through and see my little Martin – but first open the windows, Annie. Tis so hot in here.'

'The windows, ma'am? But they *are* open.'

'Oh, then tis no matter. Go see the new man of Heron and tell me what you think on him.'

'Your breakfast is going cold, ma'am.'

Hannah frowned. 'I have no appetite,' she said. 'Take the tray and set it down on the chest. My thanks.' She lay back on the pillows and dabbed at her face with the sheet. 'Oh, and a towel, Annie, if you please. Damp it first for me. I'm so hot.'

The girl did as she was bid and then went into the next room, where Hannah heard her exclaiming over the new

347

baby. Then she heard Beth's voice and closed her eyes. Later she heard Hugo's deeper voice and whispers around the bed. They did not disturb her and she didn't care to hear what was said. She only wanted to sleep . . .

That night she tossed and turned, and was glad that Hugo had chosen to sleep in one of the other bedchambers. She spread her limbs and body over the cool sheet, stretching out her toes to reach the coolest corners of the bed, aware that her eyelids burned. Her throat was painfully dry, and the jug of water beside her was soon emptied, but it did little to ease her discomfort.

When at last she fell asleep, she dreamed again, and this time the crows were closer, perching on her shoulder, fluttering against her hair, whilse she screamed soundlessly for Simon to help her. He came and stood at the top of a flight of stone steps, holding out his hands to help her. She made her way up the steps, while the black crows hopped and fluttered around her head; they were so close that she felt their small talons scratching against her bare arms, but she fought them off as best she could, afraid to open her eyes in case the cruel beaks pecked them out. Then Simon was gone, and in his place was a white skull, picked clean by the birds. She tried to scream again, but could produce no sound. Then one of the birds dislodged the skull and it rolled, bumping unevenly, down the steps towards her. With a final effort she screamed . . .

'What is it, ma'am?' asked Annie. 'Can I get you something? A fresh jug of water? Or mayhap a glass of wine, or a sleeping draught?' She was dishevelled from sleep, a candle in her hand.

'The crows,' muttered Hannah. 'The crows peck at my eyes . . .'

'What d'you say, ma'am? Crows, ma'am? Are you dreaming?'

Hannah stared at her, blinking, her eyes refusing to focus properly. She became aware of her throat.

'My throat burns,' she said. 'Ask Beth –'

'She's sleeping, ma'am,' said Annie. 'I'll fetch whatever tis you want.'

'The syrup,' said Hannah. 'You'll find it with the medicaments. Soothing syrup for my throat – and open the windows, Annie.'

'They are opened, ma'am.'

'Are they?' She sighed and blinked again. 'Is it you, Annie?'

'Aye, tis me.'

'The syrup, Annie, for my throat.'

Annie fetched it and poured a large spoonful, which Hannah took eagerly with a gasp of relief.

'So much better,' she murmured sleepily. 'Go back to bed, Annie. I am much obliged . . .'

Annie watched, disconcerted, as she dropped back onto the pillow and fell instantly asleep, breathing heavily. Her fingers clenched and unclenched themselves, and she made small, jerky movements with her head.

'Oh, ma'am,' whispered Annie. 'You're not well at all.'

Hesitating, she wondered whether to rouse Hugo or Beth, then decided it would do no good at such a late hour. No physician would leave his bed before cockcrow just for a sore throat – or was it fever? There were beads of perspiration on Hannah's face and neck, and her lips had a dry, parched look. 'In the morning,' said Annie to herself. 'Twill be time enough.' And she went back to bed.

She awoke some time later and screamed in fright. There was someone standing by the window. Beside her, the new baby stirred uneasily in his crib and gave a little cry in his sleep. The figure turned towards the sound and Annie saw that it was Hannah.

'Ma'am?' she whispered. 'What is it?'

Hannah turned in her direction. 'The crows,' she said.

With trembling fingers, Annie lit the candle and saw that Hannah's eyes were closed. She was sleepwalking!

'Sweet heaven!' muttered Annie. 'What a night this is. I'd best get her back to bed.' And she slid out of her own

349

warm sheets and approached Hannah slowly, speaking gently the while.

'. . . There now, ma'am, you'll be catching your death in that gown and no slippers to your feet. Come with Annie, now. Let me take your arm, that's the way –'

But as soon as she touched her arm, Hannah gave a startled cry and began desperately to brush at the spot.

'Get away, you hateful bird! Don't touch me – keep away! Crows . . . hateful crows . . .'

'Ma'am.' Annie spoke more firmly, one eye on the baby, who threatened to wake at any moment.

Hannah threw her arms up, hugging her head protectively.

'Damnable,' she muttered. 'Damnable crows. They are a sign of death . . . of death . . .'

Annie took hold of Hannah's gown and tugged her gently towards the door. To her relief, she followed, suddenly quiescent. But once outside on the landing, she began to flail her arms, beating off the imaginary birds that flocked round her head and screaming abuse at the top of her voice. In no time at all the whole house was roused, with Hugo struggling desperately to calm her and the baby screaming. As a delirious Hannah fought with Hugo, Allan and Beatrice watched open-mouthed and tearful, until Annie bundled them back into their bedchamber and tried to comfort them.

Hannah's delirium increased as the hours wore on, and the physician who arrived early the next morning diagnosed the dread 'child-bed fever'.

'Is Mama going to die?' Allan asked Beth.

'No, no, Allan.'

'Then why does everyone look so sad?'

'They wonder how best to treat your mama, that is all. Don't fret so, Allan. She will recover, you have my word on it.'

But her optimism was ill-founded. Hannah's condition deteriorated with terrifying rapidity. Within forty-eight hours she was reduced to a burning, aching mass of flesh and bones, mindlessly, endlessly rambling. Unable to swallow anything, she lay barely breathing, while perspiration poured off her. They gave her cooling baths, sprinkled herbs, burnt candles and prayed. They took the children in to speak to her in the hope that their familiar voices might strike a chord in the confusion of her mind; but her dreadful appearance and wild speech terrified them into silence and the experiment had to be abandoned. Blood-letting was prescribed and carried out, but Hannah only grew weaker. Hugo sat at her bedside day and night, unable to tear himself away from the dreadful spectacle.

On the fifth day after Martin's birth, Hannah's ravings grew worse and before anyone could prevent her, she threw herself out of the bed and fell heavily, striking her head against the corner of the wooden chest that stood nearby. The concussion which resulted put an end to the ravings and the sudden resulting silence unnerved everyone, robbing them of the last shreds of hope. Her comatose state lasted for another two days, until at last her life ebbed away. For a second time Hugo had lost a wife, and with Hannah's death his children were once more motherless.

The riverside garden at Heron looked tidier than at any other time in its history. Since Hannah' death, Maria had made it the focus of the children's attention, in an attempt to alleviate the gloom and distract their thoughts from their loss. Together they had pulled out weeds and cut back brambles. Little Beatrice had gathered up rocks and stones in a heap which they planned to fashion into a small rockery, and Allan, under Maria's watchful eye, had felled a small rotten tree. Jon had made a new wooden handrail for the steps, which had been scraped free of moss and soil and lovingly scrubbed by Beatrice. A few small gorse bushes had been brought down from the moor and planted beside the steps, and Melissa had contributed cuttings of lavender from the garden at Ladyford. The tallest weeds had been cut down along the river's edge and various plants long hidden and choked by weeds were now revealed to the sun, and promised to flourish. Oliver's occasional company and assistance had cheered the younger ones, and the entire project was declared a great success. Maria's ruse had worked.

Now, however, the riverside garden was the scene of a different activity. Allan, Beatrice and Oliver stood on the riverbank with Annie, while on the far side of the river Jack knocked a stake into the ground. To this he tied one end of a stout rope. The other end he threw across the water, where it was neatly caught by Jon and tied to a second stake. Minnie stood watching, with Ben propped comfortably on one hip. He was fast asleep with his thumb in his mouth and quite oblivious to the excitement.

'I'll tighten it a bit,' shouted Jon, 'or twill end up in the water and no good to anyone.' He pulled on the rope and gave it another twist round the stake before finally securing it.

Maria stood halfway up the steps, her hand on the dog's collar. Allan turned to her. 'Poor Rufus can't see from there,' he told her. 'Let him sit by me, Maria.'

Maria shook her head. 'He had his chance,' she laughed, 'and nearly knocked Beatrice into the water. He's too excitable by far. He must sit with me. Never fear, I'll tell him what is happening.'

Jon turned to her, grinning, and wondering, as they all did, whether she would ever give up her dark tunic and veil. It was whispered among the servants that she would never return to Arnsville; yet instead of returning fully to their world, she seemed to stay trapped midway between the two. If her mind was divided on the issue, however, she gave no sign of inner turmoil, and the household continued to benefit from her calm acceptance of its day-to-day problems and her quiet good humour.

Satisfied that the rope was secure, Jack plunged into the

water and began to wade across. The children screamed with excitement as the water rose to his waist and he clung to the rope for support. The river was flowing quite rapidly, swelled by recent rains, and the stony riverbed under his feet was slippery with mud, and strands of weed clutched at his legs. Jon took up two spades and waded in from his side with many exaggerated shrieks and cries for the amusement of the children.

'*Oh – Ah!* There's a fish biting my knee,' he cried, 'and a crab is nibbling at my toe. *Help!*'

Beatrice screamed and stuffed a podgy hand into her mouth to stifle her laughter.

Oliver chuckled too. 'Take care, Jon. A bigger fish may come along.'

Jon groaned loudly and stared down into the water. 'One leg gone!' he announced. 'I shall have to hop.' And he made a great commotion splashing and stumbling about. It was so convincing that Beatrice ran screaming back to the steps to stand beside Maria, reaching blindly for her hand in the trusting way that Maria always found so moving.

Minnie pointed suddenly. 'Twas about there, where Jack is. Just below the big stepping-stone. Further still – aye, about there.'

The two men began to dig. Her discovery of the silver goblet had inspired Hugo to order a full-scale search for the missing plate. Lacking Luke's guilty conscience, he had no scruples about adding it to the Heron collection, arguing that it had been legally acquired and properly paid for. He had generously overlooked Minnie's crime in stealing the piece she had found, considering that her subsequent misfortunes were punishment enough. But if more of the silver remained in the river bed he was determined it should be brought out and restored to its true splendour.

As the two spades turned up the river-bed, the water ran brown-red below the rope and excitement mounted. After a while, however, when nothing was found, Jon threw his spade out onto the far bank.

'Tis hard to tell what we're finding,' he said. 'In summer the water would be clear, but now –' He shook his head, took a deep breath and holding the rope with one hand, ducked under the water to feel about on the river bottom with his hand.

Jon and Jack moved steadily across the river, digging carefully and then making a further exploration with their hands, but time passed and still nothing came to light.

'Tis either buried too deep,' said Jack, 'or washed further downstream. We've all but covered this stretch.'

'I doubt it would be so close to the bank,' said Hugo. 'Unless it was in a sack and Luke stood on the bank and tipped it in. Minnie's find was further out, which suggests he threw it. He must have been in a state of great anxiety at the time. It can't have been above the stepping-stones, because it never could have been washed past them – they are too close together.'

So the stakes were uprooted and planted again two yards further downstream, and the search continued. Just when the children were growing restless, Jack gave a sudden cry.

'There's summat!' he shouted, and handing his spade to Jon, plunged out of sight and re-emerged with a candlestick which he waved aloft to loud cheers and congratulations. Thus encouraged, they concentrated their efforts and had soon found two goblets. By this time the afternoon sun was dropping, and Hugo decided they had had enough. The two men were hustled away to the kitchen to hot baths and spiced wine, and the goblets and candlesticks were taken off to the kitchen to be cleaned.

'If the weather holds, we'll try again tomorrow,' Hugo promised, and reluctantly they all made their way back to the house. The excitement was over for the day.

Maria rode between Allan and Oliver. Allan now rode Oliver's old pony and Oliver rode a new and lively sorrel. Maria watched anxiously as the horse tossed its head and

354

skittered in alarm at every bird and rabbit that passed within a hundred yards of them.

'Don't fret so, Maria,' said Oliver. 'I can handle him. He's highly-strung, but I like a horse to have some spirit.'

'I'll try not to forget,' said Maria, trying to keep her amusement hidden.

Oliver was nearly fifteen now and a very serious boy, very much like his father. He was tall for his age and very slim, and sat on his horse with an easy grace. He had the high cheekbones and delicate features of the Kendals, but lacked their blue eyes, his being grey like those of both parents.

Maria watched him out of the corner of her eye, admiring the proud way he held his head on the slim neck. She had a great affection for the boy. He was as close to her as the Kendal children themselves, and lately he and Allan, now ten, had become almost inseparable. Soon, however, they would be parted, for Oliver planned to join the Queen's Navy and follow in Jeffery's footsteps.

They were riding to the mine, where Hugo had long promised them a tour of inspection. The day had arrived at last, and Beatrice had been left with Melissa, while Maria took the two boys. Melissa had originally been invited, but had a horror of the dark and could not be persuaded to go down into what she insisted on calling the bowels of the earth. ''Tis only a few fathoms,' Hugo had insisted, but she had declined nonetheless and Maria had been recruited in her place. Allan had been down once before, but only as a young child and could remember very little about it. As the heir to Heron, one day to take Hugo's place at the head of its industry, Allan was expected to take an interest, which he did from an early age.

When they reached the yard, Hugo came out to greet them and the boys and Maria tied up their mounts.

'You look displeased to see us,' said Maria, puzzled by his abrupt greeting.

'Forgive me,' said Hugo. 'It has been a difficult morning and I had quite forgot you were coming.'

'If tis not suitable, we –'

'No, no. Stay, now you are here,' he said. 'I would not disappoint the boys. They have waited so patiently for this visit.'

'These difficulties,' said Maria. 'Are they serious?'

'Aye. The men are uneasy and rebellious. They jump at shadows. Ever since the Queen started to bring in foreign miners, they claim their livelihoods are in jeopardy and want to make representation to her.'

'And is there a risk to their jobs?'

'None at all. The men she imports are experts, with ideas to sell. They come with new machinery, new methods, better safeguards for the men's welfare, but these wretches are afraid of change and fear progress like the plague. They insist that the traditional ways are best and want all manner of reassurances. They have a leader, a man named Stennet, who has the audacity to challenge me with a list of articles "for my consideration"!' His voice rose with anger as he spoke. Then he shook his head. 'These troubles are mine. I shouldn't burden you with them – forgive me.'

'They are Heron's troubles,' said Maria gently. 'You shouldn't take all the burden on your own shoulders. Besides, it interests me.'

He smiled and relaxed a little. 'Tis still no excuse for me to behave so boorishly,' he said.

Oliver's face was intent. 'And will you sign their articles?'

Hugo frowned again. 'No,' he said. 'This morning I returned the document to Master Stennet. I shall suffer no such pressures and agree to no demands. If the men do not wish to work under me, they must look elsewhere. If I choose to employ a foreign adviser, I shall do so. No miner is going to dictate to me. There now, I'm raging again!'

'Would you prefer us to come another day?' said Maria seriously. 'Tis hardly a good time.'

'I shall be the one to decide if the time is right,' said Hugo sharply. 'I don't intend to change my plans for a foolish, discontented rabble. No, we'll have a look round here and then go down to the second drift, where there is some work in progress. Come along, then.'

The tour began, and Maria and the two boys found it every bit as fascinating as they had hoped. On the surface they saw the stores of oil, spare picks and shovels, coils of ropes, lamps and leather gloves. There were maps and diagrams of the underground workings and ledgers full of amounts of tin, values, and qualities.

'This book goes back to your grandfather's time,' Hugo told them. 'See, that's Luke's handwriting, and here more recently, Allan's father. Go further back in another book – here – and you see John Kendal's hand.'

'And today yours,' said Oliver. 'All Kendals.'

Hugo nodded. 'Tis a solemn thought.' He said the words lightly but Maria, catching his glance, knew that he did not consider it a light matter. He was fiercely proud of the Heron line.

'And here is my father's name,' he said. 'See – Stephen K. That's how he signed his name.'

At last it was time to go underground, and they stood at the top of the shaft, waiting for the two windlass men to pull up the bucket.

'Maria shall go first,' said Hugo. 'Then the boys, and I'll follow.'

The man nodded. Maria could not help noticing nervously that he had a surly look; no doubt he was one of the 'discontented rabble' which Hugo had spoken of so disparagingly.

Maria's courage almost failed her when she saw the size of the leather bucket and the depth of the dark shaft below her, but with the eyes of the two boys upon her she managed to smile and allowed Hugo to help her over the side. It was in fact roomier than it looked and felt reasonably stable. The boys waved and Hugo nodded to the windlass man, who began to turn the handles, and slowly, almost silently, she found herself descending. Once out of sight of the others, she closed her eyes and in a very short time, with only the slightest jar, she was at the bottom and climbing out. A man stood a few yards away working a huge pair of bellows with his feet, watching her without speaking. Once more Maria was aware of the hostility of the men and wished they could have waited for a more opportune moment to make their visit.

The bucket returned to the surface and she watched it grow smaller as it was wound up; then the whole process was repeated, and Allan joined her. Soon all four of them stood together beside the large wooden bellows, which Hugo explained was connected by long wooden ducts to the end of the tunnel, where stale air and sometimes noxious gases accumulated.

'Where does the gas come from?' Allan asked

'From the rocks,' said Hugo. ''Tis trapped between the layers of rock for years and years, and when we break up the rock the gas comes seeping out. Usually it has no colour and sometimes very little smell. The men could die of it without knowing it was there.'

They now stood in a wider chamber, but ahead of them the tunnel gleamed grey-brown with streaks of green. It was about five feet high and all of them except Allan would have to stoop to walk along it. Two torches burned, fastened one each side of the tunnel and the flames cast eerie shadows. The only sounds were the spluttering torches, the drip of water and the creaking of the bellows. Hugo nodded briefly to the man working them, but neither spoke. He had brought down a lamp for each and now filled them carefully with oil from a stone bottle. With these lit, they were ready to proceed.

Hugo went first, followed by Allan, Oliver and Maria. The man muttered something as they moved away; Maria didn't catch what he said, but Hugo's sharp ears caught the sound and he turned directly.

'What's that you say?' he demanded roughly.

The man's eyes glittered in the half light. 'I said, a woman in a mine is bad luck.'

'I'll be the judge of that,' said Hugo. 'Your job is to work the bellows. When I need your advice I'll ask for it.'

The man shrugged, but maintained his challenging gaze. The exchange at an end, they moved away along the tunnel.

Underfoot, a channel had been dug along the centre of the floor, which acted as a drain for the water which seeped and dripped down at various points along the way. They picked their way carefully past the wooden shuttering, a framework of narrow posts and cross-beams which lined the walls and roof of the tunnel. Here there were no miners, but the distant sounds of pick and shovel echoed in the enclosed space. The wooden ducts from the bellows ran along each side, and as she stumbled along, one hand holding up her skirt, Maria wondered how a man could possibly spend his working hours in such a dismal place.

'But where's the tin?' asked Allan.

Hugo laughed briefly. 'Hidden in the rock,' he said. He stopped and pointed to the rock wall. 'Even there,' he told them, 'if I were to hew out a piece of that granite and crush it up, I would find grains of tin ore. If I heated it in a pan, the tin would melt and form a small bead of metal. Here there are only a few grains of ore in each lump of rock, so we leave it where it is. Up ahead where the men are breaking into a good vein, each piece of rock will yield a greater quantity of metal – and a tin of higher quality.'

'I want to be a miner,' said Allan, but Oliver shook his head.

'I'll take my chances on the sea,' he said. 'At least there a man can see the sky!'

At last they reached the first of the wooden trucks; into it a man was shovelling lumps of rock which the men ahead of him were breaking from the rock face.

'When tis full,' Hugo explained, 'he'll pull it back along the tunnel and it'll be tipped into large buckets and taken up the shaft. From there it'll go to be crushed.'

The man, pausing in his work, regarded them for a moment, then spat. The affront was obvious and deliberate. In the light of the torch on the wall his eyes shone white in a face that was grey with dust and streaked with sweat. He opened his mouth to speak, but began to cough instead, an ugly sound which shook his large frame and left him breathless; whatever he had intended to say was left unsaid. Hugo had opened his mouth to reprove him angrily, but with an effort restrained himself.

They squeezed past the truck and now found themselves almost at the end face of the tunnel. A dozen or more men worked in the confined space, some attacking the roof, others the walls, using short-handled iron picks. The air was full of flying dust and fragments of rock, thickened by the fumes from their lamps. Instinctively, the three visitors put up their hands to cover mouth and nose, and Oliver began to cough as the harsh gritty dust reached his lungs. At this end the timbering was obviously newer and one man worked on it, his hammering adding to the noise.

'Here the mining takes precedence,' Hugo shouted. 'Temporary scaffolding goes up, and then the carpenter moves along behind the miners to replace it with the stronger permanent shuttering.'

Around them, the men had fallen silent as a mark of their disapproval. Maria was grateful that now they had reached the mine itself and would soon surely turn and retrace their steps. The men's attitude frightened her, and she felt exceedingly vulnerable. But Allan and Oliver were plying Hugo with questions. Allan wanted to try his hand, and Hugo asked one of the men to lend his pick for a moment. Maria thought at first he was going to refuse, but instead he threw it down at Allan's feet and turned away to mutter to one of his fellows. Maria felt her face burn at the insult, and prayed desperately that Hugo would keep control of his temper. Hugo picked up the pick and showed Allan how to hold it correctly and where and how to strike the rock. Then Allan wanted Oliver to try it, and he did so hurriedly, for he too was aware of the tension around them.

'That was Stennet,' Hugo said in an aside to her. 'And

Stennet spells trouble.' Maria looked at the man and saw the suppressed rage smouldering in his small, dark eyes. The grey dust mingled with the sweat on his face gave it a wild, primitive look, as though he had painted his face with warpaint. And war it might well be, reflected Maria, thinking what a terrible enemy such a man would make.

While Hugo was explaining something to the boys, Maria saw that Stennet, watched by the others, had moved back towards them, and she realised with a sudden flash of intuition that the trouble Hugo had expected and dreaded was about to materialise. As though frozen with fear, she saw him approach her, seeming to measure his steps. At the precise moment that Hugo turned back to her, Stennet reached her, and deliberately stamped in a large muddy puddle which sent a spray of filthy water all over her tunic. A few drops even reached as far as her face so that instinctively she flinched and put up a hand to protect herself, almost stumbling as he pushed past her in the confined space. A small cry escaped her lips and she saw the man smile with satisfaction. She had acted exactly as he had planned and played into his hands.

As Stennet had hoped, Hugo's control snapped and he lunged forward, catching Stennet by the arm and punching him full in the face with a blow that sent him staggering backwards to collide with another miner, who cursed violently and pushed him forward again. Stunned by the suddeness of the events, Maria could only gasp and press herself back against the rock wall in an effort to avoid the fight that now seemed inevitable.

With an oath Stennet lashed out, but Hugo side-stepped and the blow missed his cheek by a hair's breadth. Stennet was a large man and muscular, and although Hugo was sturdily built he was no match in size for the burly man now venting all the anger and frustration that had built up over the year.

'Papa!' screamed Allan, and would have rushed forward, but Oliver held him back. Maria and the two children backed away as the two men lunged at each other furiously. The other miners also retreated, some to the open end of the tunnel, others with Maria and the boys to the rock face itself. A lamp was kicked over and flame extinguished. Another was knocked from its owner's hand as Stennet's brawny arm flashed past and found its mark against Hugo's left shoulder. With a cry of pain, Hugo staggered backwards.

Now it was Oliver, his face white, who clenched his fists and made to go to Hugo's aid.

'Leave them be!' cried one of the men harshly. 'Keep well back or you'll get hurt. Twas your pa struck first.'

No one could dispute that fact.

Hugo had slipped to one knee, clutching at his shoulder, but he was up again at once, just in time to dodge another blow. Stennet's fist landed against the rock with the force of a sledge-hammer and he cried out in pain, clutching at his bleeding knuckles.

Maria longed to stop the pair before they did each other lasting harm, but her heart hammered at the thought of interfering. She sensed the inevitability of the conflict – these men were bound to fight some time, some place, and she consoled herself with that knowledge. Yet the hatred in their eyes appalled her and the violence of the struggle was terrifying.

The miners, meanwhile, watched silently, no doubt hoping for a victory for their man, yet apprehensive of the consequences. A man did not challenge his employer if he wanted to remain employed. And without a reference Stennet would never find work in another mine. He would lose his livelihood and face certain ruin. Hugo, for his part, could not afford to be challenged by one of his own men and lose. Either result led to disaster. Both men knew exactly what was at stake, and neither intended to yield.

Maria closed her eyes and began to pray for a miracle, but a cry from Stennet made her open them again. He was down, sprawled in the mud. Maria screamed as Hugo, teeth bared in a snarl, threw himself onto him. This was a new and frightening side to Hugo's character, and one that she had never guessed at. She saw him catch the man by his hair and bang his head against the floor of the tunnel; but with a tremendous effort Stennet rolled over and then he was astride Hugo, his hands clasped together in a double fist which he smashed down on the side of Hugo's head. Hugo's thrashing legs caught one of the scaffolding timbers. To Maria's horror, it was jerked sideways by the violence of the blow, unnoticed by all but herself.

'Why don't they stop?' pleaded Oliver, but Maria could only shake her head in despair. The two men were on their feet once more, but wearying rapidly. Stennet had a cut across his left cheek and Hugo's mouth was split and bleeding. Both men panted for breath, but the fury in their eyes was unabated. They sprang together and once more wrestled back and forth with a grim ferocity.

'I must help him!' cried Oliver.

'He won't forgive you if you do!' warned Maria, and Oliver knew she was right.

Hugo had freed himself from Stennet's grip and rushed with his head down, butting his opponent in the stomach. Winded, the miner staggered back against the shuttering, dislodging another prop.

Maria screamed a warning, but again it went unheeded. 'Sweet heaven!' she whispered, 'they'll have the shuttering down. They'll bring the roof down on all of us.'

Around her Maria saw that the men were growing anxious. A fight was a fight, but this was proving to be more – almost a duel to the death. Although both men were staggering drunkenly with weakness, neither would be the first to call for quarter.

Suddenly, there was an ominous creaking from overhead, and Maria saw that a section of the scaffolding was breaking away from the roof. She shrieked in terror, pointing frantically. '*The roof! The Roof!*'

In seconds the cry was taken up, and the two men on

the ground clambered up on their knees, the fearful words ringing in their ears. There was a splintering noise, and one of the roof beams parted from its support and hung crazily, uselessly.

Suddenly the men were galvanised into action and the fight was forgotten, paling into insignificance before the terrible threat of a roof fall. Maria crossed herself and tried to pray, but no words came into her mind. All she could do was stare at the collapsing shuttering and the mass of men beneath it, struggling to repair the damage before it was too late.

Stennet and Hugo were on their feet, their anger forgotten. By the light of the remaining lamps, the tunnel was filled with shouted instructions, urgent movements, dark faces, and frightened eyes glistening eerily in the gloom.

'Wedge that here – no, higher!'

'Steady it. Take the strain. Hold it, for God's sake!'

'You – put your shoulder to it, while I ease this off – Damnation take it! Tis slipping. Help me, quick. Tis going!'

Desperate arms reached up, but in spite of all their efforts new sounds of splintering wood filled their ears.

'Get them out quickly, before tis too late!' The voice was Stennet's. 'The woman and the children – take them, for God's sake, or we may all die!' Panic-stricken, Allan clung to Maria, his courage deserting him as the awful realisation of their danger dawned upon him. Oliver, too, was white and trembling, not knowing how to help, one arm round Maria's shaking shoulders.

Then Hugo was beside them, pulling them through the mass of men, who stood braced against the walls, arms upstretched against the roof to let them pass, the sound of rending rock adding to their terror.

'Tis coming down! Run while you can!'

As they ran, half stooping along the dark tunnel, more men passed them, heading back towards the rock face with fresh wooden props and tools. The sound of the men's cries faded as they reached the bottom of the shaft.

'We'll be safe now,' said Maria breathlessly. 'We'll go up one at a time. I'll see to the boys. You go back where you're needed.'

But Hugo had already turned back, and as Allan was wound up to the daylight, Maria saw him disappear into the darkness. She prayed silently. *Spare them, I beseech you, for they are good men at heart, all of them.*

Oliver put an arm comfortingly around her shoulders as they watched the bucket swaying down again. 'They saved us, those men, although they hated us,' he said.

'They did not hate us, Oliver. They quarrelled from fear. We stand for management, and in their minds the management stands for change – and that they fear most of all.'

'The bucket is here, Maria. You go next.'

'No, no –'

'I insist, Maria. You are trembling and I'll not leave you down here. Go! I'll follow.'

She looked at him, surprised by his calm, masterful attitude, and saw that he spoke as a young man now, not as a child. He had grown up during the past hour. She marvelled at the subtle change from boyhood to manhood. His arm was around her shoulders. He was concerned for her safety. The relationship had changed – it was no longer adult and child, but man and woman.

'Why do you look at me that way?' he asked, and she realised that he was not yet aware of his maturing.

''Tis nothing – I'll do as I'm bid,' she said smiling, and allowed him to help her into the bucket.

She and Allan waited at the top until Oliver joined them, and then stood, uncertain what to do next.

'We'd best ride home,' said Oliver. 'No doubt Hugo will be busy for some time yet.'

'But how will we know if they are safe?' began Maria.

'We shall know all in good time, and there is nothing we can do to help. I'll tell the windlass man to pass on a message that we are returned to Heron.'

Weak and shaken, Maria nodded and slowly they rode back to Heron. News came later that the danger had been averted. All the men were safe.

CHAPTER TWENTY

'What will you do?' Maria asked Hugo as they sat at the table later that evening. Maria had eaten earlier, but to keep him company she drank wine with him while he ate cold soused mackerel.

Hugo looked up, a twinkle in his eyes. 'I was expecting you to ask that, and I thought I knew the answer. Now I know that if I say "dismiss the man" you will make issue of it.'

'Am I so transparent?'

'Only to me, mayhap. But what if I say so? Tell me your arguments.'

'Tis not my place.'

'I am sure that won't deter you! But let me say this first. I acted hastily and allowed myself to be provoked, when I thought myself beyond such foolishness. I put you and the boys in a position of danger. I beg your pardon for that.'

'You didn't know how it would end.'

'No, but to fight in front of you! That was most unwarranted.'

'You saw that he splashed me deliberately and acted in my defence. That was honourable in intent. Don't ask my pardon, for the fault was not yours. I understand your feelings – you were provoked beyond endurance.'

He put his head on one side and considered the face which gazed on him so earnestly, framed still in the dark veil. Then he looked away.

'So I'm forgiven?' he said.

'Indeed you are. But Stennet, Hugo. Will you punish him – dismiss the man?'

367

'I must make an example of him, or I shall have a rebellion on my hands.'

'I think he is a good man, Hugo.'

'Good? You saw the wretch –'

'Aye, I saw him and others like him. Strong, brave, loyal –'

'Loyal, you say?'

'Loyal in his heart, Hugo. He was the first to cry "save the woman and the boys", even after insulting me and fighting with you. All of those men, Hugo – their first thoughts when danger threatened was to hold up the failing shuttering so that we four might escape.'

Hugo was silent.

'They all had reason, or thought they had, to hate you and could easily have run off and let us die. They are good men, Hugo, all of them.'

'But am I to be challenged by any of them and made to fight for my position? I *own* the mine, Maria. They work for me –'

'And fearful work it is!' she cried. 'Stumbling about underground, unable to stand upright, breathing foul fumes and dust, the walls running with damp –'

'Do you think I don't know all that?' he cried. 'Why do you think I want to change it? I want to pump out the standing water, freshen the air, bring in powered machines to ease their burden and better their conditions!'

'Powered machines?'

'Aye, powered by water, or air, or animals. In Spain, dogs turn wheels, ponies pull carts, birds test for noxious fumes. These things improve the men's lot – but my men will not have it. No foreigners! That's all they say. They are fearful of losing their jobs if a machine can take their place.'

'I would fear that also if I were a miner.'

He stared at her. 'But if a machine releases three men, there are three more men to work at the face.'

'And if foreign labourers come to the mine?'

'There is no question of it! All I want to do is bring

experts to advise me on the latest equipment and tell me how I can make Heron safer, more comfortable to work in, and more productive.'

'Have you told the men this?'

'I don't need to ask their permission!' he exploded. 'I am the owner! If I ask them and they refuse – as they will – what do I do then? Abandon my plans?'

'I did not say ask their permission, Hugo. I said tell them what you have told me. Reassure them, Hugo. They are frightened.'

'Frightened! Tis nonsense. Such men don't frighten easily.'

'They can be frightened for their livelihoods and for their wives and children, Hugo. How does a man explain to his family –' She stopped abruptly. 'You are not listening, Hugo! You do not hear what I say . . .'

He nodded slowly. 'I hear you,' he said. 'I was thinking – tis so long since I saw your hair. Must you cover it always with that veil?'

Astonished, she was lost for an answer and merely gazed at him in silence.

'Maria – Maria, I know how you feel about the church, but I –'

'Do you, Hugo? Do you know how I feel?'

'I believe I do. You've talked to me from time to time, and I confess I'm being selfish, yet I must ask it. Could you ever give up your life at Arnsville and come back to Heron? Oh, I know this is not the right time to ask – we were talking of other matters of great import – and yet when we sit together like this, I suddenly can't imagine Heron without you.'

For a moment she said nothing, then looked up. 'You are right, Hugo,' she said. 'This is not the right time. You give me no time to think. I don't know what to say. I suppose I'm afraid of changing one way of life for another. I have changed so much in the last five years.'

'You are afraid to give it up?'

369

'Tis the only life I know now. Does that sound cowardly?'

He smiled. 'No, honest and understandable in the circumstances. But that tunic and veil! Now tis my turn to be foolish, but I long to see you once more with your hair long and free.' He sighed. 'Forgive me. I had no right to ask it.'

Maria regarded him steadily, her mind formulating and reformulating what she wanted to say. For the last few weeks, the longing to stay on at Heron had grown in her, but she had tried to put such thoughts from her mind. She had even become conscious for the first time in years of her tunic and veil and how inappropriate they felt as she became more involved in the household and children, more interested in the mine and its problems. She was slipping back into a wordly existence with greater ease than she had believed possible.

Yet she could never fit in at Heron as Hugo's wife. Her years in the company of the nuns had had a profound effect on her emotions, and the thought of taking her place as Hugo's wife was no longer acceptable to her. Her feelings, her body, were hers alone, and she had become reconciled to her celibate life. The affection she now felt for Hugo was almost brotherly – yet in the children's eyes she knew she was rapidly taking the place of their mother. It seemed impossible for her to come to terms with her feelings.

'Hugo –' she began. 'I need to tell you how I feel, but how to begin? I don't think you will understand, because I scarcely understand myself. I'm not certain of your feelings for me –'

'They are the same as they ever were,' he said slowly. 'I haven't changed. I still love you. I would ask you to marry me, but your chosen way of life makes that impossible.'

'I realise that, and I, too, find my situation confusing. I don't properly belong anywhere now, it seems. Arnsville holds no charms for me, and yet I cannot stay here indefinitely. If I cannot be a wife to you, then you must find another who will. That is only reasonable.'

'Do you love me at all?'

'Aye, most sincerely, but I feel no passion, no desire – nothing. I would be a poor wife, Hugo.'

'Your feelings might change towards me,' he protested. 'You are changing already – you say so yourself. You no longer belong in Arnsville. A few more months here at Heron and you might feel towards me as I do towards you, for I long to take you into my arms. Aye, and into my bed. Is that so terrible?'

Maria looked at him helplessly, and he went round to her and raised her to her feet. Then, holding both her hands, he looked deep into her eyes, searching for a sign, for something that might give him hope. But there was nothing.

'Mayhap we can compromise,' he said gently. 'Will you stay on at Heron to care for us all? Give up your dark robe and veil and see if you are content to live in the world again. If, in six months' time you are of the same mind –' He paused.

'You will let me go?' she prompted.

'I will ask you to try for another six months!' he said, and they both smiled and the tension was eased. 'I beg you to stay,' he said. She was moved by the intensity of the appeal, but still she hesitated. 'Let me make a deal with you,' he said. 'If you will stay for six months, then I will keep Stennet on at the mine.'

'Hugo,' she cried, laughing in spite of herself. 'Such a devious mind!'

'The Kendals are known for it,' he assured her. 'Oh Maria, we laugh; but tis no laughing matter. I love you, and I hope in time we will grow closer and you will choose to wed me. But for now I ask only that you will stay. Half a year is such a short time. Won't you spare us half a year of your life?'

For answer, Maria raised her hands, unfastened her veil, and let the long, dark hair, so long confined, fall freely about her shoulders.

Summer passed, and the autumn golds and browns began to sweep across the moor. Melissa watched Oliver grow from a quiet boy to a withdrawn young man, whose moods were as unpredictable as the weather, and occasionally as stormy. He could no longer be persuaded to spend time with Allan, who so adored his big cousin, but would go out alone, hawking or riding or fishing for salmon, returning in a resentful silence and complaining that the horse was too old or the river too swift. Melissa wrung her hands over her son and lamented that he had suddenly become a stranger to her, but Thomas comforted her, assuring her that it was a difficult age for a boy and that he would grow out of it in time.

'But when?' she wailed. 'I cannot speak to him but he snaps my head off – nothing in the whole world is right for him. I can't believe you were this way at his age.'

'Maybe not quite so doom-laden,' he said, 'but I was moody and ill-at-ease with myself and everyone around me. Try to be in good spirits, for that may help him.'

'He was sharp with young Allan on Sunday last,' said Melissa, 'and even Maria looked strangely at him. Tis *unlike* Oliver. But let's hope you are right and twill pass with time. Did you notice that Maria has stopped wearing her tunic? I could hardly believe it – she looked so different. She wore an old russet gown that was once poor Hannah's and had let down the hem. Do you think she will stay now?'

Thomas laughed. 'Who can understand the ways of women. Nothing would surprise me. Do you hope she will?'

'Why of course I do –'

Oliver came into the room, dressed for riding. 'I shall be gone an hour or so,' he said.

'Are you hawking?' said Thomas. 'If so, and you want a companion, take Jacob with you. He would –'

'I'm not hawking,' said Oliver. 'I'm riding to Ashburton with Maria.'

They both waited for the rest of the details, but it

seemed none were forthcoming.

'And Allan?' said Melissa.

'No. Just the two of us.'

'Oh.'

'Provisioning,' he added, as though that explained every-thing. Then, with a brief nod, he left the room.

Slowly Melissa raised her eyes to meet her husband's gaze. 'Oh, *no!*' she whispered, as the truth dawned at last. 'Did I imagine the excitement in his voice?'

Thomas shook his head. 'I fear not. I heard it too.'

'But not Maria!' cried Melissa. 'He is so young. Dear Lord, he must not love Maria!'

'I think our prayers are come too late,' said Thomas wearily. 'How could we both have been so blind?'

On the way back Oliver suggested that since it was still early and the light was good, they might extend their ride to the cliff top and enjoy the sea breeze.

'Twill be more like gales if it goes on rising,' laughed Maria, 'but I agree it would be pleasant, and we're in no hurry. I haven't seen the sea since I rode back to London from Romney House. It seems so long ago. Poor Harold. And poor old Ruth – I should visit her. Tis very remiss of me to neglect her so.'

'Your heart is too soft, Maria,' said Oliver. 'For you the world is full of lame ducks, and you would return them all to perfect health.'

'I would if I could. Don't mock me, young Oliver.'

'I am not "young Oliver",' he corrected her. 'I am Oliver, rising sixteen.'

'I can't believe it.' Her eyes glowed and her cheeks were flushed, partly from the exercise and partly from the excite-ment of the morning's shopping. She had bought some blue silk for a new gown with money Hugo had given her, and was eagerly looking forward to making it, comparing the merits of this and that style in her mind's eye.

'The blue will suit you well,' he said, reading her thoughts, 'although the rose was softer.'

'And lace at the neck – or maybe braid,' she said. 'And a head-dress to match from the spare pieces.'

'You will look like a princess. Queen Elizabeth would have some competition if you were presented at court!'

'Oliver! What a charming compliment. You are right – *young* Oliver never spoke to me that way.'

He grinned. 'Stennet was kept on, did you know?' he asked.

'Aye. And twas wisely done, I think. The men will respect Hugo's generosity. Twill ease the tension among them. So you are going to sea, Oliver? You do not want to be a miner.'

'No, I love the sea. Cruel it may be, but it has a fascination for me. Do you know where I am taking you?'

'To the cliff top, I thought . . .'

'Aye. But to the spot where Simon's mother fell to her death. I have discovered the exact spot. The servants know everything, you know. I think they listen at keyholes. Ask them anything about Heron history and they can always answer you.'

'My door has a latch,' laughed Maria, 'I must be thankful for that. Come then, let's ride on to your morbid spot.'

The spot was discovered eventually and they dismounted and tied the horses to a tree. Then they stood near the cliff edge and looked down at the sea, which boiled in over the sand, curling hungrily round the rocks and boulders that littered the deserted beach. Maria stood braced against the wind blowing in from the sea, and the russet gown billowed behind her, her long hair fluttering free.

'What a sad spot,' she said, 'and yet today, with the sun shining, tis hard to imagine a death taking place here . . .'

'An accident or a suicide,' said Oliver, 'no one will ever really know.'

Maria shuddered.

'Are you cold?' he asked, and put his arm lightly around her shoulders. They stood there watching the water, the sea birds that swooped above it, and the massive grey clouds that piled one upon the other along the horizon.

'The weather is going to break,' said Maria. 'We must not stay too long.'

'Then let's sit awhile,' Oliver suggested. 'You can be a princess and I'll be your fool. Shall I sing to you, or make you laugh? Or tell a sad tale that will bring tears to your eyes –'

They made themselves comfortable, Maria sitting with her knees drawn up, her hands clasped round them, Oliver sitting beside her, chewing a piece of grass and flicking away any insects that hovered too near. Maria closed her eyes and turned her face to the sun.

'Some moments should last forever,' she said. 'This is one of them. How wonderful to be carefree for just a few moments.'

Oliver's answer seemed slow in coming, so she opened her eyes. He was shading his hand and staring out to sea.

'There's a ship out there,' he said. 'And looking mighty strange, with only two sails where there should be three. I wonder . . . See there.'

'I see it. A fishing boat? Tis very small.'

'Not so small. Tis the distance. A local man sailing home after a week's pirating, I'll wager. But tis in some kind of trouble – making for the harbour and at some speed.'

'And in that sea! The waves are increasing all the time. What should we do?'

'Nothing,' said Oliver. 'Tis daylight, and twill be seen by others – by the harbour authorities. But that harbour entrance is mighty narrow – *I* shouldn't care to bring a ship through in this wind!'

'Are you certain you want to be a sailor?' said Maria. 'Tis a dangerous life.'

He laughed. 'You listen to wild tales,' he told her. 'Life at sea is changed greatly – unless you wish to be a pirate, and I have no such ambitions. I don't fancy the gallows. I shall earn my living honestly. I promise you, Maria, a seaman is respected today – he's an honourable man. Times change.

375

The Queen needs sailors for exploration and trade, and she looks after them well.' He narrowed his eyes and shook his head. 'That ship is going on the rocks, I swear it. She will be driven against the cliff bottom. See – she is drifting past the harbour entrance.'

'Poor wretches? Can nothing be done to save them?'

'Nothing until she is aground. Then mayhap some of them will make it to land. Don't look so distressed, Maria. Tis a hazard of the sea, and always will be.'

She looked at him soberly. 'But one day it may be *your* life at risk. Imagine if the walkers on the cliff said "Tis a hazard of the sea" and did nothing to help you!'

'But what's to be done if we do help?'

Maria shrugged helplessly, and they turned back to watch the ship, which was now being driven closer to the cliff with every huge wave that lifted and dropped her. The sun went in and overhead, the heavy clouds darkened and the first few drops of rain were starting to fall. The wind was rising noticeably, and Maria shivered. Behind them the horses whinnied anxiously as a rumble of distant thunder crept across the sky.

'We must go,' he said. 'Our watching the ship cannot save it. If we stay longer, we shall have to ride back through the storm and will arrive home like drowned rats.'

'I feel we are abandong them to their fate – *Oh!*' She gave an involuntary gasp as, without warning, a clap of thunder burst overhead, followed by a vivid white flash and a roar of thunder.

'Too late!' cried Oliver. 'We daren't ride in this. We'd best make our way down to the beach and find a cave to shelter in until the worst is past.'

'But the horses?' cried Maria fearfully, as the rain fell faster and heavier, hissing into the heather-clad ground around them.

'They will have to take their chance. Give me your hand. We can climb down – tis not too steep.'

Countless feet before them had worn a recognisable path

down the sloping cliff to the beach below. And so, while the pounding of the incoming waves and the fury of the rain peppered the sand like gun-shot, Maria and Oliver began to scramble down. But the path was slippery with the rain, and Maria was hampered by the skirts of her gown. Oliver, slightly below, watched her anxiously, unable to help, for she needed one hand to steady herself and the other to hold her skirts. They were nearly half way down when she suddenly lost her footing on a loose boulder and with a gasp of fear, began to slide helplessly on the steep slope.

'Oliver!' she screamed.

He flung himself across her body in a desperate attempt to break her fall, as she slithered towards the edge of the path, where the cliff fell steeply fifty feet or more to the bottom. Panic-stricken, she clung to him, terror in her eyes, her breath ragged and uneven.

'Don't let me go!' she begged. 'Oh, Oliver, for God's sake don't let me fall!'

'You won't fall, Maria,' he told her. 'I won't let you fall. But you must rest very still while I try to find a handhold.'

'Dear God! We shall both go over!'

'No, we won't. Stay calm, Maria. Don't try to move until I have a safer footing and can steady you. Don't look down. Close your eyes and trust me. If only the rain would ease a little, it blinds me –'

He cast around for a crevice or ledge which would offer his fingers a more secure grip, while Maria closed her eyes, biting her lips in an effort to stop their trembling. Below her, she could hear the crashing of the water on the rocks, and above them the storm raged and the heavens opened, drenching the land with rain and filling the air with the fierce crackle of thunder.

Inch by inch, Oliver shifted his weight until he could reach out with his left hand and close his fingers round a small sharply-pointed tip of rock.

'Take my hand,' he urged.

For Maria the next few moments seemed like an eternity.

Her courage had quite deserted her, and as she lay helplessly clinging to the rock, fearing at any second to be prised away by the angry wind and hurled on to the rocks below, she knew real terror. But Oliver had found a secure position and was encouraging her gently to open her eyes.

'Turn towards me,' he said, keeping his voice steady. 'Don't look up or down. Look at me, and do as I say. You'll be quite safe, I swear it. I've a firm hold and I won't let go your hand. Now *slowly*, come up to kneeling . . . Grasp that rock to your right – now, slowly straighten up and stand beside me . . . There, tis done!'

'Oh Oliver!' She pressed her face into his shoulder and cried scalding tears of relief, until her anguish passed and the shaking in her limbs had ceased. Still holding to the rock with his free hand, he grasped her close with the other. Their clothes were wet through, and Maria's hair hung wet and heavy around her shoulders and clung to her face.

'Can you make the rest of the climb?' he asked gently. 'We can either climb back up or go on down. I think the storm will last a while yet.'

'We'll continue down,' said Maria after a brief hesitation.

With great caution, they made their way down the treacherous pathway to the beach and ran along to the first of several caves, where at last they found shelter from the pouring rain. Breathless and exhausted, they stared out at the wild scene before them.

'That ship,' said Maria, when she finally recovered her breath. 'I wonder what happened to it.'

'On the rocks, most likely,' he said. 'But enough about them. We have only just escaped a disaster of our own.'

'I was so fearful,' said Maria.

Oliver's voice was strong and steady. 'We are safe, and there's an end to it. Going up will be easier, and we can wait until the rain stops. Are you cold? You're shivering still.'

'Only a little. My body's still fearful, although my mind tells me I am safe.'

'Poor little body,' he laughed. 'Mayhap I can convince it.'

He put an arm round her and hugged her. 'Take heed, little body,' he said, 'Oliver is here and all is well.'

They both laughed, glad that the nightmare was at an end. Oliver's arm remained round her shoulders for a while, then fell to her waist. He was suddenly silent and unspoken words seemed to hover between them.

To Maria's surprise the pressure of Oliver's arm around her body filled her with a lightness of spirit, and an unfamiliar warmth swept through her. She dreaded the moment when he would take his arm away, and his nearness stirred her to an awakened awareness of herself. The feelings that grew in her were exquisite, fragile even, and she hardly dared breathe for fear they should melt away. Rapturously, she closed her eyes and let her body lean towards his.

As Oliver's arm tightened round her in immediate response, Maria was too overwhelmed to heed the alarm which rang in her brain. The emotion grew sweeter, and she felt her heart hammering wildly against her ribs. Surely he would sense her excitement? She did not care. She only wanted to abandon herself to the joy which was overtaking her. Oliver turned slightly, and before they knew what they did, their arms were round each other, their mouths reaching urgently in an inevitable, irresistible kiss. Maria gasped as his lips met hers with a ferocity that matched her own. There was no tenderness in it, and no restraint between them. Wordlessly they gave themselves up to the passion that had seized them both. He kissed her mouth, neck, ears, forehead; his fingers clasped her hair, his arm tightened round her, pressing them together, moulding them into one being.

'Oliver!' she whispered. 'Oh, dear God –'

'I love you. Maria, I love you –'

'Oh, my dearest Oliver, don't . . .'

But seeing his eyes so full of passionate entreaty, Maria became aware that a terrible choice lay before her – either to surrender completely to her instincts, or somehow to bridle their runaway emotions.

The truth came to her in a moment of dazzling clarity. She longed to give her body – but not to this man. Only to Hugo would she ever entrust herself. Yet this young man, so very dear to her from his early childhood, yearned for her – she was to blame for allowing this unhappy situation to develop. She had put up defences against the world around her, and now Oliver had stormed them.

Oliver waited for her response, vulnerable and so young. What could she say or do to soften the rejection?

'Maria, I beg you –'

'Oliver, wait.' Sweet heaven, help me, she asked silently; help me find a way to refuse him without shattering his self-esteem. There *was* only one way. She must tell him the truth.

Gently, she leaned back, holding him at a distance, looking into the grey eyes that now blazed with desire.

'Hear me out,' she whispered. 'Promise me you will hear me out?'

He nodded, but already his eyes were darkening with suspicion.

'Oliver, I've been foolish and blind not to see what was happening between us. It is my fault –'

'Don't talk of blame,' he cried. 'If we love each other –'

'Yes, we love each other, Oliver, I don't pretend otherwise. But in different ways.'

She saw in a flash that his love for her was a mirror of her young love for Hugo. She had grown up loving Hugo and he had rejected her. Nothing could save Oliver from his share of the unhappiness she herself had known, and she sighed for him.

'You spoke earlier, Oliver, of servants' gossip – and rumour.' He nodded. 'Then you must know of my feelings for Hugo.'

'And I believe you have refused him.'

'True.' She could not bear the dark misery growing in his eyes, but steadily she held his gaze and continued. 'Those years at Arnsville – all that time I felt like one of the nuns.

380

Thought like them. I truly did not believe I would ever think and feel as a woman again.'

'But you do, Maria, I know it.'

'Aye, much to my surprise I am a woman again, with passions and desires I had almost forgotten. Tis you who has done that for me, Oliver. You alone have made me whole again, and I cannot thank you enough for such a gift.'

He turned her face gently so that she faced him again. 'You *can* thank me, and I think you *want* to . . .'

'I do,' she whispered. 'My body cries out for you.'

'Then lie with me!'

'My dearest Oliver, would you want only the body? Would it be right for you to take my body when my heart and soul belong to someone else?'

He stared at her, and for a moment she thought, almost hoped, that he would answer 'Aye'. If that happened, what should she do? While he hesitated, she thought desperately.

'Believe me, Oliver,' she said. 'We could be lovers, this one time, and it would be very sweet for both of us. I can't deny –' she lowered her voice until it was almost a whisper '– that I do desire your body most urgently. And yet when it was over, we would look at each other with regret. Would our relationship survive? No – I think we would lose each other forever.'

'Damnation, Maria!' he said. 'You have such a way with words. You say "No" as though it were "Aye"!' He turned away angrily, and she felt tears spring to her eyes. 'Hugo will have you for the rest of his life!' he cried suddenly. 'If I should only ask for this one time, is that too much to grant, when tis what we both want? Can you look straight into my eyes and refuse me?'

Tears ran down her face. 'I think I can, Oliver, but I beseech you, don't put me to the test. I have no experience, no practice, in steering my heart through this strange emotion. Don't ask me, Oliver, if you love me.'

With a sob, she ran out of the cave and onto the rain-soaked beach, running blindly, stumbling and weeping in her distress. He let her go, his heart full of misery, his body aching with frustration and resentment. Yet even while he cursed, he knew that she was right. To take that body once and then relinquish it to another man would be a greater torment than never to know it at all. In his heart he knew she was Hugo's – maybe he had always known it.

Some of Oliver's wretchedness faded as he considered Maria's. Fresh from the convent and unschooled in the ways of love, she was indeed disturbed and confused. He had roused her from her sleep – she had confessed as much. He had released all these emotions so long imprisoned – and still thanked him for it. When at last he ran out after her, it was to find that the rain had stopped and that a rim of lighter sky had appeared along the horizon.

Maria stood about fifty yards away at the very edge of the water. He picked a small rock and flung it with all his might up into the sky so that it arched high over her head and fell into the water beyond. She turned instantly and stood, looking at him. Blindly, he reached for another and hurled that, too, though lower this time, finding that the aggressive action soothed him. He chose another. He walked nearer and, taking careful aim, hurled the rock so as to pass over her head with only two yards to spare. Maria, aware of his need, stood stock-still, trusting him. He threw another and another, with full force, and they passed her by an ever-decreasing margin so that she longed to cry out and stop him. She felt the air move as they whistled past her, but still she stood her ground, only closing her eyes so that she need not see the wild expression in his grey eyes.

'Maria!'

Slowly she opened her eyes. He was two yards away, a rock in his hand. 'I'll always love you,' he said, and she nodded. He glanced down at the rock in his hand as though surprised to find it there. He dropped it on to the sand and they ran together, comforting each other, as friends, no longer hurting each other as lovers. When the clamour in their hearts was calmed, they went back to the horses and turned towards home. Without needing to express it, both were aware that their friendship was changed and in some way stronger. They were closer instead of further apart. Neither understood how – but that was of no importance. Their love for each other had somehow survived the storm, and for that they were grateful.

As they rounded the curve of the cliff, a desolate sight met their eyes. The boat they had seen earlier now lay against the cliff, driven hard onto the rocks. The mast was broken and the rigging a hopeless tangle, whipped by the wind into an ever greater confusion. Thinly on the same wind came the sounds of her crew, some crying out in agony, others shouting orders.

'Poor wretches,' whispered Maria, as they reined in their mounts and watched the grim spectacle. They were too far away to be of any assistance, but near enough to see what was taking place. The ship lay heeled well over, with part of the hull visible. But the damage done by the first impact of ship on rocks was now being aggravated by the relentless pounding of the waves, which broke over her in clouds of white spray and carried away planks, sheets, even men.

'There's one man,' cried Maria, 'in the water between the boat and the cliff! Dear God, he will be battered to death if a wave catches him!'

Even as she spoke, a huge wave reached the tiny struggling figure and tossed it like a cork against the grey granite wall. For a moment a face floated upwards in the long green wake of the wave, then it vanished from sight. Maria shuddered.

Several others, more fortunate than him, were clinging to rocks, and one further along the beach staggered out of the water to fall exhausted onto the sand.

'Can't we do *anything*?' asked Maria, but Oliver shrugged his shoulders.

'It would take us too long to reach them,' he said.

'Twould all be over – but see there, others are going to their aid.'

Men were clambering down the cliff to the side of the wreck, where the path fell less steeply. Others were running along the beach towards it.

'The tide's full in,' said Oliver. 'Were it not for that, they might stand a greater chance, but if they abandon the ship for the waves there is little hope for them. The current curls inward there, to take the curve. Those that have reached the beach are truly fortunate.'

'What are they doing – those men on the beach?' asked Maria, her voice shrill with anxiety.

'Trying to toss a line to the boat,' said Oliver. 'If they can fasten it on the ship, then the men can hold on to it when they go overboard, and if they have the strength, prevent the waves from carrying them onto the cliff. But tis a fair distance, and the wind's against them. They'll no doubt weight the rope end with a rock or lump of wood.'

Maria pointed suddenly to the cliff top above the wreck, where men on horseback were watching the scene. 'They're going to try a rescue from the top of the cliff!' she cried.

Oliver pursed his lips thoughtfully. 'Mayhap,' he said cautiously.

'What else then?'

'Scavengers?' said Oliver.

She glanced at him, puzzled.

'They'll wait until the crew are all gone ashore, then board her and take whatever they find there of value. The human buzzards picking over the ship's carcase.'

'Why don't they help?'

'And put their lives in jeopardy?' Oliver laughed brusquely. 'No, no. They'll risk life and limb for a prize, but not for their fellow men. The sea brings out the best in some men, the worst in others.'

Maria was silent. They watched for a short while longer, then turned their horses towards home.

'Melissa will be alarmed,' said Maria.

He looked at her. 'What will you tell Hugo?' he asked.

'Only that we sheltered from the storm.'

'And will you wed him?'

'Aye. Will you wish us well, Oliver? For my sake?'

'Indeed I must, for I want your happiness above all else,' he sighed. 'If *I* cannot give you happiness, then I shall pray that he may.'

'And you?' she said softly.

'I shall go to sea as I intended and think of you as often as I may.'

'The sea is a cruel master,' said Maria. 'Don't let it change you, Oliver.'

'I'll do my best if it pleases you, ma'am.' He smiled, and she read great tenderness in his words.

She reached across and touched his sleeve briefly.

'It pleases me,' she said.

CHAPTER TWENTY ONE

The cob house finally dried out and was duly rendered, and Minnie, Jon and Ben moved into their own home. Maria, visiting them, saw with surprise that what had looked very small from outside seemed considerably larger inside. She sat on the bench and dandled Ben on her knees, jogging him while he made the clicking noises like horses' hooves and squealed with laughter.

'So you finally made up your mind,' Minnie grinned, as she wrung the clothes out with short, sharp twists of her wrists. 'Hugo jumped for joy when you told him, I'll be bound.'

'He was well pleased,' Maria admitted.

'Twas not before time, too,' said Minnie. 'Here's me with one babe already and another on the way. You'll have some catching up to do – unless you have twins. They run in the Kendal family, twins do.'

Maria let her mind dwell on the prospect without much alarm. She *was* old to be marrying for the first time. Twins would be convenient, she thought with amusement.

'And the celebration?' asked Minnie. 'Will it be at Crockern Tor?'

Maria nodded. Crockern Tor was one of the high points of the moor, where the tinners' own parliament met to discuss policies and events in which they had a common interest. The tor itself was a windy spot, and on many occasions the weather had proved hardly conducive to sitting round the giant slab of granite which served as a table. Then the men would adjourn to the Parliament Hall, a large, rough-stone building thatched with peat, where they were dry if not warm and the meeting could be conducted in a civilised way.

'Aye, tis all arranged,' she said, 'and all the miners are invited with their wives. The children shall have a separate party on the following Sunday. This is a weighty little lad! Before long he'll be dandling me on *his* knee!'

Minnie laughed proudly. 'But you haven't told me all yet, as you promised. Who's to be best man, and bride's knights and maids?'

Maria laughed. 'You are enjoying all this commotion as much as I am,' she said. 'Well, Thomas will be best man, and Abby's eldest girl the chief bridesmaid, with little Beatrice as another. Allan was to be bride's knight, but he refuses.'

'And Oliver will miss it all. I wish he had not gone so soon. What is it about the sea that lures away our menfolk?'

Maria made no answer, but smiled with a slight shrug of her shoulders. For a moment Minnie fancied a shadow crossed her face, and she wondered, as they all did, what had happened that day of the storm.

'Maggie is helping with the baking,' said Maria. 'Beth could not cook for so many. She will have no wedding breakfast to prepare, but she's getting on now and quite content to bake the wedding cake.'

Minnie groaned. 'And we all hear about nothing else! Tis cake, cake, cake from noon till dusk, and whether it shall be pink ribbon or silver, and this wording or that. So how many will dance at Crockern Tor on your wedding night?'

'Nigh on two hundred,' said Maria. 'Tis well there's no more, for the Hall will not take it.'

'I can hardly wait,' cried Minnie. 'Oh, to think that you're wedding your Hugo at last. I can scarce believe it.'

'No more can I!' laughed Maria, and made her goodbyes.

The church at Ashburton was full and the road outside was crowded. For once, Maggie thought, she was on the inside – an invited guest at a Kendal wedding. This would be something to tell her grandchildren – only she'd never have any now, having no children of her own to give her any. But Maggie was not one to waste her time on regrets. Life was life, and no harking back would change a single day of it. She had no husband either, and didn't want one. They were more trouble than they were worth, she reflected, from what she'd seen of them. She was too old to change her ways now – even too old to set her cap at the lads in the bakery, which was just as well, because she had eaten a sight too many of her own tarts and pastries over the years and they'd need bribing like as not to roll in the hay with such a dumpling! At that thought she laughed out loud, and several of the guests turned to see what amused her.

Maggie sought out her precious young Allan among the crowd. Fancy the lad refusing to be a bride knight! She grinned to herself. Young devil needs a firm hand. So like Simon, she thought wistfully – and yet there's something about the boy that sets him apart. All that stuff about dowsing and suchlike. She'd laughed when she heard, and yet again, when you looked into his eyes you could swear you saw his very soul. He came from strange folks, her beloved Allan . . .

At last they were nearly done. Passing round the bride cup and cakes and pats on the back and so many smiles, bless them. Maria looked beautiful, and so did her husband, both so dark and intense. They'd have some bonny children and no mistake. Plenty of them, too, by the way he was looking at her and her glowing up at him, flushed and glorious. Now the bells began. What a racket! That youngest ringer had no idea. A tame monkey could ring bells better. Still, can't have a wedding without bells.

Maggie looked down smugly at her best green silk, and smoothed it with her podgy hands. She looked well enough – mayhap someone would ask her for a dance. She had never been to Cockern Tor and had never fancied to see so many tinners in one place together. Wild lot, the tinners;

hasty, and would bear a grudge for generations. Oh, aye, they were a tough breed, none tougher in the West Country, and never in too great a hurry to pay their bills, either. What they'd be like after a bellyful of free wine and ale she shuddered to think, but no doubt the wives would keep them in order. If there was anyone tougher than a tinner, twas a tinner's wife!

The service was finished, and not before time. All these prayers and the old preacher ranting away! Twas hard on the knees, and Maggie's were fatter than most. God knows how bony knees would fare!

They all streamed out into the churchyard, where the late evening sun was decorating the sky with a mass of fluffy-pink clouds to rival the silks, satins, ribbons, laces and feathers of every colour and hue that adorned the guests. For this wedding was the biggest event of the year, and the people of Dartmoor had risen to the occasion.

Hugo and Maria waited at the church gate for the first of a dozen waggons that would carry the guests to Crockern Tor and later deliver them to their homes. Heron had spared no expense, and Hugo was the hero of the hour. They made a truly handsome couple, Maria in white with a head-dress of tiny seed pearls; Hugo in crimson slashed with white velvet. They waited in shower after shower of petals and rice, as the guests struggled forward to throw their share over the radiant bride and groom.

At last the cart arrived, decked with white ribbons and green boughs, and Hugo, Maria, bridesmaids and knights clambered in. The horses wore white plumes, and the sight was a dazzling one as the whole procession finally started towards Crockern Tor, to the accompaniment of the musicians who rode alongside and the jingle of horses' harness.

The Hall had been specially decorated with greenery, and colourful drapes hid the worst of the damp patches; although it was a humble dwelling, it was roomy – and nowhere was there a more fitting scene for the wedding-feast of the owner of the Heron mine.

There were a few stools for the elderly and infirm, but the guests remained for the most part standing, while Hugo and Maria went from group to group welcoming them.

Along one wall the long table was laden with cold meats and fish of every kind – fruit tarts, pasties, cakes, nuts and fruits. There was unlimited ale, cider and wine, and within the hour most of the food had been eaten and healthy inroads made into the drinks.

Mellowed by food and wine, the initial restraints vanished and everyone relaxed and prepared to enjoy themselves. The music started, and Hugo held out his hand to Maria with a courtly bow. Smiling brilliantly, she accepted and the pair of them danced their way down the centre of the hall and back again before signalling others to join them. Within seconds the floor was full of smiling women and laughing, dark-eyed men, each determined to show that they could outdance the next couple. Allan asked Maggie to dance, and her joy was complete. Thomas and Melissa danced past Abby and Adam, and next came Minnie with Jon.

'Your babe will wonder what is happening,' Maria teased her, and Minnie, remembering she was with child, danced less vigorously.

After an hour's dancing, the musicians enjoyed a well-earned rest while the entertainers took over – three jugglers, an acrobat and a ballad singer. The latter had drunk rather too well and told a string of riddles that brought the colour to the women's cheeks and made the men rock with raucous laughter and encourage him rather too well with their applause. Then it was the turn of the players, who performed 'Marriage of True Minds', a play that was hilarious without being too bawdy, so that even the most upright and sober guests could laugh without restraint. After one or two speeches, the musicians struck up once again and the Hall echoed long into the night with the beat of dancing feet and the sound of laughter. Hugo and Maria, watching hand in hand, had no doubt that, in the eyes of Dartmoor, they were well and truly wed.

As Maria struggled back to consciousness next morning, she became aware that someone was knocking at the door.

'Come in,' she called softly, for Hugo still slept beside her.

Beth came into the room, beaming broadly to see the double bed holding Master and Mistress once more.

'I wondered if you would want breakfast,' she said. ''Tis very late, but I reckoned you'd sleep on. My own head was thick as a plank this morning, but I put it under the pump and that cleared it. Not that I'm suggesting *your* head might be affected, but me – I'm not used to good wine and tis heady stuff.' She sighed happily at the memory of the night's excesses. 'I told Jack there'd be a few aching heads this morning, but I little thought mine would be one of them.' She came nearer and peered over at Hugo. 'Sleeping like a babe,' she marvelled. 'Well, I won't linger – unless you want something to eat? A coddled egg, mayhap, or a dish of porridge?'

Maria shook her head. 'But a mug of camomile tea would be perfect.'

Beth hesitated at the door and turned back. 'I didn't get a chance to say nowt yesterday, but you looked real bonny, ma'am. It brought tears to my eyes to see you so beautiful and wedded to the man you love after all this time. There's not a soul in these parts as doesn't wish you both every happiness.'

'Thank you, Beth.'

The old woman smiled, then closed the door quietly behind her. As she did so Hugo turned.

'Has she gone?' he asked.

'Hugo! You're awake!'

'Kiss me.'

'Most willingly.'

She leaned over and kissed him, and as she did so his hands closed firmly over her breasts, so that she sighed dreamily.

He laughed gently. 'I remember those beautiful breasts,' he said.

'And I recall those gentle hands, sir!'

''Twas good – very good, my sweet Maria.'

'Aye. Every bit as sweet as I had hoped.'

'And yet we were both tired. What will it be like when we are full of energy, I wonder?'

She laughed. 'Do folk die of ecstasy?' she asked him.

''Twould be a fine way to die – you have such dainty nipples.'

'I'm pleased you approve them.'

'I do indeed.' He leaned down and kissed each one in turn and without raising his head, said, 'And was I all that you hoped?'

'And more,' said Maria, stroking the dark head that lay against her breasts.

He looked up, grinning delightedly at the compliment. 'You are twenty-three years old,' he told her solemnly. 'When a virgin wife has waited so long, it behoves a husband not to disappoint her.'

The boyish boast made them both laugh and they clung together, unable to believe their good fortune.

'So you have ensnared me at last,' Hugo teased. 'You've pursued me all these years, and finally I am yours. I still recall your early tantrums. What a dreadful child you were!'

'Hugo! Tis most unkind of you to remember. A true gentleman would have more discretion.'

'Have I ever said I was a true gentleman?'

She shrugged, smiling. 'Would a true gentleman,' he said, tracing her breasts delicately with his finger, 'expect to repeat the delights of his wedding night the very next morning?'

His finger moved down over her stomach and explored

each thigh. 'A true gentleman would most surely say, "I have taken my fill of her and she is wearied. I shall restrain my longings until she is recovered." A *true* gentleman . . .'

Maria gasped with pleasure, as the finger startled her body into that new awareness which was at once a desire to take, and a desire to give. 'Then I am glad you are not a true gentleman,' she murmured. 'You are sorcerer with magical powers to excite me. Your hands touch me and I'm helpless.'

'Spellbound?'

'Aye.'

Feeling her begin to respond with small caresses of her own, his hands faltered briefly and an exquisite fire swept through him.

'I love you, Maria,' he gasped. 'I want your mind and sweet body forever.'

Maria, drifting in a haze of sensations, could only whisper, 'I'm yours Hugo,' and then give herself fully to the growing excitement which swept her to dazzling heights she had never known before. Hugo's hands were all over her; his mouth was against hers, the sweet, sour tang of his body was in her nostrils, and their skin burned with an exquisite pain as they touched. Maria, eyes closed, gasped for breath and moaned without hearing the sound. Hugo's need grew more fierce, unlike the controlled gentleness of the previous night, until she was almost overwhelmed by the wild passion which overtook him. Almost, but not entirely, for her own passions so long repressed, were now surfacing.

Beth, her hand raised to knock at the door, paused suddenly, let her hand fall and turned away, smiling. Her Mistress, she was quite certain, would not be wanting the camomile tea.

Maria re-read Oliver's letter, trying to visualise him aboard the merchantman bound for the Rhine, his second journey there. She still could not see him as a sailor, and yet he wrote calmly of storms and the hazards of shoal waters, of inadequate rations and insubordinate seamen. He had been away for four years and they had not seen him in all that time, and he wrote longingly of expeditions planned to remote corners of the world, as if the rigours of his present life were not enough for him.

Was Oliver still the quiet, sensitive young man Maria remembered? Or had the sea changed him? He enquired kindly after all at Heron and Ladyford and promised gifts for the children on his return to England. How strange to think that he would be a stranger to her own young son, Piers. She sighed, and with the letter still in her hand, crossed to the window.

The sight that met her gaze chased away the sigh and filled her with contentment. Outside, the hot July sun shimmered on the trees and baked the grass, now flattened by the dancing feet of Beatrice and Martin, as they tried to copy the steps demonstrated by their teacher, Monsieur du Près: Beatrice, at eleven, still round as a barrel, but so eager to learn, a frown of concentration on her sweet face as she held out her hand to take her brother's. No doubt that she was Hannah's daughter!

'And *one* and *two*, forward and *nod* and back and close – Don't nod so hard, Beatrice, your head will fall off! And Martin – try to take smaller steps, so – *one* and *two* and forward and *nod* – See?'

Martin nodded. He was nearly seven and looked bored. Maria knew how he hated the lessons, hated, too, poor Monsieur du Près; he called him Foxy behind his back, because his small brown eyes were so close to his long nose. But Monsieur du Près had been highly recommended as a teacher and had taught the Tucker children most successfully for the past two summers.

'Let's try again,' coaxed the teacher.

'I'm hot,' grumbled Martin.

'Tis indeed a warm day,' Monsieur du Près agreed. 'Let us move over into the shade of that oak. We will be cooler there.'

'Tis a chestnut,' said Martin, and Beatrice giggled.

'Chestnut or oak, twill give us welcome shade,' said Monsieur, and he crossed the lawn, flute in hand, moving with a mincing gait which Maria generously attributed to a lifetime of dancing.

Maria's gaze roamed the garden until she saw Annie sitting on the grass with three-year-old Piers beside her, earnestly following the rise and fall of the small wooden boat which she was sailing for him on an invisible sea. Piers was built like his father – sturdy, not tall, but with a pale skin, gold hair and blue eyes – the true Kendal colouring.

Annie cradled the baby in her arms: little Lorna, not yet a year old, with dark hair and dark eyes, and a demanding disposition. When Lorna Kendal was hungry or displeased with her small world, the entire household knew it. Hugo teasingly claimed that she had her mother's temperament.

Maria smiled and turned her attention to the last of her children: Allan, so like Simon except that his hair was silver-blond instead of gold. He was leaving his boyhood behind now, growing taller, with the slim neck and the arrogant Kendal head. He was practising his archery with the same intensity with which he attacked all his pursuits. He rode well, wrestled superbly for his age; he had a pleasant singing voice, and a fine, retentive memory – and, thought Maria, that intangible strangeness which persisted, setting him slightly apart from the others.

Maria rose. She could not idle away the entire afternoon. She would write to Oliver in the cool of the evening, unless Hugo wished to answer the letter. Beth was unwell, and Maria would have to supervise the new girl's preparations for supper. Before that, she must check the laundry and turn the two worn sheets sides to middle. She gave the children one last loving glance. Three Kendal sons. What did the future hold for them? she wondered. She turned away from the window with the suspicion of a sigh. But for today, her eyes smiled. Maria Kendal was content.